THE EYE OF THE HEART

THE EYE OF THE HEART

SHORT STORIES FROM LATIN AMERICA

EDITED BY BARBARA HOWES

AVON BOOKS NEW YORK

AVON BOOKS
A division of
The Hearst Corporation
105 Madison Avenue
New York, New York 10016

Front cover art by Donna Pacinelli
Published by arrangement with the Bobbs-Merrill Company, Inc.
Library of Congress Catalog Card Number: 72-9879
ISBN: 0-380-70942-2

First Avon Books Trade Printing: August 1990
First Avon Books Mass Market Printing: November 1974

Printed in the U.S.A.

OPM 10 9 8 7 6 5 4 3 2

For Helen, whose idea this was

Contents

Acknowledgments

"The Psychiatrist" ("O Alienista") by Machado de Assis was originally published in a collection of his stories *Papeis Avulsos* (1882). Translated by William L. Grossman and Helen Caldwell, it appeared in *The Psychiatrist and Other Stories*, published by the University of California Press (1963). Reprinted by permission of the Regents of the University of California.

"The Bourgeois King" ("El rey burgués") by Rubén Darío originally appeared in *Azul* (1888). Translated and reprinted by permission of Ben Belitt. Copyright © 1973 by Ben Belitt.

"Yzur" by Leopoldo Lugones was first published in *Las fuerzas extrañas* and appeared in English in *Classic Tales from Spanish America*, published by Barron's Educational Series, Inc. (1962). Reprinted by permission of Piri Lugones.

"The Alligator War" ("La Guerra de los yacarés") by Horacio Quiroga originally appeared in his *Cuentos de la selva* (1918), published by Sociedad Cooperativa Editorial Limitada. It was first published in English in *South American Jungle Tales*. Reprinted by permission of the publisher, Dodd, Mead and Company, Inc.

"The Devil's Twilight" ("El crepúsculo del diablo) by Rómulo Gallegos originally appeared in his *Cuentos venezolanos* (1949) and was first published in English in *Odyssey Review*. Reprinted by permission of Sonia Gallegos de Palomino.

"The Gauchos' Hearth" ("Al rescoldo") by Ricardo Güiraldes originally appeared in his *Cuentos de muerte y de sangre*. Reprinted by permission of the author's agent, International Editors Co., Buenos Aires.

"Why Reeds Are Hollow" ("Por que las cañas son huecas") by Gabriela Mistral was first published in *Elegancias* (Paris, May 1914). Copyright © 1914 by Gabriela Mistral, reprinted by permission of Doris Dana, % Joan Daves Literary Agency. Translated by W. J. Smith.

"Major Aranda's Hand" ("La mano del Comandante Aranda") by Alfonso Reyes appeared in *Quince presencias, 1915–1954* (Colección Literaria Obregón, Mexico, 1955). First published in English in *Odyssey Review* and reprinted here by permission of Alicia Reyes.

"On the Other Side of Life and Death" ("Más allá de la vida y la muerte") by César Vallejo appeared in *Escenas melografiadas*. English translation reprinted by permission of Georgette de Vallejo.

"The Other Death" ("La otra muerte") by Jorge Luis Borges published in his book *Vila Feliz*. Translated by William L. Grossman, it appeared in *Modern Brazilian Short Stories*, published by the University of California Press (1967), and reprinted by permission of the Regents of the University of California.

"The Other Death" ("La otra muerte") by Jorge Luis Borges

originally appeared in *The New Yorker*. Reprinted from *The Aleph and Other Stories: 1933–1969* by Jorge Luis Borges. English translation copyright © 1968, 1969, 1970 by Emece Editores, S. A. and Norman Thomas di Giovanni; copyright © 1970 by Jorge Luis Borges, Adolfo Bioy–Casares and Norman Thomas di Giovanni. Published by E. P. Dutton and Company. Reprinted by permission of the publisher.

"Tatuana's Tale" ("Leyenda de la Tatuana") by Miguel Angel Asturias appeared in *Leyendas de Guatemala* (Editorial Losada, S.A., Buenos Aires, 1957). Published here for the first time in English by permission of the author.

"One Sunday Afternoon" ("Una tarde de domingo") by Roberto Arlt first appeared in *El Jorobadito* (1933). Published here for the first time in English, translated by Norman Thomas di Giovanni. Copyright © 1973 by Norman Thomas di Giovanni. By permission of Mirta Arlt.

"Like the Night" ("Semejante a la noche") by Alejo Carpentier appeared in *Guerra del tiempo*. Copyright © 1958 Compañía Generales de Ediciones, S.A. Mexico, D.F. Translated by Frances Partridge, it appeared in *War of Time*, copyright © 1970 by Victor Gollancz Ltd. Reprinted by permission of Alfred A. Knopf, Inc.

"A Pine-Cone, a Toy Sheep . . ." ("Poesía y infancia") by Pablo Neruda appeared originally in *Obras completas* (1957). It was first published in English in *Evergreen Review*, English translation copyright © 1962 by Ben Belitt. Reprinted by permission of the author and Ben Belitt.

"As I Am . . . As I Was" ("A ese lugar de donde me llaman") by Lino Novás-Calvo first appeared in the Cuban periodical *Orígenes* (No. 27, 1955). It is included in his collection of short stories, *Maneras de contar*. Reprinted by permission of the author.

"The Drum Dance" ("El baile de tambor") by Arturo Uslar Pietri appeared in his collection of short stories *Treinta hombres y sus sombras* (1949). It first appeared in English in *Odyssey Review* and is reprinted by permission of the author.

"The Third Bank of the River" ("A terceira margem do rio") by João Guimarães Rosa was first published in *Primeiras estórias* (1962). Translated by William L. Grossman, it appeared in *Modern Brazilian Short Stories*, published by the University of California Press (1967) and is reprinted by permission of the Regents of the University of California.

"Jacob and the Other" ("Jacob y el otro") by Juan Carlos Onetti originally appeared in *Jacob y el otro, un sueño realizado y otros cuentos*. This translation appeared in *Prize Stories from Latin America*. Copyright © 1961, 1963 by Time, Inc. Reprinted by permission of Time-Life Books and Carmen Balcells.

"The Beautiful Soul of Don Damián" ("La bella alma de Don

Damián") by Juan Bosch appeared in *Más cuentos escritos en el exilio* (1964) and *New World Writing*. English translation copyright © 1958 by New American Library. Reprinted by permission of the author and Lysander Kemp.

"The Tree" by María-Luisa Bombal appeared in *Short Stories of Latin America* (Las Amencas Publishing Company, New York, 1963). Reprinted by permission of the author.

"Tarciso" by Dinah Silveira de Queiroz appeared originally in *As noites do morro do encanto*. Translation printed by permission of the author.

"Warma Kuyay" by José María Arguedas appeared in the book of that title (1935) and is reprinted by permission of Señora Celia Bustamante.

"How Porciúncula the Mulatto Got the Corpse Off His Back" ("De como o mulato Porciúncula descarregou seu defunto") by Jorge Amado appeared in *Historias da Bahía* (1963). Translated and reprinted by permission of Jorge Amado.

"End of the Game" ("Final del juego") by Julio Cortázar appeared in 1956. Translated by Paul Blackburn, it appeared in *End of the Game and Other Stories*. Copyright © 1967 by Random House, Inc. Reprinted by permission of Pantheon Books, a division of Random House, Inc.

"My Life with the Wave" ("Mi vida con la ola") by Octavio Paz is part of *Arenas movedizas* (1949) and is reprinted from *Eagle or Sun?* Copyright © 1970 by Eliot Weinberger. Reprinted by permission of October House, Inc.

"Miracles Cannot be Recovered" ("Los milagros no se recuperan") by Adolfo Bioy-Casares appeared in *El gran Serafín* (1967). English translation copyright © 1973 by Norman Thomas di Giovanni. Printed by permission of the author.

"Encounter with the Traitor" ("Encuentro con el traidor") by Augusto Roa Bastos first appeared in *Moriencia* (1970). English translation copyright © 1973 by Norman Thomas di Giovanni. Printed by permission of the author.

"Macario" by Juan Rulfo first appeared in *El llano en llamas* (1953). This translation first appeared in *The Burning Plain* (University of Texas Press, 1967), copyright © 1967 Fondo de Cultura Económica, Mexico 12, D.F. Translated by George D. Schade. Reprinted by permission of the University of Texas Press.

"Madness" ("Rabia") by Armonía Somers appeared in the magazine *La Mañana* (1966). Printed by permission of the author.

"The Switchman" ("El guardagujas") by Juan José Arreola appeared in *Confabulario* (1952) and in English in *TriQuarterly*. English translation copyright © 1969 by Ben Belitt. Reprinted by permission of the translator.

"Concerning Señor de la Peña" ("Del Señor de la Peña") by Eliseo Diego appeared in *Divertimientos* (1946). Printed by permission of Gloria U. Garcia.

"The Dogs" ("Los perros") by Abelardo Díaz Alfaro appeared in *El cuento:* Antología de autores puertorriqueños (1957). Printed by permission of the author.

"The Smallest Woman in the World" ("A menor mulher do mundo") and "Marmosets" by Clarice Lispector first appeared in *The Kenyon Review,* XXVI (June 1964). The former is from *Laços de Família* (1960). Reprinted by permission of Elizabeth Bishop.

"In the Beginning" by Humberto Costantini first appeared in *De por aquí nomas* (1958). Translated by Norman Thomas di Giovanni, it was published in *Mundus Artium* and is reprinted by permission of the author and translator.

"Paseo" by José Donoso was published in English in *TriQuarterly.* Copyright © 1969 by Northwestern University Press. Reprinted by permission of *TriQuarterly.*

"The Handsomest Drowned Man in the World" ("El ahogado más hermoso del mundo") by Gabriel García Márquez first appeared in *La Hojarasca* (1955). English translation is from *Leaf Storm and Other Stories.* Copyright © 1971 by Harper & Row, Publishers, Inc. Reprinted by permission of the publishers.

"A Nest of Sparrows on the Awning" ("Un nido de gorriones en un toldo") by Guillermo Cabrera Infante appeared in *Así en la paz como en la guerra* (1968). Translated here for the first time by Jill Levine. Reprinted by permission of Brandt and Brandt, Inc.

"The Two Elenas" ("Las dos Elenas") by Carlos Fuentes appeared in *Cantar de ciegos,* copyright © 1969 by Carlos Fuentes. English translation by Leonard Mades, copyright © 1972 by Carlos Fuentes. Reprinted by permission of Brandt & Brandt, Inc.

"Weight-Reducing Diet" ("Régimen para adelgazar") by Jorge Edwards appeared in *Temas y variaciones* (Editorial Universitaria, 1969). Printed by permission of Editorial Universitaria, S.A., Santiago de Chile, and Carmen Balcells.

"Sunday, Sunday" ("Día domingo") by Mario Vargas Llosa first appeared in *Los jefes.* Translated by Alastair Reid. Printed by permission of the author.

My grateful thanks are due to the following, without whose advice, encouragement, and patience this book could never have been completed:

Oscar Araujo
Ben Belitt
José Guillermo Castillo
Norman Thomas di Giovanni
Eduardo González
William L. Grossman
Daniel Halpern
Susana Hertelendy
Judy Jones
Frank MacShane
Olga Mendell
Anson C. Piper
John Schaffner
Aura Mercedes García de Truslow

Assistance in the preparation of this anthology has been given by the Center for Inter-American Relations.

B.H.

Introduction

To start off an anthology of short stories with a novella may seem unwise, as many readers (and reviewers) judge a book only from a few lines. "The Psychiatrist," by Machado de Assis, is, though, a magnificent work, and to a degree it dominates the volume because of the great Brazilian's angle of vision. I have arranged the stories in chronological order for obvious reasons—and also when one's reading moves along through history toward the present, one's knowledge of the course of any literature deepens.

But you can perfectly well open the book anywhere, as when coming to that symposium of Chinese understanding, the *I Ching;* you may thus haphazardly arrive at a story instantly meaningful to yourself. This might be by Onetti, or by Arguedas, or by Clarice Lispector. My own prejudice is that it could be by any of the forty-one writers included. But basically the collection, as you get to know it, as it manifests itself, becomes a matter of architecture. Story by story, it *builds.*

When I came across the phrase "the eye of the heart," in Jorge Amado's delightful yarn, *The Two Deaths of Quincas Wateryell,* it made a deep impression. It spoke to me about something I was beginning to realize about differences between Latin American and North American literatures, but which I had not as yet been able to set down.

The best of the writing of our neighbors to the south, it seems to me, is about *relationship*. It shows how people fit together, and how they do not. It is based on that refinement of mind and heart which makes it possible for true human change to occur. Though we have our amazing grace of talent, we have also our roughshod school, so we need to recall Octavio Paz' description of the North American as one "who wanders in an abstract world of machines, fellow citizens, and moral precepts. . . ." But difference *is* meaningful, and the sensibility of these very varied writers is a wonder and a boon.

A symbol that seems to fascinate Latin Americans is that of the labyrinth. Borges' is indeed a labyrinthine mind, and the title of the second of Neruda's autobiographical works is *La luna en el laberinto*, which covers his student days and, interestingly enough, his consular years in the Far East.

There is the maze on the outside: "Death and the Compass"; *Doña Barbara*, perhaps; perhaps *The Golden Serpent*, Ciro Alegria's notable study of a sinuous river and its riparian life; Asturais' *Strong Wind*.

Then there are accounts of those labyrinths within—Cortázar's Minotaur novel, and then *Hopscotch*; Rulfo's *Pedro Páramo*; Carpentier's *The Lost Steps*. Other labyrinths come to mind—those of the *barrio* or of the backland: Arlt, Novás-Calvo, Guimarães Rosa. The labyrinth of society, about which Bosch, Dinah Silveira de Queiroz, Donoso, Fuentes, and others have been so illuminating. Gabriel García Márquez' special study may be that of time—circular and fatal. Then other "labyrinthine ways" take the paths of fantasy and of sensibility.

It is interesting that this anthology starts off with

Machado writing about an asylum, "The Green House," in which nearly everyone in town resides at some point, and ends—or rather comes to a pause—with Mario Vargas Llosa, who was born roughly a century later. His tough jungle book about the condition and cruelty of man, *La Casa Verde*, appeared in translation in this country in 1969. "The Eye of the Heart" is wide open.

THE EYE OF THE HEART

Only now did Curió realize how close the attachment had been. Quincas's death was like an amputation; it was as though he had lost a leg or an arm, or even an eye—the eye of the heart that the voodoo priestess known as the Lady, mistress of all knowledge, had talked about. . . .

—Jorge Amado, *The Two Deaths of Quincas Wateryell*

The Psychiatrist

MACHADO DE ASSIS

I. HOW ITAGUAI ACQUIRED A MADHOUSE

The chronicles of Itaguai relate that in remote times a certain physician of noble birth, Simão Bacamarte, lived there and that he was one of the greatest doctors in all Brazil, Portugal, and the Spains. He had studied for many years in both Padua and Coimbra. When, at the age of thirty-four, he announced his decision to return to Brazil and his home town of Itaguai, the King of Portugal tried to dissuade him; he offered Bacamarte his choice between the presidency of Coimbra University and the office of Chief Expediter of Government Affairs. The doctor politely declined.

"Science," he told His Majesty, "is my only office; Itaguai, my universe."

He took up residence there and dedicated himself to the theory and practice of medicine. He alternated therapy with study and research; he demonstrated theorems with poultices.

In his fortieth year Bacamarte married the widow of a circuit judge. Her name was Dona Evarista da Costa e Mascarenhas, and she was neither beautiful nor charming. One of his uncles, an outspoken man, asked him why he had not selected a more attractive woman. The doctor replied that Dona Evarista enjoyed perfect digestion, excellent eyesight, and normal blood pressure; she had had no serious illnesses and her urinalysis was negative. It was likely she would give him healthy, robust children. If, in addition to her physiological accomplishments, Dona Evarista possessed a face composed of features neither individually pretty nor mutually compatible, he thanked God for it, for he would not be tempted to sacrifice his scientific pursuits to the contemplation of his wife's attractions.

But Dona Evarista failed to satisfy her husband's expectations. She produced no robust children, and for that matter, no puny ones either. The scientific temperament is by nature patient; Bacamarte waited three, four, five years. At the end of this period he began an exhaustive study of sterility. He reread the works of all the authorities (including the Arabian), sent inquiries to the Italian and German universities, and finally recommended a special diet. But Dona Evarista, nourished almost exclusively on succulent Itaguai pork, paid no heed; and to this lack of wifely submissiveness—understandable but regrettable—we owe the total extinction of the Bacamartian dynasty.

The pursuit of science is sometimes itself therapeutic. Dr. Bacamarte cured himself of his disappointment by plunging even deeper into his work. It was at this time that one of the byways of medicine attracted his attention: psychopathology. The entire colony and, for that matter, the kingdom itself could not boast one authority on the subject. It was a field, indeed, in which little responsible work had been done anywhere in the world. Simão Bacamarte saw an opportunity for Lusitanian and, more specifically, Brazilian science to cover itself with "imperishable laurels"—an expression he himself used, but only in a moment of ecstasy and within the confines of his home; to the outside world he was always modest and restrained, as befits a man of learning.

"The health of the soul!" he exclaimed. "The loftiest possible goal for a doctor."

"For a great doctor like yourself, yes." This emendation came from Crispim Soares, the town druggist and one of Bacamarte's most intimate friends.

The chroniclers chide the Itaguai Town Council for its neglect of the mentally ill. Violent madmen were locked up at home; peaceable lunatics were simply left at large; and none, violent or peaceable, received care of any sort. Simão Bacamarte proposed to change all this. He decided to build an asylum and he asked the Council for authority to receive and treat all the mentally ill of Itaguai and the surrounding area. He would be paid by the patient's family or, if the family was very poor, by the Council. The proposal aroused excitement and curiosity throughout the town. There was considerable opposition, for it is always difficult to uproot the established way of doing things, however absurd or evil it may be. The idea of having madmen live together in the same house seemed itself to be a symptom of madness, as many intimated even to the doctor's wife.

"Look, Dona Evarista," said Father Lopes, the local vicar, "see if you can't get your husband to take a little holiday. In Rio de Janeiro, maybe. All this intensive study, a man can take just so much of it and then his mind . . ."

Dona Evarista was terrified. She went to her husband and said that she had a consuming desire to take a trip with him to Rio de Janeiro. There, she said, she would eat whatever he thought necessary for the attainment of a certain objective. But the astute doctor immediately perceived what was on his wife's mind and replied that she need have no fear. He then went to the town hall, where the Council was debating his proposal, which he supported with such eloquence that it was approved without amendment on the first ballot. The Council also adopted a tax designed to pay for the lodging, sustenance, and treatment of the indigent mad. This involved a bit of a problem, for everything in Itaguai was already being taxed. After considerable study the Council authorized the use of two plumes on the horses drawing a funeral coach. Anyone wishing to take advantage of this privilege would pay a tax of a stated amount for each hour from the time of death to the termination of the rites at the grave. The town clerk was asked to determine the probable revenue from the new tax, but he got lost in arithmetical calculations, and one of the Councilmen, who was opposed to the doctor's undertaking, suggested that the clerk be relieved of a useless task.

"The calculations are unnecessary," he said, "because Dr. Bacamarte's project will never be executed. Who ever heard of putting a lot of crazy people together in one house?"

But the worthy Councilman was wrong. Bacamarte built his madhouse on New Street, the finest thoroughfare in Itaguai. The building had a courtyard in the center and two hundred cubicles, each with one window. The doctor, an ardent student of Arabian lore, found a passage in the Koran in which Mohammed declared that the insane were holy, for Allah had deprived them of their judgment in order to keep them from sinning. Bacamarte found the idea at once beautiful and profound, and he had the passage engraved on the façade of the house. But he feared that this might offend the Vicar and, through him, the Bishop. Accordingly, he attributed the quotation to Benedict VIII.

The asylum was called the Green House, for its windows were the first of that color ever seen in Itaguai. The formal opening was celebrated magnificently. People came from the entire region, some even from Rio de Janeiro, to witness the ceremonies, which lasted seven days. Some patients had already been admitted, and their relatives took advantage of this opportunity to observe the paternal care and Christian charity with which they were treated. Dona Evarista, delighted by her husband's glory, covered herself with silks, jewels, and flowers. She was a real queen during those memorable days. Everyone came to visit her two or three times. People not only paid court to her but praised her, for—and this fact does great honor to the society of the time—they thought of Dona Evarista in terms of the lofty spirit and presitge of her husband; they envied her, to be sure, but with the noble and blessed envy of admiration.

II. A TORRENT OF MADMEN

Three days later, talking in an expansive mood with the druggist Crispim Soares, the psychiatrist revealed his inmost thoughts.

"Charity, Soares, definitely enters into my method. It is the seasoning in the recipe, for thus I interpret the words of St. Paul to the Corinthians: 'Though I understand all mysteries and all knowledge ... and have not charity, I am nothing.' But the main thing in my work at the Green House is to study insanity in depth, to learn its various gradations, to classify the various cases, and finally to discover the cause of the phenomenon and its remedy. This is my heart's desire. I believe that in this way I can render a valuable service to humanity."

"A great service," said Crispim Soares.

"Without this asylum," continued the psychiatrist, "I might conceivably accomplish a little. But it provides far greater scope and opportunity for my studies than I would otherwise have."

"Far greater," agreed the druggist.

And he was right. From all the towns and villages in the vicinity came the violent, the depressed, the monomaniacal—the mentally ill of every type and variety. At the end of four months the Green House was a little community in itself. A gallery with thirty-seven more cubicles had to be added. Father Lopes confessed that he had not imagined there were so many madmen in the world nor that such strange cases of madness existed. One of the patients, a coarse, ignorant young man, gave a speech every day after lunch. It was an academic discourse, with metaphors, antitheses, and apostrophes, ornamented with Greek words and quotations from Cicero, Apuleius, and Tertullian. The Vicar could hardly believe his ears. What, a fellow he had seen only three months ago hanging around street corners!

"Quite so," replied the psychiatrist. "But Your Reverence has observed for himself. This happens every day."

"The only explanation I can think of," said the priest, "is the confusion of languages on the Tower of Babel. They were so completely mixed together that now, probably, when a man loses his reason, he easily slips from one into another."

"That may well be the divine explanation," agreed the psychiatrist after a moment's reflection, "but I'm looking for a purely scientific, human explanation—and I believe there is one."

"Maybe so, but I really can't imagine what it could be."

Several of the patients had been driven mad by love. One of these spent all his time wandering through the building and courtyard in search of his wife, whom he had killed in a fit of jealousy that marked the beginning of his insanity. Another thought he was the morning star. He had repeatedly proposed marriage to a certain young lady, and she had continually put him off. He knew why: she thought him dreadfully dull and was waiting to see if she could catch a more interesting husband. So he became a brilliant star, standing with feet and arms outspread like rays. He would remain in this position for hours, waiting to be supplanted by the rising sun.

There were some noteworthy cases of megalomania. One patient, the son of a cheap tailor, invented a genealogy in which he traced his ancestry back to members of royalty and, through them, ultimately to Jehovah. He would recite the entire list of his male progenitors, with a "begat" to link each father and son. Then he would slap his forehead, snap his fingers, and say it all over again. Another patient had a somewhat similar idea but developed it with more rigorous logic. Beginning with the proposition that he was a child of God, which even the Vicar would not have denied, he reasoned that, as the species of the child is the same as that of the parent, he himself must be a god. This conclusion, derived from two irrefutable premises—one Biblical, the other scientific—placed him far above the lunatics who identified themselves with Caesar, Alexander, or other mere mortals.

More remarkable even than the manias and delusions of the madmen was the patience of the psychiatrist. He began by engaging two administrative assistants—an idea that he accepted from Crispim Soares along with the druggist's two nephews. He gave these young men the task of enforcing the rules and regulations that the Town Council had approved for the asylum. They also kept the records and were in charge of the distribution of food and clothing. Thus, the doctor was free to devote all his time to psychiatry.

"The Green House," he told the Vicar, "now has its temporal government and its spiritual government."*

Father Lopes laughed. "What a delightful novelty," he said, "to find a society in which the spiritual dominates."

Relieved of administrative burdens, Dr. Bacamarte

* A play on words, for *espiritual* means both "spiritual" and "pertaining to the mind."

began an exhaustive study of each patient: his personal and family history, his habits, his likes and dislikes, his hobbies, his attitudes toward others, and so on. He also spent long hours studying, inventing, and experimenting with psychotherapeutic methods. He slept little and ate little; and while he ate he was still working, for at the dinner table he would read an old text or ponder a difficult problem. Often he sat through an entire dinner without saying a word to Dona Evarista.

III. GOD KNOWS WHAT HE IS DOING

By the end of two months the psychiatrist's wife was the most wretched of women. She did not reproach her husband but suffered in silence. She declined into a state of deep melancholy, became thin and yellowish, ate little, and sighed continually. One day, at dinner, he asked what was wrong with her. She sadly replied that it was nothing. Then she ventured for the first time to complain a little, saying she considered herself as much a widow now as before she married him.

"Who would ever have thought that a bunch of lunatics . . ."

She did not complete the sentence. Or, rather, she completed it by raising her eyes to the ceiling. Dona Evarista's eyes were her most attractive feature—large, black, and bathed in a vaporous light like the dawn. She had used them in much the same way when trying to get Simão Bacamarte to propose. Now she was brandishing her weapon again, this time for the apparent purpose of cutting science's throat. But the psychiatrist was not perturbed. His eyes remained steady, calm, enduring. No wrinkle disturbed his brow, as serene as the waters of Botafogo Bay. Perhaps a slight smile played on his lips as he said, "You may go to Rio de Janeiro."

Dona Evarista felt as if the floor had vanished and she were floating on air. She had never been to Rio, which, although hardly a shadow of what it is today, was by comparison with Itaguai a great and fascinating metropolis. Ever since childhood she had dreamed of going there. She longed for Rio as a Hebrew in The Captivity must have longed for Jerusalem, but with her husband settled so definitely in Itaguai she had lost hope. And now, of a sudden, he was permitting her to realize her dream. Dona Evarista could not hide her elation. Simão Bacamarte took her by the hand and smiled in a manner at once conjugal and philosophical.

"How strange is the therapy of the soul!" he thought. "This lady is wasting away because she thinks I do not love her. I give her Rio de Janeiro and she is well again." And he made a note of the phenomenon.

A sudden misgiving pierced Dona Evarista's heart. She concealed her anxiety, however, and merely told her husband that, if he did not go, neither would she, for of course she could not travel alone.

"Your aunt will go with you," replied the psychiatrist.

It should be noted that this expedient had occurred to Dona Evarista. She had not suggested it, for it would impose great expense on her husband. Besides, it was better for the suggestion to come from him.

"Oh, but the money it will cost!" she sighed.

"It doesn't matter," he replied. "Have you any idea of our income?"

He brought her the books of account. Dona Evarista, although impressed by the quantity of the figures, was not quite sure what they signified, so her husband took her to the chest where the money was kept.

Good heavens! There were mountains of gold, thousands upon thousands of cruzados and doubloons. A fortune! While she was drinking it in with her black eyes, the psychiatrist placed his mouth close to her and whispered mischievously: "Who would ever have thought that a bunch of lunatics . . ."

Dona Evarista understood, smiled, and replied with infinite resignation: "God knows what he is doing."

Three months later she left for Rio in the company of her aunt, the druggist's wife, one of the druggist's cousins, a priest whom Bacamarte had known in Lisbon and who happened to be in Itaguai, four maidservants, and five or six male attendants. A small crowd had come to see them off. The farewells were sad for everyone but the psychiatrist, for he was troubled by nothing outside the realm of science. Even Dona Evarista's tears, sincere and abundant as they were, did not affect him. If anything concerned him on that occasion, if he cast a restless and police-like eye over the crowd, it was only because he suspected the presence of one or two candidates for commitment to the Green House.

After the departure the druggist and the psychiatrist mounted their horses and rode homeward. Crispim Soares stared at the road, between the ears of his roan. Simão Bacamarte swept the horizon with his eyes, surveyed the distant mountains, and let his horse find the way home. Perfect symbols of the common man and of the genius! One fixes his gaze upon the present with all its tears and privations; the other looks beyond to the glorious dawns of a future that he himself will shape.

IV. A NEW THEORY

As his horse jogged along, a new and daring hypothesis occurred to Simão Bacamarte. It was so daring, indeed, that, if substantiated, it would revolutionize the bases of psychopathology. During the next few days he mulled it over. Then, in his spare time, he began to go from house to house, talking with the townspeople about a thousand and one things and punctuating the conversation with a penetrating look that terrified even the bravest.

One morning, after this had been going on for about three weeks, Crispim Soares received a message that the psychiatrist wished to see him.

"He says it's important," added the messenger.

The druggist turned pale. Something must have happened to his wife! The chroniclers of Itaguai, it should be noted, dwell upon Crispim's love for his Cesaria and point out that they had never been separated in their thirty years of marriage. Only against this background can one explain the monologue, often overheard by the servants, with which the druggist reviled himself: "You miss your wife, do you? You're going crazy without her? It serves you right! Always truckling to Dr. Bacamarte! Who told you to let Cesaria go traveling? Dr. Bacamarte, that's who. Anything he says, you say amen. So now see what you get for it, you vile, miserable, groveling little lackey! Lickspittle! Flunky!" And he added many other ugly names that a man ought not call his enemies, much less himself. The effect of the message on him, in this state of mind, can be readily imagined. He dropped the drugs he had been mixing and fairly flew to the Green House. Simão Bacamarte greeted him joyfully, but he wore his joy as a wise man should—buttoned up to the neck with circumspection.

"I am very happy," he said.

"Some news of our wives?" asked the druggist in a tremulous voice.

The psychiatrist made a magnificent gesture and replied, "It is something much more important—a scientific experiment. I say 'experiment,' for I do not yet venture to affirm the correctness of my theory. Indeed, this is the very nature of science, Soares: unending inquiry. But, although only an experiment as yet, it may change the face of the earth. Till now, madness has been thought a small island in an ocean of sanity. I am beginning to suspect that it is not an island at all but a continent."

He fell silent for a while, enjoying the druggist's amazement. Then he explained his theory at length. The number of persons suffering from insanity, he believed, was far greater than commonly supposed; and he developed this idea with an abundance of reasons, texts, and examples. He found many of these examples in Itaguai, but he recognized the fallacy of confining his data to one time and place and he therefore resorted to history. He pointed in particular to certain historical celebrities: Socrates, who thought he had a personal demon: Pascal, who sewed a report of an hallucination into the lining of his coat; Mohammed, Caracalla, Domitian, Caligula, and others. The druggist's surprise at Bacamarte's mingling of the vicious and the merely ridiculous moved the psychiatrist to explain that these apparently inconsistent attributes were really different aspects of the same thing.

"The grotesque, my friend, is simply ferocity in disguise."

"Clever, very clever!" exclaimed Crispim Soares.

As for the basic idea of enlarging the realm of insanity, the druggist found it a little far-fetched; but modesty, his chief virtue, kept him from stating his opinion. Instead, he expressed a noble enthusiasm. He declared the idea sublime and added that it was "something for the noisemaker." This expression requires explanation. Like the other towns, villages, and settlements in the colony at that time, Itaguai had no newspaper. It used two media for the publication of news: handwritten posters nailed to the doors of the town hall and of the main church, and the noisemaker.

This is how the latter medium worked: a man was hired for one or more days to go through the streets rattling a noisemaker. A crowd would gather and the man would announce whatever he had been paid to announce: a cure for malaria, a gift to the Church, some farm land for sale, and the like. He might even be engaged to read a sonnet to the people. The system continually disturbed the peace of the community, but it survived a long time because of its almost miraculous effectiveness. Incredible as it may seem, the noisemaker actually enabled merchants to sell inferior goods at superior prices and third-rate authors to pass as geniuses. Yes, indeed, not all the institutions of the old regime deserve our century's contempt.

"No, I won't announce my theory to the public," replied the psychiatrist. "I'll do something better: I'll act on it."

The druggist agreed that it might be best to begin that way. "There'll be plenty of time for the noisemaker afterwards," he concluded.

But Simão Bacamarte was not listening. He seemed lost in meditation. When he finally spoke, it was with great deliberation.

"Think of humanity," he said, "as a great oyster shell. Our first task, Soares, is to extract the pearl—that is, reason. In other words, we must determine the nature and boundaries of reason. Madness is simply all that lies beyond those limits. But what is reason if not the equilibrium of the mental faculties? An individual, therefore, who lacks this equilibrium in any particular is, to that extent, insane."

Father Lopes, to whom he also confided his theory, replied that he was quite sure he understood it but that it sounded a little dangerous and, in any case, would involve more work than one doctor could possibly handle.

"Under the present definition of insanity, which has always been accepted," he added, "the fence around the area is perfectly clear and satisfactory. Why not stay within it?"

The vague suggestion of a smile played on the fine and discreet lips of the psychiatrist, a smile in which disdain blended with pity. But he said nothing. Science merely extended its hand to theology—with such assurance that theology was undecided whether to believe in itself or in science. Itaguai and the entire world were on the brink of a revolution.

V. THE TERROR

Four days later the population of Itaguai was dismayed to hear that a certain Mr. Costa had been committed to the Green House.

"Impossible!"

"What do you mean, impossible! They took him away this morning."

Costa was one of the most highly esteemed citizens of Itaguai. He had inherited 400,000 cruzados in the good coin of King João V. As his uncle said in the will, the interest on this capital would have been enough to support him "till the end of the world." But as soon as he received the inheritance he began to make loans to people without interest: a thousand cruzados to one, two thousand to another, three hundred to another, eight hundred to another, until, at the end of five years, there was nothing left. If poverty had come to him all at once, the shock to the good people of Itaguai would have been enormous. But it came gradually. He went from opulence to wealth, from wealth to comfort, from comfort to indigence, and from indigence to poverty. People who, five years earlier, had always doffed their hats and bowed deeply to him as soon as they saw him a block away now clapped him on the shoulder, flicked him on the nose, and made coarse remarks. But Costa remained affable, smiling, sublimely resigned. He was untroubled even by the fact that the least courteous were the very ones who owed him money; on the contrary, he seemed to greet them with especial pleasure.

Once, when one of these eternal debtors jeered at him and Costa merely smiled, someone said to him: "You're nice to this fellow because you still hope you can get him to pay what he owes you." Costa did not hesitate an instant. He went to the debtor and forgave the debt. "Sure," said the man who had made the unkind remark, "Costa canceled the debt because he knew he couldn't collect it anyway." Costa was no fool; he had anticipated this reaction. Inventive and jealous of his honor, he found a way two hours later to prove the slur unmerited: he took a few coins and loaned them to the same debtor.

"Now I hope . . ." he thought.

This act of Costa's convinced the credulous and incredulous alike. Thereafter no one doubted the nobility of spirit of that worthy citizen. All the needy, no matter how timid, came in their patched cloaks and knocked on his door. The words of the man who had impugned his motive continued, however, to gnaw like worms at his soul. But this also ended, for three months later the man asked him for one hundred and twenty cruzados, promising to repay it in two days. This was all that remained of the inheritance, but Costa made the loan immediately, without hesitation or interest. It was a means of noble redress for the stain on his honor. In time the debt might have been paid; unfortunately, Costa could not wait, for five months later he was committed to the Green House.

The consternation in Itaguai, when the matter became known, can readily be imagined. No one spoke of anything else. Some said that Costa had gone mad during lunch, others said it had happened early in the morning. They told of the mental attacks he had suffered, described by some as violent and frightening, by others as mild and even amusing. Many people hurried to the Green House. There they found poor Costa calm if somewhat surprised, speaking with great lucidity and asking why he had been brought there. Some went and talked with the psychiatrist. Bacamarte approved of their esteem and compassion for the patient, but he explained that science was science and that he could not permit a madman to remain at large. The last person to intercede (for, after what I am about to relate, no one dared go to see the dreadful psychiatrist) was a lady cousin of the patient. The doctor told her that Costa must certainly be insane, for otherwise he would not have thrown away all the money that . . .

"No! Now there you are wrong!" interrupted the good woman energetically. "He was not to blame for what he did."

"No?"

"No, Doctor. I'll tell you exactly what happened. My uncle was not ordinarily a bad man, but when he became angry he was so fierce that he would not even take off his hat to a religious procession. Well, one day, a short time before he died, he discovered that a slave had stolen an ox from him. His face became as red as a pepper; he shook from head to foot; he foamed at the mouth. Then an ugly, shaggy-haired man came up to him and asked for a drink of water. My uncle (may God show him the light!) told the man to go drink in the river—or in hell, for all he cared. The man glared at him, raised his hand threateningly, and uttered this curse: 'Your money will not last more than seven years and a day, as surely as this is the Star of David!' And he showed a Star of David tattooed on his arm. That was the cause of it all, Doctor—the hex put on the money by that evil man."

Bacamarte's eyes pierced the poor woman like daggers. When she had finished, he extended his hand as courteously as if she had been the wife of the Viceroy and invited her to go and talk with her cousin. The miserable woman believed him. He took her to the Green House and locked her up in the ward for those suffering from delusions or hallucinations.

When this duplicity on the part of the illustrious Bacamarte became known, the townspeople were terrified. No one could believe that, for no reason at all, the psychiatrist would lock up a perfectly sane woman whose only offense had been to intercede on behalf of an unfortunate relative. The case was gossiped about on street corners and in barber shops. Within a short time it developed into a full-scale novel, with amorous overtures by the psychiatrist to Costa's cousin, Costa's indignation, the cousin's scorn, and finally the psychiatrist's vengeance on them both. It was all very obvious. But did not the doctor's austerity and his life of devotion to science give the lie to such a story? Not at all! This was merely a cloak by which he concealed his treachery. And one of the more credulous of the townspeople even whispered that he knew certain other things—he would not say what, for he lacked complete proof—but he knew they were true, he could almost swear to them.

"You who are his intimate friend," they asked the druggist, "can't you tell us what's going on, what happened, what reason . . . ?"

Crispim Soares was delighted. This questioning by his puzzled friends, and by the uneasy and curious in general, amounted to public recognition of his importance. There was no doubt about it, the entire population knew that he, Crispim the druggist, was the psychiatrist's confidant, the great man's collaborator. That is why they all came running to the pharmacy. All this could be read in the druggist's jocund expression and discreet smile—and in his silence, for he made no reply. One, two, perhaps three dry monosyllables at the most, cloaked in a loyal, constant half-smile and full of scientific mysteries which he could reveal to no human being without danger and dishonor.

"There's something very strange going on," thought the townspeople.

But one of them merely shrugged his shoulders and went on his way. He had more important interests. He had just built a magnificent house, with a garden that was a masterpiece of art and taste. His furniture, imported from Hungary and Holland, was visible from the street, for the windows were always open. This man, who had become rich in the manufacture of pack saddles, had always dreamed of owning a sumptuous house, an elaborate garden, and rare furniture. Now he had acquired all these things and, in semi-retirement, was devoting most of his time to the enjoyment of them. His house was undoubtedly the finest in Itaguai, more grandiose than the Green House, nobler than the town hall. There was wailing and gnashing of teeth among Itaguai's social elite whenever they heard it praised or even mentioned—indeed, when they even thought about it. Owned by a mere manufacturer of pack saddles, good God!

"There he is, staring at his own house," the passers-by would say. For it was his custom to station himself every morning in the middle of his garden and gaze lovingly at the house. He would keep this up for a good hour, until called in to lunch.

Although his neighbors always greeted him respectfully enough, they would laugh behind his back. One of them observed that Mateus could make a lot more money manufacturing pack saddles to put on himself—a somewhat unintelligible remark, which nevertheless sent the listeners into ecstasies of laughter.

Every afternoon, when the families went out for their after dinner walks (people dined early in those days), Mateus would station himself at the center window, elegantly clothed in white against a dark background. He would remain there in a majestic pose for three or four hours, until it was dark. One may reasonably infer an intention on Mateus's part to be admired and envied, although he confessed no such purpose to anyone, not even to Father Lopes. His good friend the druggist nevertheless drew the inference and communicated it to Bacamarte. The psychiatrist suggested that, as the saddler's house was of stone, he might have been suffering from petrophilia, an illness that the doctor had discovered and had been studying for some time. This continual gazing at the house . . .

"No, Doctor," interrupted Crispin Soares vigorously.

"No?"

"Pardon me, but perhaps you don't know . . ." And he told the psychiatrist what the saddler did every afternoon.

Simão Bacamarte's eyes lighted up with scientific voluptuousness. He questioned Crispim at some length, and the answers he received were apparently satisfactory, even pleasant, to him. But there was no suggestion of a sinister intent in the psychiatrist's face or manner—quite the contrary—as he asked the druggist's arm for a little stroll in the afternoon sun. It was the first time he had bestowed this honor on his confidant. Crispim, stunned and trembling, accepted the invitation. Just then, two or three people came to see the doctor. Crispim silently consigned them to all the devils. They were delaying the walk; Bacamarte might even take it into his head to invite one of them in Crispim's stead. What impatience! What anxiety! Finally the visitors left and the two men set out on their walk. The psychiatrist chose the direction of Mateus's house. He strolled by the window five or six times, slowly, stopping now and then and observing the saddler's physical attitude and facial expression. Poor Mateus noticed only that he was an object of the curiosity or admiration of the most important figure in Itaguai. He intensified the nobility of his expression, the stateliness of his pose. . . . Alas! he was merely helping to condemn himself. The next day he was committed.

"The Green House is a private prison," said an unsuccessful doctor.

Never had an opinion caught on and spread so rapidly. "A private prison"—the words were repeated from one end of Itaguai to the other. Fearfully, to be sure, for during the week following the Mateus episode twenty-odd persons, including two or three of the town's prominent citizens, had been committed to the

Green House. The psychiatrist said that only the mentally ill were admitted, but few believed him. Then came the popular explanations of the matter: revenge, greed, a punishment from God, a monomania afflicting the doctor himself, a secret plan on the part of Rio de Janeiro to destroy the budding prosperity of Itaguai and ultimately to impoverish this rival municipality, and a thousand other products of the public imagination.

At this time the party of travelers returned from their visit of several weeks to Rio de Janeiro. The psychiatrist, the druggist, Father Lopes, the Councilmen, and several other officials went to greet them. The moment when Dona Evarista laid eyes again on her husband is regarded by the chroniclers of the time as one of the most sublime instants in the moral history of man, because of the contrast between these two extreme (although both commendable) natures. Dona Evarista uttered a cry, stammered a word or two, and threw herself at her husband in a way that suggested at once the fierceness of a wildcat and the gentle affection of a dove. Not so the noble Bacamarte. With the diagnostic objectivity, without disturbing for a moment his scientific austerity, he extended his arms to the lady, who fell into them and fainted. The incident was brief; two minutes later Dona Evarista's friends were greeting her and the homeward procession began.

The psychiatrist's wife was Itaguai's great hope. Everyone counted on her to alleviate the scourge. Hence the public acclamation, the crowds in the streets, the pennants, and the flowers in the windows. The eminent Bacamarte, having entrusted her to the arm of Father Lopes, walked contemplatively with measured step. Dona Evarista, on the contrary, turned her head animatedly from side to side, observing with curiosity the unexpectedly warm reception. The priest asked about Rio de Janeiro, which he had not seen since the previous viceroyalty, and Dona Evarista replied that it was the most beautiful sight there could possibly be in the entire world. The Public Gardens, now completed, were a paradise in which she had often strolled—and the Street of Beautiful Nights, the Fountain of Ducks . . . Ah! the Fountain of Ducks. There really were ducks there, made of metal and spouting water through their mouths. A gorgeous thing. The priest said that Rio de Janeiro had been lovely even in his time there and must be much lovelier now. Small wonder, for it was so much larger than Itaguai and was, moreover, the capital. . . . But one could not call Itaguai ugly; it had some beautiful buildings, such as Mateus's mansion, the Green House . . .

"And apropos the Green House," said Father Lopes, gliding skillfully into the subject, "you will find it full of patients."

"Really?"

"Yes. Mateus is there. . . ."

"The saddler?"

"Costa is there too. So is Costa's cousin, and So-and-so, and What's-his-name, and . . ."

"All insane?"

"Apparently," replied the priest.

"But how? Why?"

Father Lopes drew down the corners of his mouth as if to say that he did not know or did not wish to tell what he knew—a vague reply, which could not be repeated to anyone. Dona Evarista found it strange indeed that all those people should have gone mad. It might easily happen to one or another—but to *all* of them? Yet she could hardly doubt the fact. Her husband was a learned man, a scientist; he would not commit anyone to the Green House without clear proof of insanity.

The priest punctuated her observations with an intermittent "undoubtedly . . . undoubtedly . . ."

A few hours later about fifty guests were seated at Simão Bacamarte's table for the home-coming dinner.

Dona Evarista was the obligatory subject of toasts, speeches, and verses, all of them highly metaphorical. She was the wife of the new Hippocrates, the muse of science, an angel, the dawn, charity, consolation, life itself. Her eyes were two stars, according to Crispim Soares, and two suns, by a Councilman's less modest figure. The psychiatrist found all this a bit tiresome but showed no signs of impatience. He merely leaned toward his wife and told her that such flights of fancy, although permissible in rhetoric, were unsubstantiated in fact. Dona Evarista tried to accept this opinion; but, even if she discounted three fourths of the flattery, there was enough left to inflate her considerably. One of the orators, for example—Martim Brito, twenty-five, a pretentious fop, much addicted to women—declaimed that the birth of Dona Evarista had come about in this manner: "After God gave the universe to man and to woman, who are the diamond and the pearl of the divine crown" (and the orator dragged this phrase triumphantly from one end of the table to the other), "God decided to outdo God and so he created Dona Evarista."

The psychiatrist's wife lowered her eyes with exemplary modesty. Two other ladies, who thought Martim Brito's expression of adulation excessive and audacious, turned to observe its effect on Dona Evarista's husband. They found his face clouded with misgivings, threats, and possibly blood. The provocation was great indeed, thought the two ladies. They prayed God to prevent any tragic occurrence—or, better yet, to postpone it until the next day. The more charitable of the two admitted (to herself) that Dona Evarista was above suspicion, for she was so very unattractive. And yet not all tastes were alike. Maybe some men . . . This idea caused her to tremble again, although less violently than before; less violently, for the psychiatrist was now smiling at Martim Brito.

When everyone had risen from the table, Bacamarte

walked over to him and complimented him on his eulogy on Dona Evarista. He said it was a brilliant improvisation, full of magnificent figures of speech. Had Brito himself originated the thought about Dona Evarista's birth or had he taken it from something he had read? No, it was entirely original; it had come to him as he was speaking and he had considered it suitable for use as a rhetorical climax. As a matter of fact, he always leaned toward the bold and daring rather than the tender or jocose. He favored the epic style. Once, for example, he had composed an ode on the fall of the Marquis of Pombal in which he had said that "the foul dragon of Nihility is crushed in the vengeful claws of the All." And he had invented many other powerful figures of speech. He liked sublime concepts, great and noble images. . . .

"Poor fellow!" thought the psychiatrist. "He's probably suffering from a cerebral lesion. Not a very serious case but worthy of study."

Three days later Dona Evarista learned, to her amazement, that Martim Brito was now living at the Green House. A young man with such beautiful thoughts! The two other ladies attributed his commitment to jealousy on the part of the psychiatrist, for the young man's words had been provocatively bold.

Jealousy? But how, then, can one explain the commitment a short time afterward of persons of whom the doctor could not possibly have been jealous: innocuous, fun-loving Chico, Fabrício the notary, and many others. The terror grew in intensity. One no longer knew who was sane and who was insane. When their husbands went out in the street, the women of Itaguai lit candles to Our Lady. And some of the men hired bodyguards to go around with them.

Everyone who could possibly get out of town did so. One of the fugitives, however, was seized just as he was leaving. He was Gil Bernardes, a friendly, polite young man; so polite, indeed, that he never said hello to anyone without doffing his hat and bowing to the ground. In the street he would sometimes run forty yards to shake the hand of a gentleman or lady—or even of a child, such as the Circuit Judge's little boy. He had a special talent for affability. He owed his acceptance by society not only to his personal charm but also to the noble tenacity with which he withstood any number of refusals, rejections, cold shoulders, and the like, without becoming discouraged. And, once he gained entry to a house, he never left it—nor did its occupants wish him to leave, for he was a delightful guest. Despite his popularity and the self-confidence it engendered, Gil Bernardes turned pale when he heard one day that the psychiatrist was watching him. The following morning he started to leave town but was apprehended and taken to the Green House.

"This must not be permitted to continue."

"Down with tyranny!"

"Despot! Outlaw! Goliath!"

At first such things were said softly and indoors. Later they were shouted in the streets. Rebellion was raising its ugly head. The thought of a petition to the government for the arrest and deportation of Simão Bacamarte occurred to many people even before Porfírio with eloquent gestures of indignation, expounded it in his barber shop. Let it be noted—and this is one of the finest pages of a somber history—that as soon as the population of the Green House began to grow rapidly, Porfírio's profits also increased for many of his customers now asked to be bled; but private interests, said the barber, have to yield to the public welfare. "The tyrant must be overthrown!" So great was his dedication to the cause that he uttered this cry shortly after he heard of the commitment of a man named Coelho who was bringing a lawsuit against him.

"How can anyone call Coelho crazy?" shouted Porfírio.

And no one answered. Everybody said he was perfectly sane. The legal action against the barber, involving some real estate, grew not out of hatred or spite but out of the obscure wording of a deed. Coelho had an excellent reputation. A few individuals, to be sure, avoided him; as soon as they saw him approaching in the distance they ran around corners, ducked into stores. The fact is, he loved conversation—long conversation, drunk down in large draughts. Consequently he was almost never alone. He preferred those who also liked to talk, but he would compromise, if necessary, for a unilateral conversation with the more taciturn. Whenever Father Lopes, who disliked Coelho, saw him taking his leave of someone, he quoted Dante, with a minor change of his own:

> *"La bocca sollevò dal fiero pasto*
> *Quel seccatore . . ."* *

But the priest's remark did not affect the general esteem in which Coelho was held, for some attributed the remark to mere personal animosity and others thought it was a prayer in Latin.

VI. THE REBELLION

About thirty people allied themselves with the barber. They prepared a formal complaint and took it to the Town Council, which rejected it on the ground that scientific research must be hampered neither by hostile legislation nor by the misconceptions and prejudices of the mob.

"My advice to you," said the president of the Council, "is to disband and go back to work."

The group could hardly contain its anger. The bar-

* "The pest raised his mouth from his savage repast." Father Lopes substituted *seccatore*, "pest," for Dante's *peccator*, "sinner." Count Ugolino, the sinner, was gnawing the head of another sinner. *Inferno*, Canto XXXIII.

ber declared that the people would march to the Green House and destroy it; that Itaguai must no longer be used as a corpse for dissection in the experiments of a medical despot; that several esteemed and even distinguished individuals, not to mention many humble but estimable persons, lay confined in the cubicles of the Green House; that the psychiatrist was clearly motivated by greed, for his compensation varied directly with the number of alleged madmen in his care—

"That's not true," interrupted the president.

"Not true?"

"About two weeks ago we received a communication from the illustrious doctor in which he stated that, in view of the great value to him as a scientist of his observations and experiments, he would no longer accept payment from the Council or from the patients' families."

In view of this noble act of self-denial, how could the rebels persist in their attitude? The psychiatrist might, indeed, make mistakes, but obviously he was not motivated by any interest alien to science; and to establish error on his part, something more would be needed than disorderly crowds in the street. So spoke the president, and the entire Council applauded.

The barber meditated for a few moments and then declared that he was invested with a public mandate; he would give Itaguai no peace until the final destruction of the Green House, "that Bastille of human reason"—an expression he had heard a local poet use and which he now repeated with great vigor. Having spoken, he gave his cohorts a signal and led them out.

The Council was faced with an emergency. It must, at all costs, prevent rebellion and bloodshed. To make matters worse, one of the Councilmen who had supported the president was so impressed by the figure of speech, "Bastille of human reason," that he changed his mind. He advocated adoption of a measure to liquidate the Green House. After the president had expressed his amazement and indignation, the dissenter observed: "I know nothing about science, but if so many men whom we considered sane are locked up as madmen, how do we know that the real madman is not the psychiatrist himself?"

This Councilman, a highly articulate fellow named Sebastião Freitas, spoke at some length. He presented the case against the Green House with restraint but with firm conviction. His colleagues were dumfounded. The president begged him at least to help preserve law and order by not expressing his opinions in the street, where they might give body and soul to what was so far merely a whirlwind of uncoordinated atoms. This figure of speech counterbalanced to some extent the one about the Bastille. Sebastião Freitas promised to take no action for the present but reserved the right to seek the elimination of the Green House by legal means. And he murmured to himself lovingly: "That Bastille of human reason!"

Nevertheless, the crowd grew. Not thirty but three hundred now followed the barber, whose nickname ought to be mentioned at this point because it gave the rebellion its name: he was called Stewed Corn, and the movement was therefore known as the Revolt of the Stewed Corners. Storming through the streets toward the Green House, they might well have been compared to the mob that stormed the Bastille, with due allowance, of course, for the difference between Paris and Itaguai.

A young child attached to the household ran in from the street and told Dona Evarista the news. The psychiatrist's wife was trying on a silk dress (one of the thirty-seven she had bought in Rio).

"It's probably just a bunch of drunks," she said as she changed the location of a pin. "Benedita, is the hem all right?"

"Yes, ma'am," replied the slave, who was squatting

on the floor, "it looks fine. Just turn a little bit. Like that. It's perfect, ma'am."

"They're not a bunch of drunks, Dona Evarista," said the child in fear. "They're shouting: 'Death to Dr. Bacamarte the tyrant.' "

"Be quiet! Benedita, look over here on the left side. Don't you think the seam is a little crooked? We'll have to rip it and sew it again. Try to make it nice and even this time."

"Death to Dr. Bacamarte! Death to the tyrant!" howled three hundred voices in the street.

The blood left Dona Evarista's face. She stood there like a statue, petrified with terror. The slave ran instinctively to the back door. The child, whom Dona Evarista had refused to believe, enjoyed a moment of unexpressed but profound satisfaction.

"Death to the psychiatrist!" shouted the voices, now closer than before.

Dona Evarista, although an easy prey to emotions of pleasure, was reasonably steadfast in adversity. She did not faint. She ran to the inside room where her husband was studying. At the moment of her precipitate entrance, the doctor was examining a passage in Averroës. His eyes, blind to external reality but highly perceptive in the realm of the inner life, rose from the book to the ceiling and returned to the book. Twice, Dona Evarista called him loudly by name without his paying her the least attention. The third time, he heard and asked what was troubling her.

"Can't you hear the shouting?"

The psychiatrist listened. The shouts were coming closer and closer, threatening, terrifying. He understood. Rising from the armchair, he shut the book and, with firm, calm step, walked over to the bookcase and put the volume back in its place. The insertion of the volume caused the books on either side of it to be slightly out of line. Simão Bacamarte carefully straightened them. Then he asked his wife to go to her room.

"No, no," begged his worthy helpmeet. "I want to die at your side where I belong."

Simão Bacamarte insisted that she go. He assured her that it was not a matter of life and death and told her that, even if it were, it would be her duty to remain alive. The unhappy lady bowed her head, tearful and obedient.

"Down with the Green House!" shouted the Stewed Corners.

The psychiatrist went out on the front balcony and faced the rebel mob, whose three hundred heads were radiant with civism and somber with fury. When they saw him they shouted: "Die! Die!" Simão Bacamarte indicated that he wished to speak, but they only shouted the louder. Then the barber waved his hat as a signal to his followers to be silent and told the psychiatrist that he might speak, provided his words did not abuse the patience of the people.

"I shall say little and, if possible, nothing at all. It depends on what it is that you have come to request."

"We aren't requesting anything," replied the barber, trembling with rage. "We are demanding that the Green House be destroyed or at least that all the prisoners in it be freed."

"I don't understand."

"You understand all right, tyrant. We want you to release the victims of your hatred, your whims, your greed. . . ."

The psychiatrist smiled, but the smile of this great man was not perceptible to the eyes of the multitude: it was a slight contraction of two or three muscles, nothing more.

"Gentlemen," he said, "science is a serious thing and it must be treated seriously. For my professional decisions I account to no one but God and the authorities in my special field. If you wish to suggest changes in the administration of the Green House, I am ready to listen to you; but if you wish me to be untrue to myself, further talk would be futile. I could invite you to appoint a committee to come and study the way I treat the madmen who have been committed to my care, but I shall not, for to do so would be to account to you for my methods and this I shall never do to a group of rebels or, for that matter, to laymen of any description."

So spoke the psychiatrist, and the people were astounded at his words. Obviously they had not expected such imperturbability and such resoluteness. Their amazement was even greater when the psychiatrist bowed gravely to them, turned his back, and walked slowly back into the house. The barber soon regained his self-possession and, waving his hat, urged the mob to demolish the Green House. The voices that took up the cry were few and weak. At this decisive moment the barber felt a surging ambition to rule. If he succeeded in overthrowing the psychiatrist and destroying the Green House, he might well take over the Town Council, dominate the other municipal authorities, and make himself the master of Itaguai. For some years now he had striven to have his name included in the ballots from which the Councilmen were selected by lot, but his petitions were denied because his position in society was considered incompatible with such a responsibility. It was a case of now or never. Besides, he had carried the street riot to such a point that defeat would mean prison and perhaps banishment or even the scaffold. Unfortunately, the psychiatrist's reply had taken most of the steam out of the Stewed Corners. When the barber perceived this, he felt like shouting: "Wretches! Cowards!" But he contained himself and merely said: "My friends, let us fight to the end! The salvation of Itaguai is in your worthy and heroic hands. Let us destroy the foul prison that confines or threatens your children and parents, your mothers and sisters, your relatives and friends, and you yourselves. Do you want to be thrown into a dungeon and starved on bread and water or maybe whipped to death?"

The mob bestirred itself, murmured, shouted, and gathered around the barber. The revolt was emerging from its stupor and threatening to demolish the Green House.

"Come on!" shouted Porfírio, waving his hat.

"Come on!" echoed his followers.

At that moment a corps of dragoons turned the corner and came marching toward the mob.

VII. THE UNEXPECTED

The mob appeared stupefied by the arrival of the dragoons; the Stewed Corners could hardly believe that the force of the law was being exerted against them. The dragoons halted and their captain ordered the crowd to disperse. Some of the rebels felt inclined to obey, but others rallied around the barber, who boldly replied to the captain:

"We shall not disperse. If you wish, you may take our lives, but nothing else: we will not yield our honor or our rights, for on them depends the salvation or Itaguai."

Nothing could have been more imprudent or more natural than this reply. It reflected the ecstasy inspired by great crises. Perhaps it reflected also an excess of confidence in the captain's forbearance, a confidence soon dispelled by the captain's order to charge. What followed is indescribable. The mob howled its fury. Some managed to escape by climbing into windows or running down the street, but the majority, inspired by the barber's words, snorted with anger and stood their ground. The defeat of the Stewed Corners appeared imminent, when suddenly one third of the dragoons, for reasons not set forth in the chronicles, went over to the side of the rebels. This unexpected reinforcement naturally heartened the Stewed Corners and discouraged the ranks of legality. The loyal soldiers refused to attack their comrades and, one by one, joined them, with the result that in a few minutes the entire aspect of the struggle had changed. The captain, defended by only a handful of his men against a compact mass of rebels and soldiers, gave up and surrendered his sword to the barber.

The triumphant rebels did not lose an instant. They carried the wounded into the nearest houses and headed for the town hall. The people and the troops fraternized. They shouted vivas for the King, the Viceroy, Itaguai, and "our great leader, Porfírio." The barber marched at their head, wielding the sword as dexterously as if it had been merely an unusually long razor. Victory hovered like a halo above him, and the dignity of government informed his every movement.

The Councilmen, watching from the windows, thought that the troops had captured the Stewed Corners. The Council formally resolved to send a petition to the Viceroy asking him to give an extra month's pay to the dragoons, "whose high devotion to duty has saved Itaguai from the chaos of rebellion and mob rule." This phrase was proposed by Sebastião Freitas, whose defense of the rebels had so scandalized his colleagues. But the legislators were soon disillusioned. They could now clearly hear the vivas for the barber and the shouts of "death to the Councilmen" and "death to the psychiatrist." The president held his head high and said: "Whatever may be our fate, let us never forget that we are the servants of His Majesty and of the people of Itaguai." Sebastião suggested that perhaps they could best serve the Crown and the town by sneaking out the back door and going to the Circuit Judge's office for advice and help, but all the other members of the Council rejected this suggestion.

A few seconds later the barber and some of his lieutenants entered the chamber and told the Town Council that it had been deposed. The Councilmen surrendered and were put in jail. Then the barber's friends urged him to assume the dictatorship of Itaguai in the name of His Majesty. Porfírio accepted this responsibility, although, as he told them, he was fully aware of its weight and of the thorny problems it entailed. He said also that he would be unable to rule without their cooperation, which they promptly promised him. The barber then went to the window and told the people what had happened; they shouted their approval. He chose the title "Town Protector in the Name of His Majesty and of the People." He immediately issued several important orders, official communications from the new government, a detailed statement to the Viceroy with many protestations of obedience to His Majesty, and finally the following short but forceful proclamation to the people:

Fellow Itaguaians:

A corrupt and irresponsible Town Council was conspiring ignominiously against His Majesty and against the people. Public opinion had condemned it, and now a handful of citizens, with the help of His Majesty's brave dragoons, have dissolved it. By unanimous consent I am empowered to rule until His Majesty chooses to take formal action in the premises. Itaguaians, I ask only for your trust and for your help in restoring peace and the public funds, recklessly squandered by the Council. You may count on me to make every personal sacrifice for the common good, and you may rest assured that we shall have the full support of the Crown.

Porfírio Caetano das Neves
Town Protector in the Name of His Majesty
and of the People

Everyone remarked that the proclamation said nothing whatever about the Green House, and some considered this ominous. The danger seemed all the greater when, in the midst of the important changes that were taking place, the psychiatrist committed to the Grēen House some seven or eight new patients, including a relative of the Protector. Everybody erroneously interpreted Bacamarte's action as a challenge to the barber and thought it likely that within twenty-four hours the terrible prison would be destroyed and the psychiatrist would be in chains.

The day ended happily. While the crier with the noisemaker went from corner to corner reading the proclamation, the people walked about the streets and swore they would be willing to die for the Protector. There were very few shouts of opposition to the Green House, for the people were confident that the government would soon liquidate it. Porfírio declared the day an official holiday and, to promote an alliance between the temporal power and the spiritual power, he asked Father Lopes to celebrate the occasion with a Te Deum. The Vicar issued a public refusal.

"May I at least assume," asked the barber with a threatening frown, "that you will not ally yourself with the enemies of the government?"

"How can I ally myself with your enemies," replied Father Lopes (if one can call it a reply), "when you have no enemies? You say in your proclamation that you are ruling by unanimous consent."

The barber could not help smiling. He really had almost no opposition. Apart from the captain of dragoons, the Council, and some of the town bigwigs, everybody acclaimed him; and even the bigwigs did not actually oppose him. Indeed, the people blessed the name of the man who would finally free Itaguai from the Green House and from the terrible Simão Bacamarte.

VII. THE DRUGGIST'S DILEMMA

The next day Porfírio and two of his aides-de-camp left the government palace (the new name of the town hall) and set out for the residence of Simão Bacamarte. The barber knew that it would have been more fitting for him to have ordered Bacamarte to come to the palace, but he was afraid the psychiatrist would refuse and so he decided to exercise forbearance in the use of his powers.

Crispim Soares was in bed at the time. The druggist was undergoing continual mental torture these days. His intimacy with Simão Bacamarte called him to the doctor's defense, and Porfírio's victory called him to the barber's side. This victory, together with the intensity of the hatred for Bacamarte, made it unprofitable and perhaps dangerous for Crispim to continue to associate with the doctor. But the druggist's wife, a masculine woman who was very close to Dona Evarista, told him that he owed the psychiatrist an obligation of loyalty. The dilemma appeared insoluble, so Crispim avoided it by the only means he could devise: he said he was sick and went to bed.

The next day his wife told him that Porfírio and some other men were headed for Simão Bacamarte's house.

"They're going to arrest him," thought the druggist.

One idea led to another. He imagined that their next step would be to arrest him, Crispim Soares, as an accessory. The therapeutic effect of this thought was remarkable. The druggist jumped out of bed and, despite his wife's protests, dressed and went out. The chroniclers all agree that Mrs. Soares found great comfort in the nobility of her husband, who, she assumed, was going to the defense of his friend, and they note with perspicacity the immense power of a thought, even if untrue; for the druggist walked not to the house of the psychiatrist but straight to the government palace. When he got there he expressed disappointment that the barber was out; he had wanted to assure him of his loyalty and support. Indeed, he had intended to do this the day before but had been prevented by illness—an illness that he now evidenced by a forced cough. The high officials to whom he spoke knew of his intimacy with the psychiatrist and therefore appreciated the significance of this declaration of loyalty. They treated the druggist with the greatest respect. They told him that the Protector had gone to the Green House on important business but would soon return. They offered him a chair, refreshments, and flattery. They told him that the cause of the illustrious Porfírio was the cause of every true patriot—a proposition with which Crispim Soares heartily agreed and which he proposed to affirm in a vigorous communication to the Viceroy.

IX. TWO BEAUTIFUL CASES

The psychiatrist received the barber immediately. He told him that he had no means of resistance and was therefore prepared to submit to the new government. He asked only that they not force him to be present at the destruction of the Green House.

"The doctor is under a misapprehension," said Porfírio after a pause. "We are not vandals. Rightly or wrongly, everybody thinks that most of the people locked up here are perfectly sane. But the government recognizes that the question is purely scientific and that scientific issues cannot be resolved by legislation. Moreover, the Green House is now an established municipal institution. We must therefore find a compromise that will both permit its continued operation and placate the public."

The psychiatrist could not conceal his amazement. He confessed that he had expected not only destruction of the Green House but also his own arrest and banishment. The last thing in the world he would have expected was—

"That is because you don't appreciate the grave responsibility of government," interrupted the barber. "The people, in their blindness, may feel righteous indignation about something that they do not understand; they have a right, then, to ask the government to act along certain lines. The government, however, must remember its duty to promote the public interest, whether or not this interest is in full accord with the demands made by the public itself. The revolution, which yesterday overthrew a corrupt and despicable Town Council, screams for destruction of the Green House. But the government must remain calm and objective. It knows that elimination of the Green House would not eliminate insanity. It knows that the mentally ill must receive treatment. It knows also that it cannot itself provide this treatment and that it even lacks the ability to distinguish the sane from the insane. These are matters for science, not for politics. They are matters requiring the sort of delicate, trained judgment that you, not we, are fitted to exercise. All I ask is that you help me give some degree of satisfaction to the people of Itaguai. If you and the government present a united front and propose a compromise of some sort, the people will accept it. Let me suggest, unless you have something better to propose, that we free those patients who are practically cured and those whose illnesses are relatively mild. In this way we can show how benign and generous we are without seriously handicapping your work."

Simão Bacamarte remained silent for about three minutes and then asked: "How many casualties were there in the fighting yesterday?"

The barber thought the question a little odd, but quickly replied that eleven had been killed and twenty-five wounded.

"Eleven dead, twenty-five wounded," repeated the psychiatrist two or three times.

Then he said that he did not like the barber's suggestion and that he would try to devise a better compromise, which he would communicate to the government within a few days. He asked a number of questions about the events of the day before: the attack by the dragoons, the defense, the change of sides by the dragoons, the Council's resistance, and so on. The barber replied in detail, with emphasis on the discredit into which the Council had fallen. He admitted that the government did not yet have the support of the most important men in the community and added that the psychiatrist might be very helpful in this connection. The government would be pleased, indeed, if it could count among its friends the loftiest spirit in Itaguai and, doubtless, in the entire kingdom. Nothing that the barber said, however, changed the expression on the doctor's austere face. Bacamarte evidenced neither vanity nor modesty; he listened in silence, as impassive as a stone god.

"Eleven dead, twenty-five wounded," repeated the psychiatrist after the visitors had left. "Two beautiful cases. This barber shows unmistakable symptoms of psychopathic duplicity. As for proof of the insanity of the people who acclaim him, what more could one ask than the fact that eleven were killed and twenty-five wounded, Two beautiful cases!"

"Long live our glorious Protector!" shouted thirty-odd people who had been awaiting the barber in front of the house.

The psychiatrist went to the window and heard part of the barber's speech:

". . . for my main concern, day and night, is to execute faithfully the will of the people. Trust in me and you will not be disappointed. I ask of you only one thing: be peaceful, maintain order. For order, my friends, is the foundation on which government must rest."

"Long live Porfírio!" shouted the people, waving their hats.

"Two beautiful cases," murmured the psychiatrist.

X. THE RESTORATION

Within a week there were fifty additional patients in the Green House, all of them strong supporters of the new government. The people felt outraged. The government was stunned; it did not know how to react. João Pina, another barber, said openly that Porfírio had "sold his birthright to Simão Bacamarte for a pot of gold"—a phrase that attracted some of the more indignant citizens to Pina's side. Porfírio, seeing his competitor at the head of a potential insurrection, knew that he would be overthrown if he did not immediately change his course. He therefore issued two decrees, one abolishing the Green House and the other banishing the psychiatrist from Itaguai.

João Pina, however, explained clearly and eloquently that these decrees were a hoax, a mere face-saving gesture. Two hours later Porfírio was deposed and João Pina assumed the heavy burden of government. Pina found copies of the proclamation to the people, the explanatory statement to the Viceroy, and other documents issued by his predecessor. He had new originals made and sent them out over his own name and signature. The chronicles note that the wording of the new documents was a little different. For example, where the other barber had spoken of "a corrupt and irresponsible Town Council," João Pina spoke of "a body contaiminated by French doctrines wholly contrary to the sacrosanct interests of His Majesty."

The new dictator barely had time to dispatch the documents when a military force sent by the Viceroy entered the town and restored order. At the psychiatrist's request, the troops immediately handed over to him Porfírio and some fifty other persons, and promised to deliver seventeen more of the barber's followers as soon as they had sufficiently recovered from their wounds.

This period in the crisis of Itaguai represents the culmination of Simão Bacamarte's influence. He got whatever he wanted. For example, the Town Council, now re-established, promptly consented to have Sebastião Freitas committed to the asylum. The psychiatrist had requested this in view of the extraordinary inconsistency of the Councilman's opinions, which Bacamarte considered a clear sign of mental illness. Subsequently the same thing happened to Crispim Soares. When the psychiatrist learned that his close friend and staunch supporter had suddenly gone over to the side of the Stewed Corners, he ordered him to be seized and taken to the Green House. The druggist did not deny his swtich of allegiance but explained that he had been motivated by an overwhelming fear of the new government. Simão Bacamarte accepted the explanation as true; he pointed out, however, that fear is a common symptom of mental abnormality.

Perhaps the most striking proof of the psychiatrist's influence was the docility with which the Town Council surrendered to him its own president. This worthy official had declared that the affront to the Council could be washed away only by the blood of the Stewed Corners. Bacamarte learned of this through the secretary of the Council, who repeated the president's words with immense enthusiasm. The psychiatrist first committed the secretary to the Green House and then proceeded to the town hall. He told the Council that its president was suffering from hemoferal mania, an illness that he planned to study in depth, with, he hoped, immense benefit to the world. The Council hesitated for a moment and then acquiesced.

From that day on, the population of the asylum increased even more rapidly than before. A person could not utter the most commonplace lie, even a lie that clearly benefited him, without being immediately committed to the Green House. Scandalmongers, dandies, people who spent hours at puzzles, people who habitually inquired into the private lives of others, officials puffed up with authority—the psychiatrist's agents brought them all in. He spared sweethearts but not flirts, for he maintained that the former obeyed a healthful impulse, but that the latter yielded to a morbid desire for conquest. He discriminated against neither the avaricious nor the prodigal: both were committed to the asylum; this led people to say that the psychiatrist's concept of madness included practically everybody.

Some of the chroniclers express doubts about Simão Bacamarte's integrity. They note that, at his instigation, the Town Council authorized all persons who boasted of noble blood to wear a silver ring on the thumb of the left hand. These chroniclers point out that, as a consequence of the ordinance, a jeweler who was a close friend of Bacamarte became rich. Another consequence, however, was the commitment of the ring-wearers to the Green House; and the treatment of these unfortunate people, rather than the enrichment of his friend, may well have been the objective of the illustrious physician. Nobody was sure what conduct on the part of the ring-wearers had betrayed their illness. Some thought it was their tendency to gesticulate a great deal, especially with the left hand, no matter where they were—at home, in the street, even in church. Everybody knows that madmen gesticulate a great deal.

"Where will this man stop," said the important people of the town. "Ah, if only we had supported the Stewed Corners!"

One day, when preparations were being made for a

ball to be held that evening in the town hall, Itaguai was shocked to hear that Simão Bacamarte had sent his own wife to the asylum. At first everyone thought it was a gag of some sort. But it was the absolute truth. Dona Evarista had been committed at two o'clock in the morning.

"I had long suspected that she was a sick woman," said the psychiatrist in response to a question from Father Lopes. "Her moderation in all other matters was hard to reconcile with her mania for silks, velvets, laces, and jewelry, a mania that began immediately after her return from Rio de Janeiro. It was then that I started to observe her closely. Her conversation was always about these objects. If I talked to her about the royal courts of earlier times, she wanted to know what kind of clothes the women wore. If a lady visited her while I was out, the first thing my wife told me, even before mentioning the purpose of the visit, was how the woman was dressed and which jewels or articles of clothing were pretty and which were ugly. Once (I think Your Reverence will remember this) she said she was going to make a new dress every year for Our Lady of the Mother Church. All these symptoms indicated a serious condition. Tonight, however, the full gravity of her illness became manifest. She had selected the entire outfit she would wear to the ball and had it all fixed and ready. All except one thing: she couldn't decide between a garnet necklace and a sapphire necklace. The day before yesterday she asked me which she should wear. I told her it didn't matter, that they both were very becoming. Yesterday at lunch she repeated the question. After dinner she was silent and pensive. I asked her what was the matter. 'I want to wear my beautiful garnet necklace, but my sapphire one is so lovely.' 'Then wear the sapphire necklace.' 'But then I can't wear the garnet necklace.' In the middle of the night, about half-past one, I awoke. She was not in bed. I got up and went to the dressing room. There she sat with the two necklaces, in front of the mirror, trying on first one and then the other. An obvious case of dementia. I had her put away immediately."

Father Lopes said nothing. The explanation did not wholly satisfy him. Perceiving this, the psychiatrist told him that the specific illness of Dona Evarista was vestimania; it was by no means incurable.

"I hope to have her well within two weeks, and, in any event, I expect to learn a great deal from the study of her case," said the psychiatrist in conclusion.

This personal sacrifice greatly enhanced the public image of the illustrious doctor. Suspicion, distrust, accusations were all negated by the commitment of his own wife whom he loved with all his heart. No one could ever again charge him with motives other than those of science itself. He was beyond doubt a man of integrity and profound objectivity, a combination of Cato and Hippocrates.

XI. RELEASE AND JOY

And now let the reader share with the people of Itaguai their amazement on learning one day that the madmen of the Green House had been released.

"All of them?"

"All of them."

"Impossible. Some, maybe. But all?"

"All. He said so himself in a communiqué that he sent today to the Town Council."

The psychiatrist informed the Council, first, that he had checked the statistics and had found that four-fifths of the population of Itaguai was in the Green House; second, that this disproportionately large number of patients had led him to re-examine his fundamental theory of mental illness, a theory that classified as sick all people who were mentally unbalanced; third, that as a consequence of this re-examination in the light of the statistics, he had concluded not only that his theory was unsound but also that the exactly contrary doctrine was true—that is, that normality lay in a lack of equilibrium and that the abnormal, the really sick, were the well balanced, the thoroughly rational; fourth, that in view of the foregoing he would release the persons now confined and would commit to the Green House all persons found to be mentally ill under the new theory; fifth, that he would continue to devote himself to the pursuit of scientific truth and trusted that the Council would continue to give him its support; and sixth, that he would give back the funds he had received for the board and lodging of the patients, less the amounts already expended, which could be verified by examination of his records and accounts.

The amazement of Itaguai was no greater than the joy of the relatives and friends of the former patients. Dinners, dances, Chinese lanterns, music, everything to celebrate the happy occasion. I shall not describe the festivities, for they are merely peripheral to this history; suffice it to say that they were elaborate, long, and memorable.

In the midst of all this rejoicing, nobody noticed the last part of the fourth item in the psychiatrist's communiqué.

XII. THE LAST PART OF THE FOURTH ITEM

The lanterns were taken down, the ex-patients resumed their former lives, everything appeared normal. Councilman Freitas and the president returned to their accustomed places, and the Council governed Itaguai without external interference. Porfírio the barber had "experienced everything," as the poet said of Napoleon; indeed, Porfírio had experienced more than Napoleon, for Napoleon was never committed to the Green House. The barber now found the obscure security of his trade preferable to the brilliant calamities of power. He was tried for his crimes and convicted, but the people begged His Majesty to pardon their ex-Protector, and His Majesty did so. The authorities decided not to prosecute João Pina, for he had overthrown an unlawful ruler. The chroniclers maintain that Pina's absolution inspired our adage:

A judge will never throw the book
At crook who steals from other crook.

An immoral adage, but immensely useful.

There were no more complaints against the psychiatrist. There was not even resentment for his past acts. Indeed, the former patients were grateful because he had declared them sane; they gave a ball in his honor. The chroniclers relate that Dona Evarista decided at first to leave her husband but changed her mind when she contemplated the emptiness of a life without him. Her devotion to this high-minded man overcame her wounded vanity, and they lived together more happily than ever before.

On the basis of the new psychiatric doctrine set forth in the communiqué, Crispim Soares concluded that his prudence in allying himself with the revolution had been a manifestation of mental health. He was deeply touched by Bacamarte's magnanimity: the psychiatrist had extended his hand to his old friend upon releasing him from the Green House.

"A great man," said the druggist to his wife.

We need not specifically note the release of Costa, Coelho, and the other patients named in this history. Each was now free to resume his previous way of life. Martim Brito, for example, who had been committed because of a speech in excessive praise of Dona Evarista, now made another in honor of the doctor, "whose exalted genius lifted its wings and flew far above the common herd until it rivaled the sun in altitude and in brilliance."

"Thank you," said the psychiatrist. "Obviously I was right to set you free."

Meanwhile, the Town Council passed, without debate, an ordinance to take care of the last part of the fourth item in Bacamarte's communiqué. The ordinance authorized the psychiatrist to commit to the Green House all persons whom he found to be mentally well balanced. But, remembering its painful experience in connection with public reaction to the asylum, the Council added a proviso in which it stated that, since the purpose of the ordinance was to provide an opportunity for the doctor to test his new theory, the authorization would remain in effect for only one year, and the Council reserved the right to close the asylum at any time if the maintenance of public order so required.

Sebastião Freitas proposed an amendment to the effect that under no circumstances were members of the Council to be committed to the Green House. The amendment was adopted almost unanimously. The only dissenting vote was cast by Councilman Galvão. He argued calmly that, in authorizing a scientific experiment on the people of Itaguai, the Council would itself be unscientific if it exempted its members or any other segment of the population from subjection to the experiment. "Our public office," he said, "does not exclude us from the human race." But he was shouted down.

Simão Bacamarte accepted the ordinance with all its restrictions. As for the exemption of the Councilmen, he declared that they were in no danger whatever of being committed, for their votes in favor of the amendment showed clearly that they were mentally unbalanced. He asked only that Galvão be delivered to him, for this Councilman had exhibited exceptional mental equilibrium, not only in his objection to the amendment but even more in the calm that he had maintained in the face of unreasonable opposition and abuse on the part of his colleagues. The Council immediately granted the request.

Under the new theory a few acts or statements by a person could not establish his abnormality: a long examination and a thorough study of his history were necessary. Father Lopes, for example, was not taken to the Green House until thirty days after the passage of the ordinance. In the case of the druggist's wife fifty days of study were required. Crispim Soares raged about the streets, telling everybody that he would tear the tyrant's ears off. One of the men to whom he spoke—a fellow who, as everyone knew, had an aversion to Bacamarte—ran and warned the psychiatrist. Bacamarte thanked him warmly and locked him up in recognition of his rectitude and his good will even toward someone he disliked, signs of perfect mental equilibrium.

"This is a very unusual case," said the doctor to Dona Evarista.

By the time Crispim Soares arrived at the psychiatrist's house, sorrow had overcome his anger. He did not tear Bacamarte's ears off. The psychiatrist tried to comfort his old friend. He told him that his wife might be suffering from a cerebral lesion, that there was a fair chance of recovery, and that meanwhile he must of course keep her confined. The psychiatrist considered it desirable, however, for Soares to spend a good deal of time with her, for the druggist's guile and intellectual dishonesty might help to overcome the moral superiority that the doctor found in his patient.

"There is no reason," he said, "why you and your wife should not eat lunch and dinner together every day at the Green House. You may even stay with her at night."

Simão Bacamarte's words placed the druggist in a new dilemma. He wanted to be with his wife, but at the same time he dreaded returning to the Green House. He remained undecided for several minutes. Then Dona Evarista released him from the dilemma: she promised to visit his wife frequently and to bear messages between the two. Crispim Soares kissed her hands in gratitude. His pusillanimous egoism struck the psychiatrist as almost sublime.

Although it took Bacamarte almost half a year to find eighteen patients for the Green House, he did not relax his efforts to discover the insane. He went from street to street, from house to house, observing, inquiring, taking notes. And when he committed someone to the asylum, it was with the same sense of accomplishment with which he had formerly committed dozens at a time. This very disproportion confirmed his new theory. At last the truth about mental illness was definitely known. One day Bacamarte committed the Circuit Judge to the Green House, after weeks of detailed study of the man's acts and thorough interrogation of his friends, who included all the important people of Itaguai.

More than once the psychiatrist was on the point of sending someone to the Green House, only to discover a serious shortcoming at the last moment. In the case of the lawyer Salustiano, for example, he thought he had found so perfect a combination of intellectual and moral qualities that it would be dangerous to leave the man at large. He told one of his agents to bring the man in, but the agent, who had known many lawyers, suspected that he might really be sane and persuaded Bacamarte to authorize a little experiment. The agent had a close friend who was charged with having falsified a will. He advised this friend to engage Salustiano as his lawyer.

"Do you really think he'll take the case?"

"Sure he will. Confess everything to him. He'll get you off."

The agent's friend went to the lawyer, admitted that

he had falsified the will, and begged him to accept the case. Salustiano did not turn the man away. He studied the charges and supporting evidence. In court he argued at great length, proving conclusively that the will was genuine. After a verdict of acquittal the defendant received the estate under the terms of the will. To this experiment both he and the learned counselor owed their freedom.

Very little escapes the comprehension of a man of genuine insight. For some time Simão Bacamarte had noted the wisdom, patience, and dedication of the agent who devised the experiment. Consequently he determined to commit him to the Green House, in which he gave him one of the choicest cubicles.

The patients were segregated into classes. In one gallery lived only those whose outstanding moral quality was modesty. The notably tolerant occupied another gallery, and still others were set aside for the truthful, the guileless, the loyal, the magnanimous, the wise. Naturally, the friends and relatives of the madmen railed against the new theory. Some even tried to persuade the Town Council to cancel the authorization it had given Bacamarte. The Councilmen, however, remembered with bitterness the words of their former colleague Galvão; they did not wish to see him back in their midst, and so they refused. Simão Bacamarte sent a message to the Council, not thanking it but congratulating it on this act of personal spite.

Some of the important people of Itaguai then went secretly to the barber Porfírio. They promised to support him with men, money, and influence if he would lead another movement against the psychiatrist and the Town Council. He replied that ambition had once led him to violent transgression of the law but that he now recognized the folly of such conduct; that the Council, in its wisdom, had authorized the psychiatrist to conduct his new experiment for a year; that anybody who objected should wait till the end of the year and then, if the Council insisted on renewing the authorization, should petition the Viceroy; that he would not recommend recourse again to a method that had done no good and had caused several deaths and other casualties, which would be an eternal burden on his conscience.

The psychiatrist listened with immense interest when one of his secret agents told him what Porfírio had said. Two days later the barber was locked up in the Green House. "You're damned if you do and you're damned if you don't," observed the new patient.

At the end of the year allowed for verification of the new theory, the Town Council authorized the psychiatrist to continue his work for another six months in order to experiment with methods of therapy. The result of this additional experimentation is so significant that it merits ten chapters, but I shall content myself with one. It will provide the reader with an inspiring example of scientific objectivity and selflessness.

XII. PLUS ULTRA

However diligent and perceptive he may have been in the discovery of madmen, Simão Bacamarte outdid himself when he undertook to cure them. All the chroniclers agree that he brought about the most amazing recoveries.

It is indeed hard to imagine a more rational system of therapy. Having divided the patients into classes according to their predominant moral qualities, the doctor now proceeded to break down those qualities. He applied a remedy in each case to inculcate exactly the opposite characteristic, selecting the specific medicine and dose best suited to the patient's age, personality, and social position.

The cases of modesty may serve as examples. In some, a wig, a fine coat, or a cane would suffice to restore reason to the madman. In more difficult cases the psychiatrist resorted to diamonds, honorary degrees, and the like. The illness of one modest lunatic, a poet, resisted every sort of therapy. Becamarte had almost given up, when an idea occurred to him: he would have the crier with the noisemaker claim the patient to be as great as Garcão or Pindar.

"It was like a miracle," said the poet's mother to one of her friends. "My boy is entirely well now. A miracle . . ."

Another patient, also in the modest class, seemed incurable. The specific remedy used for the poet would not work, for this patient was not a writer; indeed, he could barely sign his name. But Dr. Bacamarte proved equal to the challenge. He decided to have the patient made secretary to the Itaguai branch of the Royal Academy. The secretary and the president of each branch were appointed by the Crown. They enjoyed the privileges of being addressed as Excellency and of wearing a gold medallion. The government at Lisbon refused Bacamarte's request at first; but after the psychiatrist explained that he did not ask the appointment as a real honor for his patient but merely as a therapeutic device to cure a difficult case, and after the Minister of Overseas Possessions (a cousin of the patient) intervened, the government finally granted the request. The consequent cure was hailed as another miracle.

"Wonderful, really wonderful!" said everybody upon seeing the healthy, prideful expression on the faces of the two ex-madmen.

Bacamarte's method was ultimately successful in every case, although in a few the patient's dominant quality proved impregnable. In these cases the psychiatrist won out by attacking at another point, like a good military strategist.

By the end of five months all the patients had been cured. The Green House was empty. Councilman

Galvão, so cruelly afflicted with fairness and moderation, had the good fortune to lose an uncle; I say good fortune, for the uncle's will was ambiguous and Galvão obtained a favorable interpretation of it by bribing two judges. With customary integrity, the doctor admitted that the cure had been effected not by him but by nature's *vis medicatrix*. It was quite otherwise in the case of Father Lopes. Bacamarte knew that the priest was utterly ignorant of Greek, and therefore asked him to make a critical analysis of the Septuagint. Father Lopes accepted the task. In two months he had written a book on the subject and was released from the Green House. As for the druggist's wife, she remained there only a short time.

"Why doesn't Crispim come to visit me?" she asked every day.

They gave her various answers and finally told her the plain truth. The worthy matron could not contain her shame and indignation. Her explosions of wrath included such expression as "rat," "coward," and "he even cheats on prescriptions." Simão Bacamarte remarked that, whether or not these characterizations of her husband were true, they clearly established the lady's return to sanity. He promptly released her.

If you think the psychiatrist was radiant with happiness on seeing the last guest leave the Green House, you apparently do not yet understand the man. *Plus ultra* was his motto. For him the discovery of the true theory of mental illness was not enough, nor was the establishment in Itaguai of the reign of reason with the total elimination of psychological abnormality. *Plus ultra!* Something told him that his new theory bore within itself a better, newer theory.

"Let us see," he said to himself, "if I can discover the ultimate, underlying truth."

He paced the length of the immense room, past bookcase after bookcase—the largest library in His Majesty's overseas possessions. A gold-embroidered damask dressing gown (a gift from a university) enveloped the regal and austere body of the illustrious physician. The extensive top of his head, which the incessant cogitations of the scientist had rendered bald, was covered by a wig. His feet, neither dainty nor gross but perfectly proportioned to his body, were encased in a pair of ordinary shoes with plain brass buckles. Note the distinction: only those elements that bore some relationship to his work as a scientist were in any sense luxurious; the rest were simple and temperate.

And so the psychiatrist walked up and down his vast library, lost in thought, alien to everything but the dark problem of psychopathology. Suddenly he stopped. Standing before a window, with his left elbow resting on his open right hand and his chin on his closed left hand, he asked himself: "Were they all really insane? Did I really cure them? Or is not mental imbalance so natural and inherent that it was bound to assert itself with or without my help?"

He soon arrived at this conclusion: the apparently well-balanced minds that he had just "cured" had really been unbalanced all the time, just like the obviously sane minds of the rest of the people. Their apparent illness was superficial and transient.

The psychiatrist contemplated his new doctrine with mixed feelings. He was happy because, after such long study, experimentation, and struggle, he could at last affirm the ultimate truth: there never were and never would be any madmen in Itaguai or anywhere else. But he was unhappy because a doubt assailed him. In the field of psychiatry a generalization so broad, so absolute, was almost inevitably erroneous. If he could find just one undeniably well-balanced, virtuous, insane man, the new theory would be acceptable—not as an absolute, exceptionless principle, which was inadmissible, but as a general rule applicable to all but the most extraordinary cases.

According to the chroniclers, this difficulty constituted the most dreadful of the spiritual tempests through which the courageous Bacamarte passed in the course of his stormy professional life. But tempests terrify only the weak. After twenty minutes a gentle but radiant dawn dispelled the darkness from the face of the psychiatrist.

"Of course. That's it, of course."

What Simão Bacamarte meant was that he had found in himself the perfect, undeniable case of insanity. He possessed wisdom, patience, tolerance, truthfulness, loyalty, and moral fortitude—all the qualities that go to make an utter madman.

But then he questioned his own self-observation. Surely he must be imperfect in some way. To ascertain the truth about himself he convoked a gathering of his friends and questioned them. He begged them to answer with absolute frankness. They all agreed that he had not been mistaken.

"No defects?"

"None at all," they replied in chorus.

"No vices?"

"None."

"Perfect in every respect?"

"In every respect."

"No, impossible!" cried the psychiatrist. "I cannot believe that I am so far superior to my fellow men. You are letting yourselves be influenced by your affection for me."

His friends insisted. The psychiatrist hesitated, but Father Lopes made it difficult for him not to accept their judgment.

"Do you know why you are reluctant to recognize in yourself the lofty qualities which we all see so clearly?" said the priest. "It is because you have an additional quality that enhances all the others: modesty."

Simão Bacamarte bowed his head. He was both sad and happy, but more happy than sad. He immediately committed himself to the Green House. His wife and his friends begged him not to. They told him he was perfectly sane. They wept, they pleaded. All in vain.

"This is a matter of science, of a new doctrine," he said, "and I am the first instance of its application. I embody both theory and practice."

"Simão! Simão, my love!" cried his wife. Her face was bathed in tears.

But the doctor, his eyes alight with scientific conviction, gently pushed her away. He entered the Green House, shut the door behind him, and set about the business of curing himself. The chroniclers state, however, that he died seventeen months later as insane as ever. Some even venture the opinion that he was the only madman (in the vulgar or non-Bacamartian sense) ever committed to the asylum. But this opinion should not be taken seriously. It was based on remarks attributed to Father Lopes—doubtless erroneously, for, as everybody knew, the priest liked and admired the psychiatrist. In any case, the people of Itaguai buried the mortal remains of Simão Bacamarte with great pomp and solemnity.

Translated by William L. Grossman

The Bourgeois King

A Droll Story

RUBEN DARIO

A dour day, with a lusterless sky and a chill in the air: a day for a story, my friend! Something piquant to ward off the vapors and lighten our melancholy! A distraction . . . I have it . . .

They tell of a monarch—the king of a great and glittering city, a man of expensive and whimsical tastes: naked slaves, black or white as the fancy moved him, horses with oversize manes, a great pomp of arms, fleet greyhounds with hunters blowing bronze horns and filling the wind with their fanfares. A King of Poets, perhaps? Not a bit of it! A Bourgeois King, a King for the Middle Classes.

This worthy had an eye for the arts. He lavished his favors on musicians, sculptors, painters, apothecaries, barbers, fencing masters and composers of dithyrambs.

On official safaris, he carried a complement of rhetoric professors to improvise allusive songs on the spot, with the felled boar or the roebuck still bleeding to death of its wounds: his lackeys kept the winecups bubbling with gold and his houris beat time with rhythmic and spirited applause. He lived like a sun king in a Babylon of music, laughter, and convivial uproar. When he tired of the hubbub of cities he announced an imperial hunt and deafened the forests with his legions; birds fled in a panic, and the pandemonium could be heard to the remotest cavern of his realm. His dogs hurdled the hedgerows and highways on their flexible paws, and the hunters, bent to their horses' necks, raced on with purple capes billowing and hair in the wind, their faces ablaze.

In the pomp of his palace the king heaped up treasures and marvels of art. Bowers of lilac and ponds led to the palace, past snowy-necked swans and footmen marshaled stiffly at attention. All in the very best taste. One climbed a column-crammed staircase, all alabaster and smaragdite, flanked with marble lions like the throne room of Solomon. So very refined. With the swans went a great aviary to delight the most exacting connoisseur in harmony—everything billing and cooing and twittering—and in these environs paced our king, expanding his consciousness, reading novels by M. Ohmet, winsome grammatical treatises, or a ravishing critique of this, that, or the other. That's the size of it: put him down as an intrepid defender of the academic propriety of letters and the dandified posture in art: a high-minded soul, a lover of pumice and fine penmanship.

Sheer flimflam! Chinoiserie! All of it calculated to bewitch and adorn! The king could have what he pleased and it pleased him to have everything: a gallery made to order for a Goncourt or the millions of a Croesus: bronze gargoyles with wide-open gullets and gingerbread tails in fantastic and marvelous groupings; japanned lacquers monstrously encrusted with branches and leaves and fauna to baffle the expert; rare butterfly fans on the walls; fish and gamecocks in all colors; masks with infernal grimaces and eyes looking as if they were alive; halberds of antique blade and sword hilts shaped like dragons munching on lotus blossoms; eggshells packed with yellow silk tunics, spidery fine in the weave, sown with red herons and green rice shoots; vases, century-old porcelains depicting Tartar warriors covered with pelts to their navels, with drawn bows and fasces of arrows.

And so on: a Greek gallery full of marble goddesses, numphs, muses, satyrs; a hall in the style of a courtlier day, with paintings by Watteau and Chardin; two, three, four, all manner of galleries!

And our Maecenas pacing them all, his face looking drowned and majestic, with a full belly and a crown on his head—like any playing-card king.

One day a rare species of man was brought to the throne where, surrounded by courtiers, rhetoricians, dancing teachers and masters of equitation, he held court.

"And what might that be?" he asked.

"A poet, milord."

The king had pondfuls of swans, aviaries of canaries, song sparrows, mockingbirds, but a poet was something decidedly out of the ordinary.

"We will speak with this fellow."

But all the poet said was: "Milord, I haven't eaten in days."

And the king: "Then sing for your supper, sirrah!"

The poet began: "Milord, it's been a long time since I sang for posterity. I've spread my wings on the hurricane, I was born in the dawn of creation; I still seek the Elect and Awaited Ones with a lute in my hands and a hymn on my lips, the coming forth by day of the Sun. I've put behind me the noxious delusion of cities, the stink of the boudoir, the lascivious muse that belittles the spirit and mocks us with rice-powder masks. I have smashed the obsequious harp and ripped out the frail harp strings. I have smitten the cups of Bohemia, the vats where the wine that inebriates but cheers not ferments in the dark. I have put off my mountebank's cape and my woman's attire and have put on a savage and marvelous raiment: all my rags are fine purples. I have dwelt in the wilderness and kept hale and replete on a manna of milk and the nectar of life yet to come. I've walked the beaches of the world, tossing my head in raging black squalls, proud as an angel or an Olympian demigod. I have dared a new iamb and consigned the madrigal to oblivion.

"All Nature has felt my caress. I have sought in the heat of perfection the verse that is both star to the zenith and pearl in the Ocean's profundity. I covet my passion's entirety! The time of the great revolution is at hand, of the Messiah total in light, in excitement, in power. The poem to honor his spirit must be shaped like a conqueror's arch, stanzas of steel upon stanzas of gold upon stanzas of love.

"Art cannot live in the freezing containment of marble, milord, or the frills of a picture frame; the tales of the admirable M. Ohmet are not enough. Art doesn't wear knee breeches, milord; it does not speak in *bourgeois*, it does not steadfastly dot all its 'i's.' It walks as it pleases, augustly in gold, with a nimbus of fire, or it moves in its nakedness, kneading the feverish clay and painting with light. Art is opulent. It beats the air with its wings like an eagle, or it bares its claws like a lion. If the choice is between Apollo and the geese of this world, choose Apollo, milord, though the geese be carved out of ivory and Apollo be baked in terracotta.

"O Poesy!

"What a pass we have come to! Our rhythms grow whorish, we honor the moles on the skin of our women and fabricate unguents of verses. Every shoemaker abuses my hendecasyllables; a Professor of Pharmacy puts the finishing periods and commas to my heart's inspiration. And all this in your name, milord! . . . Perfection, perfection itself—"

Here the king interrupted: "Have you heard enough, gentlemen? What is your pleasure, my lords?"

A philosopher replied in his kind: "If his Majesty will allow me, let the wretch sweat for his bread with a hand organ. Put him in the garden with the rest of the swans, to sing to you from the pond."

"Capital!" the king said. Then, turning again to the poet: "You'll grind tunes on a hand organ, sirrah. You'll keep your mouth shut. You will crank up your music box till it plays only waltzes, quadrilles, and galops, if you don't fancy dying of starvation. A piece of music for a piece of bread! Let's have no more twaddle about great things to come. Dismissed!"

From that very day, our famishing poet began cranking his hand organ by the banks of the swan pond for everyone to see. *Tooraloo! Tooralee!* ... shamed in the full glare of the sun. Did the king ever stroll in these purlieus? *Tralalalady!* Did our bard fill his belly? *Tooraloo! Tooralee!* Only the mockingbird came and went as he pleased, drinking dew in the flowering lilacs: bees buzzed at him, stinging his face and bringing tears to his eyes. Tears rolled down his cheeks and plopped bitterly in the black clay.

In midwinter, our poor poet froze, body and soul. His brain petrified; all his great hymns were forgotten, while this bard of the eagles and mountains withered away like any other poor devil, whirling the crank of his hand organ. *Tralalady!*

By the first snow, he was totally forgotten by the king and his vassals. They had buttoned their birds into blankets, but the poet was left to the glacial air that gnaws at the flesh and lashes the face with its thongs.

One night while a frost of white feathers rained from the spaces, there was a great palace banquet; a spidery light laughed gaily on everything—on the marble, the gold, the tunics of mandarins cut in old porcelain. The Professor of Rhetoric performed marvels of prosody—blood-curdling dactyls, anapests, pyrrhic extravaganzas—to the insane applause of the court, and the cups of cut crystal seethed with champagne and fine, luminous bubbles. A midwinter festival! And still that unfortunate beggar, at his post by the pond with only his hand organ to warm him, cranking the handle in trembling and fear, covered with snow and mocked by the wind, the implacable freeze and the dazzle, in bitter-dark night, kept grinding out lunatic galops and quadrilles while the stripped forest echoed. He gave up the ghost still awaiting the sun of a goldener time that would bring with it his dream of perfection—an art without knee breeches, cloaked in gold and wearing a nimbus. The very next day he was found by the king and his court—frozen to death like a sparrow, poor devil of a poet, with a bitter smile on his lips and his fingers still clutching his hand organ.

A dour day, a lusterless sky with a chill in the air. There you have it, my friend! The vapors, the doldrums are on us.

But should a chance phrase have touched any spirit in passing—a round of applause for the teller!

Hasta la vista!

Translated by Ben Belitt

Yzur

LEOPOLDO LUGONES

I bought the monkey at the auction sale of a circus that had gone bankrupt.

The first time it occurred to me to try the experiment described in these lines was one afternoon as I was reading in some article or other that the natives of Java used to attribute the lack of speech in monkeys not to the fact that they cannot talk, but simply that they will not. "They refrain from speech," it said, "so that people will not put them to work."

This idea, which I did not take seriously at first, came to engross me until it evolved into this anthropological theory: monkeys were men who for some reason or other stopped speaking. This caused the vocal organs and the brain centers that control speech to atrophy to the point where the relationship between the two grew so weak that it virtually disappeared. The language of the species was reduced to inarticulate cries, and the primitive human sank to animal level.

It is obvious that if this could be demonstrated, all the strange characteristics that make monkeys such unusual creatures would be readily explained. But there could be only one possible proof of this: to get a monkey to talk again.

Meanwhile I had traveled all over the world with my monkey, drawing him closer and closer to me through our wanderings and adventures. In Europe he attracted everyone's attention, and had I wanted to I could have made him as much a celebrity as Consul;* but my status as a businessman was out of keeping with such foolishness.

Inspired by my firm convictions about speech in monkeys, I went through the entire bibliography on the subject without any appreciable result. The only thing I knew with absolute certainty was that *there is no scientific reason why a monkey cannot speak.* This took five years of study and thought.

Yzur—where he got this name I never could find out, since his former owner did not know either—Yzur was certainly a remarkable animal. The training he received in the circus, although limited almost entirely to mimicry, had greatly developed his faculties; this was what impelled me even more to try out my apparently absurd theory upon him. Moreover, it is known that the chimpanzee (which Yzur was) is one of the most docile of monkeys and the best equipped mentally, which increased my chances of success. Every time I saw him walking along on two feet with his hands behind his back to keep his balance, cutting a figure like a drunken sailor, the conviction that he was a retarded human grew stronger in me.

Actually, there is no reason why a monkey should not form words with precision. His natural speech—that is to say the combination of cries by which he communicates with his fellow creatures—is quite diversified; his larynx, although different from a human being's, does not differ as much as a parrot's does—yet parrots can speak; and as for his brain, in addition to the fact that comparison with that of a parrot dispels all doubt, it should be recalled that an idiot's brain is

* Consul, the Almost-Human, a nineteenth-century hoax.

also undeveloped—and in spite of this, there are idiots who can pronounce some words. As far as Broca's convolution is concerned, this depends, of course, upon the total development of the brain; moreover, it has not been proved conclusively that this is the area that controls speech. Although it is the most likely area anatomically, there are, nevertheless, incontrovertible arguments to the contrary.

Happily, a monkey has—added to his many bad characteristics—a love of learning, as his flair for imitation reveals: good memory, powers of reflection developed even to the point of skillful pretending, and an attention span better developed, comparatively, than that of a child. He is, then, a pedagogical subject of the most promising type.

Moreover, mine was young, and it is known that youth is a monkey's most intelligent period. The only difficulty lay in the method I should use to teach him words. I was acquainted with all the unfruitful attempts of my predecessors, and it goes without saying that in view of the competence of some of them and the completely negative results of all their efforts, my determination faltered on more than one occasion. But all my thoughts on the subject kept drawing me to this conclusion: *the first step is to develop the monkey's organs of sound production.*

This is, indeed, the way one proceeds with deaf mutes before getting them to articulate. And scarcely had I begun to think about this when analogies between monkeys and deaf mutes came abundantly to mind. First of all, there is their extraordinary facility for imitation, which compensates for articulated speech and shows that failure to speak does not mean failure to think, even though there may be a lessening of this latter faculty due to the paralysis of the former. Then there are other characteristics, more peculiar because they are more specific: diligence in work, fidelity, and courage, which are increased certainly by two factors whose interrelation is surely revealing—a knack for balancing tricks and resistance to dizziness.

I decided, then, to begin my work with practical lip and tongue exercises for my monkey, thus treating him like a deaf mute. After that, his hearing would help me to establish direct verbal communication without the need for recourse to the sense of touch. The reader will note that in this I was planning ahead too optimistically.

Fortunately, among all the great apes the chimpanzee has the most mobile lips, and in this particular case Yzur, who had suffered from sore throats, knew how to open his mouth wide so they could examine it. The first inspection confirmed—in part—my suspicions: his tongue lay at the bottom of his mouth like an inert mass, motionless except when swallowing. The exercises soon had their effect, for after two months he knew how to stick out his tongue to sass me. This was the first connection he made between moving his tongue and an idea—a relationship, moreover, quite in keeping with his make-up.

The lips caused greater trouble: it was even necessary to stretch them with tweezers. But he appreciated—perhaps by my expression—the importance of that strange task, and set about it with a will. While I practiced the movements for him to imitate, he would sit there with his arm twisted behind him scratching his rump and blinking in quizzical concentration; or else he would stroke his hairy cheeks with the air of a man who is marshaling his thoughts by helping them along with rhythmic gestures. At last he learned how to move his lips.

But language skills are not easily mastered, as is shown by a child's long period of prattling, which leads him to the acquisition of speech habits only as his intellect develops. Indeed, it has been shown that the center of voice production is associated with the speech center of the brain in such a way that their normal development depends upon their working in tandem. This had already been foreseen as a logical deduction in 1785 by Heinicke, inventor of the oral method of teaching deaf mutes. He used to speak of the "dynamic concatenation of ideas," a phrase so crystal clear that it would do honor to more than one contemporary psychologist.

As for language arts, Yzur was in the same situation as a child who understands many words before beginning to speak; but he was much more adept at forming proper decisions about things because of his greater experience with life. These decisions must have been the result not only of impressions but also of intellectual curiosity and investigation, to judge by their varied character. Since this presupposes abstract reasoning, it revealed in him a high degree of intelligence, which was certainly very helpful for my purpose.

If my theories seem too bold, it should be borne in mind that the syllogism, which is the basis of logical reasoning, is not alien to the mind of many animals. This is true because the syllogism is basically a comparison between two sensations; if not, why do animals who know man flee from him, while those who never knew him do not?

I began, then, the phonetic education of Yzur. It was a question of teaching him first the mechanics of speech, and then leading him gradually into speaking meaningfully. The monkey had this much of an advantage over a deaf mute: he possessed a voice and had better control over his organs of articulation. It was a question of teaching him how to modulate his voice—that is, how to pronounce sounds, which teachers call static if they are vowels and dynamic if they are consonants.

In view of a monkey's fondness for food—and following in this instance a method employed by Heinicke with deaf mutes—I decided to associate each vowel with something good to eat: a with *potato*, e with *beet*, *i* with *pie*, *o* with *cocoa*, and *u* with *prune*, working things out so that the vowel should be contained in the name of the tidbit, either alone and repeated, as in *cocoa*, or combining the basic sounds in both stressed and unstressed syllables, as in *potato*. All went well as far as the vowels were concerned—that is, sounds formed with the mouth open. Yzur learned them in two weeks. The *u* was the hardest for him to pronounce.

The consonants gave me a devilish amount of work. I soon came to the conclusion that he would never succeed in pronouncing those formed by using both the teeth and gums: his long eyeteeth completely prevented this. His vocabulary was limited, then, to the five vowels plus *b*, *k*, *m*, *g*, *f*, and *c*—that is, all the consonants formed by using only the palate and the tongue. Even for this, the aural method was not enough; I had to resort to the sense of touch as with a deaf mute, resting his hand on my chest and then on his own so that he could feel the sound vibrations.

And so three years went by without getting him to form a single word. He tended to name things after the letter that predominated in them. That was all.

In the circus he had learned to bark like a dog, for they were his working companions; and when he saw me lose hope in the face of my vain attempts to elicit speech from him, he would bark loudly as if he were showing me all he knew. He would pronounce the vowels and consonants separately, but he was unable to combine them. At most he would come out with a giddy succession of *p*'s and *m*'s.

Despite the slow progress, a great change had come over his character. He moved his features less, his expression was more intelligent, and he struck thoughtful poses. He had acquired, for example, the habit of staring at the stars. His sensitivity had likewise increased: he was more inclined to cry easily.

The lessons continued with unyielding determination, although with no greater success. The whole business had become a painful obsession, and little by little I felt inclined to use force. My disposition was becoming more bitter with failure, until it reached the point of unconscious hostility toward Yzur.

He was becoming more moody in his deep, stubborn silence, and was beginning to convince me that I would never get him out of it, when suddenly I realized that he wasn't speaking because he didn't want to!

The cook came in horror to tell me one evening that he had surprised the monkey "speaking real words." According to his story, Yzur was squatting next to a fig tree in the garden; but terror prevented the cook from recalling the heart of the matter—that is, the words themselves. He thought he could remember only two: *bed* and *pipe*. I almost kicked him for his stupidity.

Needless to say, I spent the night in the grip of great emotion. And what I hadn't done for three years—the error that ruined everything—came as the result of the irritability brought on by that sleepless night, and by excessive curiosity as well.

Instead of letting the monkey come to the point of showing his command of speech naturally, I summoned him the next day and tried to get it out of him by making him obey me. All I got was the *p*'s and *m*'s with which I was fed up, the hypocritical winks, and—may Heaven forgive me—a certain hint of ridicule in the restless mobility of his grimaces. I became angry, and without thinking I whipped him. The only result was tears, and an absolute silence unbroken even by moaning.

Three days later he fell ill with a kind of mental depression complicated by symptoms of meningitis. Leeches, cold showers, purgatives, counterirritants, alcoholatures, bromides—every remedy for the terrible illness was given to him. With determination born of desperation I struggled on, driven by remorse and fear, the former because I believed the animal to be a victim of my cruelty, the latter because I feared for the secret he was carrying, perhaps, to the grave.

He improved after a great while, but was so weak, however, that he could not stir from his bed. The nearness of death had ennobled and humanized him: his eyes, full of gratitude, were never off me and followed me all around the room like two rotating globes even though I went behind him; his hand sought mine in the companionship of convalescence. In my great solitude, he was rapidly acquiring the status of a person.

Nonetheless, the demon of investigation, which is nothing but the spirit of perversity, drove me to renew my experiments. The monkey had really talked. I just couldn't leave it at that.

I began very slowly, asking him for the letters he knew how to pronounce. Not a sound! I left him alone for hours and watched him through a little hole in the partition. Not a sound! I spoke to him in short sentences, trying to play upon his faithfulness or his liking for food. Not a sound! When my sentences were sad, his eyes would fill with tears. When I used a familiar sentence such as "I am your master," with which I used to begin all my lessons, or "You are my monkey," with which I used to follow up my first statement in order to convey to his mind the finality of a complete truth, he would denote agreement by closing his eyelids. But he would not utter a sound, not even go so far as to move his lips.

He had gone back to signs as his only means of communicating with me, and this fact, coupled with his points of similarity with deaf mutes, caused me to redouble my precautions, since everyone knows how very prone deaf mutes are to mental illness. At times I wanted him to lose his mind to see if delirium would finally break his silence.

His convalescence was not progressing: the same emaciation, the same sadness. It was obvious that he was mentally and emotionally ill; his whole constitution had been undermined by some malfunction of the brain, and sooner or later his case would be hopeless. But in spite of the increasing submissiveness caused by the disease, his silence—that maddening silence brought on by my desperate action—continued unbroken. From some dim background of tradition which had become instinct, the species was imposing its millennial silence upon the animal, whose ancestral will was strengthened by his own inner being. The primitive men of the jungle who had been forced into silence—that is, into intellectual suicide—by some unknown and barbaric injustice, were keeping their secret; forest mysteries dating from the dawn of history still held sway across the enormous gulf of time in his now unconscious decision.

The great families of four-handed anthropoids, unfortunately retarded in the course of evolution and surpassed by man, who oppressed them with brutal barbarism, had doubtless been dethroned and had lost their sway in the leafy realm of their primitive Eden. Their ranks had been decimated, and their females had been captured so that organized slavery might begin with the mother's womb. In their helpless, conquered state they had been impelled to express their human dignity by breaking the unhappy but higher bond—speech—that linked them to their enemies, and as a final safeguard they had taken refuge in the obscurity of the animal kingdom.

And what horrors, what monstrous excesses of cruelty must the conquerors have committed upon these half-beasts during the course of their evolution to cause them—after having known intellectual pleasure, the forbidden fruit of the Scriptures—to resign themselves to that stultification of their species in degrading equality with inferior creatures; to that retrogression which fixed their intelligence forever at the level of the gestures made by an acrobatic automaton; to that great fear of life which would eventually bend their backs in bondage as a mark of their animal state and imprint upon them the wistful bewilderment that forms a basic trait of their tragicomic nature!

This is what had aroused my ill humor, buried deep in some atavistic limbo, on the very verge of success. Through millions of years the magic power of speech kept stirring in the simian soul; but against that temptation which was about to pierce the dark shadows of animal instinct, ancestral recollections that permeated his species with some instinctive horror were also raising an age-old barrier.

Yzur began to breathe his last without losing consciousness. It was a gentle death, with eyes closed, soft breathing, faint pulse, and complete tranquillity, interrupted only from time to time when he turned his sad, old mulatto-like face toward me with a heartbreaking expression of eternity. And the last afternoon, the afternoon of his death, there occurred the extraordinary event that made me decide to write this story.

Overcome by the warmth and the quiet of the growing dusk, I was dozing at his bedside when I suddenly felt myself seized by the wrist. I awoke, startled. The monkey, with his eyes wide open, was definitely dying now, and his expression was so human that it horrified me; but his hand, his eyes, drew me toward him with such eloquence that I bent over close to his face. And then, with his final breath, the final breath that crowned and dashed my hopes simultaneously, he pronounced—I am sure of it—he pronounced in a murmur (how can I classify the tone of a voice that had not spoken for ten thousand centuries?) these words, whose deep humanity served to bridge the gap between our species:

"Water, master. Master, my master. . . ."

Translated by William E. Colford

The Alligator War

HORACIO QUIROGA

It was a very big river in a region of South America that had never been visited by white men; and in it lived many, many alligators—perhaps a hundred, perhaps a thousand. For dinner they ate fish, which they caught in the stream, and for supper they ate deer and other animals that came down to the waterside to drink. On hot afternoons in summer they stretched out and sunned themselves on the bank. But they liked nights when the moon was shining best of all. Then they swam out into the river and sported and played, lashing the water to foam with their tails, while the spray ran off their beautiful skins in all the colors of the rainbow.

These alligators had lived quite happy lives for a long, long time. But at last one afternoon, when they were all sleeping on the sand, snoring and snoring, one alligator woke up and cocked his ears—the way alligators cock their ears. He listened and listened, and, to be sure, faintly, and from a great distance, came a sound: *Chug! Chug! Chug!*

"Hey!" the alligator called to the alligator sleeping next to him, "Hey! Wake up! Danger!"

"Danger of what?" asked the other, opening his eyes sleepily and getting up.

"I don't know!" replied the first alligator. "That's a noise I never heard before. Listen!"

The other alligator listened: *Chug! Chug! Chug!*

In great alarm the two alligators went calling up and down the riverbank: "Danger! Danger!" And all their sisters and brothers and mothers and fathers and uncles and aunts woke up and began running this way and that with their tails curled up in the air. But the excitement did not serve to calm their fears. *Chug! Chug! Chug!* The noise was growing louder every moment; and at last, away off down the stream, they could see something moving along the surface of the river, leaving a trail of gray smoke behind it and beating the water on either side to foam: *Chush! Chush! Chush!*

The alligators looked at each other in the greatest astonishment: "What on earth is that?"

But there was one old alligator, the wisest and most experienced of them all. He was so old that only two sound teeth were left in his jaws—one in the upper jaw and one in the lower jaw. Once, also, when he was a boy, fond of adventure, he had made a trip down the river all the way to the sea.

"I know what it is," said he. "It's a whale. Whales are big fish, they shoot water up through their noses, and it falls down on them behind."

At this news, the little alligators began to scream at the top of their lungs, "It's a whale! It's a whale! It's a whale!" and they made for the water intending to duck out of sight.

But the big alligator cuffed with his tail a little alligator that was screaming nearby with his mouth open wide. "Dry up!" said he. "There's nothing to be afraid of! I know all about whales! Whales are the afraidest people there are!" And the little alligators stopped their noise.

But they grew frightened again a moment afterward. The gray smoke suddenly turned to an inky black, and the *Chush! Chush! Chush!* was now so loud that all the alligators took to the water, with only their eyes and the tips of their noses showing at the surface.

Cho-ash-h-h! Cho-ash-h-h! Cho-ash-h-h! The strange monster came rapidly up the stream. The alligators saw it go crashing past them, belching great clouds of smoke from the middle of its back and splashing into the water heavily with the big revolving things it had on either side.

It was a steamer, the first steamer that had ever made its way up to the Parana. *Chush! Chush! Chush!* It seemed to be getting farther away again. *Chug! Chug! Chug!* It had disappeared from view.

One by one, the alligators climbed up out of the water onto the bank again. They were all quite cross with the old alligator who had told them wrongly that it was a whale.

"It was not a whale!" they shouted in his ear—for he was rather hard of hearing. "Well, what was it that just went by?"

The old alligator then explained that it was a steamboat full of fire and that the alligators would all die if the boat continued to go up and down the river.

The other alligators only laughed, however. Why would the alligators die if the boat kept going up and down the river? It had passed by without so much as speaking to them! That old alligator didn't really know so much as he pretended to! And since they were very hungry they all went fishing in the stream. But alas! There was not a fish to be found! The steamboat had frightened every single one of them away.

"Well, what did I tell you?" said the old alligator. "You see, we haven't anything left to eat! All the fish have been frightened away! However—let's just wait till tomorrow. Perhaps the boat won't come back again. In that case, the fish will get over their fright and come back so that we can eat them." But the next day the steamboat came crashing by again on its way back down the river, spouting black smoke as it had done before, and setting the whole river boiling with its paddle wheels.

"Well!" exclaimed the alligators. "What do you think of that? The boat came yesterday. The boat came today. The boat will come tomorrow. The fish will stay away and nothing will come down here at night to drink. We are done for!"

But an idea occurred to one of the brighter alligators: "Let's dam the river!" he proposed. "The steamboat won't be able to climb a dam!"

"That's the talk! That's the talk! A dam. A dam! Let's build a dam!" And the alligators all made for the shore as fast as they could.

They went up into the woods along the bank and began to cut down trees of the hardest wood they could find—walnut and mahogany, mostly. They felled more than ten thousand of them altogether, sawing the trunks through with the kind of saw that alligators have on the tops of their tails. They dragged the trees down into the water and stood them up about a yard apart, all the way across the river, driving the pointed ends deep into the mud and weaving the branches together. No steamboat, big or little, would ever be able to pass that dam! No one would frighten the fish again! They would have a good dinner the following day and every day! And since it was late at night by the time the dam was done, they all fell sound asleep on the riverbank.

Chug! Chug! Chug! Chush! Chush! Chush! Cho-ash-h-h-h-h! Cho-ash-h-h-h-h! Cho-ash-h-h-h-h!

They were still asleep the next day when the boat came up; but the alligators barely opened their eyes and then tried to go to sleep again. What did they care about the boat? It could make all the noise it wanted but it would never get by the dam!

And that is what happened. Soon the noise from the boat stopped. The men who were steering on the bridge took out their spyglasses and began to study the strange obstruction that had been thrown up across the river. Finally a small boat was sent to look into it more closely. Only then did the alligators get up from where they were sleeping, run down into the water, and swim out behind the dam, where they lay floating and looking downstream between the piles. They could not help laughing, nevertheless, at the joke they had played on the steamboat!

The small boat came up, and the men in it saw how the alligators had made a dam across the river. They went back to the steamer but soon after came rowing up toward the dam again.

"Hey, you alligators!"

"What can we do for you?" answered the alligators, sticking their heads thorugh between the piles in the dam.

"That dam is in our way!" said the men.

"Tell us something we don't know!" answered the alligators.

"But we can't get by!"

"I'll say so!"

"Well, take the old thing out of the way!"

"Nosireesir!"

The men in the boat talked it over for a while and then they called: "Alligators!"

"What can we do for you?"

"Will you take the dam away?"

"No!"

"No?"

"No!"

"Very well! See you later!"

"The later the better," said the alligators.

The rowboat went back to the steamer, while the alligators, as happy as could be, clapped their tails as loud as they could on the water. No boat could ever get by that dam and drive the fish away again!

But the next day the steamboat returned; and when the alligators looked at it, they could not say a word from their surprise: it was not the same boat at all but a larger one, painted gray like a mouse! How many steamboats were there, anyway? And this one probably would want to pass the dam! Well, just let it try! No, sir! No steamboat, little or big, would ever get through that dam!

"They shall not pass!" said the alligators, each taking up his station behind the piles in the dam.

The new boat, like the other one, stopped some distance below the dam; and again a little boat came rowing toward them. This time there were eight sailors in it, with one officer. The officer shouted: "Hey, you alligators!"

"What's the matter?" answered the alligators.

"Going to get that dam out of there?"

"No!"

"No?"

"No!"

"Very well!" said the officer. "In that case, we shall have to shoot it down!"

"Shoot it up if you want to!" said the alligators.

And the boat returned to the steamer.

But now, this mouse-gray steamboat was not an ordinary steamboat; it was a warship, with armor plate and terribly powerful guns. The old alligator who had made the trip to the river mouth suddenly remembered and just in time to shout to the other alligators, "Duck for your lives! Duck! She's going to shoot! Keep down deep under water."

The alligators dived all at the same time and headed for the shore, where they halted, keeping all their bodies out of sight except for their noses and their eyes. A great cloud of flame and smoke burst from the vessel's side, followed by a deafening report. An immense solid shot hurtled through the air and struck the dam exactly in the middle. Two or three tree trunks were cut away into splinters and drifted off downstream. Another shot, a third, and finally a fourth, each tearing a great hole in the dam. Finally the piles were entirely destroyed; not a tree, not a splinter, not a piece of bark was left; and the alligators, still sitting with their eyes and noses just out of water, saw the warship come steaming by and blowing its whistle in derision at them.

Then the alligators came out on the bank and held a council of war. "Our dam was not strong enough," said they; "we must make a new and much thicker one."

So they worked again all that afternoon and night, cutting down the very biggest trees they could find and making a much better dam than they had built before. When the gunboat appeared the next day, they were sleeping soundly and had to hurry to get behind the piles of the dam by the time the rowboat arrived there.

"Hey, alligators!" called the same officer.

"See who's here again!" said the alligators, jeeringly.

"Get that new dam out of there!"

"Never in the world!"

"Well, we'll blow it up, the way we did the other!"

"Blaze away, and good luck to you!"

You see, the alligators talked so big because they were sure the dam they had made this time would hold up against the most terrible cannonballs in the world. And the sailors must have thought so, too; for after they had fired the first shot a tremendous explosion occurred in the dam. The gunboat was using shells, which burst among the timbers of the dam and broke the thickest trees into tiny, tiny bits. A second shell exploded right near the first, and a third near the second. So the shots went all along the dam, each tearing away a long strip of it till nothing, nothing, nothing was left. Again the warship came steaming by, closer in toward shore on this occasion, so that the sailors could make fun of the alligators by putting their hands to their mouths and holloing.

"So that's it!" said the alligators, climbing up out of the water. "We must all die, because the steamboats will keep coming and going, up and down, and leaving us not a fish in the world to eat!"

The littlest alligators were already whimpering, for they had had no dinner for three days; and it was a crowd of very sad alligators that gathered on the river shore to hear what the old alligator now had to say.

"We have only one hope left," he began. "We must go and see the Sturgeon! When I was a boy, I took that trip down to the sea along with him. He liked the salt water better than I did and went quite a way out into the ocean. There he saw a sea fight between two of these boats; and he brought home a torpedo that had failed to explode. Suppose we go and ask him to give it to us. It is true the Sturgeon has never liked us alligators; but I got along with him pretty well myself. He is a good fellow, at bottom, and surely he will not want to see us all starve!"

The fact was that some years before an alligator had eaten one of the Sturgeon's favorite grandchildren, and for that reason the Sturgeon had refused ever since to call on the alligators or receive visits from them. Nevertheless, the alligators now trouped off in a body to the big cave under the bank of the river where they knew the Sturgeon stayed, with his torpedo beside him. There are sturgeons as much as six feet long, you know, and this one with the torpedo was of that kind.

"Mr. Sturgeon! Mr. Sturgeon!" called the alligators at the entrance of the cave. No one of them dared go in, you see, on account of that matter of the Sturgeon's grandchild.

"Who is it?" answered the Sturgeon.

"We're the alligators," the latter replied in a chorus.

"I have nothing to do with alligators," grumbled the Sturgeon crossly.

But now the old alligator with the two teeth stepped forward and said, "Why, hello, Sturgy. Don't you remember Ally, your old friend that took that trip down the river when we were boys?"

"Well, well! Where have you been keeping yourself all these years?" said the Sturgeon, surprised and pleased to hear his old friend's voice. "Sorry I didn't know it was you! How goes it? What can I do for you?"

"We've come to ask you for that torpedo you found, remember? You see, there's a warship keeps coming up and down our river scaring all the fish away. She's a whopper, I'll tell you, armor plate, guns, the whole thing! We made one dam and she knocked it down. We made another and she blew it up. The fish have all gone away and we haven't had a bite to eat in near onto a week. Now you give us your torpedo and we'll do the rest!"

The Sturgeon sat thinking for a long time, scratching his chin with one of his fins. At last he answered: "As for the torpedo, all right! You can have it in spite of what you did to my eldest son's first-born. But there's one trouble: who knows how to work the thing?"

The alligators were all silent. Not one of them had ever seen a torpedo.

"Well," said the Sturgeon proudly, "I can see I'll have to go with you myself. I've lived next to that torpedo a long time. I know all about torpedoes."

The first task was to bring the torpedo down to the dam. The alligators got into line, the one behind taking in his mouth the tail of the one in front. When the line was formed it was fully a quarter of a mile long. The Sturgeon pushed the torpedo out into the current and got under it so as to hold it up near the top of the water on his back. Then he took the tail of the last alligator in his teeth and gave the signal to go ahead. The Sturgeon kept the torpedo afloat, while the alligators towed him along. In this way they went so fast that a wide wake followed on after the torpedo, and by the next morning they were back at the place where the dam was made.

As the little alligators who had stayed at home reported, the warship had already gone by upstream. But this pleased the others all the more. Now they would build a new dam, stronger than ever before, and catch the steamer in a trap, so that it would never get home again.

They worked all that day and all the next night, making a thick, almost solid dike, with barely enough room between the piles for the alligators to stick their heads through. They had just finished when the gunboat came into view.

Again the rowboat approached with the eight men and their officer. The alligators crowded behind the dam in great excitement, moving their paws to hold their own with the current, for this time they were downstream.

"Hey, alligators!" called the officer.

"Well?" answered the alligators.

"Still another dam?"

"If at first you don't succeed, try, try, again!"

"Get that dam out of there!"

"No, sir!"

"You won't?"

"We won't!"

"Very well! Now you alligators just listen! If you won't be reasonable, we are going to knock this dam down, too. But to save you the trouble of building a fourth, we are going to shoot every blessed alligator around here. Yes, every single last alligator, women and children, big ones, little ones, fat ones, lean ones, and even that old codger sitting there with only two teeth left in his jaws!"

The old alligator understood that the officer was trying to insult him with that reference to his two teeth, and he answered: "Young man, what you say is true. I have only two teeth left, not counting one or two others that are broken off. But do you know what those two teeth are going to eat for dinner?" As he said this the old alligator opened his mouth wide, wide, wide.

"Well, what are they going to eat?" asked one of the sailors.

"A little dude of a naval officer I see in a boat over there!"—and the old alligator dived under water and disappeared from view.

Meantime the Sturgeon had brought the torpedo to the very center of the dam, where four alligators were holding it fast to the river bottom waiting for orders to bring it up to the top of the water. The other alligators had gathered along the shore, with their noses and eyes alone in sight as usual.

The rowboat went back to the ship. When he saw the men climbing aboard, the Sturgeon went down to his torpedo.

Suddenly there was a loud detonation. The warship had begun firing, and the first shell struck and exploded in the middle of the dam. A great gap opened in it.

"Now! Now!" called the Sturgeon sharply, on seeing that there was room for the torpedo to go through. "Let her go! Let her go!"

As the torpedo came to the surface, the Sturgeon steered it to the opening in the dam, took aim hurriedly with one eye closed, and pulled at the trigger of the torpedo with his teeth. The propeller of the torpedo began to revolve, and it started off upstream toward the gunboat.

And it was high time. At that instant a second shot exploded in the dam, tearing away another large section.

From the wake the torpedo left behind it in the

water the men on the vessel saw the danger they were in, but it was too late to do anything about it. The torpedo struck the ship in the middle, and went off.

You can never guess the terrible noise that torpedo made. It blew the warship into fifteen thousand million pieces, tossing guns and smokestacks and shells and rowboats—everything—hundreds and hundreds of yards away.

The alligators all screamed with triumph and made as fast as they could for the dam. Down through the opening bits of wood came floating, with a number of sailors swimming as hard as they could for the shore. As the men passed through, the alligators put their paws to their mouths and holloed, as the men had done to them three days before. They decided not to eat a single one of the sailors, though some of them deserved it without a doubt. Except that when a man dressed in a blue uniform with gold braid came by, the old alligator jumped into the water off the dam and snap! snap! ate him in two mouthfuls.

"Who was that man?" asked an ignorant young alligator, who never learned his lessons in school and never knew what was going on.

"It's the officer of the boat," answered the Sturgeon. "My old friend, Ally, said he was going to eat him, and eaten him he has!"

The alligators tore down the rest of the dam, because they knew that no boats would be coming by that way again.

The Sturgeon, who had quite fallen in love with the gold lace of the officer, asked that it be given him in payment for the use of his torpedo. The alligators said he might have it for the trouble of picking it out of the old alligator's mouth, where it had caught on the two teeth. They also gave him the officer's belt and sword. The Sturgeon put the belt on just behind his front fins and buckled the sword to it. Thus togged out, he swam up and down for more than an hour in front of the assembled alligators, who admired his beautiful spotted skin as something almost as pretty as the coral snake's, and who opened their mouths wide at the splendor of his uniform. Finally they escorted him in honor back to his cave under the riverbank, thanking him over and over again and giving him three cheers as they went off.

When they returned to their usual place they found the fish had already returned. The next day another steamboat came by; but the alligators did not care, because the fish were getting used to it by this time and seemed not to be afraid. Since then the boats have been going back and forth all the time, carrying oranges. And the alligators open their eyes when they hear the *chug! chug! chug!* of a steamboat and laugh at the thought of how scared they were the first time and of how they sank the warship.

But no warship has ever gone up the river since the old alligator ate the officer.

Translated by Arthur Livingston

The Devil's Twilight

RÓMULO GALLEGOS

On the rim of a trough that displays its dry basin under the leafless branches of the trees in the square it would decorate if fresh water gushed singing from its faucet, the Devil sits looking at the carnival procession.

A noisy flow of people pours steadily into the square. People lean on the verandas that face the street where the "parade" goes by, mill like drunken ants around the stalls where candies, fried stuff, soft drinks and conefuls of confetti and painted rice are sold, eddy around the musicians, working out wild steps to the rhythm of the native *joropo* dance whose savage melody breaks on the hardness of the atmosphere tarnished by the dry season like a rag shredded by the wind.

Both hands holding onto the finely corded *araguaney* tree, his hat at the back of his neck and tobacco in his mouth, the Devil is listening to the music that stirs up vague nostalgic memories he cannot quite figure out deep inside of him. Sometimes sad, heartbreaking, like a cry lost in the loneliness of the plains, sometimes erotic, exciting, the music is the song of an obscure race, sad and lascivious, whose gaiety is a disturbing thing that has much tragedy in it.

Sections of desolate landscape never seen before pass briefly through the Devil's mind, shadows heavy with a sadness his heart has never felt, lightnings of blood that flashed through his life before, but he does not remember when. It is the music's spell digging down into the Devil's heart like a nest of scorpions. Under the influence of such thoughts he begins to feel depressed. His sucked-in cheeks shudder slightly; the quiet hard pupil of his eye bores a vision of hatred into the air in an unhappy way. The unconscious cause of all this is probably the presence of the crowd that awakens diabolical desires for power in him. His rough long-nailed fingers curve like ready claws around cords of the *araguaney*.

Beside him, one of those sitting on the rim of the trough with him says: "Ah, Pedro Nolasco, my friend, nowadays you don't see costumes like in the old days, do you?"

The Devil answers sullenly: "It isn't a carnival or anything else anymore."

"Those tight-rope dancers that used to stretch their ropes from window to window! The gangs of black boys that used to cudgel each other. They sure slammed each other around! Those devils!"

Pedro Nolasco's memory is working along those same lines.

He was one of the most respected devils and would start the popular celebration on its typical predominant note. At noon he plunged into the street in his devil's costume, all red, and with his long whip. From then on he went tirelessly up and down the neighborhood streets all afternoon, followed by a noisy mob so numerous that it sometimes stretched several blocks long, on which he would suddenly turn, wielding his whip that did not always just crack idly through the air in false threats.

More than once his diabolical lash raised some good welts on the calves of small boys and bigger fellows.

And every one of them took it, without protest or resentment, as punishment deserved for his deafening howls, as if the whipping came from "on High." It was the custom. No one resorted to anything except flight before the onslaught of the devils' whips.

Possessed by his part, Pedro Nolasco would lash out with what seemed to him the most righteous indignation because once he put on his devil's clothes and started down the street he forgot that it was a farce and considered the irreverent screams of the children an insult to his authority.

For their part, the mob of kids acted as if with this thought: a devil is a superior being; not everyone who wants to can be a devil, for it has its dangers, and you have to accept the whip cuts of anyone who knows how to be one the right way.

Pedro Nolasco was the best devil in Caracas. His territory was Candelaria parish and its limits. There was not a boy who did not run behind him howling until he was hoarse, risking his skin.

They respected him like an idol. When carnival time approached they began to talk about him, and his mysterious personality was the object of enthusiastic comments. Most people knew him only by name and many pictured him in the most fantastic manner. For some, Pedro Nolasco could not be like other men who worked and lived an ordinary life, but a mysterious being who did not leave his house all year, appearing in public just for the carnival in his absurdly sacred role of devil. Knowing Pedro Nolasco, where he lived and personal things about him made anyone proud. If you had spoken with him, it was like being the favorite of a prince. Anyone who had had this privilege could truly boast, for this was enough to make you grow in the eyes of all the kids in the parish.

This prestige increased even more because of a story in which Pedro Nolasco appeared as a sort of guardian-hero. The story ran that on Carnival Tuesday, many years back, Pedro Nolasco had done a very brave thing that showed his loyalty to his followers. Around that time in Caracas there was a rival devil, the devil of San Juan, who had as big a following as the Candelaria devil whose territory he had said he would invade that day and make use of his whip on him and his crowd. Pedro Nolasco got wind of this and went in search of him together with his yelling followers. The two mobs met and the San Juan devil drove into the other's people, whip swinging high. The one from Candelaria came to their defense, and before the other could bring down his arm to give him a whipping, Pedro Nolasco gave him a terrific butt in the face that broke his own horns and cut up the other's mouth. It was a fight Dante would not have been ashamed to sing.

From then on Pedro Nolasco was the only devil nobody would defy, feared by his shamefaced rivals who drew ridiculous crowds along out-of-the-way streets, looked up to and liked by his people, in spite of stinging calves and perhaps just because of them.

But time ran on and Pedro Nolasco's empire began to crumble. A poorly aimed lash landed on the shoulders of a boy from an influential family and he was taken to the police station. Pedro Nolasco felt humiliation at that arrest authorized by a single protest against his rod, undisputed until then. And, rather than acknowledge the deterioration of his power, he decided never to get into costume again.

Now he is in the square watching the masquerade go by. Among the large number of masqueraders, ridiculous devils pass, purely ornamental, who stick together and carry harmless tridents of silver-foiled cardboard in their hands. Nowhere the single devil with his traditional ruler's switch that was the terror and fascination of the crowd. No doubt, the carnival had degenerated.

Pedro Nolasco was busy with these thoughts when

he saw a large mob of boys coming into the square. In the lead came an absurd clown carrying a tiny parasol in one hand and in the other a fan which he fluttered in front of his sloppily painted face in an ambiguous and repugnant effeminate manner. That was his only attraction and yet the crowd ran behind that parasol fascinated, as if it were a special lure.

Anger and shame flooded through Pedro Nolasco. How could a man possibly masquerade that way? And, above all, how was it possible that a crowd was following him? You have to lose all your manly qualities to become a shameful, stupid following like that. Just look at how they troop after a clown that fans himself like a woman! The carnival could not be more degenerate!

But Pedro Nolasco loved his people and wanted to save them from such shame. A resolution flashed like lightning through his quiet hard eye.

The next day, Carnival Tuesday, the devil of Candelaria appeared in the streets of Caracas again.

At first it looked as if he would recover all of his old prestige because in just a few moments he gathered behind him a crowd that shook the streets with its sinister *awoooo's!* But suddenly the clown with the tiny parasol appeared and Pedro Nolasco's crowd went after the ridiculous lure that offered delightful fun without the risks of the devil's switch.

He was left behind alone, and under his cloth mask crowned by two real goat's horns two tears of sad despair slid down.

But suddenly he changed again and, prompted by an instinct experience had made wise, he dashed after the deserting mob, confident that the legendary authority of his whip would bring it back to his power, submissive and fascinated.

The crowd turned. There was a moment of hesitation. The devil was about to impose himself, recovering with the strength of his switch the control that grotesque idol had wrenched from him. The voice of the centuries rang out in their hearts.

But the clown understood the signs of the time and, waving his parasol like a false flag, set his followers on the Devil.

There was a loud reaction as in the good old days, deafening howls like those of an eager pack of dogs, but this time it meant hate, not fear.

Pedro Nolasco realized what had happened: he was hopelessly dethroned. Whether a feeling of humiliation made him decide to give up completely the power he had hoped to re-establish over that degenerate mob or whether his diabolic heart shrank back in authentic fear, he turned his back on the clown and began to move away forever into retirement.

But success fired the clown. Stirring up the mob, he shouted: "Come on, fellows! Rocks for the devil!"

This was enough for all hands to arm themselves with stones and turn with vengeance on the old idol that was now disgraced.

Pedro Nolasco ran from that rain of stones that came down on him and in his mad flight he crossed the suburb and rushed into the fields on the edge of town. The mob's thirst for blood grew as they ran after him under the guiding parasol of the clown, in whose hand the treacherous fan was a triumphant sword that day.

Evening was beginning to fall. A purplish twilight was spilling out over the fields like an omen. The devil was running, running over a lonely stretch along a dirt road banked with mounds of trash which vultures, like evil signs, were turning up. Seeing him approach, they rose in lazy, noisy flight, letting out prophetic murmurs, took to the safety of the empty branches of a tree that stood spectrally on that barren landscape.

The stones continued to rain down on him with even more zest, more fury. Pedro Nolasco felt his strength leaving him. His exhausted legs were folding under him. He fell twice as he ran. His heart was choking him horribly.

And it filled with pain, as it always does in the case of redeemers when they are persecuted by the creatures they love. For he felt that he was a redeemer misunderstood and betrayed by everyone. He had wanted to free "his people" from the shameful spell of the grotesque clown, to bring them back to themselves, to inspire them by his whip with the manliness that had once drawn them to follow him, driven by the voluptuousness that playing with danger can produce.

Finally a rock aimed by a sure, powerful arm, landed on his head. His sight clouded; he felt that everything around him was spinning dizzily and the earth was escaping under his feet. He screamed once and fell down on his face on the trash dump. The mob stopped, frightened at what it had done, and began to break up.

There was a tragic silence. The clown stayed nailed to the spot for a minute, mechanically fluttering his fan. Under the laughter painted on his face with white lead his amazement took on a macabre intensity. From the gloomy tree the vultures extended their necks toward the victim lying on the dump.

Then the clown took to his heels.

As he climbed over the back of a small hill, his parasol stood out like a rope dancer's against the sunset's light.

Translated by George M. Molinari

The Gauchos' Hearth

RICARDO GÜIRALDES

Steeped in silence, the coals turned velvety with ash as they died. The oil lamp threw off a wild flame, blackening the wall, and the last flicker from the hearth wearily lapped about the bellows.

One night followed another, all alike. I let myself slip into a general lethargy, sometimes thinking, sometimes absently listening to the hoarse cry of the peacock, the fluid strum of some refrain, the half-audible murmur of voices, calming as a lullaby.

At the table, a perpetual game of *tute* came to an end. Everyone moved back to the fire to drink the last cups of *mate* and to spend the rest of the evening in leisurely conversation.

Silverio, a big fellow of nineteen, brought a seat next to mine. He punched me playfully on the thigh.

"Drink up! Don't fall asleep on us!"

I took the *mate* someone was offering me, which until then I had not even noticed.

Silverio broke into his boyish laugh. An explosion of white teeth in a face browned by wind and sun.

He turned his humor on someone else.

"Don Segundo, your fingers'll grow together. Come tell us a story . . . pull up a seat."

A great, swarthy man was struggling with a tune too difficult for his callused hands. His tiny hat, the crown smashed in, made him seem even bigger than he was.

He left the instrument in a corner. It was covered with nicks and scratches, its strings as twisted as old veins.

"Come on over with us," someone said, making room. "Aren't any ghosts around here."

He was alluding to the old gaucho's superstitions, known to everyone and considered an integral part of his character.

"Talkin' about ghosts," he said; "I'll tell you a story." He gathered his *chiripá* about his knees so that it wouldn't drag on the floor.

For some people, a story is an excuse for pretty phrasing; for others, a lesson; for others, a way to put off sleep.

But for a gaucho, a story is such a special treat that he lives for the moment right alongside the hero; he gestures, even shouts out during the tense passages. His feelings are so real that if someone were to say to him, "Those are the villains! That's the one who did it!" there's many a gaucho would jump to help the man whose heart had touched his own through a noble deed, a proud word or a brave front to misfortune.

They let him think awhile, a preliminary to any good story, while they prepared to whet their fears. Each one brought up whatever he had seen of those phenomena which, because no one in the room could explain them, were attributed to supernatural causes.

One man had met up with the Horseman; another, the lantern that guides a man to his death; the Hound had rushed out at another, and still another got lost in a cemetery full of strange noises.

"There was this Englishman," the storyteller began: "Big, strong fellow who'd done business with more'n a few hide dealers and got himself the reputation of a slick operator.

Once on a time he was going to buy a drove of fat, crossbred yearlings from a rich widow. And he wasn't above using them calf's eyes of his to promote the sale.

It was a pitch-black night. The man was thinking over what tricks he'd use with the widow to fatten the tidy sum he'd put together buying beef for the slaughterhouses.

Seven miles from her place, the mare on the team got out of step. The driver figured it was best to give them a breather and whip them on again next morning when it was cooler. But the Englishman was in a hurry for his money. He wasn't about to wait around, so he made ready to go it afoot.

The driver showed him two roads: one going direct south to a general store from where he could follow the lane to the farm; and another shorter one heading straight for the mountain they could see from where they stood. Once across the mountain, he could make for a tall *ombu*, whose branches leaned across the farm's boundary line. But the road was dangerous, and plenty of stories had been told by those as had chosen to take it. It ran through property belonging to Alvarez, whom even the Englishman had heard of.

It was said a spirit haunted that road. The driver told him all about it.

Seems that one day the widow's son disappeared. Left nothing behind but a scrap of paper begging them to remember his soul, which was condemned to wander the earth, and that every day they set out a slice of beef and two pesos in a clearing off the road.

The widow did what her dead son asked, and next morning the plate was empty. The two pesos were gone, and the word "thanks" was scratched across the dirt. This surprised no one since the dead man was well brought up. Didn't matter that he hadn't wrote a letter while alive; his soul was a different case entirely.

Since then no white man dared cross of nights. Even the most cocksure turned back halfway.

The old woman would bring the food and the two pesos during the day, so nothing happened to her, only she'd hear the voice of her son's soul, which gratified her.

The driver concluded his story and, wishing the Englishman a good night, he headed for town. But the Englishman made straight for the mountain. He was a headstrong man and didn't hold with ghosts.

Directly on reaching it, he struck out to find the clearing.

That dark could have froze the heart out of anyone, but the Englishman was bristling with curiosity. He found the plate with the food and two pesos just like the widow had left it, as it wasn't time yet for the spirits to turn up.

He hid himself in the brush, took out a sawed-off shotgun, and waited to see what would happen.

He was already in the grip of sleep when a thrashing in the underbrush startled him. He looked all around, and soon made out a gaucho dressed in rags.

This gaucho carried a white poncho over his arm, so long it dragged on the ground; he had coltskin boots that reached midcalf and a short *chiripá* with more holes than a poor man's got worries.

Well, he sat down by the plate, and right off he pulled out a knife long as a man's arm and commenced swallowing whole chunks of meat.

God seemed to be setting up the Englishman's hand; suddenly, a whirlwind blew in and carried off the two pesos. That varmint let go his knife and give chase like a man possessed, when his luck failed and the Englishman grabbed him by the scruff of the neck. He knew this man could kill him, and he begged for his life. He claimed that, though he'd fallen on bad times, he wasn't no bandit and told how he'd come to play ghost.

Well, sir.

More'n twenty years back, when still only a kid, this fellow'd sworn to cut the comb off the cock luring away his girl; but that cock was Jacinto, a powerful man in the territory at the time. So they whipped the widow's son for a troublemaker.

Right then he promised he'd never rest easy till he'd got even. As fate would have it, one night he found Jacinto alone and he killed him, but in a clean fight.

Afterwards, he'd buried the body. Taking a chance on being spotted, he crept over to the widow's that night and left the note that would assure him food and some money to get out of his fix in due course.

That was his story; and he'd wrapped himself in his white poncho and scared folk account of was afraid they might recognize him.

He begged for mercy again; said he'd been punished enough by the life he'd lived. Though he wasn't the sort to shield a fugitive, the Englishman promised to keep silent and let the poor devil suffer in peace.

This happened years ago. They say the Englishman cleared the best deal ever as a reward for his kind heart."

Don Segundo paused; his bronze face seemed moved, and he tapped the pot's smooth belly with a stick from the fire. His listeners waited quietly for the conclusion.

"Well. So happened the Englishman was on the move a lot, but he had occasion to return years later.

He stopped off at the widow's. Couldn't help but think on what had happened to him in his younger days, so at suppertime, although it was a ticklish subject, he inquired after her son's ghost. The old woman started crying. She said she never heard his voice anymore; said he never wrote "thanks" in the dirt like he used to.

She surely must have offended him someways, for

she just didn't know how to deal with spirits. He no longer even took the two pesos, though he always ate what she brought. Many's the time she'd cried and begged his spirit to answer, but it never did.

The Englishman's curiosity was roused. Though the years had half-crippled him, just remembering that night made him feel young enough to handle himself in any pass. He told the widow to string his gear up under the eaves as it was a warm night; and when everyone else was asleep, he set out for the mountain, his step not near so firm and sure as it had been years back. He was puzzling why that buzzard had changed his ways.

He'd no more'n reached the grove when a strong wind come up. He took it for an evil omen. He cleared a way through the underbrush as best he could, and after running in circles a right smart while, he stumbled onto the clearing. Time he got there he was sweating; his breath was caught in his windpipe, and he set himself down to wait for the choking to pass. He wondered if it wasn't fear had brought it on. It's bad when a man asks himself that question, and now he jumped at every little sound.

A storm'll bring on strange noises in a wood. At times the wind sounds like a woman's wailing; a broken branch will groan like a human being, and I've even stopped short at sound of rushes whacking a tree trunk, thinking it might be some soul condemned to chop wood forever. Next day, as happens when God punishes a sinner, he finds his work undone and he's got to go on chopping and chopping in the hope that someday his ax blade might break the spell.

Times like that I've felt my heart shrivel thinking on what fate might have in store for each of us. And I consider how the Englishman must have felt—an old man with sins piled high around him who thought he'd reached that hour when he'd meet his Maker.

But seeing as he didn't believe in ghosts, he got up

courage to draw near the clearing. He found the plate same as before, and again he hid himself to wait.

He'd been there a stretch, what seemed like forever. It was too dark to check his watch. He wanted to get up, but he felt something like a hand pass across his jaw, and he crouched down lower. The chill was seeping into him, and the only reason he didn't make for the houses was because he was scared.

He caught a sound; something was walking amongst the dry leaves in front of him. The wind had stopped and he could hear real plain the footsteps of a man prowling about.

He held his breath and looked toward where the sound come from. A handspan ahead, he saw two gleaming eyes fixed on him. He felt his heart somersault, and squeezed the knife he'd drawn, swearing that if it was a joke, whoever gave him this fright would pay plenty. But he looked again: closer yet was two other eyes. He heard a ruckus behind him. It sounded like someone was laughing, and finally, half angry, half scared to death, he leapt into the clearing.

"Come on, come on," he yelled, "whoever you are, I'm gonna stomp your . . ." But just then something run against his legs. The man staggered a couple steps and fell face down on the empty brass plate. More shadows trotted over him; something yelped in his ear, ripping off half of it. He felt like the hairy paws of devils was trampling and scratching his face.

He yanked himself up and shot off for the mountain, without once looking back. This fellow run through the trees, crashing into trunks, stumbling, tangling himself in the underbrush, catching himself on brambles and bawling like a lost calf for the Lord to deliver him out of this hell."

Don Segundo laughed.

"Sweet Jesus, that man had a scare!"

"Look how that stiff-lipped Englishman melted. Soft as butter at the end," someone stated. "And he learned his lesson the hard way. That is, if the devil really had a hand in it," Silverio laughed.

"Seems the so-called ghost had saved a few pesos and left the territory to live like God meant us," Don Segundo continued. "But the widow still put out food. A fox smelled it one night, and the whole pack commenced to visit the clearing from then on. Whoever'd a notion to take the food away had best go forewarned and not make any slips."

Everyone was happy with the story. Of course, Don Segundo had stretched it so that they wouldn't tease him for another; but it was as good as a true one.

There was a general stir. The kindling had grown cold on those feeding the fire. Some men went off to sleep, while those who were least tired returned to the table, where the old, well-worn deck of cards awaited the familiar grip of strong hands.

Translated by Patricia Emigh

Why Reeds Are Hollow

GABRIELA MISTRAL

For don Max. Salas Marchant

I

Even in the peaceful world of plants, a social revolution once took place. It is told that in this case the leaders were those vain reeds. A master of rebellion, the wind, disseminated propaganda, and in no time at all there was talk of nothing else in the vegetal centers. Virgin forests fraternized with silly gardens, in a common struggle for equality.

Equality of what? Of their thickness of trunk, the excellence of their fruit, their right to pure water?

No, simply equality of height. The ideal was that all should raise their heads uniformly. The corn had no thought of making itself strong like the oak, but only of stirring its hairy tassels at the same elevation. The rose did not strive to be useful like the rubber plant, but just wanted to reach that high crown, and make of it a pillow on which to lull its flowers to sleep.

Vanity, vanity! Delusions of grandeur, even if they went against Nature, caricatured their aims. In vain, some modest flowers—the shy violet and flat-nosed lily—spoke of divine law and the evils of pride. Their voices seemed dotty.

An old poet, bearded like the River God, condemned the project in the name of beauty, and had some wise things to say about uniformity, hateful to him in every respect.

II

How did it all turn out? People tell of strange influences at work. Earth spirits blew upon the plants with their monstrous vitality, and so it was that an ugly miracle took place.

One night, the world of lawn and shrub grew dozens of feet, as if obeying some imperious appeal from the stars.

Next day, the country people were dismayed—when they came out of their huts—to find clover high as a cathedral and wheat fields wild with gold!

It was maddening. Animals roared with fright, lost in the darkness of their pastures. Birds chirped in desperation, their nests having risen to unheard-of heights. Nor could they fly down in search of seed: gone was the sunbathed soil, the grass's humble tapestry.

Shepherds lingered by their flocks beside dark pastures; their sheep refused to enter anything so dense, afraid they might be swallowed up completely.

Meanwhile, victorious, the reeds laughed aloud, whipping their riotous leaves against the blue tops of the eucalyptus.

III

Thus a month is said to have passed. Then the decline set in.

And it came about in this fashion: violets, which delight in shade, dried up when their purple heads were exposed to full sunlight.

"It doesn't matter," the reeds hastened to say. "They're a mere nothing."

(But in the country of the spirits, they were mourned.)

Lilies, stretching their height to fifty feet, broke in

two. Like the heads of queens, white marble heads lay lopped off all around.

The reeds argued as before. (But the Graces ran wild through the wood, lamenting.)

Lemon trees at that height lost all their blossoms to the violent winds. *Adios*, harvest!

"It doesn't matter," the reeds stated yet again. "Their fruit was so bitter."

The clover dried out, its stems twisting like threads in a fire.

Corn tassels drooped, but no longer from gentle lassitude. In all their extravagant length they fell upon the earth, heavy as rails.

Potatoes, to strengthen their stems, put forth feeble tubers; these were little bigger than apple seeds.

Now the reeds laughed no more; at last they grew serious.

Blossoms of shrub or grass were no longer being fertilized: the insects could not reach them without overheating their little wings.

Furthermore, it was said that man had neither bread nor fruit nor forage for his animals; hunger and sorrow were abroad in the land.

In such a state of things, only the tall trees remained sound, trunks rising strongly as ever: they had not yielded to temptation.

The reeds were the last to fall, signaling the total disaster of their tree-level theory; roots rotted from excessive humidity, and even the network of foliage could not keep them from drying out.

It was then clear that, compared with their former solid bulk, they'd become hollow. They reached hungry leagues upward, but, their insides being empty, they were laughable, like marionettes or dolls.

In the face of such evidence, no one could defend their philosophy; no more was said about it for thousands of years.

Nature—generous always—repaired the damage in six

months, seeing to it that all wild plants would again spring up in the usual way.

The poet, bearded like the River God, appeared after a long absence and, rejoicing, sang of the new era.

"So be it, dear people. Beautiful is the violet for its minuteness, and the lemon tree for its gentle shape. Beautiful are all things as God made them: the noble oak and the brittle barley."

The earth bore fruit once again; flocks fattened, the people were nourished.

But the reeds—those rebel chieftains—bore for all time the mark of their disgrace: they were hollow, hollow ...

Translated by William Jay Smith

Major Aranda's Hand

ALFONSO REYES

Major Aranda suffered the loss of a hand in battle, and, unfortunately for him, it was his right hand. Other people make collections of hands of bronze, of ivory, of glass and of wood; at times they come from religious statues or images; at times they are antique door knockers. And surgeons keep worse things in jars of alcohol. Why not preserve this severed hand, testimony to a glorious deed? Are we sure that the hand is of less value than the brain or the heart?

Let us meditate about it. Aranda did not meditate, but was impelled by a secret instinct. Theological man has been shaped in clay, like a doll, by the hand of God. Biological man evolves thanks to the service of his hand, and his hand has endowed the world with a new natural kingdom, the kingdom of the industries and the arts. If the strong walls of Thebes rose to the music of Amphion's lyre, it was his brother Zethus, the mason, who raised the stones with his hand. Manual laborers appear therefore in archaic mythologies, enveloped in magic vapor: they are the wonder-workers. They are "The Hands Delivering the Fire" that Orozco has painted. In Diego Rivera's mural the hand grasps the cosmic globe that contains the powers of creation and destruction; and in Chapingo the proletarian hands are ready to reclaim the patrimony of the earth.

The other senses remain passive, but the manual sense experiments and adds and, from the spoils of the earth, constructs a human order, the son of man. It models both the jar and the planet; it moves the potter's wheel and opens the Suez Canal.

A delicate and powerful instrument, it possesses the most fortunate physical resources: hinges, pincers, tongs, hooks, bony little chains, nerves, ligaments, canals, cushions, valleys and hillocks. It is soft and hard, aggressive and loving.

A marvelous flower with five petals that open and close like the sensitive plant, at the slightest provocation! Is five an essential number in the universal harmonies? Does the hand belong to the order of the dog rose, the forget-me-not, the scarlet pimpernel? Palmists perhaps are right in substance although not in their interpretations. And if the physiognomists of long ago had gone on from the face to the hand, completing their vague observations, undoubtedly they would have figured out correctly that the face mirrors and expresses but that the hand acts.

There is no doubt about it, the hand deserves unusual respect, and it could indeed occupy the favorite position among the household gods of Major Aranda.

The hand was carefully deposited in a quilted jewel case. The folds of white satin seemed a diminutive Alpine landscape. From time to time intimate friends were granted the privilege of looking at it for a few minutes. It was a pleasing, robust, intelligent hand, still in a rather tense position from grasping the hilt of the sword. It was perfectly preserved.

Gradually this mysterious object, this hidden talisman, became familiar. And then it emigrated from the treasure chest to the showcase in the living room, and a place was made for it among the campaign and high military decorations.

Its nails began to grow, revealing a slow, silent, surreptitious life. At one moment this growth seemed something brought on by inertia, at another it was evident that it was a natural virtue. With some repugnance at first, the manicurist of the family consented to take care of those nails each week. The hand was always polished and well cared for.

Without the family knowing how it happened—that's how man is, he converts the statue of the god into a small art object—the hand descended in rank; it suffered a *manus diminutio*; it ceased to be a relic and entered into domestic circulation. After six months it acted as a paperweight or served to hold the leaves of the manuscripts—the major was writing his memoirs now with his left hand; for the severed hand was flexible and plastic and the docile fingers maintained the position imposed upon them.

In spite of its repulsive coldness, the children of the house ended up by losing respect for it. At the end of a year, they were already scratching themselves with it or amused themselves by folding its fingers in the form of various obscene gestures of international folklore.

The hand thus recalled many things that it had completely forgotten. Its personality was becoming noticeable. It acquired its own consciousness and character. It began to put out feelers. Then it moved like a tarantula. Everything seemed an occasion for play. And one day, when it was evident that it had put on a glove all by itself and had adjusted a bracelet on the severed wrist, it did not attract the attention of anyone.

It went freely from one place to another, a monstrous little lap dog, rather crablike. Later it learned to run, with a hop very similar to that of hares, and, sitting back on the fingers, it began to jump in a prodigious manner. One day it was seen spread out on a current of air: it had acquired the ability to fly.

But in doing all these things, how did it orient itself, how did it see? Ah! Certain sages say that there is a faint light, imperceptible to the retina, perhaps perceptible to other organs, particularly if they are trained by education and exercise. Should not the hand see also? Of course it complements its vision with its sense of touch; it almost has eyes in its fingers, and the palm is able to find its bearings through the gust of air like the membranes of a bat. Nanook, the Eskimo, on his cloudy polar steppes, raises and waves the weather vanes to orient himself in an apparently uniform environment. The hand captures a thousand fleeting things and penetrates the translucent currents that escape the eye and the muscles, those currents that are not visible and that barely offer any resistance.

The fact is that the hand, as soon as it got around by itself, became ungovernable, became temperamental. We can say that it was then that it really "got out of hand." It came and went as it pleased. It disappeared when it felt like it; returned when it took a fancy to do so. It constructed castles of improbable balance out of bottles and wineglasses. It is said that it even became intoxicated; in any case, it stayed up all night.

It did not obey anyone. It was prankish and mischievous. It pinched the noses of callers, it slapped collectors at the door. It remained motionless, playing dead, allowing itself to be contemplated by those who were not acquainted with it, and then suddenly it would make an obscene gesture. It took singular pleasure in chucking its former owner under the chin, and it got into the habit of scaring the flies away from him. He would regard it with tenderness, his eyes brimming with tears, as he would regard a son who had proved to be a black sheep.

It upset everything. Sometimes it took a notion to

sweep and tidy the house; other times it would mix up the shoes of the family with a true arithmetical genius for permutations, combinations and changes; it would break the window panes by throwing rocks, or it would hide the balls of the boys who were playing in the street.

The major observed it and suffered in silence. His wife hated it, and of course was its preferred victim. The hand, while it was going on to other exercises, humiliated her by giving her lessons in needlework or cooking.

The truth is that the family became demoralized. The one-handed man was depressed and melancholy, in great contrast to his former happiness. His wife became distrustful and easily frightened, almost paranoid. The children became negligent, abandoned their studies, and forgot their good manners. Everything was sudden frights, useless drudgery, voices, doors slamming, as if an evil spirit had entered the house. The meals were served late, sometimes in the parlor, sometimes in a bedroom because, to the consternation of the major, to the frantic protest of his wife, and to the furtive delight of the children, the hand had taken possession of the dining room for its gymnastic exercises, locking itself inside, and receiving those who tried to expel it by throwing plates at their heads. One just had to yield, to surrender with weapons and baggage, as Aranda said.

The old servants, even the nurse who had reared the lady of the house, were put to flight. The new servants could not endure the bewitched house for a single day. Friends and relatives deserted the family. The police began to be disturbed by the constant complaints of the neighbors. The last silver grate that remained in the National Palace disappeared as if by magic. An epidemic of robberies took place, for which the mysterious hand was blamed, though it was often innocent.

The most cruel aspect of the case was that people

did not blame the hand, did not believe that there was such a hand animated by its own life, but attributed everything to the wicked devices of the poor one-handed man, whose severed member was now threatening to cost us what Santa Aña's leg cost us. Undoubtedly Aranda was a wizard who had made a pact with Satan. People made the sign of the cross.

In the meantime the hand, indifferent to the harm done to others, acquired an athletic musculature, became robust, steadily got into better shape, and learned how to do more and more things. Did it not try to continue the major's memoirs for him? The night when it decided to get some fresh air in the automobile, the Aranda family, incapable of restraining it, believed that the world was collapsing; but there was not a single accident, nor fines nor bribes to pay the police. The major said that at least the car, which had been getting rusty after the flight of the chauffeur, would be kept in good condition that way.

Left to its own nature, the hand gradually came to embody the Platonic idea that gave it being, the idea of seizing, the eagerness to acquire control. When it was seen how hens perished with their necks twisted or how art objects belonging to other people arrived at the house—which Aranda went to all kinds of trouble to return to their owners, with stammerings and incomprehensible excuses—it was evident that the hand was an animal of prey and a thief.

People now began to doubt Aranda's sanity. They spoke of hallucinations, of "raps" or noises of spirits, and of other things of a like nature. The twenty or thirty persons who really had seen the hand did not appear trustworthy when they were of the servant class, easily swayed by superstitions; and when they were people of moderate culture, they remained silent and answered with evasive remarks for fear of compromising themselves or being subject to ridicule. A round table of the Faculty of Philosophy and Literature devoted itself to discussing a certain anthropological thesis concerning the origin of myths.

There is, however, something tender and terrible in this story. Aranda awoke one night at midnight with shrieks of terror: in strange nuptials the severed hand, the right one, had come to link itself with the left hand, its companion of other days, as if longing to be close to it. It was impossible to detach it. It passed the remainder of the night there, and there it resolved to spend the nights from then on. Custom makes monsters familiar. The major ended by paying no attention to the hand. It even seemed to him that the strange contact made the mutilation more bearable and in some manner comforted his only hand.

The poor left hand, the female, needed the kiss and company of the right hand, the male. Let us not belittle it; in its slowness it tenaciously preserves as a precious ballast the prehistoric virtues: slowness, the inertia of centuries in which our species has developed. It corrects the crazy audacities, the ambitions of the right hand. It has been said that it is fortunate that we do not have two right hands, for in that case we would become lost among the pure subtleties and complexities of virtuosity; we would not be real men; no, we would be sleight-of-hand performers. Gauguin knows well what he is doing when, to restrain his refined sensitivity, he teaches the right hand to paint again with the candor of the left hand.

One night, however, the hand pushed open the library door and became deeply absorbed in reading. It came upon a story by de Maupassant about a severed hand that ends by strangling its enemy. It came upon a beautiful fantasy by Nerval in which an enchanted hand travels the world, creating beauty and casting evil spells. It came upon some notes by the philosopher Gaos about the phenomenology of the hand. . . . Good heavens! What will be the result of this fearful incursion into the alphabet?

The result is sad and serene. The haughty independent hand that believed it was a person, an autonomous entity, an inventor of its own conduct, became convinced that it was only a literary theme, a matter of fantasy already very much worked over by the pen of writers. With sorrow and difficulty—and, I might almost say, shedding abundant tears—it made its way to the showcase in the living room, settled down in its jewel case, which it first placed carefully among the campaign and high military decorations; and, disillusioned and sorrowful, it committed suicide in its fashion: it let itself die.

The sun was rising when the major, who had spent a sleepless night tossing about, upset by the prolonged absence of his hand, discovered it inert in the jewel case, somewhat darkened, with signs of asphyxiation. He could not believe his eyes. When he understood the situation, he nervously crumpled the paper on which he was about to submit his resignation from active service. He straightened up to his full height, reassumed his military haughtiness, and, startling his household, shouted at the top of his voice: "Attention! Fall in! All to their posts! Bugler, sound the bugle call of victory!"

Translated by Mildred Johnson

On the Other Side of Life and Death

CÉSAR VALLEJO

July's motionless brambles. Wind moored to each stalk crippled by too much grain pulling it down. Dead lust over navel-like mounds of the midsummer sierra. Wait. None of this. Let's sing some other time. Ah, what a pleasant dream.

My horse was heading that way. After eleven years of absence, I was finally nearing Santiago, my birthplace. The poor brute moved along, and I wept from the depths of my being out to my worn fingers, and maybe my weeping passed through the very reins I held, into the horse's cocked ears and then down and back through the clatter of the hooves that seemed to dance in the same spot, strange dance-steps measuring the road and the unknown ahead—I wept for my mother, two years dead, who no longer had to await the return of her footloose son. The entire region, the lovely weather, the lemon afternoon with its harvest colors, and here and there a hacienda that my soul recognized, all of it began to stir in me an ecstasy of homesickness, and my lips almost crinkled, as if they would root at my mother's imperishable breast, always full of milk; yes, even on the other side of death.

I must have passed that way with her as a child. Yes,

right. But no. It wasn't with me that she traveled over that countryside—I was too young then. It was with my father. It must have been soooo many years ago. . . ! It was also in July, close to the feast of Santiago. Father and mother on horseback, he in the lead. The royal road. All at once my father, who had just avoided running into a cactus suddenly looming round a bend: "Careful, ma'am!"

But it was too late for my poor mother; she was thrown from the saddle to the rocks in the path. They carried her back to town on a stretcher. I cried so much for my mother, and they wouldn't tell me what had happened. But she got better. Late into the night before the fiesta, she was already cheerful and full of laughter. She was no longer confined to her bed, and everything was beautiful.

But now I was crying more, remembering her that way, sick, bedridden, when she showed me more love and fussed over me more and gave me more cookies too from under her pillow and from the drawer of the night table. I was crying more now, as I approached Santiago, where I could only find her dead, buried under the ripe whispering mustard of a humble graveyard.

It was not two years since my mother had died. I had had the first news of her death in Lima, where I also learned that Papa and my brothers had set out for a distant hacienda owned by an uncle, to do whatever they could to dull the pain of such an overwhelming loss. The estate was in a very remote area in the jungle, on the other side of the Marañon River. From Santiago I would continue in that direction, eating up endless paths through steep highlands and unfamiliar, scorching jungles.

My horse snorted suddenly. Chaff blew thickly on the light breeze, almost blinding me. A mound of barley. And then Santiago slid into view on its rugged mesa, with its burnt roofs under the setting sun. And eastwards on the abutment of a reddish yellow promontory, I could still see the graveyard, retouched at the hour by the sixth color of the afternoon; and it was more than I could take, and a vast inconsolable sorrow made me numb.

I got to the village as night fell. I turned the last corner, and as I entered the street my house was on, I made out a figure sitting alone on the stone bench by the door. Alone. Very much alone—so much so that it frightened me, drowning out the deep grief in my soul. Perhaps it was also because of the almost frozen peace with which the silhouette, stiffened by the wavering half-light, clung to the whitewashed face of my tears. A unique attack of nerves dried my tears. I went forward. My older brother Angel jumped up from the seat and embraced me. He had come in from the hacienda on business a few days before.

That night, after a frugal meal, we mounted a vigil until dawn. I visited all the rooms in the house, the corridors and stables, and although he made obvious efforts to turn aside my eagerness to explore the rambling old house we loved so well, Angel himself seemed to enjoy this self-torture of going throught the hallucinating domain of life's deepest past.

During the few days of his stay in Santiago, Angel had lived alone in the house, where, he said, everything was as it had been left at Mama's death. He also gave me an account of her last healthy days before the fatal illness, and of her final moments. How often then did our brotherly embraces pierce us to the heart!

"Ah, this larder where I used to ask Mama for bread, with fake tears!" And I opened a small door with rickety panels.

As in all rural houses of the Peruvian sierras, that almost always have a stone seat built-in next to the door, there was one leaning back by the threshold I had just crossed, doubtless the same ancient bench of my childhood, filled in and plastered innumerable times. With the shabby door open, we sat on the bench, and there too we placed the sad-eyed lantern we carried with us. Its light fell squarely on Angel's face, which went paler moment by moment, as the night slipped by, until his face seemed nearly transparent. Once, seeing him like that, I kissed his grave, bearded cheek.

A flash of lightning, the kind that comes in summer in the sierras, from far off, with its thunder already spent, turned the night inside out. Rubbing my eyelids, I faced Angel. And there was nothing there—neither he nor the lantern nor the seat—nothing. And I heard nothing. I felt as if I were in a grave . . .

Then I saw again my brother, the lantern, the seat. But now I thought that Angel's face looked refreshed and serene, and—maybe I was wrong—as if he had recovered from his earlier misery and weakness. Again, maybe this was a trick my eyes were playing on me, for such a change is inconceivable.

"I can see her still," I went on, "and the poor thing never knew what to do, what with giving me cookies and scolding me: 'I caught you, you little fibber, you pretend to cry but you're laughing!' And she kissed me more than all the rest of you, because I was the youngest."

At the end of our grieving vigil, Angel again seemed crushed and, as before the flash of lightning, astonishingly haggard. So no doubt I had suffered a freak of vision from the sudden bolt of light, seeing a relaxation and exuberance in his face that could not, of course, have been there.

It was not yet dawn the following day when I mounted and rode off toward the hacienda, taking leave of Angel, who was staying on a few more days to look after the business that had brought him to Santiago.

At the end of the first day's journey, something amazing happened. I was leaning back on a wall bench outside the inn, resting, when suddenly an old woman of the place gave me a frightened look and asked sympathetically: "What's happened to your face, sir? My Lord! Looks like there's blood all over it . . ."

I sprang up from the seat. And in fact I saw my face in the mirror, splotched with stains of dried blood. A shudder ran through me, and I longed to run away from myself. Blood? Where from? I had pressed my face against Angel's as he wept . . . But . . . No, no. Where did the blood come from? You can imagine the terror and shock that knotted up in my breast. That seizure of the heart was like nothing else I had ever felt. There are no words to express it, now or ever. And even today, it's all here in this solitary room where I am writing, the stale blood and my face smeared with it and the old woman at the inn and that day and my brother weeping, whom my dead mother did not kiss . . .

. . . After I wrote those last sentences, I fled to my balcony, panting, in a cold sweat, so shattering was the memory of that strange blood.

Night of nightmare in that unforgettable hut, where my dead mother's image, in a contention of wild threads, endless threads that broke as soon as glimpsed, alternated with Angel's, who was weeping live rubies—forever and ever.

I continued on my way. And at last, after a week of jogging over ridges and hot jungles, after crossing the Marañon, one morning I approached the vicinity of the hacienda. Its cloudy sky echoed by fits and starts the distant thunder and let through momentary gleams of sun.

I dismounted by the tethering post at the roadside gate. A few dogs barked in the sad stillness of the mountain haze. I had returned now, after so many years, to that solitary mansion planted in the deepest hollows of the jungle.

Through the warning chatter of nervous fowl came a voice, calling and holding back the mastiffs inside—and strange as it seems, my trembling and exhausted horse seemed to sniff at its sound, and he snorted again and again, pushed his ears almost straight forward and, rearing up, tried to jerk the reins out of my hands and bolt. The enormous outer gate was closed. I must have rapped on it automatically. Then, inside the walls, that same voice rang out, and the next moment, as the immense gate opened with a spine-chilling sound, that ringing voice came to a dead stop on all my twenty-six years and left me staring at Eternity. The doors swung back.

Consider for a moment this incredible event that broke the laws of life and death and leapt beyond all possibility; word of hope and faith between the absurd and the infinite, undeniable disjuncture of time and place—all nebula, made of unharmonic unknown harmonies that make one cry!

My mother came out to receive me.

"My son!" she cried out, stupefied. "You're alive? Have you come back to life? Dear God in Heaven, what am I seeing?"

Mother! My mother, body and soul, alive! And so alive that today I think that as I stood before her, I felt two hailstones suddenly visible at the edges of my nostrils, two desolate hailstones of decrepitude falling on my heart and weighing it down till I was stooped like an old man, as if, by some fantastic trick of fate, my mother had just been born and I in turn was coming from days so far back in time that I felt for her the emotions of a father.

Yes. My mother was there. Dressed totally in black. Alive. Not dead anymore. Was it possible? No. How could it be? Impossible. That lady was not my mother. She couldn't be. And then, what had she said when she saw me? Did she think *I* was dead?

"My precious son!" She broke into tears and rushed to press me against her breast, with that frenzy of joyous weeping with which she had always greeted my comings and goings.

I turned to stone. I saw her throw her beloved arms around my neck, kiss me hungrily and as if she wanted to eat me up, sobbing out endearments that will never again rain down on the depths of my being. She took my expressionless face abruptly in her two hands, she looked at me thus, face to face, smothering me with questions. And, after a few seconds, I started crying too, but without changing expression or even moving: my tears were like pure water oozing from the eyes of a statue.

Finally I managed to focus all the dispersed lights of my spirit. I moved back a few steps. And then, oh dear God! I made my mother appear, the mother my heart would not accept, whom it denied and feared; I made her appear at God knows what sacred point in time, unknown to me until that moment, and I gave a silent, double-edged cry in her full presence, with the same rhythm of the hammer that rises and falls on the anvil, of the first wail a child lets loose as it is torn from its mother's womb, as if to let her know that there he goes, alive, into the world, and to give her at the same time a sign and a password that they may recognize each other forever after. And I moaned, beside myself.

"Never! Never! My mother died a long time ago. It can't be . . ."

She stood up, frightened by my words, as if doubting that I was really I. She drew me into her arms again and the two of us went on weeping tears no living creature has wept or will ever weep aain.

"Yes," I repeated, "my mother's already dead. My brother Angel knows this."

And at this point the blood stains I had seen on my face went through my mind like signs from another world.

"Son of my heart!" she whispered: "Are you the dead son I myself saw in his coffin? Yes. It's you, you yourself! I believe in God! Come to my arms! Can't you see I'm your mother? Look at me! Look at me! Touch me, son! Is it possible you don't believe it?"

Again I observed her. I touched her venerable little head, covered with white hair. Nothing. I believed nothing.

"Yes, I see you," I answered her. "I touch you. But I don't believe. So many impossible things can't be happening."

And I laughed as hard as I could.

Translated by Hardie St. Martin and Robert Mezey

The Piano

ANÍBAL MONTEIRO MACHADO

"Rosália!" shouted João de Oliveira to his wife, who was upstairs. "I told the guy to get out. What a nerve! He laughted at it. He said it wasn't worth even five hundred cruzeiros."

"It's an old trick," she replied. "He wants to get it for nothing and then sell it to somebody else. That's how these fellows get rich."

But Rosália and Sara looked somewhat alarmed as they came downstairs. The family approached the old piano respectfully, as if to console it after the insult.

"We'll get a good price for it, you'll see," asserted Oliveira, gazing at the piano with a mixture of affection and apprehension. "They don't make them like this any more."

"Put an ad in the paper," said Rosália, "and they'll come flocking. The house will be like *this* with people." She joined the tips of the fingers of her right hand in customary token of an immense crowd. "It's a pity to have to give it up."

"Ah, it's a love of a piano!" said João. "Just looking at it your think you hear music." He caressed its oaken case.

"Well, come on, João. Let's put the ad in."

It had to be sold so that the little parlor could be

made into a bedroom for Sara and her intended, a lieutenant in the artillery. Besides, the price would pay for her trousseau.

Three mornings later, the piano was adorned with flowers for the sacrifice, and the house was ready to receive prospective buyers.

The first to arrive were a lady and her daughter. The girl opened the piano and played a few chords.

"It's no good at all, Mama."

The lady stood up, looked at it, and noticed that the ivory was missing from some of the keys. She took her daughter by the hand and walked out, muttering as she went: "Think of coming all this distance to look at a piece of junk."

The Oliveira family had no time to feel resentment, for three new candidates appeared, all at the same time: an elderly lady who smelled like a rich widow, a young girl wearing glasses and carrying a music portfolio, and a redheaded man in a worn, wrinkled suit.

"I was here ahead of you," said the young girl to the old lady. "It doesn't really matter. I only came because my mother wanted me to. There must be plenty of others for sale. But I'd just like to say that I was ringing the doorbell while you were still getting off the bus. We came in together but I got here first."

This rivalry for priority pleased the Oliveiras. They thought it wise, however, to break up the argument, so they smiled at everyone and offered them all coffee. The young girl went over to the piano, while the redheaded man stood at a distance and evaluated it with a cool eye. At this moment a lady entered holding a schoolgirl by the hand. They sat down distrustfully.

Suddenly the young girl began to play, and the whole room hung on the notes that she extracted from the keyboard. Off-pitch, metallic, horrible notes. The Oliveiras anxiously studied the faces of their visitors. The redheaded man remained utterly impassive. The others glanced at one another as if seeking a common understanding. The newly arrived lady made a wry face. The perfumed old lady seemed more tolerant and looked indulgently at the old piano case.

It was a jury trial and the piano was the accused. The young girl continued to play, as if she were wringing a confession from it. The timbre suggested that of a decrepit, cracked-voiced soprano with stomach trouble. Some of the notes did not play at all. Doli joined in with her barking, a bitch's well-considered verdict. A smile passed around the room. No one was laughing, however. The girl seemed to be playing now out of pure malice, hammering at the dead keys and emphasizing the cacophony. It was a dreadful situation.

"There's something you ought to know about this piano," explained João de Oliveira. "It's very sensitive to the weather, it changes a great deal with variations in temperature."

The young girl stopped abruptly. She rose, put on some lipstick, and picked up her music portfolio.

"I don't know how you had the nerve to advertise this horror," she said, speaking to João but looking disdainfully as Rosália as if she had been the horror.

And she left.

João said nothing for a moment. After all, the insult had been directed at the old piano, not at him. Nevertheless, he felt constrained to declare that it was a genuine antique.

"They don't make them like this any more," he said emphatically. "They just don't make them."

There was a long silence. The status of the piano had reached its nadir. Finally the redheaded man spoke: "What are you asking for it?"

In view of what had happened, João de Oliveira lowered substantially the price he had had in mind.

"Five contos," he said timidly.

He looked at everyone to see the effect. There was a silent response. Oliveira felt cold. Was the price monstrously high? Only the old lady showed any delicacy at all: she said she would think it over. But, through her veil of mercy, João perceived her decision.

As they all were leaving, a man about to enter stepped out of their way.

"Did you come about the piano?" asked one of them. "Well, you'll . . . ."

But Oliveira interrupted.

"Come in," he said cheerfully. "It's right here. Lots of people have been looking at it."

The man was middle-aged, with a shock of grayish hair. He lifted the lid of the piano and examined the instrument at length. "Probably a music teacher," thought João.

The man did not ask the price. "Thank you," he said and left.

The house was empty again. Sara returned to her room. Rosália and João looked at each other in disappointment.

"Nobody understands its value," commented João sadly. "If I can't get a decent price for it, I'd rather not sell it at all."

"But how about Sara's trousseau?" said Rosália.

"I'll borrow the money."

"You'd never be able to pay it back out of your salary."

"We'll postpone the marriage."

"They love each other, João. They'll want to get married no matter what, trousseau or no trousseau."

At this moment, Sara could be heard shouting from her room that she could not possibly get married without two new slips and so forth.

"The thing is," Rosália went on, "this house is about the size of a matchbox. Where can we put the newlyweds? We'll have to give up the piano to make room for them. Nobody nowadays has enough room."

Sara's voice was heard again: "No, don't sell the piano. It's so pretty . . ."

"It's also so silent," interrupted her mother. "You

never play it any more. All you ever play is the victrola."

She went to her daughter's room to speak further with her. Strange that Sara should talk like that. Rosália put the dilemma flatly: "A husband or a piano. Choose."

"Oh, a husband!" replied Sara with voluptuous conviction. "Of course."

She hugged her pillow.

"So . . . ?"

"You're always against it, Rosália," shouted João de Oliveira.

"Against what?"

"Our piano."

"Oh, João, how can you say such a thing!"

The next day, as soon as he got back from work, João de Oliveira asked about the piano.

"Did any people answer the ad, Rosália?"

Yes, there had been several telephone calls for information about the piano, and an old man had come and looked at it. Also, the redheaded man had come again.

"Did any of them say anything about buying it?" asked João.

"No. But the two men who came to the house looked at it a long time."

"They did? Did they look at it with interest? With admiration?"

"It's hard to say."

"Yes, they admired it," said Sara. "Especially the old man. He almost ate it with his eyes."

João de Oliveira was touched. It was no longer a matter of price. He just wanted his piano to be treated with consideration and respect, that's all. Maybe it wasn't worth a lot of money but it certainly deserved some courteous attention. He was sorry he hadn't been there, but what his daughter told him of the old man's respectful attitude consoled him for the contumely of the day before. That man must understand the soul of antique furniture.

"Did he leave his address, Sara? No? Oh, well ... he'll probably be back."

He rose from his chair and walked around the old instrument. He smiled at it lovingly.

"My piano," he said softly. He ran his hand over the varnished wood as if he were caressing an animal.

No candidate the next day. Only a voice with a foreign accent asking if it was new. Rosália replied that it wasn't but that they had taken such good care of it that it almost looked like new.

"Tomorrow is Saturday," thought Oliveira. "There's bound to be a lot of people."

There were two, a man and a little girl, and they came in a limousine. The man looked at the modest house of the Oliveira family and considered it useless to go in. Nevertheless, he went to the door and asked the make and age of the piano.

"Thank you. There's no need for me to see it," he replied to João's insistence that he look at it. "I thought it would be a fairly new piano. Good luck ..."

And he went away.

João was grief-stricken. Ever since he had inherited the piano he had prized it dearly. He had never thought he would have to part with it. Worst of all, no one appreciated it, no one understood its value.

No one, except possibly the fellow who came the next Wednesday. He praised the piano in the most enthusiastic terms, said it was marvelous, and refused to buy. He said that if he paid so low a price for it he would feel he was stealing it, and that João and Rosália were virtually committing a crime in letting this precious thing get out of their hands. Oliveira did not exactly understand.

"Does he mean what he says?" he asked Rosália.

"I think he's just trying to be funny," she replied.

"I don't know. Maybe not."

Rosália was the first to lose hope. Her main concern now, when her husband came home from work, was to alleviate his suffering.

"How many today?"

"Nobody. Two telephone calls. They didn't give their names but they said they'd probably come and look at it."

Her voice was calm, soothing.

"How about the redheaded fellow?"

"I'm sure he'll be back."

For several days no one came or telephoned. João de Oliveira's feelings may be compared to those of a man who sees his friend miss a train: he is sad for his friend's sake and he is happy because he will continue for a time to have the pleasure of his company. João sat down near the piano and enjoyed these last moments with it. He admired its dignity. He confided his thoughts to it. Three generations had played it. How many people it had induced to dream or to dance! All this had passed away, but the piano remained. It was the only piece of furniture that bespoke the presence of his forebears. It was sort of eternal. It and the old oratory upstairs.

"Sara, come and play that little piece by Chopin. See if you remember it."

"I couldn't Papa. The piano sounds terrible."

"Don't say that," Rosália whispered. "Can't you see how your father feels?"

Whenever Sara's eyes lit on the piano, they transformed it into a nuptial bed in which she and the lieutenant were kissing and hugging.

For days and days no prospective buyer appeared. Nothing but an occasional telephone call from the redheaded man, as if he had been a doctor verifying the progress of a terminal case. The advertisement was withdrawn.

"Well, João, what are we going to do about it?"

"What are we going to do about what, Rosália?"

"The piano!"

"I'm not going to sell it," João shouted. "These leeches don't give a damn about the piano; they just want a bargain. I'd rather give it away to someone who'll take good care of it, who knows what it represents."

He was walking back and forth agitatedly. Suddenly the expression of his face changed.

"Listen, Rosália. Let's phone our relatives in Tijuca."

Rosália understood his purpose and was pleased.

"Hello! Is Messias there? He went out? Oh, is this Cousin Miquita? Look . . . I want to give you our piano as a present. . . . Yes, as a present. . . . No, it's not a joke. . . . Really. . . . Right. . . . Exactly. . . . So it won't go out of the family. . . Fine. Have it picked up here sometime soon. . . . You're welcome. I'm glad to do it. . . ."

After he had hung up he turned to his wife.

"You know what? She didn't believe me at first. She thought it was All Fools' Day."

Rosália was delighted. João walked over to the old piano as if to confer with it about what he had just done.

"My conscience is clear," he thought. "You will not be rejected. You will stay in the family, with people of the same blood. My children's children will know and respect you; you will play for them. I'm sure you understand and won't be angry with us."

"When will they come for it?" interrupted Rosália, eager to get the room ready for the bridal couple.

The next day Messias telephones his relatives in Ipanema. Did they really mean to give him a piano? It was too much. He was grateful but they really shouldn't. When his wife told him, he could hardly believe it.

"No, it's true, Messias. You know, our house is about as big as a nutshell. We can't keep the piano here, and João doesn't want it to fall into the hands of strangers. If you people have it, it's almost the same as if it were still with us. Are you going to send for it soon?"

Several days went by. No moving van came. Mr. and Mrs. Oliveira thought the silence of their relatives in Tijuca extremely odd.

"Something's wrong. Telephone them, Rosália."

Cousin Miquita answered. She was embarrassed. The moving men asked a fortune for the job.

"I guess it's the gasoline shortage. . . . Wait a few more days. Messias will arrange something. We're delighted about getting the piano. We think of nothing else, Rosália."

This last sentence struck a false note, thought Rosália. After a week, João de Oliveira telephoned again.

"Do you want it or don't you, Messias?"

"João, you can't imagine how terrible we feel about this," came the stammered reply. "You give us a fine present and we can't accept it. They're asking an arm and a leg to move it here. And, anyway, we really have no room for it. We haven't even got enough room for the stuff we have now. We should have thought of this before. Miquita feels awful about it."

"In short, you don't want the piano."

"We want it . . . But we don't . . . we can't . . ."

João de Oliveira hung up. He was beginning to understand.

"You see, Rosália. We can't even give the piano away. We can't even give it away."

"What can you do, João! Everything ends up with nobody wanting it."

After a few minutes of silent despondence, they were aroused by Sara, who interspersed her sobs with words of bitter desperation. Her mother comforted her.

"Don't worry, child. It'll be all right. We'll sell it for whatever we can get."

"I want it out right away, Mama. In a few days I'm to be married and my room isn't even ready yet. None of our things are in here. Only that terrible piano ruining my life, that piano that nobody wants."

"Speak softly, dear. Your father can hear you."

"I want him to hear me," she cried, with another sob. She wiped her eyes.

João de Oliveira slept little that night. He was meditating about life. His thoughts were confused and generally melancholy. They induced in him a fierce rage against both life and the piano. He left the house early and went to a nearby bar, where he talked with several men.

"What is my husband doing in a place like that?" Rosália asked herself. João was never a drinker.

Oliveira came back accompanied by a shabbily dressed Negro and two husky Portuguese in work clothes. He showed them the piano. They hefted it and said they doubted if they could handle it, just the three of them.

Rosália and Sara looked on in amazement.

"Have you found a buyer?" asked Rosália.

"No, wife. Nobody will buy this piano."

"You're giving it away?"

"No, wife. Nobody wants it even for free."

"Then what are you doing, João? What in the world are you doing?"

João's eyes watered but his face hardened.

"I'm going to throw it the ocean."

"Oh, no, Papa!" exclaimed Sara. "That's crazy!"

The Oliveiras could not see the ocean from their windows, but they could smell it and hear it, for they were only three blocks from the avenue that ran along the beach.

The men were waiting, talking among themselves.

"What a courageous thing to do, João!" said his wife. "But shouldn't we talk it over first? Is there no other way out? People will think it funny, throwing a piano into the water."

"What else can we do, Rosália? Lots of ships go to the bottom of the ocean. Some of them have pianos on board."

This irrefutable logic silenced his wife. João seemed to take heart.

"Okay, you fellows," he cried. "Up with it! Let's go!"

One of the Portuguese came forward and said humbly, on behalf of his colleagues and himself, that they couldn't do it. They hoped he would excuse them, but it would hurt their conscience to throw something like that in the sea. It almost seemed like a crime.

"Boss, why don't you put an ad in the paper? The piano is in such good condition."

"Yes, I know," replied Oliveira ironically. "You may go."

The men left. For a moment the Negro entertained the idea that he might take the piano for himself. He stared at it. He was fascinated by the idea of owning something, and a fine, luxurious thing at that. It was a dream that could become an immediate reality. But where would he take it? He had no house.

Rosália rested her head on her husband's shoulder and fought back the tears.

"Ah, João, what a decision you have made!"

"But if nobody wants it, and if it can't stay here ..."

"I know, João. But I can't help feeling sad. It's always been with us. Doesn't it seem cruel, after all these years, to throw it in the ocean? Look at it, standing there, knowing nothing about what's going to happen to it. It's been there almost twenty years, in that corner, never doing any harm ..."

"We must try to avoid sentimentality, Rosália."

She looked at him with admiration.

"All right, João. Do what you must."

Groups of Negro boys, ragged but happy, start out from the huts at Pinto and Latolandia where they live and stroll through the wealthy neighborhoods. One can always find them begging nickels for ice cream, gazing in rapture at the posters outside the movie houses, or rolling on the sand in Leblon.

That morning a southwester was whipping the Atlantic into a fury. The piano, needless to say, remained as tranquil as ever. And imposing in the severity of its lines.

Preparations for the departure were under way. João de Oliveira asked his wife and daughter to remove the parts that might possibly be useful. Accordingly, the bronze candlesticks were taken off, then the pedals and metal ornaments, and finally the oak top.

"Ugh!" exclaimed Sara. "It looks so different."

Without mentioning it to his family, João de Oliveira had recruited a bunch of Negro boys. They were waiting impatiently outside the door. Oliveira now told them to come in, the strongest ones first.

It was twenty after four in the afternoon when the funeral cortege started out. A small crowd on the sidewalk made way for it. The piano moved slowly and irregularly. Some people came up to observe it more closely. Rosália and her daughter contemplated it sadly from the porch, their arms around each other's shoulders. They could not bring themselves to accompany it. The cook was wiping her eyes on her apron.

"Which way?" asked the Negro boys when the procession reached the corner. They were all trying to hold the piano at the same time, with the result that it almost fell.

"Which way?" they repeated.

"To the sea!" cried João de Oliveira. And with the grand gesture of a naval commander he pointed toward the Atlantic.

"To the sea! To the sea!" echoed the boys in chorus.

They began to understand that the piano was going

to be destroyed, and this knowledge excited them. They laughed and talked animatedly among themselves. The hubbub inspired the little bitch Doli to leap in the air and bark furiously.

The balconies of the houses were crowded, chiefly with young girls.

"Mother of heaven!" they exclaimed. "What is it?" And, incredulously, "A piano!"

"It came from ninety-nine," cried a Negro urchin, running from house to house to inform the families.

"Why, that's where Sara lives."

"It's João de Oliveira's house."

An acquaintance ran out to learn the facts from Oliveira himself.

"What's wrong, João?"

"Nothing's wrong. I know what I'm doing. Just everybody keep out of the way."

"But why don't you sell it?"

"I'll sell it, all right. I'll sell it to the Atlantic Ocean. See it there? The ocean . . ."

With the air of a somewhat flustered executioner, he resumed his command.

"More to the left, fellows. . . . Careful, don't let it drop. . . . Just the big boys now, everybody else let go."

From time to time one of the boys would put his arm inside the piano and run his hand along the strings. The sound was a sort of death rattle.

A lady on a balcony shouted at João, "Would you sell it?"

"No, madam, it's not for sale. I'll give it away. You want it?"

The lady reddened, felt offended, and went into her house. João made his offer more general.

"Anyone around here want a piano?"

At number forty-three a family of Polish refugees accepted. They were astounded, but they accepted.

"Then it's yours," shouted João de Oliveira.

The Polish family came down and stood around the piano.

"We'll take it, all right. . . .But . . . our house is very small. Give us a couple of days to get ready for it."

"Now or never!" replied Oliveira. "Here it is, right outside your house. You don't want it? Okay, fellows, let's go."

The piano moved closer and closer to the sea. It swayed like a dead cockroach carried by ants.

João de Oliveira distinguished only a few of the exclamations coming from the doors, windows, and balconies of the houses.

"This is the craziest thing I ever heard of," someone shouted from a balcony.

"Crazy?" replied João de Oliveira, looking up at the speaker. "Okay then you take it. Take it. . . ."

Farther on, the scene was repeated. Everyone thought it was a crazy thing to do and everyone wanted the piano; but as soon as the owner offered immediate possession, there was just embarrassed silence. After all, who is prepared to receive a piano at a moment's notice?

João de Oliveira proceeded resolutely, accompanied by a buzz of comments and lamentations. He decided to make no more replies.

A group of motorcycle policemen stopped the procession and surrounded the old piano. João de Oliveira gave a detailed explanation. They asked to see his documents. He went back to the house and got them. He thought the requirement natural enough, for the nation was at war. But he resented having had to give an explanation, for he was acting pursuant to a personal decision for which he was accountable to no one outside the family. He certainly had a right to throw away his own property. This thought reawakened his affection for the instrument. Placing his hand on the piano as if on the forehead of a deceased friend, he felt deeply moved and began to discourse on its life.

"It's an antique, one of the oldest pianos in Brazil."

It had belonged to his grandparents, who had been in the service of the Empire.

"It was a fine piano, you may believe me. Famous musicians played on it. They say that Chopin preferred it over all others. But what does this matter? No one appreciates it any more. Times have changed. . . . Sara, my daughter, is getting married. She'll live with us. The house is small. What can I do? No one wants it. This is the only way out."

And he nodded toward the sea.

The Negro boys were growing impatient with the interruptions. They were eager to see the piano sink beneath the waves. Almost as impatient as these improvised movers, were the people who had joined the procession, including delivery men, messenger boys, a few women, and a great many children.

The police examined the interior of the piano but found nothing suspicious. They returned Oliveira's papers and suggested that he hurry so that traffic would not be impeded.

A photographer asked some of the people to form a group and snapped their picture. João de Oliveira was on the left side in a pose expressing sadness. Then he became annoyed with all these interruptions that prolonged the agony of his piano.

Night fell rapidly. A policeman observed that after six o'clock they would not be permitted to go on. They would have to wait till the next day.

The Negro boys dispersed. They were to be paid later, at Oliveira's house. People were amazed that evening at the number of young Negroes strolling around with small, ivory-plated pieces of wood in their hands.

The piano remained there on the street where they had left it, keeled over against the curb. A ridiculous position. Young men and women on their evening promenade soon surrounded it and made comments.

When he got home, João de Oliveira found some of Sara's girl friends there, eagerly questioning her about the piano.

It was still dark when João and his wife awoke to the loud sound of rain. Wind, rain, and the roar of the surf. They lit the light and looked at each other.

"I was thinking about the piano, Rosália."

"So was I, João. Poor thing! Out in the rain there ... and it's so cold!"

The water must be getting into the works and ruining everything ... the felt, the strings. It's terrible, isn't it, Rosália?"

"We did an ungrateful thing, João."

"I don't even like to think about it, Rosália."

João de Oliveira looked out the window. Flashes of lightning illuminated the trees, revealing branches swaying wildly in the wind. João went back to bed and slept fitfully. He awoke again and told his wife that he had been listening to the piano.

"I heard everything that was ever played on it. Many different hands. My grandmother's hands, my mother's, yours, my aunt's, Sara's. More than twenty hands, more than a hundred white fingers were pressing the keys. I never heard such pretty music. It was sublime, Rosália. The dead hands sometimes played better than the live ones. Lots of young girls from earlier generations were standing around the piano, listening. Couples who later got married were sitting nearby, holding hands. I don't know why, but after a while they all looked at me—with contempt. Suddenly the hands left the piano, but it kept on playing. The Funeral March. Then the piano shut by itself.... There was a torrent of water. The piano let itself get swept along ... toward the ocean. I shouted to it but it wouldn't listen to me. It seemed to be offended, Rosália, and it just kept on going.... I stood there in the street, all alone. I began to cry...."

João de Oliveira was breathing hard. The mysterious

concert had left him in a state of emotion. He felt remorseful.

The rain stopped. As soon as it was light, João went out to round up the Negro boys. All he wanted now was to get the thing over with as quickly as possible.

The wind was still strong, and the ocean growled as if it were digesting the storm of the night before. The boys came, but in smaller numbers than before. Several grown men were among them. João de Oliveira, in a hoarse voice, assumed command again.

On the beach the piano moved more slowly. Finally the long tongues of the waves began to lick it.

Some families stood on the sidewalk, watching the spectacle. Oliveira's crew carried and pushed the piano far enough for the surf to take charge and drag it out to sea. Two enormous waves broke over it without effect. The third made it tremble. The fourth carried it away forever.

João de Oliveira stood there, knee deep in water, with his mouth open. The sea seemed enormously silent. No one could tell that he was crying, for the tears on his cheeks were indistinguishable from the drops of spray.

Far off, he saw Sara with her head resting on the lieutenant's shoulder. Doli was with her, her snout expressing inquiry and incipient dismay; she had always slept next to the piano. João was glad that Rosália had not come.

Many people appeared later on the beach, asking one another what had happened. It seemed at first that an entire Polish family had drowned. Subsequently, it was learned that only one person had drowned. Some said it was a child. Others insisted that it was a lady who had had an unhappy love affair. Only later was it generally known that the person who had drowned was a piano.

People posted themselves at their windows to watch João de Oliveira come back from the beach.

"That's the man!" someone announced.

Oliveira walked slowly, staring at the ground. Everyone felt respect for him.

"It's gone, Rosália," he said as he entered the house. "It has passed the point of no return."

"Before we talk about it, João, go change your clothes."

"Our piano will never come back, Rosália."

"Of course it won't come back. That's why you threw it in the sea."

"Who knows," said Sara. "Maybe it'll be washed up on a beach somewhere."

"Let's not think about it any more. It's over. It's finished. Sara, it's time you did your room."

There was a pause, after which João resumed his lamentation.

"I saw the waves swallow it."

"Enough, my husband. Enough!"

"It came back to the surface twice."

"It's all over! Let's not think about it anymore."

"I didn't mention it to anybody so they wouldn't think I went crazy ... though they're beginning to think I'm crazy anyway.... The fact is, I'm probably the most rational man in the whole neighborhood.... But a little while ago I clearly heard the piano play the Funeral March."

"That was in your dream last night," Rosália reminded him.

"No, it was there by the sea, in broad daylight. Didn't you hear it, Sara? Right afterward, it was covered all with foam, and the music stopped."

He nodded his head, expressing hopelessness before the inevitable. He was talking as if to himself.

"It must be far away by now. Under the water, moving along past strange sights. The wrecks of ships. Submarines. Fishes. Until yesterday it had never left this room.... Years from now it will be washed up on some island in an ocean on the other side of the world.

And when Sara, Rosália, and I are dead, it will still remember the music it made in this house."

He left the room. Sara, alone, looked at the place where the piano had been. Again, she pictured the conjugal bed there, but this time she felt a little guilty.

Her thoughts were interrupted by a knock at the door. A fellow came in with an official notice. Some unidentified person had told the police that a secret radio was hidden in the piano and that her father had wanted to get rid of it. He was to appear at the district police station and answer questions. Well, it was the sort of thing you had to expect in wartime. Nothing anyone could do about it.

Oliveira spent the rest of the day at the police station. He came home late.

"What a life, Rosália!" he said as he fell dejected into the armchair. "What a life! We can't even throw away things that belong to us."

João felt oppressed, stifled. He meditated awhile and then spoke again.

"Have you ever noticed, Rosália, how people hate to get rid of old things? How they cling to them?"

"Not only old things," replied Rosália. "Old ideas too."

Doli was sniffing the area where the piano had been. She wailed a little and fell asleep.

The doorbell rang. A man entered and drew some papers from a briefcase. He said he came from the Port Captain's office.

"Are you João de Oliveira?"

"Yes, I am João de Oliveira."

"What did you cast in the sea this morning?"

Oliveira was stupefied.

"Out here we're not in that port, my dear sir. It's ocean."

"Are you going to give me a vocabulary lesson, Mr. Oliveira?"

The man repeated his previous question and explained that regulations now forbade the placing of objects in or on the sea without a license.

"Have you a license?"

Oliveira humbly asked whether what he had done was in any way offensive or bad.

"That's not the question. Don't you know that we're at war? That our coasts must be protected? That the Nazis are always watching for an opportunity?"

"But it was just a piano, sir."

"It's still a violation. Anyway, was it really a piano? Are you absolutely sure?"

"I think I am," João blurted, looking at his daughter and his wife. "Wasn't it a piano, Rosália? Wasn't it, Sara?"

"Where's your head, João?" exclaimed Rosália. "You know it was a piano."

Her husband's doubt surprised everyone. He seemed to be musing.

"I thought a person could throw anything in the ocean that he wanted to."

"No, indeed! That's all we need. . . ."

João arose. He looked delirious.

"Suppose I want to throw myself in the sea. Can I?"

"It all depends," replied the man from the Port Captain's office.

"Depends on whom? On me and nobody else! I'm a free man. My life belongs to me."

"Much less than you think," said the man.

Sara broke into the smile with which she always greeted the lieutenant, who had just come in. She ran to kiss him.

"See our room, darling. It looks good now, doesn't it?"

"Yes, real good. Where are you going to put the new one?"

"The new one?"

"Yes. Aren't you going to get another?"

Sara and her mother exchanged glances of amazement.

"I'm crazy for a piano," said Sara's fiancé. "You have no idea how it relaxes me. All day long I have to hear guns shooting. A little soft music in the evening ..."

Sara had a fit of coughing. João de Oliveira went out the door. He felt suffocated; he needed to breathe.

Who else would come out of the night and make new demands of him? How could he have known that a piano hidden from the world, living in quiet anonymity, was really an object of public concern? Why hadn't he just left it where it was?

It was miles away now, traveling.... Far away, riding the southern seas.... And free. More so than he or Sara or Rosália. It was he, João de Oliveira, who now felt abandoned. For himself and for his family. It wasn't their piano any more. It was a creature loose in the world. Full of life and pride, moving boldly through the seven seas. Sounding forth. Embraced by all the waters of the world. Free to go where it wished, to do what it wished.

Beneath the trees in front of the house, the Negro boys were waiting for their second day's pay. They had worked hard. It was so dark that he could scarcely distinguish their shaved heads. In the midst of them he saw a vaguely familiar form. The person opened the garden gate and asked permission to enter.

With some difficulty João recognized the redheaded man, but he was wholly unprepared for what the man was about to say:

"I've come back about the piano. I think I can make you a reasonable offer."

Translated by William L. Grossman

The Other Death

JORGE LUIS BORGES

I have mislaid the letter, but a couple of years or so ago Gannon wrote me from his ranch up in Gualeguaychú saying he would send me a translation, perhaps the very first into Spanish, of Ralph Waldo Emerson's poem "The Past," and adding in a P.S. that don Pedro Damián, whom I might recall, had died of a lung ailment a few nights earlier. The man (Gannon went on), wasted by fever, had in his delirium relived the long ordeal of the battle of Masoller. It seemed to me there was nothing unreasonable or out of the ordinary about this news since don Pedro, when he was nineteen or twenty, had been a follower of the banners of Aparicio Saravia. Pedro Damián had been working as a hand up north on a ranch in Río Negro or Paysandú when the 1904 revolution broke out. Although he was from Gualeguaychú, in the province of Entre Ríos, he went along with his friends and, being as cocky and ignorant as they were, joined the rebel army. He fought in one or two skirmishes and in the final battle. Returned home in 1905, Damián, with a kind of humble stubbornness, once more took up his work as a cowhand. For all I know, he never left his native province again. He spent his last thirty years living in a small lonely cabin eight or ten miles from Ñancay. It was in that out-of-the-way place that I spoke with him one evening (that I tried to speak with him one evening) back around 1942; he was a man of few words, and not very bright. Masoller, it turned out, was the whole of his personal history. And so I was not surprised to find out that he had lived the sound and fury of that battle over again at the hour of his death. When I knew I would never see Damián another time, I wanted to remember him, but so poor is my memory for faces that all I could recall was the snapshot Gannon had taken of him. There is nothing unusual in this fact, considering that I saw the man only once at the beginning of 1942, but had looked at his picture many times. Gannon sent me the photograph and it, too, has been misplaced. I think now that if I were to come across it, I would feel afraid.

The second episode took place in Montevideo, months later. Don Pedro's fever and his agony gave me the idea for a tale of fantasy based on the defeat at Masoller; Emir Rodríguez Monegal, to whom I had told the plot, wrote me an introduction to Colonel Dionisio Tabares, who had fought in that campaign. The Colonel received me one evening after dinner. From a rocking chair out in the side yard, he recalled the old days with great feeling but at the same time with a faulty sense of chronology. He spoke of ammunition that never reached him and of reserves of horses that arrived worn out, of sleepy dust-covered men weaving labyrinths of marches, of Saravia, who might have ridden into Montevideo but who passed it by "because the gaucho has a fear of towns," of throats hacked from ear to ear, of a civil war that seemed to me less a military operation than the dream of a cattle thief or an outlaw. Names of battles kept coming up: Illescas, Tupambaé, Masoller. The Colonel's pauses were so effective and his manner so vivid that I realized he had told and retold these same things many times before, and I feared that behind his words almost no true memories remained. When he stopped for a breath, I managed to get in Damián's name.

"Damián? Pedro Damián?" said the Colonel. "He served with me. A little half-breed. I remember the bovs used to call him Daymán—after the river." The Colonel let out a burst of loud laughter, then cut it off all at once. I could not tell whether his discomfort was real or put on.

In another voice, he stated that war, like women, served as a test of men, and that nobody knew who he really was until he had been under fire. A man might think himself a coward and actually be brave. And the other way around, too, as had happened to that poor Damián, who bragged his way in and out of saloons with his white ribbon marking him as a Blanco, and later on lost his nerve at Masoller. In one exchange of gunfire with the regulars, he handled himself like a man, but then it was something else again when the two armies met face to face and the artillery began pounding away and every man felt as though there were five thousand other men out there grouping to kill him. That poor kid. He'd spent his life on a farm dipping sheep, and then all of a sudden he gets himself dragged along and mixed up in the grim reality of war....

For some absurd reason Tabares' version of the story made me uncomfortable. I would have preferred things to have happened differently. Without being aware of it, I had made a kind of idol out of old Damián—a man I had seen only once on a single evening many years earlier. Tabares' story destroyed everything. Suddenly the reasons for Damián's aloofness and his stubborn insistence on keeping to himself were clear to me. They had not sprung from modesty but from shame. In vain, I told myself that a man pursued by an act of cowardice is more complex and more interesting than one who is merely courageous. The gaucho Martín

Fierro, I thought, is less memorable than Lord Jim or Razumov. Yes, but Damián, as a gaucho, should have been Martín Fierro—especially in the presence of Uruguayan gauchos. In what Tabares left unsaid, I felt his assumption (perhaps undeniable) that Uruguay is more primitive than Argentina and therefore physically braver. I remember we said good-by to each other that night with a cordiality that was a bit marked.

During the winter, the need of one or two details for my story (which somehow was slow in taking shape) sent me back to Colonel Tabares again. I found him with another man of his own age, a Dr. Juan Francisco Amaro from Paysandú, who had also fought in Saravia's revolution. They spoke, naturally, of Masoller.

Amaro told a few anecdotes, then slowly added, in the manner of someone who is thinking aloud, "We camped for the night at Santa Irene, I recall, and some of the men from around there joined us. Among them a French veterinarian, who died the night before the battle, and a boy, a sheepshearer from Entre Ríos. Pedro Damián was his name."

I cut him off sharply. "Yes, I know," I said. "The Argentine who couldn't face the bullets."

I stopped. The two of them were looking at me, puzzled.

"You are mistaken, sir," Amaro said after a while. "Pedro Damián died as any man might wish to die. It was about four o'clock in the afternoon. The regular troops had dug themselves in on the top of a hill and our men charged them with lances. Damián rode at the head, shouting, and a bullet struck him square in the chest. He stood up in his stirrups, finished his shout, and then rolled to the ground, where he lay under the horses' hooves. He was dead, and the whole last charge of Masoller trampled over him. So fearless, and barely twenty."

He was speaking, doubtless, of another Damián, but

something made me ask what it was the boy had shouted.

"Filth," said the Colonel. "That's what men shout in action."

"Maybe," said Amaro, "but he also cried out, 'Long live Urquiza!' "

We were silent. Finally the Colonel murmured, "Not as if we were fighting at Masoller, but at Cagancha or India Muerta a hundred years ago." He added, genuinely bewildered, "I commanded those troops, and I could swear it's the first time I've ever heard of this Damián."

We had no luck in getting the Colonel to remember him.

Back in Buenos Aires, the amazement that his forgetfulness produced in me repeated itself. Browsing through the eleven pleasurable volumes of Emerson's works in the basement of Mitchell's, the English bookstore, I met Patricio Gannon one afternoon. I asked him for his translation of "The Past." He told me that he had no translation of it in mind, and that, besides, Spanish literature was so boring it made Emerson quite superfluous. I reminded him that he had promised me the translation in the same letter in which he wrote me of Damián's death. He asked me who was Damián. I told him in vain. With rising terror, I noticed that he was listening to me very strangely, and I took refuge in a literary discussion on the detractors of Emerson, a poet far more complex, far more skilled, and truly more extraordinary than the unfortunate Poe.

I must put down some additional facts. In April, I had a letter from Colonel Dionisio Tabares; his mind was no longer vague and now he remembered quite well the boy from Entre Ríos who spearheaded the charge at Masoller and whom his men buried that night in a grave at the foot of the hill. In July, I passed through Gualeguaychú; I did not come across

Damián's cabin, and nobody there seemed to remember him now. I wanted to question the foreman Diego Abaroa, who saw Damián die, but Abaroa had passed away himself at the beginning of the winter. I tried to call to mind Damián's features; months later, leafing through some old albums, I found that the dark face I had attempted to evoke really belonged to the famous tenor Tamberlik, playing the role of Othello.

Now I move on to conjectures. The easiest, but at the same time the least satisfactory, assumes two Damiáns: the coward who died in Entre Ríos around 1946, and the man of courage who died at Masoller in 1904. But this falls apart in its inability to explain what are really the puzzles: the strange fluctuations of Colonel Tabares' memory, for one, and the general forgetfulness, which in so short a time could blot out the image and even the name of the man who came back. (I cannot accept, I do not want to accept, a simpler possibility—that of my having dreamed the first man.) Stranger still is the supernatural conjecture thought up by Ulrike von Kühlmann. Pedro Damián, said Ulrike, was killed in the battle and at the hour of his death asked God to carry him back to Entre Ríos. God hesitated a moment before granting the request, but by then the man was already dead and had been seen by others to have fallen. God, who cannot unmake the past but can affect its images, altered the image of Damián's violent death into one of falling into a faint. And so it was the boy's ghost that came back to his native province. Came back, but we must not forget that it did so as a ghost. It lived in isolation without a woman and without friends; it loved and possessed everything but from a distance, as from the other side of a mirror; ultimately it "died" and its frail image just disappeared, like water in water. This conjecture is faulty, but it may have been responsible for pointing out to me the true one (the one I now believe to be true), which is at the same time simpler and more unprecedented. In a mysterious way I discovered it in the treatise *De Omnipotentia* by Pier Damiani, after having been referred to him by two lines in Canto XXI of the *Paradiso*, in which the problem of Damiani's identity is brought up. In the fifth chapter of that treatise, Pier Damiani asserts—against Aristotle and against Fredegarius de Tours—that it is within God's power to make what once was into something that has never been. Reading those old theological discussions, I began to understand don Pedro Damián's tragic story.

This is my solution. Damián handled himself like a coward on the battlefield at Masoller and spent the rest of his life setting right that shameful weakness. He returned to Entre Ríos; he never lifted a hand against another man, he never cut anyone up, he never sought fame as a man of courage. Instead, living out there in the hill country of Ñancay and struggling with the backwoods and with wild cattle, he made himself tough, hard. Probably without realizing it, he was preparing the way for the miracle. He thought from his innermost self, If destiny brings me another battle, I'll be ready for it. For forty years he waited and waited, with an inarticulate hope, and then, in the end, at the hour of his death, fate brought him his battle. It came in the form of delirium, for, as the Greeks knew, we are all shadows of a dream. In his final agony he lived his battle over again, conducted himself as a man, and in heading the last charge he was struck by a bullet in the middle of the chest. And so, in 1946, through the working out of a long, slow-burning passion, Pedro Damián died in the defeat at Masoller, which took place between winter and spring in 1904.

In the *Summa Theologiae*, it is denied that God can unmake the past, but nothing is said of the complicated concatenation of causes and effects which is so vast and so intimate that perhaps it might prove impossible to annul a *single* remote fact, insignificant as it may seem, without invalidating the present. To modify the past is not to modify a single fact; it is to annul the consequences of that fact, which tend to be infinite. In other words, it involves the creation of two universal histories. In the first, let us say, Pedro Damián died in Entre Ríos in 1946; in the second, at Masoller in 1904. It is this second history that we are living now, but the suppression of the first was not immediate and produced the odd contradictions that I have related. It was in Colonel Dionisio Tabares that the different stages took place. At first, he remembered that Damián acted as a coward; next, he forgot him entirely; then he remembered Damián's fearless death. No less illuminating is the case of the foreman Abaroa; he had to die, as I understand it, because he held too many memories of don Pedro Damián.

As for myself, I do not think I am running a similar risk. I have guessed at and set down a process beyond man's understanding, a kind of exposure of reason; but there are certain circumstances that lessen the dangers of this privilege of mine. For the present, I am not sure of having always written the truth. I suspect that in my story there are a few false memories. It is my suspicion that Pedro Damián (if he ever existed) was not called Pedro Damián and that I remember him by that name so as to believe someday that the whole story was suggested to me by Pier Damiani's thesis. Something similar happens with the poem I mentioned in the first paragraph, which centers around the irrevocability of the past. A few years from now, I shall believe I made up a fantastic tale, and I will actually have recorded an event that was real, just as some two thousand years ago in all innocence Virgil believed he was setting down the birth of a man and foretold the birth of Christ.

Poor Damián! Death carried him off at the age of twenty in a local battle of a sad and little-known war, but in the end he got what he longed for in his heart, and he was a long time getting it, and perhaps there is no greater happiness.

Translated by Norman Thomas di Giovanni

Tatuana's Tale

MIGUEL ÁNGEL ASTURIAS

Father Almond Tree, with his pale pink beard, was one of the priests who were so richly dressed that the white men touched them to see if they were made of gold. He knew the secret of medicinal plants, the language of the gods that spoke through translucent obsidian, and he could read the hieroglyphics of the stars.

One day he appeared in the forest, without being planted, as though brought there by spirits. He was so tall he prodded the clouds, he measured the years by the moons he saw, and was already old when he came from the Garden of Tulan.

On the full moon of Owl-Fish (one of the twenty months of the four-hundred-day year), Father Almond Tree divided his soul among the four roads. These led to the four quarters of the sky: the black quarter, the Sorcerer Night; the green quarter, Spring Storm; the red quarter, Tropical Ecstasy; the white quarter, Promise of New Lands.

"O Road! Little Road!" said a dove to White Road, but White Road did not listen. The dove wanted Father Almond Tree's soul so that it would cure its dreams. Doves and children both suffer from dreams.

"O Road! Little Road!" said a heart to Red Road, but Red Road did not listen. The heart wanted to distract Red Road so it would forget Father Almond Tree's soul. Hearts, like thieves, don't return what others leave behind.

"O Road! Little Road!" said a vine trellis to Green Road, but Green Road did not listen. It wanted the Father's soul to get back some of the leaves and shade it had squandered.

How many moons have the roads been traveling?

The fastest, Black Road, whom no one spoke to along the way, entered the city, crossed the plaza and went to the merchants' quarter, where it gave Father Almond Tree's soul to the Merchant of Priceless Jewels in exchange for a little rest.

It was the hour of white cats. They prowled back and forth through the streets. Wonder of rosebushes! The clouds looked like laundry strung across the sky.

When Father Almond Tree found out what Black Road had done, he once again took on human form, shedding his tree-like shape in a small stream that appeared like an almond blossom beneath the crimson moon. Then he left for the city.

He reached the valley after a day's travel, just at evening time when the flocks are driven home. The shepherds were dumbfounded by this man in a green cloak and pale pink beard. They thought he was an apparition and answered his questions in monosyllables.

Once in the city, he made his way to the western part of town. Men and women were standing around the public fountains. The water made a kissing sound as it filled their pitchers. Following the shadows to the merchants' quarter, he found that part of his soul Black Road had sold. The Merchant of Priceless Jewels kept it in a crystal box with gold locks. He went up to the Merchant, who was smoking in a corner, and offered him two thousand pounds of pearls for the piece of soul.

The Merchant smiled at the Father's absurd suggestion. Two thousand pounds of pearls? No, his jewels were priceless.

Father Almond Tree increased his offer. He would give him emeralds, big as kernels of corn, fifty acres of them, enough to make a lake.

The Merchant smiled again. A lake of emeralds? No, his jewels were priceless.

He would give him amulets, deer's eyes that bring rain, feathers to keep storms away, marijuana to mix with his tobacco.

The Merchant refused.

He would give him enough precious stones to build a fairy-tale palace in the middle of the emerald lake!

The Merchant still refused. His jewels were priceless—why go on talking about it? Besides, he planned to exchange this piece of soul for the most beautiful slave in the slave market.

It was useless for Father Almond Tree to keep on making offers and show how much he wanted to get his soul back. Merchants have no hearts.

A thread of tobacco smoke separated reality from dream, black cats from white cats, the Merchant from his strange customer. As he left, Father Almond Tree banged his sandals against the doorway to rid himself of the cursed dust of the house.

After a year of four hundred days, the Merchant was returning across the mountains with the slave he had bought with Father Almond Tree's soul. He was accompanied by a flower bird who turned honey into hyacinths, and by a retinue of thirty servants on horseback.

The slave was naked. Her long black hair, wrapped in a single braid like a snake, fell across her breasts and down to her legs. The Merchant was dressed in gold and his shoulders were covered with a cape woven from goat hair. His thirty servants on horseback stretched out behind like figures in a dream.

"You've no idea," said the Merchant to the slave, reining in his horse alongside hers, "what your life will be like in the city! Your house will be a palace, and all my servants will be at your call, including me, if you like." His face was half lit by the sun. "There," he continued, "everything will be yours. Do you know I refused a lake of emeralds for the piece of soul I exchanged for you? We'll lie all day in a hammock and have nothing to do but listen to a wise old woman tell stories. She knows my fate and says that it rests in a gigantic hand. She'll tell your fortune as well, if you ask her."

The slave turned to look at the countryside. It was a landscape of muted blues, growing dimmer in the distance. The trees on either side formed so fanciful a design it might have appeared on a woman's shawl. The sky was calm, and the birds seemed to be flying asleep, winglessly. In the granite silence, the panting of the horses as they went uphill sounded human.

Suddenly, huge solitary raindrops began to spatter on the road. On the slopes below, shepherds shouted as they gathered their frightened flocks. The horses stepped up their pace to find shelter, but there wasn't enough time. The wind rose, lashing the clouds, and ripping through the forest until it reached the valley, which vanished from sight under blankets of mist, while the first lightning bolts lit up the countryside like the flashes of a mad photographer.

As the horses stampeded, fleeing in fear, reins broken, legs flying, manes tangled in the wind and ears pressed back, the Merchant's horse stumbled and threw the man to the foot of a tree which at that instant, split by lightning, wrapped its roots about him like a hand snatching up a stone and hurled him into the ravine.

Meanwhile Father Almond Tree, who had remained in the city, wandered the streets like a madman, frightening children, going through garbage, talking to donkeys, oxen and stray dogs, which, like men, are all sad-eyed animals.

"How many moons have the roads been traveling?" he asked from door to door, but the people were dumfounded by this man in a green cloak and pale pink beard, and they slammed them shut without answering as though they'd seen a specter.

At length Father Almond Tree stopped at the door of the Merchant of Priceless Jewels and spoke to the slave, who alone had survived the storm.

"How many moons have the roads been traveling?"

The answer which began to form froze on her lips. Father Almond Tree was silent. It was the full moon of Owl-Fish. In silence their eyes caressed each other's faces like two lovers who have met after a long separation.

They were interrupted by raucous shouts. They were arrested in the name of God and the King, he as a warlock and she as his accomplice. Surrounded by crosses and swords, they were taken to prison, Father Almond Tree with his pale pink beard and green cloak, the slave displaying flesh so firm it seemed to be made of gold.

Seven months later, they were condemned to be burned alive in the Plaza Mayor. On the eve of the execution, Father Almond Tree tattooed a little boat on the slave's arm with his fingernail.

"Tatuana, by means of this tattoo," he said, "you will be able to flee whenever you are in danger. I want you to be as free as my spirit. Trace this little boat on a wall, on the ground, in the air, wherever you wish. Then close your eyes, climb aboard and go . . .

"Go, my spirit is stronger than a clay idol.

"My spirit is sweeter than the honey gathered by bees sipping from the honeysuckle.

"As my spirit, you'll become invisible."

At once, Tatuana did what Father Almond Tree

said: she drew a little boat, closed her eyes, and, as she got in, the boat began to move. So she escaped from prison and death.

On the following morning, day of the execution, the guards found in the cell only a withered tree, whose few almond blossoms still retained their pale pink color.

Translated by Patricia Emigh and Frank MacShane

One Sunday Afternoon

ROBERTO ARLT

Eugene Karl went out into the street that Sunday afternoon telling himself, Something strange is going to happen to me today—it's almost dead sure.

Eugene traced the origin of such premonitions to the odd, wild beatings of his heart, and these palpitations he attributed to the agency of some remote thought upon his sensibility. In the grip of a dim presentiment, it was not uncommon for him to take deliberate precautions or else to act in a rather strange way. Usually his tactic depended on his psychic state. If he were happy he conceded that the nature of his premonition was benign. But if he were in a state of gloom he went so far as to shut himself indoors, fearing that the cornice of some skyscraper or some electric cable might otherwise come toppling down on his head. Most of the time, however, he enjoyed riding the wave of a premonition, of giving in to that dark yearning for adventure found even in men of the dourest and most pessimistic outlook.

For half an hour or more Eugene followed the luck of the streets, when suddenly he noticed a woman wrapped in a black coat. She was coming toward him, smiling openly. Eugene looked at her again, his face screwed up, unable to place her, and at the same time thought, Every day—isn't it lucky?—women are becoming freer and freer in their ways.

All at once the woman exclaimed, "Hello there, Eugene!"

And immediately Karl came out of his mind's fog. "Oh, is that you? Hello there."

For a fraction of a second Leonilda shot him a languid, ambiguous smile. Eugene asked, "And John?"

"Out as usual. As you see, he left me all alone. Do you want to come and have tea with me?"

Leonilda spoke slowly, hesitantly, her smile softened by a sensual languor which, as she tilted her head to one shoulder, made her look at the man from between half-shut lids, as if she were looking into brilliant sunlight. A sparkle of gray water trembled in the depths of her pupils. Karl said to himself, She's out for bedding down with someone other than her husband, and he had no sooner thought this when his pulse rate leaped from seventy-five to a hundred and ten. The emotion unleashed by this unknown door laxly being opened before him by Leonilda was such that he felt he had just sprinted a couple of hundred yards. Still, he could not help having his misgivings. Alone. Have tea with her. She doesn't know a woman ought not receive her husband's friends alone.

And then he mumbled, "No. Thank you, really—If John were—." His voice was that of the child who says "No, thanks" when a coin is offered because he's been told not to accept gifts. So much so that he immediately told himself, Why am I so foolish? I should have accepted. Maybe she'll ask me again.

Aloud now he said, "Imagine my not recognizing you, Leonilda." But his thoughts dwelled elsewhere, and the woman appeared to understand the various feelings that stirred the man, and Karl told himself, Why did I foolishly refuse her invitation? But Eugene, trying to stifle a budding obsession, persisted.

"I didn't recognize you," he said. "And when I saw you smile I asked myself, Who can this woman be?"

As he spoke, a wish danced inside him. Will she ask me again? I wonder.

Leonilda looked suggestively into his eyes. Her smile was languid and wry, and it shrewdly penetrated the hypocrisy of the man, who was pointlessly playing the upright citizen. Her silence itself seemed to Eugene the raging of a storm, through the thick of which one caught her insinuation: Dare to. I'm alone. No one will find out.

They no longer had anything to say to each other now, but the call of their sex and the contradiction of their buried emotions kept them pinned to the sidewalk. Eugene, lips stiff with nervous tension, blurted awkwardly, "So your husband isn't home? He's off somewhere, and he left you—all alone?"

She laughed; then lightly laying her head upon her left shoulder, she kept up her laughter, twisted the strap of her handbag, and, looking at him, challenging, answered, "He left me alone. Completely alone. And I got so bored I decided to go for a walk. Why don't you come and have tea with me?"

Karl's pulse rose from eighty to a hundred and ten. There was a tremor of hesitation in the depths of her eyes. Maybe lose a friend. The two of us all by ourselves. How far might she go?

Leonilda studied him half mockingly. She detected his qualms, and there, standing on the sidewalk, with her head resting lightly on one shoulder and with a suggestive streetwalker's smile, she watched him through narrowed eyelids, saying in a soft, mocking voice, "You see, I keep telling John that if he's going to leave me alone I'm going to have to find me a sweetheart. Ha, ha! How funny! A sweetheart at my age. Could anyone want me? But, really, why don't you come? You have a cup of tea and you leave. Why must you look so sad?"

It was true. Never had Karl felt sadness as in that moment. He thought he was going to betray a friend. What remorse later on when withdrawing his unclean sex from this woman's sex! Still, Leonilda's smile was so suggestive. And he told himself again, Betray a friend for a woman. He'd have the right to say to me then: Don't you know the world is crawling with women? And you had to approach my wife, my one woman. You. And the world full of women. Here's the surprise I felt in store for me today.

Eugene's heart beat as if he had run a two-hundred-yard sprint. And he was unable to resist. Leonilda was seducing him with that static pose of hers—head resting on her left shoulder and a shameless smile that gave a glimpse of white teeth and rosy gums.

A terrible laxity gripped his limbs. It fell perpendicularly between them, and on the sidewalk veneered with yellow light, lazily, obliquely, he perceived the mobility of space, as if he found himself at the pinnacle of a cloud, with worlds and cities at his feet. At the same time, he was eager to dissolve into the unfamiliar world of sensuality offered by the married woman, but despite his desire he was helpless to overcome the inertia that held him on the undulating sidewalk, obliquely, under her gaze.

She, very softly, went back to her charge. "You have tea and afterward you leave . . ."

He, his mind made up, said: "All right, then. I'll come with you. We'll have tea together." But in the meantime he thought, When we're alone I'll take her hand, then I'll kiss her, and after that touch her breast. All or nothing, it's the same thing. She may say 'No, don't,' but I'll take her to the bed—to her wide, wide marriage bed, where for years now she's been sleeping with John.

Now she walked by his side with quiet intimacy. Karl felt ridiculous, like a wooden man swaying on sawdust feet.

To say something, Leonilda asked, "Are you still separated from your wife?"

"Yes."

"And don't you miss her?"

"No."

"Ah, you men! How you . . ."

For a second or two, Eugene had an overwhelming desire to burst into noisy laughter, and he repeated to himself, We men! And you—you, taking me to have tea in your husband's absence? But returning to the thought of being alone in a room with Leonilda, he could not shut out John's image. He saw him rushing after work to some secret brothel, picking out whores with extraordinary bottoms; and then he studied Leonilda with a certain curiosity, wondering whether John had adapted her to his sexual predilections; and suddenly he found himself before a wooden door. Leonilda took out her keys and, smiling languidly, opened up. They climbed a set of stairs, now barely able to look each other in the eye.

If I were alongside a cataract, Eugene thought, there'd be no more noise in my ears.

Another lock creaked, it got darker, then he glimpsed the furniture of a study; a key turned, and curves of yellow light jumped back off the sofas. He made out green filing cabinets suspended from the walls, and suddenly, utterly exhausted, he dropped into an armchair. His joints pained him. Mentally he had hurtled himself too rapidly toward his desire, and now his joints were stiff with anxiety. His blood seemed to plummet headlong in an immense congealed block toward the center of his heart, and a certain limpness creeping into the bend of his knees left him overcome in his cold leather armchair, while the voice of the absent husband seemed to whisper in his ear, 'Scoundrel—my one woman. Didn't you know that? My only woman in the whole world!' A mocking smile formed on Eugene's face. All husbands have only one woman when she's in danger of slipping into bed with another man.

He realized she was still in the room when she said, "Pardon me, Eugene, I'm going to take off my coat."

Leonilda disappeared. With great effort Karl got up from the chair and, holding his shoulders motionless, began shaking his head vigorously. He knew this trick from having seen boxers use it when they were at the point of being knocked out. He took a deep breath and then, in control again, sat at one end of the sofa. He now turned his attention inward. How should he behave in this woman's presence?

Leonilda came back wearing a dark woolen street dress. She too seemed in control of herself, and then, almost mockingly, Eugene popped the sly question: "So you're often bored, are you?"

She, seated in an armchair adjacent to the sofa, crossing her legs, pretended to think, and then, determined, answered, "Yes, quite often."

There was a dark silence, in which each shot the other a glance, looking each other in the eye, and as in a movie these words slipped into Karl's ears: The two of us alone. Ten minutes earlier you were making your way along the city streets, infected by the Sunday boredom, not knowing what to do with your time and hoping for a scintillating adventure. O life! And now you don't know quite how to get all this started. Take her around the waist, kiss her hand, accidentally touch her breast. No woman can resist a man when he plays with her breasts.

The din of falling water was shattering in the man's ears, and then once more forcing out the words that were caught there at the back of his dry throat and thick tongue, he murmured with the false smile of a person who finds nothing to talk about, "And what do you do to keep from getting bored?"

"I go to the movies."

"Ah. Who's your favorite actress?"

They eyed each other again with dense looks. Sitting sideways on the arm of her chair, Leonilda smiled incoherently, her eyes narrowed in such a way that her pupils sparkled with an unbearable, evil glint, as if she were singling out each of Karl's thoughts and mocking him for not being bold. Clasping a knee between her fine, long hands, at certain moments she appeared to be drunk with her adventure, and Karl harped back on: "So you get bored?"

"Yes."

"And what does he say?"

"John? What would you expect him to say? Sometimes he thinks we should never have married. Other times he tells me I have all the look of a woman born to have a lover. Do you think I have the figure to be loved by anyone? And I too ask myself, What did we ever get married for?"

Eugene resorted to a cigarette. He had noticed that restlessness can be unconsciously dispelled by some intimate mechanical busywork. He slowly inhaled, filling his mouth with smoke, then slowly blew it into the air, and, in an extremely calm voice, now in control of himself, he asked, "And John never questioned whether you wanted a lover? I mean, he never insinuated that you might have a lover?"

"No—"

"Then why have you asked me to come here today? You want to be unfaithful to your husband. Have you chosen me for that?"

"No, Eugene. How outrageous! John is very good. He works hard all day—"

"And because he's good and works hard all day you invite me to have tea with you?"

"What's wrong with that?"

"That's just it—nothing's wrong with it. The only thing is that someday you may run into a man who'll try to tumble you into bed."

Leonilda stood up abruptly. "I would let out a

shout, Eugene, rest assured of that. Furthermore, I'm bored, and I work all day too. But I'm bored with these four walls. It's horrible. Have you any idea what goes on in the mind of a woman stuck all day inside the four walls of an apartment?"

She was fighting back. He had to be careful.

"And he has no inkling of what's going on inside you?"

"Yes, he does."

"And?"

"I'm tired."

"Why don't you amuse yourself reading?"

"Please, spare me from books. They're horrible! What would you have me read? Can I learn anything from books?"

Now, relaxing in the big armchair, she seemed sad in the confused light that colored her skin a shade of wood. She anxiously disclosed her yearnings. "You know, Eugene, I'd like to live someplace else . . ."

"Where?"

"I don't know. I'd like to get far away, without a fixed destination. John's the other way. You know the first thing he does when we arrive anywhere? He reads the newspapers."

"Very interesting things appear in the papers."

"I know, I know . . . You're very funny. He reads the papers and answers everything I ask him with a yes or a no. That's all the talking we do. We have nothing to say to each other. I'd really like to get far away . . . Travel by train, with a lot of rain, eat in station restaurants . . . Don't think I'm crazy, Eugene."

"I don't think anything."

"He doesn't stir from the house—except when I won't put up with it anymore. He's a homebody. That's it, Eugene. A homebody. It seems that all men over thirty are homebodies; they don't want to budge out of their corners. But me—I'd love to get far, far away. To live like a screen star. Do you think what the papers say about a screen star's life is true?"

"Sure, maybe ten percent of it is true."

"You see, Eugene . . . that's the life I'd love to have. But that's impossible now."

"So it is. But why did you invite me here?"

"I longed to talk to you." She shook her head as if she were rejecting a thought that was out of place. "No, I could never be unfaithful to John. No. God forbid. You realize—if his friends ever found out . . . What a horrible humiliation for him. And you'd be the first to bandy it about: 'John's wife cheats on him—and with me . . .' "

"And were you hoping I'd kiss you?"

"No."

"Are you sure of that?" Eugene could not suppress a sly smile, and he became insistent. "I don't know why but I think you're lying."

Leonilda hesitated for a moment. She looked about her as if she were perched on a shaky height. And even if Eugene had tried to unravel her secret, it would have been impossible just then. She seemed suffused with the transparency of an unreal atmosphere, as though she stood somewhere between heaven and earth.

"You promise not to tell anyone?"

"I promise."

"All right, then. Once a friend of John's kissed me."

"And were you hoping he'd kiss you?"

"No. It came as—as a surprise."

"And were you pleased or not?"

"When it happened I was furious. I threw him out of the house. This was some years ago."

"Did he ever come back?"

"No—but you're going to think badly of me."

"Not at all."

"Well, I've often thought back with regret, Why hasn't he come around again?"

"Would you have given yourself to him?"

"No . . . no . . . But tell me, Eugene, what comes over a man when he suddenly kisses the wife of a friend like that? A friend he cares about—because he cared about John."

"Speaking from a metaphysical point of view, it's generally difficult to say what happens. Now, if you take the question from a materialistic viewpoint, what may have happened is that the man was excited by your presence and that—possibly—you knew he was. And it's more probable that you deliberately contributed to stirring him up. You're the kind of woman who likes firing up her husband's friends."

"That's hardly true, Eugene—because, as you see . . . nothing's happening between us . . ."

"Because I'm in control of myself."

"Are you? I hadn't noticed."

"That's why you invited me to tea. But I am in control and, besides, I find that it amuses me."

"In what way . . . does it amuse you?"

"Observing the other party. It's something like the game of cat and mouse. I look into your eyes and deep inside I see a storm of desire and misgiving."

"Eugene."

"Yes?"

"Will you tell your wife I invited you to tea?"

"No—because I'm separated from her. And even if I weren't I wouldn't tell her, because she'd lose no time spreading it among her friends. 'Do you know that John's wife invited my husband to have tea alone with her?' "

"How awful!"

"Not at all. She's an upright woman. All upright women are more or less like her. More or less shameless and more or less bored. Occasionally they'd like to go to bed with the men who are attracted to them; but then they pull back and will barely sleep with their own husbands even."

"And what did you think when I invited you to—?"

"The first time, I refused; then immediately I thought, It was foolish of me not to accept. If she asks me again I'll say yes. When you insisted that I come along I experienced a great surge of emotion and curiosity . . ."

"Go on, go on—I enjoy listening to you."

"Curiosity and emotion. Yes. Future adventure. That's what I thought walking along beside you. It's been a long time since I've been to bed with a married woman, especially with the wife of a friend."

"You're a savage. I won't allow you to speak like that."

"Then I'll shut up."

"No, go on."

"All right. As I was saying—where was I? During these past years I've dedicated myself to spiritual love—meaning the love of girls. I'll never understand why people say young women are spiritual."

"Did you fall in love with any of them?"

"Oh no, but I had small affairs that proved to me that the most intelligent girls have incredibly set minds. Here's an example. A while back I met a girl who was half literary and half tubercular. We were having coffee together; in five minutes she was talking about her pastel pajamas, about her "pale, ivory hands," about Virginia tobacco, about Debussy. You know what I did? I left her arty confidences high and dry, asking her if she menstruated regularly and moved her bowels every day."

Leonilda roared with laughter. "Eugene, Eugene—you're a perfect barbarian."

Karl went on. "She didn't get angry, and seeing she was so thin, I felt sorry for her. I decided to do something for her. I drew her up a wonderful program—physical exercises, citrus fruit for breakfast, and, believe me, Leonilda, it got to the point where I worried not only whether she performed her bodily functions but even about the consistency of her stools, teaching her that the ideal should look something like stewed apple."

"Eugene, change the subject—"

"No, Leonilda. I want you to see what a good heart I have. It's not the heart of a savage. I used to tell that girl, 'First you must gain twenty pounds and then lose your virginity.' Don't you agree that women over fourteen ought to be free to go to bed with anyone they like?"

"And pregnancy?"

"That can be avoided. But it's horrible to force a woman to stand guard over her own virginity. Anyway, the girl found my lessons somehow spiritually wanting and she dropped me—for a man with curly hair, no doubt, who reads Jean Cocteau and wears fawn-colored gloves."

While Karl was speaking, Leonilda said to herself, What a charlatan this man is. But to cover up the sudden fit of anger that shot through her nerves, she reached out an arm to rearrange a paper flower in its vase, and she said, "You were saying, Eugene?"

"Are you being bored?"

"Where did you get that idea?"

"Your mind was off somewhere else."

"You're right, Eugene. I was remembering what you thought when we met."

"My first reaction, as I told you, was that of finding myself at the outset of a wonderful adventure. Or at least at the outset of a dark affair. On the other hand, in a way there's a certain pleasure in running the risk of being shot down by the friend and husband. Though perhaps not even that. What do you think—would John actually kill me?"

"No . . . I don't think so. The poor man would be so upset."

"You see, we modern husbands aren't even up to wringing the neck of a scoundrel who preys on our wife. Of course, the fact of not wringing our wife's neck is a triumph of reason and civilization. But, anyway, sometimes it's pleasurable to commit murder—in the name of a superstition. And besides, Leonilda, if John were not to kill you or me, it wouldn't be out of kindness but simply because he realized that in putting horns as big as a house on him you were only taking a bit of justice into your own hands. But let's go back to the beginning. When I came in I was thinking about how I might make the first move with you—kiss your hand or take hold of one of your breasts."

"Eugene!"

"That's what I thought."

"I won't allow you—"

"Cut out the acting."

"All right, but don't talk that way."

"Fine. Description of massage section suppressed."

"Eugene!"

"Leonilda, you're not letting me get out what I have to say,"

"Speak with some decency."

"It's like this. When we came in I expected you to begin flitting about and say, 'See how brave I am, today I've decided to be unfaithful to my husband.' I wanted you to say that, Leonilda. Or else, unfastening your negligee, to say, 'Come kiss my breasts.' Or if not that, 'Kneel here at my feet and rest your head on my lap.' When you came in, for a second I told myself, How wonderful if she were to appear naked, but wrapped in a robe."

"But you're out of your senses."

"Leonilda, these are conjectures. I'm not saying you should necessarily have done any of it. I'm only suggesting how pleasant it might have been had it happened."

"Thank God—"

"I know—that it didn't. When we came in and you said, 'I'm bored,' and then, believe me, my heart sank down to my shoes."

"Why?"

"I don't know. I felt instinctively sorry for you and John."

"Sorry ... sorry for him ..."

"And for you." Now Eugene paced from one end of the study to the other. "Of course. I pitied you. I saw what your problem was, and your problem was the same that all married women have. The husband always at the office; they forever alone within the four walls you described."

"He and I have nothing to say to each other, Eugene."

"That's natural, Leonilda. How long have you been married?"

"Ten years."

"And you expect to have something new to say to a man you've lived with for ten years—for some three thousand six hundred days? No, Leonilda. I'm afraid not."

"He comes home, sinks down in that armchair, and reads his newspapers. Newspapers are the fifth wall in this house. We look at each other, and either we don't know what to say or we know it all by heart."

"You're not telling me anything new. It happens to all couples—married and even unmarried. Unmarried couples get tremendously bored when they're not outright fools. You and I, Leonilda, if we went on seeing each other, would end up in the same situation ourselves."

"That's possible."

"I'm glad you see it. Really, knowing a woman is to pile on one sorrow more. Every girl who enters our life damages something precious inside us. Probably every man who enters a woman's life destroys a facet of kindness in her previously left undestroyed by others, simply because they never found the way to do it. It evens out. We're all a pack of scoundrels."

"You don't believe in anything."

"You want me to believe in you, maybe?"

"Is this what life is all about, then?"

"And how would you like it to be?"

"I don't really know. I mean—that all married couples get along like John and me."

"Maybe ninety percent do."

"Then what can one do?"

To this point their conversation had developed in an easygoing if mischievous flow, but suddenly a swell of emotion exploded in Karl. Roughly seizing the woman's hand, he pulled her toward him and kissed her face. She avoided his lips. He let her go, looked at her affectionately, and said, "I kissed you because you're an unfortunate little creature. A typical little creature who swallows all the nonsense of the movies. Look into my eyes." (Leonilda had withdrawn to her chair, scarlet with shame.) "You see now. I'm rid of desire. Try to love John. He's a good man. I'm a good man too. We're all good men. But each one of us is ridiculed by some woman, each woman is ridiculed somewhere by some man. As I said earlier, it evens out."

Face to face, nearly composed, they studied one another as if they had come across each other completely alone on the face of the planet. Neither had a thing to learn or say. Karl stood up.

"Well, so long."

She smiled ambiguously, cautiously asking, "Will you be angry? When John comes in tonight I'll tell him you were here."

"What? You're going to tell him?"

"Have we done something wrong, perhaps?"

"You're right. Good-by."

Without moving from her seat, Leonilda watched him advance—his back to her—toward the massive wooden door.

Translated by Norman Thomas di Giovanni

Like the Night

ALEJO CARPENTIER

And he traveled like the night.
—Iliad, Book I.

I

Although the headlands still lay in shadow, the sea between them was beginning to turn green when the lookout blew his conch to announce that the fifty black ships sent us by King Agamemnon had arrived. Hearing the signal, those who had been waiting for so many days on the dung-covered threshing floors began carrying the wheat toward the shore, where rollers were already being made ready so that the vessels could be brought right up to the walls of the fortress. When the keels touched the sand, there was a certain amount of wrangling with the steersmen, because the Mycenaeans had so often been told about our complete ignorance of nautical matters that they tried to keep us at a distance with their poles. Moreover, the beach was now crowded with children, who got between the soldiers' legs, hindered their movements, and scrambled up the sides of the ships to steal nuts from under the oarsmen's benches. The transparent waves of dawn were breaking amid cries, insults, tussles, and blows, and our leading citizens could not make their speeches of welcome in the middle of such pandemonium. I had been expecting something more solemn, more ceremonious, from our meeting with these men who had come to fetch us to fight for them, and I walked off, feeling somewhat disillusioned, toward the fig tree on whose thickest branch I often sat astride, gripping the wood with my knees, because it reminded me somewhat of a woman's body.

As the ships were drawn out of the water and the tops of the mountains behind began to catch the sun, my first bad impression gradually faded; it had clearly been the result of a sleepless night of waiting, and also of my having drunk too heavily the day before with the young men recently arrived on the coast from inland, who were to embark with us soon after dawn. As I watched the procession of men carrying jars, black wineskins, and baskets moving toward the ships, a warm pride swelled within me, and a sense of my superiority as a soldier. That oil, that resinated wine, and above all that wheat from which biscuits would be cooked under the cinders at night while we slept in the shelter of the wet prows in some mysterious and unknown bay on the way to the Great City of Ships—the grain that I had helped to winnow with my shovel—all these things were being put on board for me; nor need I tire my long, muscular limbs, and arms designed for handling an ashwood pile, with tasks fit only for men who knew nothing but the smell of the soil, men who looked at the earth over the sweating backs of their animals or spent their lives crouched over it, weeding, uprooting, and raking, in almost the same attitudes as their own browsing cattle. These men would never pass under the clouds that at this time of day darken the distant green islands, whence the acrid-scented silphium was brought. They would never know the wide streets of the Trojans' city, the city we were now going to surround, attack, and destroy.

For days and days, the messengers sent us by the Mycenaean king had been telling us about Priam's insolence and the sufferings that threatened our people because of the arrogant behavior of his subjects. They had been jeering at our manly way of life; and, trembling with rage, we had heard of the challenges hurled at us long-haired Achaeans by the men of Ilium although our courage is unmatched by any other race. Cries of rage were heard, fists clenched and shaken, oaths sworn with the hands palm upward, and shields thrown against the walls, when we heard of the abduction of Helen of Sparta. While wine flowed from skins into helmets, in loud voices the emissaries told us of her marvelous beauty, her noble bearing and adorable way of walking, and described the cruelties she had endured in her miserable captivity. That same evening, when the whole town was seething with indignation, we were told that the fifty black ships were being sent. Fires were lighted in the bronze foundries while old women brought wood from the mountains.

And now, several days later, here I was gazing at the vessels drawn up at my feet, with their powerful keels and their masts at rest between the bulwarks like a man's virility between his thighs; I felt as if in some sense I was the owner of those timbers, transformed by some portentous carpentry unknown to our people into racehorses of the ocean, ready to carry us where the greatest adventure of all time was now unfolding like an epic. And I, son of a harness maker and grandson of a castrator of bulls, was to have the good fortune to go where those deeds were being done whose luster reached us in sailors' stories; I was to have the honor of seeing the walls of Troy, of following noble leaders and contributing my energy and strength to the cause of rescuing Helen of Sparta—a manly undertaking and the supreme triumph of a war that would give us prosperity, happiness, and pride in ourselves forever. I took a deep breath of the breeze blowing from the olive-covered hillside and thought how splendid it would be to die in such a just conflict, for the cause of Reason itself. But the idea of being pierced by an enemy lance made me think of my mother's grief and also of another, perhaps even profounder grief, though in this case the news would have to be heard with dry eyes because the hearer was head of the family. I walked slowly down to the town by the shepherds' path. Three kids were gamboling in the thyme-scented air. Down on the beach the loading of wheat was still going on.

II

The impending departure of the ships was being celebrated on all sides with thrumming of guitars and clashing of cymbals. The sailors from *La Gallarda* were dancing the zarambeque with enfranchised Negresses, and singing familiar *coplas*—like the song of the *Moza del Retoño*, wherein groping hands supplied the blanks left in the words. Meanwhile the loading of wine, oil, and grain was still going on, with the help of the overseer's Indian servants, who were impatient to return to their native land. Our future chaplain was on his way to the harbor, driving before him two mules loaded with the bellows and pipes of a wooden organ. Whenever I met any of the men from the ships, there were noisy embraces, exaggerated gestures, and enough laughter and boasting to bring the women to their windows. We seemed to be men of a different race, expressly created to carry out exploits beyond the ken of the baker, the wool carder, and the merchant who hawked holland shirts embroidered by parties of nuns in their patios. In the middle of the square, their brass instruments flashing in the sun, the Captain's six trumpeters were playing popular airs while the Burgundian drummers thundered on their instruments, and a sackbut with a mouthpiece like a dragon was bellowing as if it wanted to bite.

In his shop, smelling of calfskin and Cordovan leather, my father was driving his awl into a stirrup strap with the half-heartedness of someone whose mind is elsewhere. When he saw me, he took me in his arms with serene sadness, perhaps remembering the horrible death of Cristobalillo, the companion of my youthful escapades, whom the Indians of the Dragon's Mouth had pierced with their arrows. But he knew that everyone was wild to embark for the Indies then—although most men in possession of their senses were already realizing that it was the "madness of many for the gain of a few." He spoke in praise of good craftsmanship and told me that a man could gain as much respect by carrying the harness maker's standard in the Corpus Christi procession as from dangerous exploits. He pointed out the advantages of a well-provided table, a full coffer, and a peaceful old age. But, probably having realized that the excitement in the town was steadily increasing and that my mood was not attuned to such sensible reasoning, he gently led me to the door of my mother's room.

This was the moment I had most dreaded, and I could hardly restrain my own tears when I saw hers, for we had put off telling her of my departure until everyone knew that my name had been entered in the books of the Casa de la Contratación. I thanked her for the vows she had made to the Virgin of Navigators in exchange for my speedy return, and promised her everything she asked of me, such as to have no sinful dealings with the women of those far-off countries, whom the Devil kept in a state of paradisiac nakedness in order to confuse and mislead unwary Christians, even if they were not actually corrupted by the sight of such a careless display of flesh. Then, realizing that it was useless to make demands of someone who was already dreaming of what lay beyond the horizon, my mother began asking me anxiously about the safety of the ships and the skill of their pilots. I exaggerated the solidity and seaworthiness of *La Gallarda*, declaring that her pilot was a veteran of the Indies and a comrade of Nuño García. And to distract her from her fears, I told her about the wonders of the New World, where all diseases could be cured by the Claw of the Great Beast and by bezoar stones; I told her, too, that in the country of the Omeguas there was a city built entirely of gold, so large that it would take a good walker a night and two days to cross it, and that we should surely go there unless we found our fortune in some not-yet-discovered regions inhabited by rich tribes for us to conquer. Gently shaking her head, my mother then said that travelers returned from the Indies told lying, boastful stories, and spoke of Amazons and anthropophagi, of terrible Bermudan tempests and poisoned spears that transformed into a statue anyone they pierced.

Seeing that she confronted all my hopeful remarks with unpleasant facts, I talked to her of our high-minded aims and tried to make her see the plight of all the poor idol worshippers who did not even know the sign of the Cross. We should win thousands of souls to our holy religion and carry out Christ's commandments to the Apostles. We were soldiers of God as well as soldiers of the King, and by baptizing the Indians and freeing them from their barbarous superstitions our nation would win imperishable glory and greater happiness, prosperity, and power than all the kingdoms of Europe. Soothed by my remarks, my mother hung a scapulary around my neck and gave me various ointments against the bites of poisonous creatures, at the same time making me promise that I would never go to sleep without wearing some woolen socks she had made for me herself. And as the cathedral bells began to peal, she went to look for an embroidered shawl that she wore only on very important occasions. On the way to church I noticed that in spite of everything my parents had, as it were, grown in stature because of their pride in having a son in the Captain's fleet, and that they greeted people more often and more demonstratively than usual. It is always gratifying to have a brave son on his way to fight for a splendid and just cause. I looked toward the harbor. Grain was still being carried onto the ships.

III

I used to call her my sweetheart, although no one yet knew that we were in love. When I saw her father near the ships, I realized that she would be alone, so I followed the dreary jetty battered by the winds, splashed with green water, and edged with chains and rings green with slime until I reached the last house, the one with green shutters that were always closed. Hardly had I sounded the tarnished knocker when the door opened, and I entered the house along with a gust of wind full of sea spray. The lamps had already been lighted because of the mist. My sweetheart sat down beside me in a deep armchair covered in old brocade and rested her head on my shoulder witth such a sad air of resignation that I did not dare question those beloved eyes, which seemed to be gazing at nothing, but with an air of amazement. The strange objects that filled the room now took on a new significance for me. Some link bound me to the astrolabe, the compass, and the wind rose, as well as to the sawfish hanging from the beams of the ceiling and the charts by Mercator and Ortelius spread out on either side of the fireplace among maps of the heavens populated by Bears, Dogs, and Archers.

Above the whistling of the wind as it crept under the doors, I heard the voice of my sweetheart asking how our preparations were going. Reassured to find that it was possible to talk of something other than ourselves, I told her about the Sulpicians and Recollects who were to embark with us, and praised the piety of the gentlemen and farmers chosen by the man who would take possession of these far-off countries in the name of the King of France. I told her what I knew of the great River Colbert, bordered with ancient trees draped in silvery moss, its red waters flowing majestically beneath a sky white with herons. We were taking provisions for six months. The lowest decks of the *Belle* and the *Amiable* were full of corn. We were undertaking the important task of civilizing the vast areas of forest lying between the burning Gulf of Mexico and Chicagua, and we would teach new skills to the inhabitants.

Just when I thought my sweetheart was listening most attentively to what I was saying, she suddenly sat up, and said with unexpected vehemence that there was nothing glorious about the enterprise that had set all the town bells ringing since dawn. Last night, with her eyes inflamed with weeping, her anxiety to know something about the world across the sea to which I was going had driven her to pick up Montaigne's *Essais* and read everything to do with America in the chapter on Coaches. There she had learned about the treachery of the Spaniards, and how they had succeeded in passing themselves off as gods, with their horses and bombards. Aflame with virginal indignation, my sweetheart showed me the passage in which the skeptical Bordelais says of the Indians that "we have made use of their ignorance and inexperience to draw them more easily into fraud, luxury, avarice, and all manner of inhumanity and cruelty by the example of our life and pattern of our customs." Blinded by her distress at such perfidy, this devout young woman who always wore a gold cross on her bosom actually approved of a writer who could impiously declare that the savages of the New World had no reason to exchange their religion for ours, their own having served them very well for a long time.

I realized that these errors came only from the resentment of a girl in love—and a very charming girl—against the man who was forcing her to wait for him so long merely because he wanted to make his fortune quickly in a much-proclaimed undertaking. But although I understood this, I felt deeply wounded by her scorn for my courage and her lack of interest in an adventure that would make my name famous; for the news of some exploit of mine, or of some region I had pacified, might well lead to the King's conferring a title on me, even though it might involve a few Indians dying by my hand. No great deed is achieved without a struggle, and as for our holy faith, the Word must be imposed with blood. But it was jealousy that made my sweetheart paint such an ugly picture of the island of Santo Domingo, where we were to make a landing, describing it in adorably unsuitable words as "a paradise of wicked women." It was obvious that in spite of her chastity, she knew what sort of women they were who often embarked for Cap Français from a jetty nearby under the supervision of the police and amid shouts of laughter and coarse jokes from the sailors. Someone, perhaps one of the servants, may have told her that a certain sort of abstinence is not healthy for a man, and she was imagining me beset by greater perils than the floods, storms, and water dragons that abound in American rivers, in some Eden of nudity and demoralizing heat.

In the end I began to be annoyed that we should be having this wrangle instead of the tender farewells I had expected at such a moment. I started abusing the cowardice of women, their incapacity for heroism, the way their philosophy was bounded by baby linen and workboxes, when a loud knocking announced the untimely return of her father. I jumped out of a back window, unnoticed by anyone in the marketplace, for passersby, fishermen, and drunkards—already numerous even so early in the evening—had gathered around a table on which a man stood shouting. I took him at first for a hawker trying to sell Orvieto elixir, but he turned out to be a hermit demanding the liberation of the holy places, I shrugged my shoulder and went on my way. Some time ago I had been on the point of enlisting in Foulque de Neuilly's crusade. A malignant fever—cured thanks to God and my sainted mother's ointments—most opportunely kept me shivering in bed on the day of departure: that adventure ended, as everyone knows, in a war between Christians and Christians. The crusades had fallen into disrepute. Besides, I had other things to think about.

IV

The wind had died down. Still annoyed by my stupid quarrel with my betrothed, I went off to the harbor to look at the ships. They were all moored to the jetty, side by side, with hatches open, receiving thousands of sacks of wheat flour between their brightly camouflaged sides. The infantry regiments were slowly going up the gangways amid the shouts of stevedores, blasts from the boatswain's whistle, and signals tearing through the mist to set the cranes in motion. On the decks, shapeless objects and menacing machines were being heaped together under tarpaulins. From time to time an aluminum wing revolved slowly above the bulwarks before disappearing into the darkness of the hold. The generals' horses, suspended from webbing bands, traveled over the roofs of the shops like the horses of the Valkyries. I was standing on a high iron gangway watching the final preparations, when suddenly I became agonizingly aware that there were only a few hours left—scarcely thirteen—before I too should have to board one of those ships now being loaded with weapons for my use. Then I thought of women; of the days of abstinence lying ahead; of the sadness of dying without having once more taken my pleasure from another warm body.

Full of impatience, and still angry because I had not got even a kiss from my sweetheart, I struck off toward the house where the dancers lived. Christopher, very drunk, was already shut into his girl's room. My girl embraced me, laughing and crying, saying that she was proud of me, that I looked very handsome in my uniform, and that a fortuneteller had read the cards and told her that no harm would come to me during the Great Landing. She more than once called me a "hero," as if she knew how cruelly her flattery contrasted with my sweetheart's unjust remarks. I went out onto the roof. The lights were coming on in the town, outlining the gigantic geometry of the buildings in luminous points. Below, in the streets, was a confused swarm of heads and hats.

At this distance, it was impossible to tell women from men in the evening mist. Yet it was in order that this crowd of unknown human beings should go on existing, that I was due to make my way to the ships soon after dawn. I should plow the stormy ocean during the winter months and land on a remote shore under attack from steel and fire, in defense of my countrymen's principles. It was the last time a sword would be brandished over the maps of the West. This time we should finish off the new Teutonic Order for good and all, and advance as victors into that longed-for future when man would be reconciled with man. My mistress laid her trembling hand on my head, perhaps guessing at the nobility of my thoughts. She was naked under the half-open flaps of her dressing gown.

V

I returned home a few hours before dawn, walking unsteadily from the wine with which I had tried to cheat the fatigue of a body surfeited with enjoyment of another body. I was hungry and sleepy, and at the same time deeply disturbed by the thought of my approaching departure. I laid my weapons and belt on a stool and threw myself on my bed. Then I realized, with a start of surprise, that someone was lying under the thick woolen blanket; and I was just stretching out my hand for my knife when I found myself embraced by two burning-hot arms, which clasped me around the neck like the arms of a drowning man while two inexpressibly smooth legs twined themselves between mine. I was struck dumb with astonishment when I saw that the person who had slipped into my bed was my sweetheart. Between her sobs, she told me how she had escaped in the darkness, had run away in terror from barking dogs and crept furtively through my father's garden to the window of my room. Here she had waited for me in terror and impatience. After our stupid quarrel that afternoon, she had thought of the dangers and sufferings lying in wait for me, with that sense of impotent longing to lighten a soldier's hazardous lot which women so often express by offering their own bodies, as if the sacrifice of their jealously guarded virginity at the moment of departure and without hope of enjoyment, this reckless abandonment to another's pleasure, could have the propitiatory power of ritual oblation.

There is a unique and special freshness in an encounter with a chaste body never touched by a lover's hands, a felicitious clumsiness of response, an intuitive candor that, responding to some obscure promptings, divines and adopts the attitudes that favor the closest possible physical union. As I lay in my sweetheart's arms and felt the little fleece that timidly brushed against one of my thighs, I grew more and more angry at having exhausted my strength in all-too-familiar coupling, in the absurd belief that I was ensuring my future serenity by means of present excesses. And now that I was being offered this so desirable compliance, I lay almost insensible beneath my sweetheart's tremulous and impatient body. I would not say that my youth was incapable of catching fire once again that night under the stimulus of this new pleasure. But the idea that it was a virgin who was offering herself to me, and that her closed and intact flesh would require a slow and sustained effort on my part, filled me with an obsessive fear of failure.

I pushed my sweetheart to one side, kissing her gently on the shoulders, and began telling her with assumed sincerity what a mistake it would be for our nuptial joys to be marred by the hurry of departure; how ashamed she would be if she became pregnant and how sad it was for children to grow up with no father to teach them how to get green honey out of hollow tree trunks and look for cuttlefish under stones. She listened, her large bright eyes burning in the darkness, and I was aware that she was in the grip of a resentment drawn from the underworld of the instincts and felt nothing but scorn for a man who, when offered such an opportunity, invoked reason and prudence instead of taking her by force, leaving her bleeding on the bed like a trophy of the chase, defiled, with breasts bitten, but having become a woman in her hour of defeat.

Just then we heard the lowing of cattle going to be sacrificed on the shore and the watchmen blowing their conchs. With scorn showing clearly in her face, my sweetheart got quickly out of bed without letting me touch her, and with a gesture not so much of modesty as of someone taking back what he had been on the point of selling too cheap, she covered those charms which had suddenly begun to enflame my desire. Before I could stop her, she had jumped out of the window. I saw her running away as fast as she could among the olives, and I realized in that instant that it would be easier for me to enter the city of Troy without a scratch than to regain what I had lost.

When I went down to the ships with my parents, my soldier's pride had been replaced by an intolerable sense of disgust, of inner emptiness and self-depreciation. And when the steersmen pushed the ships away from the shore with their strong poles, and the masts stood erect between the row of oarsmen, I realized that the display, excesses, and feasting that precede the departure of soldiers to the battlefield were now over. There was no time now for garlands, laurel wreaths, wine drinking in every house, envious glances from weaklings, and favors from women. Instead, our lot would consist of bugle calls, mud, rainsoaked bread, the arrogance of our leaders, blood spilled in error, the sickly, tainted smell of gangrene. I already felt less confident that my courage would contribute to the power and happiness of the long-haired Achaeans. A veteran soldier, going to war because it was his profession and with no more enthusiasm than a sheep shearer on his way to the pen, was telling anyone prepared to listen that Helen of Sparta was very happy to be in Troy, and that when she disported herself in Paris' bed, her hoarse cries of enjoyment brought blushes to the cheeks of the virgins who lived in Priam's palace. It was said that the whole story of the unhappy captivity of Leda's daughter, and of the insults and humiliations the Trojans had subjected her to, was simply war propaganda, inspired by Agamemnon with the consent of Menelaus. In fact, behind this enterprise and the noble ideals it had set up as a screen, a great many aims were concealed which would not benefit the combatants in the very least: above all, so the old soldier said, to sell more pottery, more cloth, more vases decorated with scenes from chariot races, and to open new ways of access to Asia, whose peoples had a passion for barter, and so put an end once and for all to Trojan competition.

Too heavily loaded with flour and men, the ship responded slowly to the oars. I gazed for a long time at the sunlit houses of my native town. I was nearly in tears, I took off my helmet and hid my eyes behind its crest; I had taken great trouble to make it round and smooth, like the magnificent crests of the men who could order their accouterments of war from the most highly skilled craftsmen and who were voyaging on the swiftest and longest ship.

Translated by Frances Partridge

A Pine-Cone, a Toy Sheep...

PABLO NERUDA

The poet's heart, like all other hearts, is an interminable artichoke. . . .

I

My great-great grandparents came to the *pampas* of Parral and planted their vines. Their acres were scant and their offspring prodigious. Time passed and the family multiplied: indoors and out, they kept coming. The wine-making went on as before—a strong and acidulous wine, undistilled, in the hogshead. Little by little things worsened; my grandparents abandoned their homestead, moved off, and came back to die in the dust bowls midway in Chile.

My father died in Temuco: he was made for a kindlier climate. He lies buried in one of the rainiest graveyards of the world. He was a nondescript farmer, a mediocre laborer assigned to the Talcahuano dike, but a first-class railroader. Railroading, with my father, was a passion. My mother could pick out in the dark, among all the other trains, precisely the train that was bringing my father into the station house at Temuco, or taking him away.

Few people today know about gravel trains. In the north, in the typhoon country, the rains would wash away the rails, if there were not men on hand all hours around the clock to pack down the crossties with gravel. They had to carry the slabs from the quarries in baskets and empty the cobble into flatcars. Forty years ago, a crew of that sort must have been something to reckon with. They had no choice but to live alone at isolated points, slashing away at the flint. Company salaries were menial. References were not required of those who signed up to work on the gravel trains. Teams were recruited from the gigantic and muscular peons: from the fields, from the suburbs, from the prison cells. My father was a train conductor, used to giving orders and obeying them. Sometimes, when my teachers put me in a rage, I signed for a stint on the gravel trains too. We hacked stone in Boroa, in the wilderness heart of the frontier, the scene of those bloody encounters between Spaniards and Araucanian Indians.

Nature went to my head like whisky. I was ten, or thereabouts, already a poet. The rhymes did not come; but the beetles and birds and partridge eggs of the *pampas* enchanted me. Coming on them by chance in the gorges—blue-tinted, shadowy, glowing, colored like the barrel of a shotgun—was a miracle. I was stunned by the perfection of the insect world. I went looking for "snake-mothers"—that was our extravagant name for the largest coleopter of all, black, burnished, and powerful, the Titan of Chilean insects. It thrilled me to see them there, all at once, on the ginger-tree trunks, or the wild-apple, or the boughs of the *coigue* trees:[1] I knew I could throw the weight of my feet on them, without cracking their shells....

My forays attracted the curiosity of the workers: they began to interest themselves in my discoveries. Heedless of even my father, they took off for the virgin timber, and, with greater agility, stamina, and cunning than I could ever muster, returned with incredible prizes for me. There was one fellow, Monge by name,

[1] *coigue:* A species of cupuliferous beech tree much valued for its wood, in Patagonia and Tierra del Fuego. In Chile, a tree of considerable height similar to the oak, with an inferior wood.

whom my father regarded as a dangerous knife slinger. Two long gashes scored the swarthiness of his face: one, the vertical scar of a knife slash, the other, a horizontal white grin full of guile and good fellowship. It was Monge who brought me white *copihues*,[2] great, shaggy spiders and sucking pigeons; and once he tracked down the most dazzling prize of them all: "snake-mothers," moon beetles. . . . I saw only one in my lifetime—a lightning flash disguised as a rainbow. His caparison glowed yellow and violet and crimson and green, and then he was gone from my hands like a bolt and lost in the timber. Soon Monge himself was not there to hunt me another. . . . My father told me how he died. He fell from a freight car and bowled down a precipice. They held up the convoy for him, but, as my father said, Monge was nothing but a sack of bones. I mourned for a week.

II

It is hard to give a true picture of the house that we lived in—the typical frontiersman's home of forty years ago. All the family dwellings intercommunicated. In the well of the patios, the Reyes, the Ortegas, the Candias, and the Massons exchanged hardware or books, birthday cakes and rubbing unguents, tables and chairs and umbrellas. All the hamlet's activities were rooted in the homestead. There, Don Carlos Masson, looking like Emerson—North American, with a mane of white hair—was the reigning patriarch of the communal household. His sons, the young Massons, were Creole to the core. A first founder rather than an empire builder, Don Carlos lived by the Law and the Writ. Out of that clan, without whom we all would have been

[2] *copihue:* The liliaceous climber of Chile, with red and white blossoms of striking beauty, and berries similar to the chili. In Chile, a symbol of the Araucanian forests.

destitute, came the hotels and the slaughterhouses and the printing presses. Some of the Massons were newspaper editors, others worked for a wage in the printing house. All fell away with the passing of time and poverty was general, as before. Only the Germans, in the typical pattern of the frontier, preserved the cache of their worldly goods irreducibly intact.

All the houses had the air of a bivouac encampment or an explorer's safari. One saw, upon entering, great sixty-gallon casks, farm implements, saddle gear, and other indescribable objects. They remained "temporary" to the end, with abortive stairs going nowhere. All my life, there was talk of bringing things to completion. Parents began to think of sending their sons to the University.

In the house of Don Carlos Masson the great feast days were celebrated.

Name day solemnities always concentrated on turkey with celery, roast lamb on skewers, with snowy milk for dessert.... Heading the interminable table sat the white-headed patriarch with his wife, Doña Micaela Candia. Behind was the huge flag of Chile, to which a diminutive North American pennant had been pinned, as if to indicate the ratio of blood. The lone star of Chile predominated.

One room of the Masson house we youngsters entered only very rarely. The color of the furniture is unknown to me to this day, since all was hidden from sight under white sheaths, until fire carried them away. There, also, the album of family photographs was kept, with finer and more delicate images than the dreadful tinted enlargements that later invaded the frontier.

Among them was a portrait of my mother, dead in Parral not long after I was born; a lady slenderly built and bemused, dressed in black. She wrote verses once, I am told, but all I ever saw of her was the lovely family portrait. My father had taken a second wife, Doña Trinidad Candia, my stepmother. It is strange now to have to invoke that tutelary angel of my childhood in such terms. She was diligent and lovable, with a countrywoman's sense of humor and an indefatigable gusto for kindness. Like all the women of that day and that region, she turned into an amenable and undeviating phantom, once my father appeared on the scene.

In that room I saw the dancers go by in quadrilles and mazurkas.

In my house was a trunkful of fascinating keepsakes. From its depths, a fabulous parrot glittered on a calendar. One day, when my mother was rifling that magical casket, I plunged in to salvage the parrot. Later on, as I grew older, I plundered it secretly; there were precious, impalpable fans.

The trunk had other associations: the first love story to inflame my imagination. In it were hundreds of post cards, all signed in one hand—was it Enrique or Umberto?—and addressed to a Maria Thielman. Each was a marvel: all the era's great actresses set into little embossed transparencies, sometimes cemented with patches of real hair. There were castles and cities and exotic perspectives. At first, I had eyes for only the figures; but as I grew older, I turned to the messages of love set down in a perfect calligraphy. I imagined the lover: a gallant in a slouch hat, with a walking stick and a diamond in his cravat. His words were words of unmitigated passion, mailed from all points of the compass by a man on the move, full of glittering turns of phrase and incandescent audacity. I, too, began to yearn for Maria Theilman of the letters: I evoked her in the guise of a pitiless prima donna, with pearls in her hair. How did those letters end up in the trunk of my mother? I never learned the answer.

III

The boys in the public school neither acknowledged nor reverenced my status as poet. The frontier still retained its "Far-Western" stamp of a country without prejudice. My classmates were the Schnakes, the Schelers, the Hausers, the Smiths, the Taitos, the Seranis. All was equal between us: Arcenas, Ramirez, and Reyes. Basque names were absent; but Sephardic Albalas and Francos mingled freely with Irish McGintys and Polish Yanichewskys. Araucanian Indian names—Melivilus, Catrileos—glowed with a shadowy brilliance, smelling of timber and water.

We battled together in a great, barnlike barrack, with holm oak acorns: only those who have stopped one can judge of their sting. Before coming to school, which was close to the river bank, we all primed our pockets with artillery. I had little physical endurance, no strength to speak of, and limited cunning. I always came off badly in those sallies. While I gaped at the cut of a holm acorn, green, with a high polish, in its rugged, gray frieze-cap, or tried languidly to carve out of its cup one of those pipes that enchanted me so, I went down under a hail of acorns aimed at my head. It occurred to me, in my second year, to protect myself with a waterproof hat, bright green in color. It was my father's hat, originally, charged with the same fascination as his *manta de castilla* and his red and green signal lanterns—which I could hardly hope to carry off with me to dazzle my classmates....

Little by little, I armed myself with verses.

In the schoolhouse, the cold was glacial. Forty years ago, I sat quaking with cold, just as the boys in the new Liceo de Temuco do to this day. They have built a grand modern structure with large windows and no heating facilities: that's life for you, out on the frontier! We made men of ourselves in my day. There was plenty of reason to. Southern houses are all ramshackle, hastily clapped together out of freshly cut boards, with zinc roofing. Incessant great rainfalls made music on the roofs. Then, one fine morning a house facing the front would awake to find itself roofless: wind had carried it off two hundred meters. The streets were great quagmires; everywhere wagons fouled on the road. On the footpaths, picking our way from boulder to boulder, we slogged toward the schoolhouse in the rain and the cold. Our umbrellas spun away on the wind. Raincoats were costly, shoes were soon waterlogged; gloves I despised. I shall never forget all the drenched stockings close to the braziers, the multitude of shoes sending up steam like small locomotives. Later, the floods came, sweeping away whole settlements—the most wretched of all, those who lived closest to the river. The earth rocked with temblors. Sometimes on the highest ranges of all a plume of terrible light stood up: the Llaima volcano was active again.

And worst of all, fires. In 1906 or '07, I don't recall which, all Temuco went up in a holocaust. Houses blazed like match boxes; twenty-two street blocks were razed to the ground; nothing was left. But if there is one thing Southerners know how to build in a hurry, it is houses. They don't build for the ages; but they build. A man who has lived in the South all his life must expect to live through three or four holocausts. I remember myself first as a child planted on blankets in front of our house, watching it blaze for the second or third time.

But the saws sang. Timber was piled in the stations again; there was a tang of fresh boards in the villages. Some of my verses are still scrawled on the walls there: the paper-smooth boards, grained with mysterious veins, always tempted me. Since then, wood has been—not an obsession with me, for I admit to none—but a staple of my natural life:

Oh, whatever it is that I know
or invoke again
among all of the things of the world,
it is wood that abides

as my playfellow,
I take through the world
in my flesh and my clothing
the smell
of the sawyer;
the reek of red boards;
my breast and my senses
soaked up
in my childhood the bulk
of felled trees coming down,
great stands in the forest, crammed
with coming constructions;
I smelled in the whiplash
the gigantic length of the larch tree
and the laurel branch, forty yards high.

IV

People who live in plank houses have different habits of thinking and feeling from the folk of central Chile. In some ways, they are like the people of the great North country and the desolate wastelands. Being born in a house of mud bricks is not the same thing as being born in a house just hewn from the forest. In those houses, birth happens for the first time. The graveyards are still fresh.

For that reason, too, one finds neither religious ceremony nor written poetry. My mother used to lead me to church by the hand. The courts of the Church of the Heart of Mary were planted with lilacs, and at the novena, all was drenched in their powerful aroma.

The church itself was always empty. At twelve, I was almost the only young male in the temple. Mother let me do as I pleased in the temple. Not being religious by nature, I never troubled my head about ritual and remained erect on my feet almost always, while the others were chanting and genuflecting. I never learned how to cross myself; but no one in the Church of Temuco ever called attention to the young infidel at large in their midst, upright on his feet. Perhaps that is why I have entered all churches with respect ever since. In that very same parish, my first romance flourished. The name might have been Maria; I can never be sure. But I well remember the whole of that baffling first love, or whatever it was; it was splendid and woeful, full of tremors and torments, soaked through and through with the reek of conventual lilies.

Most of the city folk were agnostics. My father, my uncles, my innumerable in-laws and godparents gathered around the big dining-room table, were of no mind to say grace. Instead, they swapped tales of *el huaso Rios*: how he crossed the bridge at Malleco on horseback, and lassoed Saint Joseph.

Everywhere there were hammers and handsaws—men working in wood and sowing spring wheat. Pioneers, it appears, require little of their god. Blanca Hauser—a Temucan with a house on the Manzano Plaza, on whose benches I wrote seas of bad verse—tells the story of an old codger and his wife who came running up in the midst of an earthquake. The old lady was beating her breast and crying loud cries: "Lord have mercy on us! *Misericordia!*" The old fellow overtook her and asked: "What's that you say? What's that you say?" "*Misericordia*, imbecile!" the old lady told him. And the old man, finding that too much to manage, came trotting after her, thumping his chest at odd moments and repeating: "It's just what she says it is! It's just what she says it is!"

V

From time to time my uncles summoned me to the great rite of roast lamb. Eston Masson, as I have said, had North American blood in his veins, but the Massons were true Creoles. The tough virgin soil had soaked into its humors all the Nordic and Mediterranean strain, leaving only the Araucanian. Wine flowed under the willows and sometimes the guitar could be heard through the week. A salad of green peas was prepared in great washing troughs. Each morning I heard the terrible shriek of stuck pigs, but the most frightful of all was the preparation of the *ñachi.*[3] They slit the throat of the lamb and the blood gushed into washbowls seasoned with strong spices. My uncles asked me to drink down the blood.

I went clad in the garb of a poet, as in deep mourning: I mourned for the rain, for the grief of the world, for no one at all. And the barbarous ones raised their goblet of blood.

I overcame my compunction and drank with the others. One must learn how to live like a man.

The centaurs held festival, a true revel of centaurs: a jousting bout. Wherever two foals made a name for themselves—just as the prowess of two men might win them a local notoriety—first the talk, and then, little by little, the plans for the tourney began to take shape. The contest of the Thunderbolt and the Condor was already legendary: two colts of colossal proportions, one black and one gray. Came the day of the pike-thrust!

The men had already come down from the mountains—horsemen from all parts of the country: from Cholchol and Curacautin, from Pitrufquen and Gorbea, from Lanchoche and Lautaro, from Quepa, from Quitratue, from Labranza, from Boroa and from Carahue. There the two centaurs, might matched to might, tried to sweep all before them, or make the first pass with the pike. The colts quivered from their hooves to their froth-clabbered nostrils. The moments when nobody budged were deathly to live through; then the Thunderbolt or the Condor was victorious and we saw

[3] *ñachi:* In Chile, a blood sauce, served warm from the slaughtered lamb, spiced with chili and salt; believed to be an aid to digestion.

the hero pace by with his great flashing spurs on a soaked horse. The great feast followed, with its hundreds of trenchermen. The wits of the South put it this way:

With an olive's brine
and a lake of wine
and the sweet of the roast
till the belly burst.

Out of this violent fellowship came the Romantic who exercised a powerful influence on my life: Orlando Masson. He was the first man I ever knew to enlist in the social struggle. He founded a newspaper and printed my first verses: I drank in the odor of newsprint, rubbed elbows with compositors and dyed my fingers with printer's ink. He launched passionate campaigns at the abuses of the powerful; for with progress had come exploitation. On the pretext of liquidating the bandits, land was ceded to "colonizers," and Indians exterminated like rabbits. Araucanians are not timid or taciturn or crack-brained by nature: they became so under the shock of excruciating experience. After the Independence, after 1810, the good people of Chile took up the slaughter of Indians with the exaltation of Spanish conquistadors. Temuco was the last refuge of the Araucanian.

Against all these excesses Orlando made voluble protest. It was good, in a barbarous and violent land, to see his newspaper plead the cause of the just against the cruel, the weak against the all-powerful. The last fire I remember in Temuco was the newspaper plant of Orlando Masson. . . .

He was a jovial man, full of battles.

VI

The summers of Cautín are searing. The wheat and the sky burn. Earth struggles to throw off its lethargy.

The houses are as little prepared for the summer as for the winter. I head toward the open country, looking for poems. I walk and I walk: on the Nielal summit, I get lost. I am alone, with a pocketful of beetles and a great, hairy spider, in a box, newly caught. I can no longer see the sky over my head. In the eternal damp of the jungle I slither unsteadily, a bird cries out suddenly, the hallucinated cry of the *chucao*.[4] It wells from below like a sinister warning. The *copihues* glimmer faintly, like blood drops. I walk very small under gargantuan ferns. Close to my mouth darts a wild pigeon, with a dry thrashing of feathers. Higher up, other birds mock me with a jarring sound of laughter. The going is hard; it grows late.

Father is not home yet: he is due at three or four in the morning. I go up to my cubicle. I open a page of Salgari.[5] The rain smashes down like a cataract: in a moment, night and the rain have covered the world. Alone there, I write verses in my arithmetic notebook. I am up early the next morning. The plums are all green. I vault over fences, carrying my little packet of salt, I clamber up a tree, make myself comfortable, nibble a plum circumspectly; I bite and I spit out a morsel; I douse it with salt; I eat it. I bolt down a hundred—far too many, I think now.

Our old house has burned down, and the new one seems strange to me. I stand on a fence post and look all around. Nobody. I turn up some old timber: a few, miserable spiders insignificant in size—nothing at all.

[4] *chucao:* In Chile, the onomatopoeic name for a small bird gifted with the faculty of predicting good or bad luck on journeys. Heard from the right, his song portends a safe journey; heard from the left, it portends misfortune. About the size of a thrush, with dusky brown plumage, found in densely wooded areas.

[5] Emilio Salgari, born Verona, Italy, August 1863; died, a suicide, Turin, Italy, November 1911. Merchant marine officer and prolific writer of adventure fiction translated into a number of languages. His novels of piratical blood and thunder in the Malay Seas include *Sandokan* (bearded, bejeweled *kriss* in hand), *Los piratas de la Malasia, Una venganza malasia.*

In the rear, the latrine; near it, the trees teem with caterpillars. The almond trees show me their fruits sheathed in white plush. I know how to catch horseflies with a handkerchief—that way no harm comes to them. I keep them caged for a few days, holding them up to my ears. What a glorious humming!

Solitude; a child-poet dressed in black, on the spacious and terrible frontier. Little by little my life and my books trace the harrowing signs of a mystery, uncertainly.

I call to mind what I read the night before: how the breadfruit saved Sandokan and his friends in far-off Malaysia. I have no love for the Indian-killer, Buffalo Bill—but what a terror on horseback! The meadows are lovely to me and the conical tents of the redskins. I begin to read voraciously—leaping from Jules Verne to Vargas Vila, to Strindberg, to Gorki, to Felipe Trigo, to Diderot. The pages of *Les Misérables* leave me sick with pity and misery and I blubber my love into Bernardin de Saint-Pierre.

Human wisdom has split wide for me like a grain bag and scattered its seed in the night of Temuco . . .

VII

In the recesses of the world, knowledge waits for us. For some, revelation comes in a geometrical treatise; for others, in the lines of a poem. For me, books were a jungle in which I could lose myself, press farther and farther away from myself. They were another world of sumptuous flowers, another steep and crepuscular foliage, a mysterious silence, voices out of the sky; but also they were lives on the other side of the mountain peaks, on the other side of the ferns, beyond the rain.

There came to Temuco a tall lady in flat heels and voluminous draperies, dressed in sand-color. She was the Principal of the Liceo; she came from a southerly city, from the snows of Magellan. Her name was Gabriela Mistral.[6]

I saw her only rarely, because I shrank from the contact of outlanders. I had little to say. I lived mournfully, mutely, and avidly.

Gabriela had an ample, white smile in a tawny face flayed by blood and the weathers. I remembered that face from before: except for the absence of scars, it was the face of the pile driver, Monge! There was the very same smile, half friendly, half wary, the same knotting of eyebrows stung by snow or the glare of the *pampas*. She took books from the folds of her clerical robes and delivered them into my hands; it never seemed strange to me; I devoured them. It was she who first urged on me the great Russian masters who influenced me so.

The she went North. I wasted no tears on her; my friends now were legion, the agonized lives of my books. I knew where to find them....

VIII

I'll tell you a story about birds. On Lake Budi some years ago, they were hunting down the swans without mercy. The procedure was to approach them steathily in little boats and then rapidly—very rapidly—row into their midst. Swans like albatrosses have difficulty in flying; they must skim the surface of the water at a run. In the first phase of their flight they raise their big wings with great effort. It is then that they can be seized; a few blows with a bludgeon finish them off.

Someone made me a present of a swan: more dead than alive. It was of a marvelous species I have never seen since anywhere else in the world: a black-throated swan—a snow boat with a neck packed, as it were, into

[6] Gabriela Mistral: The distinguished poetess of Chile, winner of the Nobel Prize for Literature (1945) and author of *Tala*, *Ternura*, and other volumes of verse little known in this country.

a tight stocking of black silk. Orange-beaked, red-eyed.

This happened near the sea, in Puerto Saavedra, Imperial del Sur.

They brought it to me half dead. I bathed its wounds and pressed little pellets of bread and fish into its throat; but nothing stayed down. Nevertheless the wounds slowly healed, and the swan came to regard me as a friend. At the same time, it was apparent to me that the bird was wasting away with nostalgia. So, cradling the heavy burden in my arms through the streets, I carried it down to the river. It paddled a few strokes, very close to me. I had hoped it might learn how to fish for itself, and pointed to some pebbles far below, where they flashed in the sand like the silvery fish of the South. The swan looked at them remotely, sad-eyed.

For the next twenty days or more, day after day, I carried the bird to the river and toiled back with it to my house. It was almost as large as I was. One afternoon it seemed more abstracted than usual, swimming very close and ignoring the lure of the insects with which I tried vainly to tempt it to fish again. It became very quiet; so I lifted it into my arms to carry it home again. It was breast-high, when I suddenly felt a great ribbon unfurl, like a black arm encircling my face: it was the big coil of the neck, dropping down.

It was then that I learned swans do not sing at their death, if they die of grief.

I have said little about my poems. I know very little about such things, really. I prefer instead to move among the evocations of my childhood. Perhaps, out of these plants and these solitudes and this violent life come the truths and the secret things—the profoundest *Poetics* of all, unknown because no one has written them down. We come upon poetry a step at a time, among the beings and things of this world: nothing is taken away without adding to the sum of all that exists in a blind extension of love.

Once, looking for little trophies and creaturely things of my world in the back of our house in Temuco, I came on a knothole in a neighboring fence post. I peered through the opening and saw a plot very like our own, all wilderness and waste. I withdrew a few steps, with the vague sense of portents to come. Suddenly a hand appeared—the tiny hand of a child just my age. I came closer, and the hand disappeared; in its place was a lovely white sheep—a toy sheep of nondescript wool. The wheels had fallen away—but that only made it more lifelike. I have never seen a more ravishing animal. I peered through the knothole, but the child was nowhere in sight. I went back to the house and returned with a prize of my own which I left in the very same spot; a pine-cone I treasured above all things, half open, balsamic, sweet-smelling. I left it there and I went away with the little toy sheep....

Translated by Ben Belitt

As I Am . . . As I Was

LINO NOVÁS-CALVO

As I recall, it all began at the end of September. My birthday was about to arrive, and my mother was making me a new shirt. As she sat working on it, her face turned pale and she began to cough. Her eyes grew wide and she stood up, clutching her bosom. Then she walked into the other room.

The doctor was not called. When she seemed worse and her temperature was fluctuating wildly, my Aunt Sol came to see us, bearing news of some kind. She stood in the doorway, an expression of secrecy on her face, and looked into the room where my mother lay in bed. When my mother saw her, she became radiant. Then she began to weep silently.

Aunt Sol left immediately. When she was gone, my mother got up and put on her best dress. She arranged her hair and applied make-up. But at dusk Aunt Sol came back, and the animation in my mother's face suddenly disappeared. They spoke in low voices for a moment. Aunt Sol was exhausted; her eyelids closed as she said: Maybe they're mistaken about the date. He could be coming on another ship.

She went slowly toward the door. My mother stood

in the middle of the room, her hands across her chest. Thanks, anyway, Sol, she said weakly.

That was the beginning. For a period of several months I was obliged to watch these changes. And I understood nothing. Or perhaps I should say that I understood them without explaining them to myself. I knew that each month *someone* was supposed to be arriving on a ship, but this someone did not come. Meanwhile my mother would fall ill and then suddenly recover, or at least it seemed that she did. Another arrival date would be approaching, bringing with it a fresh hope. Then Aunt Sol would appear, looking disappointed, and my mother would go back to being ill once again.

But she did not complain of feeling sick, merely sometimes of being tired. She never stopped sewing. One day after Sol had left she said: It was all the work of the Devil. There's no help for it!

I can see her now, pale and thin, taller than the little door at the end of the room. I imagine her going out with her head bent over and then coming into the other room through the little doorway, as if she were emerging from a crypt. At that time the two of us lived alone at El Cerro. She had told me: I'm going to take in a lodger. She'll live in the sitting room. She's a seamstress too. We've got plenty of space, and I can do my work in our room.

This room faced the little garden, where I played with the other children of the neighborhood. The seamstress who came to live in the sitting room was a solid woman with shiny black skin. My mother shut the door between the two rooms, and we went in and out through the garden to the street behind.

We don't need the sitting room, she would say. And that street in front of the house is full of holes and there are puddles when it rains. In the back you can see the country. You can watch the sun go down.

I did not feel that she was talking to me. She had

brought the sewing machine in and installed it in our room, and the stacks of unfinished work were in the bathroom. The women who ran the shops no longer came to the house. Sometimes she went out early to deliver finished things and pick up new work. There was not much of that. She worked slowly now. Sometimes I would look in through the window from the garden and see her from behind. She would stop the sewing machine and sit there stiffly, merely looking at the wall. When she began to pedal again she would keep her bust erect, as a person does when he has been seized by a paralyzing pain.

One day she told me: I'm going to send you to your Aunt Sol's house for a few weeks. Or maybe to your Uncle Martín's. I've got to go away to the country and do some work there. It may take me several weeks.

I had never gone to the country. I had not mentioned it to her except once in a while back in Spain, and again coming over on the ship, and finally here in El Cerro, in that lean-to. I said: And my other uncles?

They're all right. They're somewhere around. The trouble is that they think I'm bad. It was the Devil that did it!

Martín came that evening. He had visited us before, passing through. He was a languid man with a dark, sad, pock-marked face, and he did not like to talk. I always saw him wearing a wide belt that held files, pliers and hammers. As he was leaving he said to my mother: You think about it. Send me the boy if you want.

She added quickly for my benefit, but speaking to her brother: I'm coming right back, you know. It's just some work I've got to do there in Artemisa. But it might be better for him with his Aunt Sol. It's country there, and there are flowers.

Martín squinted at us both. Then he looked around the room as if in wonder. As you like, he said. But anyway, you know.

He went out slowly, a bit hunched over, through the little garden. She turned out the light, set me on the edge of the bed, and let herself fall into the rocking chair.

Your uncles are good men, she told me. Maybe I was the bad one. But I didn't want them doing favors for me; neither they nor anybody else. I brought you here so you wouldn't have to grow up with Adam. He's the one who's bad. God forgive him! God forgive us all! It was the work of the Devil!

I did not understand what she was saying. I had heard her speak of Adam before, and although I had never seen him, I knew he was my father. She went on.

He's your father, but if ever you see him, just remember one thing. He never recognized you. Besides, you don't look like him. You're a Román.

She was silent, and I felt that she was weeping somewhere inside, Then, raising her voice, she exclaimed irritably: Go to bed! I don't know why I'm telling you all this.

The following day she was herself once again, dignified, reserved and haughty. When I think of it now, it seems strange that a personality such as hers should have belonged to a village woman. But nothing about her made one think of the country. Furthermore, she lived in such a state of tension that one did not think of what she was, but only of what she felt. She astonished those around her. One day she said to the black woman: You're surprised that I know how to speak and dress properly. According to you I ought to be working as a maid!

The woman opened her eyes very wide, shrugged her shoulders, and began to mutter. My mother turned to a client who was there and whispered: I realize that sometimes I lose my temper. I was very young when I went through all that. There was nobody to help me. All my brothers were in Cuba.

She would get up and dress before dawn, looking ghostlike but beautiful in her light-colored, flowing dress, with those unmoving green eyes and her black hair all around her head like a halo. To me she seemed very tall—taller than Martín and taller than the black woman—perhaps because she was being whetted for death.

A serving maid! She reiterated on another occasion. No one in my family has ever been a servant. God forbid!

Uncle Martín returned the following night. My mother seemed to be full of life. That morning Sol had sent a neighbor, Romalia, with a message. Once again a ship was about to arrive.

I've put off the trip to Artemisa, she told my uncle. Today's Saturday, I'd like to spend Sunday here, and I may stay on for another week. But the boy's going to Sol's. She has more room where she lives. I don't want to go off and leave him shut into your little cubicle. It's like a grave in there.

They were both silent. Martín shut his eyes briefly and went out, his head bent forward in front of him. He looked back sadly at me, but he did not look at her. And he never again saw her alive!

In the morning Sabina the black woman called timidly at the door in the partition. Teresa! Teresa! Are you all right?

That night I had slept like a drugged person. Perhaps that actually was the case. As I was going to bed my mother had given me a herbal brew she had made. At times in my sleep it seemed that I heard her coughing, but I was not certain. My sleep was leaden. Sometimes I had dreams in which I thought I heard moans, but there was no way of knowing whether they were real or imaginary. In the morning my mother was up, her hair all arranged, wearing a clean starched houserobe with flower designs on it. She partially opened the little door and with great aplomb looked at the black woman.

Yes, thank you, Sabina. I'm all right. I had a nightmare, that's all. And she repeated: Thank you, Sabina!

Never yet had I heard her say she was ill. Nor had the doctor come to the house. Sometimes she would be away all one morning or afternoon. Finally she explained to me that now she was sewing at other people's houses as well as at home.

I've put off the trip to the country until next week. I have some clothes here I've got to finish first. She spoke without looking at me, and she moved carefully, as if she suspected that something inside her were about to break. Sitting down at the sewing machine, she began to hem a piece of cloth. Now and then she stopped and stared fixedly out through the doorway, across the countryside. Once she caught me staring at her, and said severely: Come on, drink your milk and go and play. Pretty soon you've got to go for you lesson.

I did not go to school. It was a long way from our house, whereas the woman who taught me lived across the street. She gave me classes after breakfast and again after lunch.

Be careful! my mother went on. We don't want them throwing stones at you again.

I went outside, but not to play. I threw myself onto the grass and began to sniff, the way a dog does. I had an exceptionally acute sense of smell, and certain of the neighbors, aware of this, had remarked upon it. Once I had claimed that a room smelled of a dead body, and three days later the old woman who lived in it had died. My mother knew about this.

When I returned at noon, Sabina was with her. They were sorting the sewing. Romalia was there as well. She was a sad, bony, toothless woman, with a little round belly that stuck out in front.

My mother handed her a package, saying: Take this

to my sister Sol. Tell her to come by here tomorrow.

She turned to explain to Sabina: My half-sister. I have only one brother, Antón, and he works for her in the garden. My half-brothers are all over the place. Martín, in the sack factory down there. Javier, riding around in his mule cart. And Sol, my half-sister, in Jesus del Monte. Románes everywhere!

She tried to smile, but by now her smile had become a mere grimace. She was horribly pale, and the make-up she had put on only augmented her pallor. But she forced herself to stand erect, as a healthy person does. Seeing me in the doorway, she said: And this one. This one too is named Román. He has no other family name. And he doesn't need any other!

And she added to herself in a deep, angry voice: A spineless jellyfish!

The others, Sabina and Romalia, listened to her quietly, saying nothing, pretending to be unconcerned. But their eyes went from her to me.

My mother repeated: A jellyfish! I can't see how . . . But God forgive me!

She looked downward, crossing her hands on her breast.

And God forgive him, too!

Slowly her voice had grown softer; her body hunched over slightly. Then she became aware of this, straightened herself, and said in a strained, almost imperious voice: Go along, Romalia. Take the bundle with you. Tell Sol to come tomorrow. Perhaps one of these days I'll be going along to the country.

Romalia backed up little by little, staring at us. She went out through Sabina's room. Sabina remained seated on the stool near the sewing machine, leaning first one way and then the other in order to see us better. Then my mother said to me: I've been thinking, I may stay quite a while in Artemisa. I've been offered better work there. In the meantime, where would you like to stay? With your Aunt Sol or your Uncle Martín? Sol has country; there are flowers.

It was getting dark. She went to the door and looked out at the countryside for a long time, without speaking. When she turned back, it seemed to me that her eyes were moist, but she would not let me see them. She walked to the end of the room and began to ladle out the food that had been bought at a stall in the street. And she began to hum.

The next morning Aunt Sol arrived. She was nothing like my mother: older, somewhat blond, and with the wide body and the gross voice of a country woman. She looked at my mother with the same expression of surprise and compassion that I had seen in the neighbors' faces.

I'll wait another week, said my mother. Today's the twentieth, On the twenty-seventh the *Alfonso XII* is docking, isn't it?

She saw me and changed the subject. If I stay there, she told them, send him to school. He'll have to study. He's never going to take to farm work.

Then, in a burst of confidence, she said: Today I feel well. Really, I do feel much better. Do you think the *Alfonso* . . .

For the first time I was aware, if only vaguely so, of the reason for her alternating depressions and exaltations. Another ship was on the way.

Sol said: Don't you worry about the boy. We'll take care of him.

And perhaps you won't have to, my mother said, her face flushing, forgetting that I was there. These last days I've been praying all the time.

Then an idea occurred to her, and her face clouded over. It's true that maybe I don't deserve it. They say I'm bad.

She regained control of herself and stood up with a grimace. Each day she changed her dress, and that day she was wearing the prettiest one. But she was busy making another, and she had bought a bottle of perfume. This scent made me more aware of another odor, still extremely faint, but unmistakable, that was beginning to be noticeable in the house. Then I realized that she was getting worse; for months she had been failing. At the moment she was lively, she looked younger, but she was like a light that flickered on and off. She had no muscles left—only skin, bones and tendons.

When Sol said good-by she seemed to be leaving against her will. Tell me the truth. How do you feel? You still don't want me to take him?

My mother seemed to be slightly delirious as she spoke. She was not looking at the others, and from time to time she seemed to be addressing someone who was not present.

I was saying to Sabina, there are terrible people in the world. They trample you underfoot, then tease you and humiliate you. And nobody calls them to account for it. There's no justice.

She shook her head, clutched her bosom, and cried in a low voice: God forgive me!

After a silence she said: No. Don't take him yet. We'll wait another week. Will you do me this favor once more? Go to the dock. . . .

Sol went away shaking her small head. I saw her clench her fists, and I heard her murmur to herself: Poor sister! It's not right that she should have all this trouble!

My mother did not follow her out. When the door was shut she stood against it, facing the little doorway opposite. On the other side of the partition Sabina's sewing machine no longer hummed. Without looking at me, my mother said: That package on the chair there. It's the dress for the lady at number eleven. You take it over to her.

I went out, but I stood on the other side of the door, listening. I heard Sabina go in.

You look much better today, said the black woman. But if I were you I wouldn't put off going to the hospital any longer. You'll be better taken care of there.

There was a silence, and my mother said: I want to stretch the time as far as I can. I want to be with the boy. But I don't want him to see me haggard and ugly. I want him to remember me as I am . . . as I was. When I come back I'll look young again. I'll be like a young girl. She paused. But it's still not certain that I'll go. Something may still happen, you know.

When I got back to the house I found her leaning over, clutching the edge of the table. Then she went behind the curtain, and for a long time I heard her heavy breathing. But the following day she got up looking rested, and put on the new dress she had finished making. Aunt Sol came in early, very lively. They talked together in low voices. Soon Sol hurried out, and my mother seemed to be waiting for her to return. The fire had come back to her eyes, and she moved with a lightness she had not shown for many months. She showered, put her new dress back on, and made up her face. Then she sat down again at the sewing machine and began to sing under her breath. All afternoon she gave no sign of having noticed my return to the room. Sabina opened the door a crack and looked in at her with concern.

Come in, Sabina, come in. You know, I feel fine. And I think we're going to have a visitor.

She did not make any explanation. I went out and in, and for several hours she did not seem to be aware of my presence.

You know, Sabina, no one can judge anyone. Each one of us has his own soul, and sometimes it's not what others think it is. If we have a visitor, we'll invite you to the party. Because we're going to have a little party. You're a good friend, Sabina.

Then I saw that she was weeping, and that it was because she was happy. The black woman moved her eyes from one side to the other as if she expected to see a ghost.

I tell you my sister Sol heard that a certain personage was coming on the *Alfonso XII*. And if it's true . . .

Then she looked in the direction of the door, remained poised, inmovable for an instant, and in a lower tone of voice added doubtfully: I don't mean to be presumptuous. I'm like the Chinese. Let us wait and hope. Do you know this child's name? Román is his second name, my father's name. But he must have another. Everybody has two family names. Why did he have to be something less than other people? His other name is Pérez. My sister says a certain important person is arriving on the *Alfonso*. And if he's coming, I know why. You'll see, Sabina! You'll see yet how everything will all be settled!

I was stretched out on the floor behind the curtain, sniffing. She did not seem to realize this.

You'll see, Sabina, you'll see, said my mother.

Slowly the black woman shut the door behind her, as one does with sick people. But she was frightened. I ran around the outside of the house and went in through the street entrance to stand in front of Sabina's open door. She was piling up pieces of clothing and saying to herself: an important person, a certain important personage . . . The poor thing's out of her mind!

She saw me and stopped talking. I ran out. Something was bothering me. Perhaps it was the new smell. When I got back to the room my mother had turned on all the lights. She sent me to take a shower, and dressed me in my best suit.

Put this on, just for today, she told me. It's Sunday. And you're growing. What's the use of saving your clothes? Besides, we may have a visitor. You'll see! You'll see!

She was exhilarated. She had been working up to

this little by little. Soon she was quite beside herself with excitement. Then, suddenly, she was still. Nothing happened. No one came. It was so quiet I could hear a fly go past me in the air. But some message had reached her innermost being, and when, hours later, Aunt Sol came back with the news (or rather the lack of news), it was as if she had already prepared herself to hear it.

My aunt said: It's no good, Teresa. Things are the way they are. What's the use of pretending? There must have been a mistake. He's not coming here. He's gone to Buenos Aires!

My mother stood looking at her. She had no expression. In the past few hours her face had gone dead, like a fire that has burned itself out. It was only a ghost of itself, no longer a face, but a mask. Yet her voice was still firm when she said: It's all right. You can take the boy with you. I think I'll go where I have to go.

At the time (and for long afterward) it was this memory of my mother that stayed in my mind. But then, slowly, it began to dissolve, and in its place I was left with the other picture, the one she had meant to leave with me the day when she had said: I don't want him to remember me haggard and ugly. I want him to remember me as I am . . . as I was.

Translated by Paul Bowles

The Drum Dance

ARTURO USLAR PIETRI

They threw him down on the brick floor of the cell and shut the door. Everything was dark. The bricks were cool and it felt good to be lying on them. To be calm and quiet. To let himself slide down into sleep without being suddenly surprised.

The heavy footsteps of the provost marshal were going away. They were Ño Gaspar's steps, who was bowlegged and square-shouldered as a sack of cocoa beans, with his white sandals, his shirt unbuttoned at the throat, his chest crossed by the shoulder belt of yellow silk for the rooster's-tale saber.

The sound of the drums came into the cell, a harsh, infinite, unchanging rhythm—the tenor drum clear and the bass husky—and you could imagine in the darkness the sound of the Negroes' feet, beating up the dust in the square.

A few smoking lamps that streaked rays of light across the sweaty faces of the Negroes in the darkness hung from the leafy *saman* trees.

That's where Ño Gaspar had found him. He had kept coming closer and closer, slowly, timidly, sticking to the side of a wall, hiding behind a tree, away from the lights. But his feet shuffled to the rhythm and he chewed the vibrant tune between his teeth. He started to dance by himself. And then, without knowing how, he was dancing with the colored girl, her eyes, laughter, fragrance, on fire in the dark.

"Wow, Soledad, we're dancing together."

"Wow, Hilario, you're back."

But just then or a little later or much later Ño Gaspar got there. He didn't have to see him to know it was he. He knew his voice, knew his steps, could feel him coming. He knew that he had come.

"So, Hilario. I knew you were going to come back to your own accord. That you were going to be caught easy. When the search parties went to look for you, I sent them for the hell of it. I know my men. And there it is. You came all by yourself."

They tied his hands behind his back quickly with a piece of rope. The drum dance did not stop but many of those present got wind of what was happening and began to come over to them.

"It's Hilario."

"Yeah. The peon from El Manteco."

"He deserted from the camp in Caucagua."

"They're going to skin him for sure."

He let them lead him away without putting up a fight. From the darkness the eyes of the Negroes converged on him. As he passed under the lamps you could see how emaciated he was; his skin had become discolored and leathery, his lips cracked, his eyes sunken, dull.

The provost marshal himself was led to observe: "You're a sack of bones, Hilario. There's not enough meat on you for a meatball. Ah, the black boy was so solid."

But he said nothing. He hardly seemed to see. He only heard in snatches, confusedly. The voices of some of the women:

"Poor thing. Letting himself get caught that way!"

"He's all bones. He won't be able to stand the whip."

He wasn't sure if he was hearing all that or just imagining it, as he went from the square that was full of the drumbeat, into the dark entry hall of Headquarters, and, too weak to resist the push they gave him, fell onto the bricks of the cell.

Strangled by the rope, his wrists were pounding like the drum, almost with the same beat. He was thirsty. He pressed his dry lips against a damp brick.

He had known that all this was going to happen. He had thought about it an infinite number of times. He had constantly imagined it while he hid, starving, in the forest and came down at night to drink at the river or steal from the farms. He had known it since the day he had run away from camp.

He would have to come back to town and Ño Gaspar would come to get him and tie his hands behind his back, as he had them now, as he had had them when Ño Gaspar tied them on recruiting day.

"So that you'll know what's good for you and become a man."

But he felt like sleeping. To make up for all those days and nights in the bush. He felt peaceful there on the bricks.

He pressed his face to the floor and couldn't feel his own weight.

"I feel sort of light."

He could no longer hear the drum. It must be very late at night. But he could sort of feel the weight of the houses resting on the ground. They weren't many. The six on their lots around the square. There were more corrals than farmhouses. But he felt how they weighed down the ground. And he could feel the sleepy, dark water of the River Tuy sliding near or far off. And the wind passing over the roofs, and the trees and the water, and he stroked the dirt on the ground. The wind sped faster than the Tuy toward the sea.

He also seemed to be sliding along and floating.

But suddenly he felt as if he had fallen and he opened his eyes in the darkness.

"And now all that's left is Corporal Cirguelo's whip," he said between his teeth, and he felt a chill.

While he had been in camp he had seen a deserter flogged.

"Taiiiiin . . . shun!" the officer roared. The company came to attention.

It was time for the punishment. Long before daybreak. Corporal Cirguelo and an assistant prepared the whips. They had placed the deserter in front of the company. They had pulled down his pants. It was as cold then as now. They had tied his hands and, put into a crouching position, they had stuck guns down through his arms and his hams, as a brace.

The corporal shoved him with his foot until he came to rest on his side, and before he swung his whip the band started right off playing the "turkey trot" so that they wouldn't hear the cries of the man they were "skinning."

One lash, two lashes, three lashes. The soliders in the company groaned at each stroke, but the screams of the one being punished could not be heard because the band was playing the trot without stopping and as loud as possible. The black boy, Hilario, was humming it.

"Tara rara rarah, the turkey."

"Tara rara rarah, the gobbler."

Before turning him on his other side to continue, they threw a bucket of salt water on the flayed cheek.

Corporal Cirguelo swung his whip. Now you could hardly hear the groans of the punished soldier.

"Tara rara rarah, the turkey."

Now he couldn't get the catchy tune of the "turkey trot" out of his head. Corporal Cirguelo wore long sideburns and had a gold-capped tooth. He must still be there at the barracks in Caucagua.

Next morning the search party would come to take him. They would put him on a boat on the river. Without untying his hands. They would land him ashore again. When they passed by the houses the people would come out to see him.

"It's a deserter they're taking in."

They would enter Caucagua. Late in the afternoon. Through the back street. They would go by the Islander's general store. And there, around the corner, was the camp. And there, at the door or outside, Corporal Cirguelo would no doubt be waiting.

There was a lot of walking to do. Before they got there. They had to take him out of here. Go down the river to the coast. Spend the morning. Time to sleep in the boat. To see, from the bottom where he would be lying, the treetops turning over in the sky. Tie up again. People would come to the riverbank. It would be very late afternoon. And the questions would begin again.

"How did they catch him?"

"Where was he hiding?"

"Did the search party find him?"

And that word that they were going to repeat, were repeating just as he had been repeating it so many times: The skinning. They're going to skin him. He can't get out of the skinning. One hundred lashes. Ah, good skinning. Two hundred lashes on each cheek. A skinning for a complete man, Corporal Cirguelo's gold-capped tooth, Tara, rara, rarah, the turkey.

He couldn't get that out of his head from the time he ran away from camp. From the time he had seen that other deserter flogged. From the time he had seen them pick him up sagging and wobbly as a rag-doll effigy of Judas.

And now, lying on the floor of the cell, he felt so helpless, without any strength. He wouldn't be able to resist the blows. He wouldn't even be able to resist half of them. One, sang the corporal. Two. Three. The first ones burned like a live coal. Then the bleeding would begin. And then it was as if they were tearing off strips of flesh little by little. Then it began to hurt inside. Thirty. Thirty-one. Along his guts. His spleen. His lungs. Sixty-six. Sixty-seven. And that's where the groaning started. Where they stayed on. Where they went away. Where they began to feel numb.

The brick on which his cheek rested was hot now. He dragged himself farther along the ground until he lay on a cool piece of floor. Everything was still dark and quiet. He started to listen. Not even the wind was going by now. But somewhere in the distance a dog had barked.

Far beyond the guardhouse, the building, the square. The barking came from somewhere outside the village. Somewhere near the river. The forest. The night. The solitude.

"Oh damn."

The barking was coming from the forest. Who could ever catch him now if he were there again. He used to hear the dogs barking far away like that whenever he peered out of the bushes on a slope and saw a farm in a clearing on a little hill. Hunger brought him out of the forest at night. He had learned to walk noiselessly and stop to listen like the deer. To cock his ear into the wind. Sometimes he heard something, would hide in a cluster of corn, and see the men in the search party going by with machetes, guns, and blankets slung diagonally across chest and shoulder.

When a dog scented him and barked, he had to stop. He would lose sight of the farm again and go back into the forest. He ate guavas and roots. Sometimes he got dizzy from hunger. Sometimes he managed to approach a farm without a dog's barking, grabbed everything there was to eat on the stove, and scampered away.

He had never actually gone far from the village. If he appeared somewhere else, where he was a stranger, they could discover him. He kept on foraging through the woods near the waterfalls. He would look at the river from a distance. The Tuy rolled along quietly. Sometimes a canoe passed and he recognized some of the peons from where he was.

"Oh damn."

Sometimes, after drinking on his stomach at the river's edge, he released a dry leaf to see it go down the current and remained watching it in a sort of daze until the cry of a *guacharaca* in the forest or the babble of a flock of parrots crossing the sky shook him out of it.

He could see the village from certain points. The *saman* trees in the square, the church, Headquarters, the long street. People at the door of the general store. If he were there where his eyes were, where that man was, leaning against the door. Wouldn't that cause a stir!

"Wow. Here's Hilario."

"The deserter."

"Grab him!"

But he was far off among those trees where the wind made noise. At night all you could see were the lights flickering in the darkness. The village seemed farther away and smaller.

He hadn't kept track of how long he had been in the forest. He was becoming thinner. His skin was getting lighter. He was changing from black to a greenish color, like the alligator's tail. He was less nimble as he walked. He got tired faster when he climbed. He lost his breath and had to rest a while. Doubled over, breathing hard, he would sit there looking at his feet and hands. They were bonier and more skinny. The palms of his hands were purplish and his nails yellow. There were nights when he didn't have the strength to go near the farms. He would stay under a tree, chattering with the cold. All that was left of his trousers were rags. But it was very cold. If he heard a sound, he was too weak to get up. It could be an animal. It could be a search party. If it was the search party they would capture him. He didn't have the will to resist or even listen. He would remain there for a while, worried, waiting, but the sound was not repeated and he sighed, at ease.

Instead of going farther away, the more ill and weaker he felt, he kept coming closer to town. Every once in a while he would think: "If they catch me now, I won't be able to resist the whip. I won't survive the whip."

But something inside him made him feel that distant, inevitable thing that kept coming dangerously closer.

On two or three occasions, he had gone so far as to follow the riverbank up to the first houses in town. He had even dared sneak into a yard to steal a piece of beef hanging out to dry in the sun.

Some day they would catch him. If it pleased God.

"Oh damn!"

He neither sleeps nor stays awake. He feels the floor turning warm under his body. His whole body throbbing without stopping, on the bricks. A cold tickling sensation in his hands, strangled by the rope behind his back. His bones aching with the sweet pain of a fever. He closes his eyes hard in order to sleep. Vague sparks pass through them. Red spots, rushing through. His pulse keeps on knocking and shaking him without relief.

Prrrm. Prrrrrm. Prrrrrmpumpum. Prrrrmpumpum. Pum. Pumpum. Like the drum. Sometimes clear like the tenor, sometimes thick and husky like the bass. Like the drum.

Even from the river he could already hear it like that. From the time he started to sneak nearer, in the shadow of the first houses. He hadn't heard the drum for a long time. All he had heard was the sound of the branches, dogs barking, the songs of birds. But not the hot beat of the drum. As he crouched low, hiding, he beat on the ground with his foot and his hand. Dum dum, dum dum, dum dum. It was like a hot wave of water going around his body.

He was near the lights in the square now and he heard the heavy rhythm of the steps. The shadow of the Negroes moved as one solid mass. The lights seemed to go up and down under the branches of the *saman* trees.

Under the protection of a wall, he has drawn near the square. Something like a feverish tremor carries him along with the drum. Everything sounds inside and outside his head like the drumskin sounded by the black fists. He is all worked up. Everything comes and goes with the drum. Women. Lights. The names of things. His own name which calls and calls him without stopping.

Hilario, it says. Hilario, it repeats. Hilario, the drum. Hilario the shadows. Hilario, Hilarito, Hilarion. Larito, larion. Larito, ito, ito, ito. The rhythm resounds. Everything makes him shake. Sounds and resounds. Booms in the darkness. Booms.

Everything staggers. Tum tum. Tum tum. Hilario staggers. So much darkness. So much night. So much drumming. The drum keeps time in the darkness. Hilario trembles. Hilario shuffles. So many women are shaking in the darkness. Hilario, Hilarito, Hilarion.

Leaping shadows moved past him. They and the drum and the square and the lights. He was in their midst. The rhythm beat in his bones and his eyes. Panting mouths and clouded eyes went by.

And that woman in front of him, brought, carried by the drumbeat. Shaking together with him. Bound to him. Beat together with him.

"Yeah! Yeah! Yeah!"

"Wow, Soledad, we're dancing together!"

"Wow, Hilario, you're back!"

And that's where he felt him coming. Felt his footstep without seeing him. He could distinguish his footsteps between the drumbeats. Ño Gaspar's steps. The heavy, solid, sure step. He recognized his step without turning his head.

He could count them. One. A moment went by. Two. He was coming closer. All you could hear was the footstep of Ño Gaspar, the provost marshal. You couldn't hear the drum of the dance. All you could hear was that footstep.

The door squeaked. His eyes were open. From the brick floor he noticed the cell filled with the ashes of dawn and, in the doorway, tall and broad. Ño Gaspar, and behind Ño Gaspar the faces, the blankets, the guns and the machetes of the men in the search party.

Translated by Hardie St. Martin

The Third Bank of the River

JOÃO GUIMARÃES ROSA

My father was a dutiful, orderly, straightforward man. And according to several reliable people of whom I inquired, he had had these qualities since adolescence or even childhood. By my own recollection, he was neither jollier nor more melancholy than the other men we knew. Maybe a little quieter. It was Mother, not Father, who ruled the house. She scolded us daily—my sister, my brother, and me. But it happened one day that Father ordered a boat.

He was very serious about it. It was to be made specially for him, of mimosa wood. It was to be sturdy enough to last twenty or thirty years and just large enough for one person. Mother carried on plenty about it. Was her husband going to become a fisherman all of a sudden? Or a hunter? Father said nothing. Our house was less than a mile from the river, which around there was deep, quiet, and so wide you couldn't see across it.

I can never forget the day the rowboat was delivered. Father showed no joy or other emotion. He just put on his hat as he always did and said good-by to us. He took along no food or bundle of any sort. We expected Mother to rant and rave, but she didn't. She looked very pale and bit her lip, but all she said was: "If you go away, stay away. Don't ever come back!"

Father made no reply. He looked gently at me and motioned me to walk along with him. I feared Mother's wrath, yet I eagerly obeyed. We headed toward the river together. I felt bold and exhilarated, so much so that I said: "Father, will you take me with you in your boat?"

He just looked at me, gave me his blessing, and by a gesture, told me to go back. I made as if to do so but, when his back was turned, I ducked behind some bushes to watch him. Father got into the boat and rowed away. Its shadow slid across the water like a crocodile, long and quiet.

Father did not come back. Nor did he go anywhere, really. He just rowed and floated across and around, out there in the river. Everyone was appalled. What had never happened, what could not possibly happen, was happening. Our relatives, neighbors, and friends came over to discuss the phenomenon.

Mother was ashamed. She said little and conducted herself with great composure. As a consequence, almost everyone thought (though no one said it) that Father had gone insane. A few, however, suggested that Father might be fulfilling a promise he had made to God or to a saint, or that he might have some horrible disease, maybe leprosy, and that he left for the sake of the family, at the same time wishing to remain fairly near them.

Travelers along the river and people living near the bank on one side or the other reported that Father never put foot on land, by day or night. He just moved about on the river, solitary, aimless, like a derelict. Mother and our relatives agreed that the food which he had doubtless hidden in the boat would soon give out and that then he would either leave the river and travel off somewhere (which would be at least a little more respectable) or he would repent and come home.

How far from the truth they were! Father had a secret source of provisions: me. Every day I stole food and brought it to him. The first night after he left, we all lit fires on the shore and prayed and called to him. I was deeply distressed and felt a need to do something more. The following day I went down to the river with a loaf of corn bread, a bunch of bananas, and some bricks of raw brown sugar. I waited impatiently a long, long hour. Then I saw the boat, far off, alone, gliding almost imperceptibly on the smoothness of the river. Father was sitting in the bottom of the boat. He saw me but he did not row toward me or make any gesture. I showed him the food and then I placed it in a hollow rock on the river bank; it was safe there from animals, rain, and dew. I did this day after day, on and on and on. Later I learned, to my surprise, that Mother knew what I was doing and left food around where I could easily steal it. She had a lot of feelings she didn't show.

Mother sent for her brother to come and help on the farm and in business matters. She had the schoolteacher come and tutor us children at home because of the time we had lost. One day, at her request, the priest put on his vestments, went down to the shore, and tried to exorcise the devils that had got into my father. He shouted that Father had a duty to cease his unholy obstinacy. Another day she arranged to have two soldiers come and try to frighten him. All to no avail. My father went by in the distance, sometimes so far away he could barely be seen. He never replied to anyone and no one ever got close to him. When some newspapermen came in a launch to take his picture, Father headed his boat to the other side of the river and into the marshes, which he knew like the palm of his hand but in which other people quickly got lost. There in his private maze, which extended for miles, with heavy foliage overhead and rushes on all sides, he was safe.

We had to get accustomed to the idea of Father's being out on the river. We had to but we couldn't, we never could. I think I was the only one who understood to some degree what our father wanted and what he did not want. The thing I could not understand at all was how he stood the hardship. Day and night, in sun and rain, in heat and in the terrible midyear cold spells, with his old hat on his head and very little other clothing, week after week, month after month, year after year, unheedful of the waste and emptiness in which his life was slipping by. He never set foot on earth or grass, on isle or mainland shore. No doubt he sometimes tied up the boat at a secret place, perhaps at the tip of some island, to get a little sleep. He never lit a fire or even struck a match and he had no flashlight. He took only a small part of the food that I left in the hollow rock—not enough, it seemed to me, for survival. What could his state of health have been? How about the continual drain on his energy, pulling and pushing the oars to control the boat? And how did he survive the annual floods, when the river rose and swept along with it all sorts of dangerous objects—branches of trees, dead bodies of animals—that might suddenly crash against his little boat?

He never talked to a living soul. And we never talked about him. We just thought. No, we could never put our father out of mind. If for a short time we seemed to, it was just a lull from which we would be sharply awakened by the realization of his frightening situation.

My sister got married, but Mother didn't want a wedding party. It would have been a sad affair, for we thought of him every time we ate some especially tasty food. Just as we thought of him in our cozy beds on a cold, stormy night—out there, alone and unprotected, trying to bail out the boat with only his hands and a gourd. Now and then someone would say that I was getting to look more and more like my father. But I knew that by then his hair and beard must have been shaggy and his nails long. I pictured him thin and sickly, black with hair and sunburn, and almost naked despite the articles of clothing I occasionally left for him.

He didn't seem to care about us at all. But I felt affection and respect for him, and, whenever they praised me because I had done something good, I said: "My father taught me to act that way."

It wasn't exactly accurate but it was a truthful sort of lie. As I said, Father didn't seem to care about us. But then why did he stay around there? Why didn't he go up the river or down the river, beyond the possibility of seeing us or being seen by us? He alone knew the answer.

My sister had a baby boy. She insisted on showing Father his grandson. One beautiful day we all went down to the riverbank, my sister in her white wedding dress, and she lifted the baby high. Her husband held a parasol above them. We shouted to Father and waited. He did not appear. My sister cried; we all cried in each other's arms.

My sister and her husband moved far away. My brother went to live in a city. Times changed, with their usual imperceptible rapidity. Mother finally moved too; she was old and went to live with her daughter. I remained behind, a leftover. I could never think of marrying. I just stayed there with the impedimenta of my life. Father, wandering alone and forlorn on the river, needed me. I knew he needed me, although he never even told me why he was doing it. When I put the question to people bluntly and insistently, all they told me was that they heard that Father had explained it to the man who made the boat. But now this man was dead and nobody knew or remembered anything. There was just some foolish talk, when the rains were especially severe and persistent, that my father was wise like Noah and had the boat built in anticipation of a new flood; I dimly remember people saying this. In any case, I would not condemn my father for what he was doing. My hair was beginning to turn gray.

I have only sad things to say. What bad had I done, what was my great guilt? My father always away and his absence always with me. And the river, always the river, perpetually renewing itself. The river, always. I was beginning to suffer from old age, in which life is just a sort of lingering. I had attacks of illness and of anxiety. I had a nagging rheumatism. And he? Why, why was he doing it? He must have been suffering terribly. He was so old. One day, in his failing strength, he might let the boat capsize; or he might let the current carry it downstream, on and on, until it plunged over the waterfall to the boiling turmoil below. It pressed upon my heart. He was out there and I was forever robbed of my peace. I am guilty of I know not what, and my pain is an open wound inside me. Perhaps I would know—if things were different. I began to guess what was wrong.

Out with it! Had I gone crazy? No, in our house that word was never spoken, never through all the years. No one called anybody crazy, for nobody is crazy. Or maybe everybody. All I did was go there and wave a handkerchief so he would be more likely to see me. I was in complete command of myself. I waited. Finally he appeared in the distance, there, then over there, a vague shape sitting in the back of the boat. I called to him several times. And I said what I was so eager to say, to state formally and under oath. I said it as loud as I could:

"Father, you have been out there long enough. You are old. . . . Come back, you don't have to do it anymore. . . . Come back and I'll go instead. Right now, if you want. Any time. I'll get into the boat. I'll take your place."

And when I had said this my heart beat more firmly.

He heard me. He stood up. He maneuvered with his oars and headed the boat toward me. He had accepted my offer. And suddenly I trembled, down deep. For he had raised his arm and waved—the first time in so many, so many years. And I couldn't ... In terror, my hair on end, I ran, I fled madly. For he seemed to come from another world. And I'm begging forgiveness, begging, begging.

I experienced the dreadful sense of cold that comes from deadly fear, and I became ill. Nobody ever saw or heard about him again. Am I a man, after such a failure? I am what never should have been. I am what must be silent. I know it is too late. I must stay in the deserts and unmarked plains of my life, and I fear I shall shorten it. But when death comes I want them to take me and put me in a little boat in this perpetual water between the long shores; and I, down the river, lost in the river, inside the river ... the river ...

Translated by William L. Grossman

Jacob and the Other

JUAN CARLOS ONETTI

I. THE DOCTOR'S STORY

Half the town must have been present last night at the Apollo Cinema, seeing the thing and participating in the tumultuous finale. I was having a boring time at the club's poker table and intervened only when the porter gave me an urgent message from the hospital. The club has only one telephone line; but by the time I left the booth everybody knew more about the news than I. I returned to the table to cash my chips and to pay my losses.

Burmestein hadn't moved. He sucked at his cigar a little more and told me in his smooth and unctuous voice: "Forgive me, but if I were you, I'd stay and exploit your lucky streak. After all, you can just as well sign the death certificate here!"

"Not yet, it seems," I replied and tried to laugh. I looked at my hands as they handled the chips and the money: they were calm, rather tired. I had slept barely a couple of hours the previous night, but that had already become almost a habit; I had drunk two cognacs tonight and mineral water with my dinner.

The people at the hospital knew my car and remembered all its diseases. And so an ambulance was waiting for me at the club entrance. I sat down next to the

Galician[1] driver and heard only his greeting: he remained silent—out of respect or emotion—and waited for me to begin the conversation. I started smoking and did not speak until we turned the Tabarez curve and the ambulance entered the spring night of the cement highway, white and windy, cool and mild, with disorderly clouds grazing the mill and the high trees.

"Herminio," I asked him, "what is the diagnosis?"

I saw the joy the Galician was trying to conceal and imagined the inward sigh with which he celebrated this return to the habitual, to the old sacred rites. He started talking, in his most humble and astute tones. I realized that the case was serious or lost.

"I barely saw him, Doctor. I lifted him from the theater into the ambulance and took him to the hospital at ninety or a hundred because young Fernández was telling me to hurry and also because it was my duty. I helped to take him out, and right away they ordered me to fetch you at the club."

"Fernández, hm. But who is on duty?"

"Doctor Rius, Doctor."

"Why doesn't Rius operate?" I asked him, raising my voice.

"Well," Herminio replied and took his time avoiding a puddle full of bright water, "he must have got ready to operate at once, I'd say. But if he has you at his side . . ."

"You loaded and unloaded him. That's enough. What's the diagnosis?"

"What a doctor!" the Galician exclaimed with an affectionate smile. We were beginning to see the lights of the hospital, the whiteness of its walls under the moon. "He didn't move or moan, he started to swell like a balloon, ribs in the lung, a shinbone laid bare, almost certain concussion. But he hit a couple of chairs with his back when he fell and, if you forgive

[1] Galician: native of Galicia, the northwest corner of Spain, from which many people emigrated to Latin America. Tr.

my opinion, it's the backbone that'll decide. Whether it's broken or not."

"Will he die or won't he? You've never been wrong, Herminio." (He had been wrong many times, but always with some good excuse.)

"This time I won't talk," he said, shaking his head as he braked.

I changed clothes and was starting to wash my hands when Rius came in.

"If you want to operate," he said, "I'll have everything ready in two minutes. I've done little or nothing so far because there's nothing to be done. Morphine, of course, to keep him—and us—quiet. And if you want to know where to start, I'd advise you to toss a coin."

"Is there that much?"

"Multiple trauma, deep coma, pallor, filiform, pulse, great polypnoea, cyanosis. The right hemithorax doesn't breathe. Collapsed. Crepitation and angulation of the sixth rib on the right. Dullness in the right pulmonary base with hypersonority in the pulmonary apex. The coma is getting deeper all the time, and the syndrome of acute anemia is becoming accentuated. Is that enough? I would leave him in peace."

It was then that I resorted to my worn-out phrase of mediocre heroics, to the legend that surrounds me as the lettering of a coin or medal encircles a portrait, and which may possibly stick to my name some years after my death. But that night I was no longer twenty-five or thirty; I was old and tired, and the phrase so often repeated was, to Rius, no more than a familiar joke. I said it with a nostalgia for my lost faith, as I was putting on my gloves. I repeated it and heard myself saying it, like a child who pronounces an absurd magical formula that gives him permission to enter a game or stay in it: "My patients die on the table."

Rius laughed as usual, gave my arm a friendly squeeze, and left. But almost immediately, as I was trying to locate a damanged pipe that leaked into the washbasins, he looked in again to tell me: "There's a piece missing in the picture I gave you, my friend. I didn't tell you about the woman. I don't know who she is, she kicked or tried to kick 'the corpse-to-be' in the movie theater and then pushed her way to the ambulance to spit at him as the Galician and Fernández were putting him in. I was on duty there and had her thrown out; but she swore she'd come back tomorrow because she had a right to see the dead man—maybe to spit on him at leisure."

I worked with Rius till five in the morning and then sent out for a container of coffee to help us wait. At seven, Fernández came into the office with the suspicious face that God makes him put on to confront important events. On such occasions, his narrow and childish face turns his eyes into slits, he leans forward a little and says through his watchful mouth: "Somebody's robbing me and life is nothing but a conspiracy to cheat me."

He moved toward the table and remained there standing, white and twisted, without a word.

Rius stopped tinkering with the grafts, did not look at him, and grabbed the last sandwich from the plate. Then he wiped his lips with a napkin and asked of the iron inkpot, with its eagle and its two dried-up inkholes: "Already?"

Fernández breathed audibly and put a hand on the table. We turned our heads and saw his suspicion and his confusion, his thinness and his weariness. Idiotized by lack of food and sleep, the boy drew himself up to remain true to his mania for changing the order of things, of the world in which we can understand one another.

The woman is in the corridor, sitting on a bench, with a thermos and a *mate* gourd. They forgot all about her and let her in. She says she doesn't mind waiting, she must see him. That man."

"Yes, my boy," Rius said slowly, and I recognized in his voice the malignity that comes of nights of fatigue, the needling that he administers so skillfully. "Did she bring flowers, at least? Winter is over and every ditch of Santa Maria must be full of *yuyos*. I'd like to push her face in, and I'll ask the chief's permission in a moment for a trip around the corridors. But meanwhile that mare of a woman can visit the body, throw it a flower, spit on it, and throw it another flower."

I was the chief, and so I asked: "What happened?"

Fernández gave a fleeting caress to his lean face, discovered without too much exertion that it contained all the bones promised him by his reading of Testut, and then looked at me as if I were responsible for all the tricks and deceits that jumped out of nowhere to surprise him with mysterious regularity. He discarded Rius without hatred and without violence, kept his suspicious eyes glued to my face and recited: "Improved pulse, respiration, and cyanosis. Sporadically recovers consciousness."

This was much better than I had expected to hear at seven in the morning. But I couldn't be quite sure yet, and so I just thanked him with a nod and took my turn looking at the bronzed eagle of the inkstand.

"Dimas arrived a while ago," Fernández said. "I gave him all the details. May I go?"

"Yes, of course." Rius had thrown himself against the back of his armchair and looked at me with the beginning of a smile. Perhaps he had never seen me so old, perhaps he had never loved me as much as he did that spring morning—or maybe he was trying to find out who I was and why he loved me.

"No, my friend," he said when we were alone again. "With me you can play any farce you like—but not the farce of modesty, of indifference, the kind of garbage that's put into sober words like: 'I have once again only done my duty.' Well, Chief, you did it. If that animal hasn't croaked yet, it won't. They advised you at the club to do nothing but sign his death certificate—that's what I would have done, with a lot of morphine, of course, if you hadn't happened to be in Santa Maria—and now I advise you to give that character a certificate of immortality. With a quiet conscience and with a signature endorsed by Doctor Rius. Do it, Chief. And then steal yourself a sleeping-pill cocktail from the lab and go to sleep for twenty-four hours. I'll take care of the judge and the police. I also promise you to take care of the spitting sessions of the lady who's stoking up on *mate* in the corridor."

He got up and shook my hand, only once but pausing to transmit the weight and the warmth of his own.

"Okay," I told him. "You'll decide if it's necessary to wake me."

While removing my surgical gown, with a slowness and dignity not entirely produced by weariness, I admitted to myself that the success of the operation, of all operations for that matter, mattered to me as much as the fulfillment of an old and unrealizable dream of mine: to repair my old car with my own hands—and forever. But I couldn't tell this to Rius because he would understand without effort and with enthusiasm; nor could I tell it to Fernández because, fortunately, he could never believe me.

So I kept my mouth shut and, on the way back in the ambulance, heard out with equanimity the clumsily put praises of the Galician Herminio. With my silence, I accepted before history that the resurrection that had just occurred at the Santa Maria Hospital could not have been achieved by the doctors of the capital itself.

I decided that my car could spend another night outside the club and made the ambulance take me home. The morning, furiously white, smelled of honeysuckle, and there was already a breath of the river in the air.

"They threw stones and said they'd burn the theater down," the Galician said when we reached the plaza. "But the police came and they only threw stones, as I've already told you."

Before taking my pills I realized that I could never know the whole truth of that story. With patience and luck on my side I might find out half of it, the half that concerned the people of the town. But I had to resign myself to the fact that the other half would remain forever out of my reach. It was brought here by the two strangers who would, in their different ways, carry it out again, forever unknown.

At that very moment, with the glass of water in my hand, I recalled that I had first got involved in this story a week earlier, on a warm and cloudy Sunday, while I was watching people coming and going on the plaza from a window of the hotel bar.

The lively, charming man and the moribund giant made their way diagonally across the plaza and the first yellowish sunlight of spring. The smaller of the two was carrying a wreath, the little wreath of a distant relative for a modest wake. They advanced indifferent to the curiosity aroused by the slow beast nearly six and a half feet tall: unhurried but resolved, the lively one marched along with an inherent dignity, as if he were flanked by soldiers in gala uniform and some high personage and a stand, decorated with flags and filled with solemn men and old women, were expecting him. The word spread that they had laid the wreath at the foot of the Brausen monument, to the accompaniment of children's jeers and a few stones.

From then on the tracks became somewhat tangled. The smaller man, the ambassador, went into the Berne to rent a room, to take an *apéritif*, and to discuss prices without passion, lifting his hat to anyone in sight and offering deep bows and cheap invitations. He was about forty to forty-five, of medium height, broad-chested; he had been born to convince, to create the mild and humid climate in which friendship flourishes and hopes are born. He had also been born for happiness, or at least for obstinately believing in happiness, against all odds, against life itself and its errors. He had been born, above all and most important of all, to impose quotas of happiness on all possible kinds of people. And all this with a natural and invincible shrewdness, never neglecting his personal purposes or worrying unduly over the uncontrollable future of others.

At noon he called at the editorial offices of *El Liberal*. He returned in the afternoon to see the people from the sports section and get some free publicity. He unwrapped a scrapbook of yellowing photographs and newspaper cuttings, with big headlines in foreign languages, and exhibited diplomas and documents reinforced at the edges with Scotch tape. He made his smile, his unwearying and uncompromising love, float above the ancient memories, the passing years, melancholy, and failure.

"Right now he's better than ever. Maybe he weighs a kilo or two more. This is, of course, why we're on this grand tour of South America. Next year, at the Palais de Glace, he'll regain his title. Nobody can beat him, in Europe or in America. And how could we possibly skip Santa Maria on a tour that is a prologue to a world championship? Ah, Santa Maria! What a coast, what a beach, what air, what culture!"

His voice had an Italian tone, but not exactly. There was always in his vowels and his s's a sound that could not be localized, a friendly contact with the complicated surface of the globe. He traversed the newspaper building from top to bottom, played with the linotypes, hugged the typesetters, improvised astonishment while standing under the rotary press. The next day he obtained his first headline, cool but unpaid: FORMER WORLD WRESTLING CHAMPION IN SANTA MARIA. He called at the editorial office every night of the week, and the space devoted to Jacob van Oppen grew bigger every day, until the Saturday of the challenge and the fight.

At noon that Sunday when I saw them parading across the plaza, the moribund giant spent half an hour in church, kneeling before the new altar of the Immaculate Conception. They saw he went to confession, and some people swear they saw him beating his chest—presumably before he emerged and hesitatingly pushed his enormous baby face, wet with tears, into the gilded light outside the church.

II. THE NARRATOR'S STORY

The visiting cards read: "Comendatore Orsini," and the restless and talkative man handed them out generously all over town. A few are still preserved, some decorated with autographs and adjectives.

From that first—and last—Sunday, Orsini rented the hall of the Apollo Cinema for training sessions, with a peso admission charged on Monday and Tuesday, half a peso on Wednesday, and two pesos on Thursday and Friday, when the challenge was picked up and the curiosity and the local patriotism of Santa Maria began to fill the Apollo. It was that Sunday, too, that the announcement of the challenge was posted on the new plaza, with proper permission from the municipal authorities. On an old photograph, the former World Wrestling Champion of All Weights exhibited his biceps and his gold belt, while aggressive red letters spelled out the challenge: 500 PESOS 500 to whoever enters the ring and is not pinned by Jacob van Oppen in three minutes.

Just a line below the challenge was forgotten; an announcement promised exhibition bouts of Graeco-Roman wrestling between the world champion—he would regain his title within a year—and the best athletes of Santa Maria.

Orsini and the giant had entered South America through Colombia and were now descending it by way of Peru, Ecuador, and Bolivia. The challenge had been picked up in only a few places, and the giant could always dispose of it in a matter of seconds, with the first clinch.

The posters evoked nights of heat and noise, theaters and big tents, audiences composed mostly of Indians and drunks, shouts of admiration, and laughter. The referee lifted his arm, van Oppen went back to his sadness and thought anxiously of the bottle of rotgut waiting in his hotel room, as Orsini was making his smiling progress under the white lights of the ring, drying his forehead with a handkerchief that was even whiter.

"Ladies and gentlemen. . . ."—this was the moment for giving thanks, for talking of unforgettable memories, for shouting *vivas!* to the country and to the city. For months now these memories had been forming for the two of them an image of South America: sometime, some night, within a year, when they already would be far away, they would be able to recall it without difficulty, with the aid of only three or four repeated moments of devotion.

On Tuesday or Wednesday Orsini took the champion in his car to the Berne, after an almost deserted training session. The tour had become a routine, and estimates of pesos to be earned differed little from pesos actually earned. But Orsini still felt he had to keep the giant under his wing, for mutual benefit. Van Oppen sat down on the bed and drank from the bottle; Orsini gently took it away from him and fetched from the bathroom the plastic glass he used to give his dentures a morning rinse. And he repeated, in friendship, the old cliché: "No morality without discipline." He spoke French as he spoke Spanish; his accent was never definitely Italian. "The bottle is here and nobody wants to steal it from you. But drinking with a glass makes all the difference. There is discipline, there is chivalry."

The giant turned his head to look at him: his blue eyes were turbid and he seemed to see instead with his half-opened mouth. "Dyspnea again, black anguish," thought Orsini. "Best for him to get drunk and sleep it off till tomorrow." He filled the glass with rum, took a swallow, and stretched out his hand to van Oppen. But the beast bent down to take off his shoes and then—second symptom—got up and examined the room. First, with his hands in his belt, he looked at the beds, the useless floor rug, the table, and the ceiling; then he walked around to test with his shoulder the resistance of the doors leading to the corridor and the bathroom, and of the window with the blocked view.

"No it's starting all over again," Orsini continued. "Last time it was in Guayaquil. It must be a cyclical affair, but I don't understand the cycle. Some night he'll strangle me and not because he hates me—but just because I happen to be at hand. He knows, surely he knows, that I am his only friend."

The barefoot giant slowly returned to the center of the room. His shoulders were bent slightly forward and his face wore a sneering and contemptuous smile. Orsini sat down at the flimsy table and dipped his tongue into the glass of rum.

"*Gott*," said van Oppen and began to sway as if he were listening to some distant and interrupted music. He wore the black knitted shirt, too tight for him, and the *vaquero* pants Orsini had bought him in Quito. "No. Where am I? What am I doing here?" With his enormous feet gripping the floor, he moved his body and stared at the wall above Orsini's head.

"I'm waiting. Always I find myself in a hotel room in a land of stinking niggers and always waiting. Gimme the glass. I'm not afraid; for that's the worst thing about it—nobody ever comes."

Orsini filled the glass and rose to give it to him. He examined his face, the hysteria in his voice, touched his moving shoulder. "Not yet," he thought. "But almost."

The giant emptied the glass and coughed without bending his head.

"Nobody," he said. "Footwork. Flexions. Holds. Lewis. To Lewis!—at least he was a man and lived like one. Gymnastics is not a man, wrestling is not a man, all this is not a man. A hotel room, a gymnasium, filthy Indians. It's pure hell, Orsini."

Orsini made another calculation and rose again with the rum bottle. He filled the glass van Oppen was clutching to his belly and passed his hand over the giant's shoulder and cheek.

"Nobody," said van Oppen. "Nobody!" he shouted. His eyes turned desperate, then raging. But he emptied the glass with a wise and merry smile.

"Now," thought Orsini. He grabbed the bottle and started pushing against the giant's thigh with his hip, to guide him toward the bath.

"A few more months, a few weeks," thought Orsini. "And then it's over. They'll all come later and we will be with them. We'll go to the other side."

Sprawling on the bed, the giant drank from the bottle and snorted, shaking his head. Orsini lit the table lamp and turned off the ceiling light. He sat down again at the table, adjusted his voice, and sang gently:

> Vor der Kaserne
> vor dem grossen Tor
> steht eine Laterne
> Und steht sie noch davor
> wenn wir uns einmal wiedersehen,
> bei der Laterne wollen wir stehen
> wie einst, Lili Marlene
> wie einst, Lili Marlene . . .

He sang the whole song and was halfway through it again when van Oppen put the bottle on the floor and started crying. Then Orsini got up with a sigh and an affectionate insult and walked on tiptoe to the door and the passage. And as on nights of glory he descended the Berne staircase, drying his forehead with a spotless handkerchief.

III

He walked downstairs without meeting anyone on whom he could bestow a smile or a lift of his hat; but his face remained affable, on guard. The woman, who had waited for hours with determination and without impatience, was sunk in the leather armchair of the lobby, paying no attention to the magazines on the low table and smoking one cigarette after another. She got up and confronted him. Prince Orsini had no escape; nor was he looking for one. He heard his name, raised his hat to the lady, and bent down to kiss her hand. He wondered what favor he could grant her and was ready to grant her whatever she requested. She was small, intrepid, and young. Her complexion was quite dark, her small nose hooked, her eyes very bright and cold. "Jewish or something like that," thought Orsini. "She's pretty." Suddenly the prince heard a language so concise as to be almost incomprehensible, unheard of.

"That poster in the plaza, the ads in the paper. Five hundred pesos. My fiancé will fight the champion. But today or tomorrow, that's Wednesday, you'll have to deposit the money at the bank of *El Liberal*."

"*Signorina*," the prince said with a smile and swayed with a disconsolate gesture, "fight the champion? You'll lose your fiancé. And I would be so sad to see a pretty young lady like you . . ."

But she, looking even smaller and more determined, effortlessly defied the gallantry of a man in his fifties.

"Tonight I'll go to *El Liberal* to take up the challenge. I saw the champion at mass. He's old. We need the five hundred pesos to get married. My fiancé is twenty and I'm twenty-two. He owns the Porfilio store. Come and see him."

"But, *señorita*," said the prince with a wider smile. "Your fiancé, a fortunate man if you'll permit me to say so, is twenty. What has he done so far? Buying and selling."

"He has also lived in the country."

"The country." The prince hummed the word with ecstasy. "But the champion has dedicated his whole life to this, to fighting. What if he is a few years older than your fiancé? I fully agree, *señorita*."

"Thirty, at least," she said. She felt no need to smile, relying on the coldness of her eyes. "I saw him."

"But these were the years he devoted to learning how to break, without an effort, arms and ribs, how to remove, gently, a collarbone from its proper place, how to dislocate a leg. And since you have a fiancé of twenty, and healthy . . ."

"You issued a challenge. Five hundred pesos for three minutes. I'll go to *El Liberal* tonight, Mr. . . ."

"Prince Orsini," said the prince.

She nodded her head, without wasting any time for sneers. She was small, compact, pretty, and hard as iron.

"I am happy for Santa Maria." The prince smiled and bowed. "It will be a great sporting spectacle. But you, *señorita*, are you going to the newspaper in the name of your fiancé?"

"Yes, he gave me a paper. Go and see him. The Porfilio store. They call him the Turk. But he's a Syrian. He has the document."

The prince understood that it wouldn't be right to kiss her hand again.

"Well," he joked. "First a spinster, then a widow. After Saturday. A very sad destiny, *señorita*."

She offered him her hand and walked toward the hotel door. She was hard as a lance and had barely enough charm to make the prince look at her back. Suddenly she stopped and returned.

"A spinster, no, because with these five hundred pesos we'll get married. A widow neither, because that champion of yours is very old. He's bigger than Mario but could never beat him. I saw him."

"Agreed. You saw him leaving the church after mass. But I assure you that when things really get going he becomes a wild beast and I swear to you that he knows his trade. World Champion of All Weights, *señorita.*"

"Well," she repeated with a sudden weariness. "As I told you, the Porfilio Brothers store. Tonight I'll go to *El Liberal;* but you will find me tomorrow, as always, at the store."

"*Señorita*. . . ." He kissed her hand again.

The woman was clearly looking for a deal. And so Orsini went to the restaurant and ordered a dish of meat and spaghetti. Later he worked on his accounts and, sucking at his gold-ringed cigarette mouthpiece, kept a watch on the sleep, grunts, and movements of Jacob van Oppen.

About to fall asleep above the silence of the plaza, he granted himself a twenty-four hours' vacation. It wasn't advisable to hurry his visit to the Turk. Moreover, as he put it to himself while turning off the light and interpreting the snores of the giant: "I have suffered enough, oh Lord; we have suffered enough. I see no reason for hurry."

The next day Orsini took care of the champion's awakening, brought him aspirins and hot water. He listened with satisfaction to van Oppen's curses under the shower and observed with joy the transformation of his rude noises into an almost submarine version of *Ich hatte einen Kameraden*. Like all other men, he decided to lie, to lie to himself and to trust his luck. He organized van Oppen's morning, the slow walk through the town, his enormous torso covered by the knitted woolen sweather bearing in front a giant blue C, the letter which spelled out—in all alphabets and in all languages—the words WORLD WRESTLING CHAMPION OF ALL WEIGHTS. Orsini accompanied him, at a lively step, as far as the streets that descended toward the Promenade. There, for the benefit of the few curious onlookers of eight o'clock in the morning, he repeated a scene from the old farce. He stopped to raise his hat and wipe his forehead, to smile like a good loser, and to give Jacob van Oppen a pat on the back.

"What a man!" he murmured to no one in particular. His head turned away, his arms lowered, his mouth snapping for air, he repeated for the benefit of all of Santa Maria: "What a man!"

Van Oppen kept walking toward the Promenade at the same moderate speed, his shoulders hunched toward the future, his jaw hanging. Then he took the street to the cannery and braved the astonishment of fishermen, loafers, and ferry employees: he was too big for anyone to make fun of him.

But the sneers, though never spoken aloud, hovered all around Orsini that day, around his clothes, his manners, his inadequate education. However, he had made a bet with himself to be happy that day, and so only good and pleasant things could get through to him. He held what he would later call press conferences at the offices of *El Liberal*, at the Berne, and at the Plaza; he drank and chatted with the curious and the idle, told anecdotes and atrocious lies, exhibited once again his yellowing and fragile press cuttings. There had been a time, no doubt about it, when things really were that way: van Oppen, world champion, young, with an irresistible bolt grip, with tours that were not exiles, besieged by offers that could be rejected. The words and pictures in the newspapers, though discolored and outdated, tenaciously refused to become ashes and offered irrefutable proofs. Never quite drunk, Orsini believed after the fifth or sixth glass that the testimonies of the past were a guarantee of the future. He needed no change of personality to dwell comfortably in an impossible paradise. He had been born a man of fifty, cynical, kindly, a friend of life, waiting for things to happen to him. All that was needed for the miracle was a transformation of van Oppen, his return to the years before the war, to his bulgeless stomach, sparkling skin, and needle-cold shower in the mornings.

Yes, the future Mrs. Turk—a charming and obstinate woman, with all due respect—had been at *El Liberal* to pick up the challenge. The head of the sports section already had photos of Mario doing his gymnastics, but only by paying for them with a speech on democracy, free press, and freedom of information. On patriotism, too, Sports Section added.

"And the Turk would have knocked our heads off, mine and the photographer's, if his bride hadn't intervened and calmed him with a couple of words. They had been muttering to each other in the rear of the store, and then the Turk came out, not so big, I think, as van Oppen, but much more of a brute, more dangerous. Well, you know more about these things than I."

"I understand," smiled the prince. "Poor boy. He's not the first." And he let his sadness float over the olives and potato chips of the Berne.

"The man was fighting mad but got himself under control, put on his short fishing pants, and started doing his gymnastics out in the open. He did everything that Humberto, our photographer, asked of him or invented for him, and all this only to get his revenge and get even for the shock we had given him. And she was there too, sitting on a barrel like his mother or his teacher, smoking, not saying a word, but watching him all the time. And when one thinks that she's less than five feet tall and weighs less than ninety pounds . . ."

"I know the lady," Orsini agreed nostalgically. "And I have seen so many cases. . . . Ah, human personality is a mysterious thing; it doesn't come from muscles."

"It's not for publication, of course," said Sports Section. "But will you make the deposit?"

"The deposit?" The prince opened his hands in a pious gesture. "This afternoon or tomorrow morning. It depends on the bank. How do you feel about tomorrow morning at your office? It'll be good publicity and free at that. To hold van Oppen for three minutes . . . As I always say"—and here he showed his golden molars and called the waiter—"sport is one thing and business another. What can one do, what can we do when a candidate for suicide suddenly appears at the end of our training tour? And when—what's worse—he gets help."

IV

Life had always been difficult and beautiful and unique, and Prince Orsini did not have the five hundred pesos. He understood the woman and there was an adjective at the tip of his tongue to define her and to enshrine her in his past; but then he began to think of the man whom the woman represented and fronted for, the Turk who had accepted the challenge. And so he said good-by to happiness and the easy life. He checked the champion's mood and pulse, then told him a lie and, at nightfall, started walking toward the Porfilio Brothers store with the yellow scrapbook under his arm.

First the worm-eaten ombu tree, then the lamp that hung from it and produced a circle of intimidated light. Suddenly, barking dogs and contending shouts: "Go away!" "Quiet!" "Down!" Orsini crossed the first light, saw the round and watery moon, reached the store sign, and made a respectful entry. A man wearing rope sandals and ballooned country pants was finishing his gin by the counter. He left and they were alone: he—Prince Orsini—the Turk and the woman.

"Good evening, *señorita*," Orsini smiled and bowed. The woman was sitting on a straw-backed chair, knitting; she withdrew her eyes from the needles to look at him and—perhaps—to smile. "Baby clothes," Orsini thought indignantly. "She's pregnant, she's preparing her baby's layette, that's why she wants to get married, that's why she wants to rob me of five hundred pesos."

He walked straight toward the man who had stopped filling paper bags with *mate* and was waiting for him stolidly across the counter.

"That's the one I told you about," the woman stated. "The manager."

"Manager and friend," Orsini corrected. "After so many years . . ."

He shook the man's stiffly opened hand and raised his arm to pat him on the back.

"At your orders," said the storekeeper and lifted his thick black whiskers to show his teeth.

"Pleased to meet you, very pleased to meet you." But he had already breathed the sour and deathly smell of defeat, had calculated the Turk's unspent youth, the perfect manner in which his hundred kilos were distributed over his body. "There isn't one surplus gram of fat here, not one gram of intelligence or sensitivity; there is no hope. Three minutes: poor Jacob van Oppen!"

"I've come about these five hundred pesos," Orsini started, testing the density of the air, the poorness of the light, the hostility of the couple. "It's not against me; it's against life," he thought. "I have come here to set your minds at rest. Tomorrow, as soon as I receive a money order from the capital, I'll make the deposit at *El Liberal*. But I'd also like to talk of other things."

"Haven't we already talked about everything?" the woman asked. She was too small for the shaky straw-backed chair; her shiny knitting needles were too big for her. She could be good or evil; now she had chosen to be implacable, to make up for some long and obscure delay, to take revenge. In the light of the lamp, the shape of her nose was perfect and her bright eyes shone like glass.

"That's quite true, *señorita*. I don't want to say anything I haven't already said before. But I thought it my duty to say it directly. To tell the truth to señor Mario." He smiled while repeating his greeting with his head; his truculence barely vibrated, deep and muted. "And that's why, *patrón*, I'd like you to serve drinks for three. It's on me, of course; have whatever you like."

"He doesn't drink," said the woman without hurry and without lifting her eyes from her knitting, nestling in her aura of ice and irony.

The hairy beast behind the counter finished sealing a package of *mate* and turned around slowly to look at the woman. "Gorilla chest; two centimeters of forehead; never had any expression in his eyes," Orsini noted. "Never really thought, suffered, or imagined that tomorrow might bring a surprise or not come at all."

"Adriana," the Turk muttered, remaining motionless until she turned her eyes toward him. "Adriana, vermouth I do take."

She gave him a rapid smile and shrugged her shoulders. The Turk pursed his lips to drink the vermouth in small swallows. The prince, his heavy green hat tilted backward, was leaning over the counter, touching the wrapping of his scrapbook. Looking for inspiration and sympathy, he talked of crops, rains, and droughts, of farming methods and means of transport, of Europe's aging beauty and of America's youth. He improvised, distributing prophecies and hopes, while the Turk nodded silent agreement.

"The Apollo was full this afternoon," the prince launched a sudden attack. "As soon as it became known that you've picked up the challenge, everybody wanted to see the champion training. I don't want him bothered too much, so I raised the entrance price; but the public still insists on paying it. And now," he said while starting to unwrap the scrapbook, "I'd like you to take a little look at this." He caressed the leather cover and lifted it. "It's almost all words, but the photographs help. Look, it's quite clear: world champion, gold belt."

"Former world champion," the woman corrected out of the crackling of her straw-backed chair.

"But, *señorita*," Orsini said without turning, exclusively for the Turk's benefit, as he flipped the pages of decaying clippings, "he'll be champion again before six months are out. A false decision, the International Wrestling Federation has already intervened. . . . Look at the headlines, eight columns, front pages, look at the photographs. See, that's a world champion: nobody in this world can beat him. Nobody can hold him for three minutes and not be pinned. Why! One minute against him would be a miracle. The champion of Europe couldn't do it; the champion of the United States couldn't do it either. I'm talking to you seriously, man to man; I've come to see you because, as soon as I spoke to the *señorita*, I understood the problem, the situation."

"Adriana," the Turk reminded him.

"That's it," said the prince. "I understood everything. But there is always a solution. If you climb into the Apollo ring on Saturday . . . Jacob van Oppen is my friend, and his friendship has only one limit; it disappears when the bell rings and he starts fighting. Then he is no longer my friend, no longer an ordinary man: he is the world champion, he has to win and he knows how."

Dozens of salesmen had stopped their Fords outside

the Porfilio Brothers store, to smile at its late owners or at Mario, to have a drink, to show samples, catalogues, and lists, to sell sugar, rice, wine, and maize. But what Orsini was trying to sell to the Turk between smiles, friendly pats on the back, and compassionate pleas was a strange and difficult merchandise: fear. Alerted by the presence of the woman and counseled by his memories and instincts, he limited himself to selling prudence and tried to make a deal.

The Turk still had half a glass of vermouth left; he lifted it to wet his small pink lips, without drinking.

"It's five hundred pesos," said Adriana from her chair. "And it's time to close."

"You said . . ." The Turk started. His voice and thought tried to understand, to be calm, to free themselves from three generations of stupidity and greed. "Adriana, I'll have to take down the *mate* first. You said that if I climb into the ring at the Apollo on Saturday . . ."

"I said this: if you get into the ring, the champion will break you some ribs or other bones; he'll have you pinned in half a minute. There'll be no five hundred pesos then—though you may well have to spend more than that on doctors. And who'll take care of your business while you're at the hospital? And on top of it all, you'll lose your reputation and the whole town will laugh at you." Orsini felt that the time had come for pause and meditation; he asked for another gin, tried to fathom the Turk's stolid face and anxious movements, and heard a sardonic little laugh from the woman, who had dropped her knitting on her thighs.

Orsini took a sip of gin and started to wrap up the rickety scrapbook. The Turk was smelling the vermouth and trying to think.

"I don't mean to say," the prince murmured in a low distracted voice whose tone was that of an epilogue accepted by both parties, "I don't mean to say that you may not be stronger than Jacob van Oppen. I know much about these things; I have dedicated my life and my money to the discovery of strong men. Moreover, as *señorita* Adriana so intelligently reminded me, you are much younger than the champion. More youth, more vigor; I'm prepared to put this in writing. If the champion—just to take an example—bought this store, he'd be out begging in the streets in six months. While you, on the other hand, will be a rich man in less than two years. Because you, my friend Mario, know about business and the champion doesn't." The scarpbook was already wrapped; he put it on the counter and leaned on it to get on with his drink and the conversation. "In exactly the same way, the champion knows how to break bones, how to bend your knees and your waist backward so he can pin you on the 'mat.' That's how it's put—or, at least, that's how they used to put it. On the rug. Everybody to his trade."

The woman had risen to put out a lamp in the corner; she was now standing with her knitting between her stomach and the counter, small and hard, not looking at either man.

The Turk examined her face and then grunted: "You said that if I didn't climb into the ring at the Apollo on Saturday . . ."

"I said?" Orsini asked with surprise. "I think that I offered you some advice, But, in any case, if you withdraw your acceptance of the challenge, we might agree on something, a compensation. We could talk."

"How much?" asked the Turk.

The woman lifted a hand and dug her nails into the beast's hairy arm; when the man turned his face to look at her, she said: "Five hundred pesos, no more and no less, right? And we're not going to lose them. If you don't show up on Saturday, all Santa Maria will know that you're a coward. I'll tell them, house by house and person by person."

She spoke without passion. Still sticking her nails into the Turk's arms, she spoke to him with patience and good humor, as a mother speaks to the child she reprimands and threatens.

"One moment," said Orsini. He raised a hand and used the other to lift the glass of gin to his mouth until it was empty. "I have thought of that, too. The comments that people, that the town will make if you don't turn up on Saturday." He smiled at the two hostile faces and his tone became more cautious. "For example . . . let us suppose that you do turn up and climb into the ring. Don't try to provoke the champion: that would be fatal for what we're planning. You climb into the ring, realize with the first clinch that the champion knows his job and let him pin you, cleanly, without a scratch."

The woman was again digging her nails into the giant hairy arm; the Turk removed her with a bark.

"I understand," he said then. "I go in and I lose. How much?"

Suddenly Orsini accepted what he had suspected from the beginning of the meeting: whatever agreement he might reach with the Turk, the stubborn little woman would wipe it out before the night was over. He realized without any room for doubt that Jacob van Oppen was doomed to fight the Turk on Saturday.

"How much?" he murmured while adjusting the scrapbook under his arm. "Let's say a hundred, a hundred and fifty pesos. You climb into the ring. . . ."

The woman moved a step away from the counter and stuck the needles into the ball of wool. She was looking at the earth and cement floor and her voice sounded tranquil and drowsy:

"We need five hundred pesos and he will win them for us on Saturday, with no tricks and no deals. There's nobody stronger, nobody can bend him backward. Least of all that exhausted old man, whatever champion he may have been in his day. Shall we close?"

"I've got to take down the *mate*," the Turk said again.

"Well, so that's that. Take out what I owe you and give me a last glass." He put a ten-peso note on the counter and lit a cigarette. "We'll celebrate, and you'll be my guests."

But the woman relit the corner lamp and sat down again in the straw-backed chair, picked up her knitting, and smoked a cigarette; and the Turk served only one glass of gin. Then he started with a yawn to carry the bags of *mate*, piled up against the wall, toward the cellar trap door.

Without knowing why, Orsini tossed a visiting card on the counter. He stayed in the store ten minutes more, watching with clouded eyes, perspiring, the Turk's methodical handling of the *mate* bags. He saw him moving them with the same ease, with as much visible effort as he, Prince Orsini, would use to move a box of cigarettes or a bottle.

"Poor Jacob van Oppen," Orsini meditated. "To grow old is all right for me. But he was born to be always twenty; and it's not he who is twenty now but that giant son of a bitch who is wrapped round the little finger of the fetus in her belly. He's twenty, the animal, nobody can take it away from him to give it back afterward, and he'll be twenty on Saturday night at the Apollo."

V

From the editorial office of *El Liberal*, almost elbow to elbow with the sports section, Orsini made a telephone call to the capital to ask for an urgent remittance of a thousand pesos. To escape the operator's curiosity, he used the direct line; he told loud lies for the benefit of the editorial office, now occupied by thin and bewhiskered youths and a girl smoking through a cigarette holder. It was seven in the evening; he almost made some coarse comments in reply to the obvious hesitation of the man who was listening to him from a distant telephone in some room that couldn't be imagined, making grimaces of disagreement in some cubicle of the capital, on an October evening.

He broke off the conversation with a weary and tolerant smile.

"At last," he said, and blew his nose into a linen handkerchief. "Tomorrow morning we'll have the money. Troubles. Tomorrow noon I'll make the deposit in the managing editor's office. The managing editor's office sounds businesslike, right? . . . Ah, there's the boy. If any of you would like some refreshment . . ."

They thanked him, and one typewriter or another stopped its noise, but no one accepted his invitation. Sports Section, with his thick glasses, was bending over a table marking some photographs.

Leaning against a table and smoking a cigarette, Orsini looked at the men bent over their machines and their jobs. He knew that he no longer existed for them, was no longer in the editorial office. "And I won't exist for them tomorrow either," he thought with a touch of sadness and a smile of resignation. Because everything had been postponed until Friday night and Friday night was just beginning to bud in the fade-out of the sweet and rosy dusk beyond the windows of *El Liberal*, on the river, above the first shadow that wrapped the deep sirens of the barges.

He bridged mistrust and indifference and made Sports Section shake hands with him.

"I hope that tomorrow will be a great night for Santa Maria; I hope that the best man wins."

But this phrase would not be printed in the newspaper to serve as support for his smiling and benevolent face. From the lobby of the Apollo—Jacob van Oppen, World Champion, Trains Here from 6 to 8 P.M. Entrance: 3 pesos—he heard the murmurs of the public and the thumping of van Oppen's feet on the improvised ring. Van Oppen could no longer fight, break bones, or risk having them broken. But he could skip a rope, indefinitely, without tiring.

Seated in the narrow ticket office, Orsini checked the statement of receipts and expenditures and tallied his accounts. Even without the triumphant Saturday night, seats at five pesos, the visit to Santa Maria showed some profit. Orsini offered the other man a coffee, counted the money, and put his signature at the foot of the lists.

He remained alone in the dark and smelly office. The rhythmical tapping of van Oppen's feet on the boards could be heard.

"One hundred and ten animals sitting there open-mouthed because the champion skips a rope, the way all school girls skip in the playground—and they probably do it better."

He remembered van Oppen as a young man, or at least not yet grown old; he thought of Europe and the United States, of the true Lost World; tried to convince himself that van Oppen was responsible for the passing of the years, his decline, and his repugnant old age, as if these were vices he had freely acquired and accepted. He tried to hate van Oppen in order to protect himself.

"I should have spoken to him before, maybe yesterday or this morning on those walks of his on the Promenade where he minces along like an old woman. Maybe I should have spoken to him out in the open, facing the river, the trees, the sky, all that these Germans call nature. But Friday has come; it is now Friday night."

He gently felt the bank notes in his pocket and got up. Outside, Friday night was waiting for him, punctual and mild. The hundred and ten imbeciles were shouting inside the movie house; the champion had started his last number, the gymnastics session in which all his muscles swelled and overflowed.

Orsini walked slowly toward the hotel, his hands clasped behind his back, looking for details of the town to dismiss and to remember, to mingle them with details of other distant towns to join them all into a whole and to keep on living.

The hotel bar stretched out till it became the receptionist's counter. Over a drink with much soda the prince planned his battle. To occupy a hill may prove more important than to lose an ammunition dump. He put some money on the counter and asked for his hotel bill.

"It's for tomorrow really, excuse me, but I'd rather have it now and avoid the rush. Tomorrow, as soon as the fight is over, we have to leave by car, at midnight or at dawn. I phoned from *El Liberal* today and they mentioned some new contracts. Everybody wants to see the champion, naturally, before the Antwerp tournament."

He paid the bill with an outsize tip and went up to his room with a bottle of gin under his arm to pack the suitcases. One, old and black, belonged to Jacob and could not be touched; there was also an impressive heap of his belongings on the stage of the Apollo: robes, sweaters, stretcher springs, ropes, fleece-lined boots. But all this could be picked up later on any pretext. He packed his suitcases and those of Jacob's that had not been proclaimed sacred; he was taking a shower, potbellied and determined, when he heard the room door bang. Beyond the noise of the water he heard steps and silence. "It's Friday night," he thought, "and I don't even know whether it's best to get him drunk before or after talking to him. Or maybe before *and* after."

Jacob was sitting on the bed, cross-legged, contemplating with childish joy the trademark on the sole of his shoe: CHAMPION. Somebody, maybe Orsini himself, had once told him as a joke that those shoes were manufactured for the exclusive benefit of van Oppen, to remind people of him and to make thousands upon thousands of strangers pay homage to him with their feet.

Wrapped in his bathrobe, and dripping water, Orsini entered the room, jovial and shrewd. The champion had grabbed the gin bottle and, after taking a drink, continued to contemplate his shoe without listening to Orsini.

"Why did you pack the suitcases? The fight is tomorrow."

"To gain time," said Orsini. "That's why I began to pack them. But afterward . . ."

"Is it at nine? But it always starts late. And after the three minutes I still have to swing the clubs and lift the weights. And also to celebrate."

"All right," Orsini said, looking at the bottle tilted against the champion's mouth, counting the drinks, calculating.

The champion had put away the bottle and was now massaging the white crepe sole of his shoe. He was smiling a mysterious and incredulous smile, as if he were listening to some distant music that he hadn't heard since childhood. Suddenly he became serious, took in both hands the foot bearing the allusive trademark, and lowered it slowly until the sole was resting on the narrow rug by the bed. Orsini saw the short, dry grimace that had replaced the vanished smile; he hesitatingly moved toward the champion's bed and lifted the bottle. While pretending to drink, he could estimate that there were still two thirds of a liter of gin left.

Motionless, collapsed, with his elbows leaning on his knees, the champion prayed: "*Verdammt, verdammt, verdammt.*"

Without making a noise, Orsini moved his feet from the ground and with his back to the champion, yawning, took out a gun from his jacket hanging from a chair and put it in a pocket of his bathrobe. Then he sat on his bed and waited. He had never needed the gun, not even to threaten Jacob. But the years had taught him to anticipate the champion's actions and reactions, to estimate his violence, his degree of madness, and also the exact point of the compass at which madness began.

"*Verdammt*," Jacob kept praying. He filled his lungs with air and rose to his feet. He joined his hands at the nape of his neck and dipped from the waist, hard, bending his chest first right, then left toward the midriff.

"*Verdammt!*" he shouted as if looking at somebody who challenged him, then remade his distrustful smile and began to undress. Orsini lit a cigarette and put a hand into his bathrobe pocket, his knuckles resting against the coolness of the gun. The champion took off his sweater, his undershirt, his pants and the shoes with his trademark; he threw them all into the corner between the wall and the closet, where they formed a pile on the floor.

Leaning against the bed and the pillow, Orsini tried to remember other outbursts, other prologues, and match them against what he saw. "Nobody said we should go. Who told you we must go tonight?"

Jacob was wearing only his wrestling trunks. He lifted the bottle and drank half its remaining contents. Then, keeping up his smile of mystery, allusions, and memories, began to do gymnastics exercises, stretching and bending his arms while bending his knees to squat.

"All this flesh," Orsini thought with his fingers on the trigger of the gun, "the same muscles, or bigger, as twenty years ago; a little more fat on the belly, the loins, the midriff. White, timid enemy of the sun, gringo and womanish. But these arms and these legs are as strong as ever, maybe stronger. The years didn't pass him by; but they always come, search, and find a place to enter and to stay. We were all promised old age and death, sudden or by inches. This poor devil didn't believe these promises; and to that extent the result is unjust."

Illuminated by Friday's last light and by the lamp Orsini had lit in the bathroom, the giant was shining with sweat. He finished his gymnastics session by lying down flat on his back and lifting himself up on his arms. Then he gave a short and slow salute with his head to the pile of clothes by the closet. Panting, he took another drink from the bottle, lifted it into the ash-colored air, and moved toward Orsini's bed without stopping to look at it. He remained standing, enormous and sweating, breathing with much effort and noise, with an openmouthed expression of fury from end to end. He kept looking at the bottle, looking for explanations from its label, rounded and secret.

"Champion," Orsini said, withdrawing but not touching the wall, raising a leg to get an easier grip on his gun. "Champion, we must order another bottle. We must start celebrating right away."

"Celebrating? But I always win."

"Yes, the champion always wins. And he'll also win in Europe."

Orsini raised himself from the bed and maneuvered his legs until he was seated, his hand still in his bathrobe pocket.

In front of him, Jacob's enormous contracted muscles were expanding. "There have never been better legs than his," Orsini thought with fear and sadness. "All he needs to knock me out is to bring down the bottle; it takes a lot less than a minute to crush a man's head with the bottom of a bottle." He got up slowly and limped away, showing a bland paternal smile all the way to the opposite corner of the room. He leaned against the table and remained for a moment with his eyes ajar, muttering to himself a Catholic and magical formula.

Jacob hadn't moved. He remained standing by the bed, now with his back toward it, the bottle still in the air. The room was almost dusky now, and the bathroom light was weak and yellowish.

Maneuvering with his left hand, Orsini lit a cigarette. "I have never pushed him that far," he thought.

"We can celebrate now, Champion. We'll celebrate till dawn and at four we'll take the bus. Good-by Santa Maria. Good-by and thanks, you didn't treat us too badly."

White, magnified by the shadow, Jacob slowly put down the arm with the bottle and clinked the glass against his knee.

"We're going away, Champion," Orsini added. "He's thinking about it now, and let's hope he'll understand it in less than three minutes."

Jacob turned his body around as if he were in a saltwater pool and doubled up to sit on the bed. His hair, scanty but still untouched by gray, showed through the dark the tilt of his head.

"We have contracts, genuine contracts," Orsini continued, "if we go south. But it must be at once, it must be by the four-o'clock bus. I made a phone call from the newspaper office this afternoon, Champion. I called a manager in the capital."

"Today. Today is Friday," said Jacob slowly and without drunkenness in his voice. "So the fight is tomorrow night. We can't leave at four."

"There is no fight, Champion. There are no problems. We go at four; but first we celebrate. I'll order another bottle right away."

"No," said Jacob.

Again Orsini leaned motionless against the table. His pity for the champion, so exacerbated and long-suffering in the last few months, turned into pity for Prince Orsini, condemned to a nurse's life of coddling, lying, and boredom with this creature whom fate assigned him to earn a living. Then his pity became depersonalized, almost universal. "Here, in a South American hole that has a name only because someone wanted to comply with the local custom of baptizing any heap of houses. He, more lost and exhausted than I; I, older, gayer, and more intelligent than he, watching him with a gun that may or may not shoot, determined to threaten him with it but certain that I'll never pull the trigger. Pity human existence, pity whoever arranges things in this clumsy and absurd manner. Pity the people I have had to cheat so that I could keep alive. Pity the Turk of the store and his fiancée, all those who don't really have the privilege of choice."

From far away, disjointed, the sound of the conservatory piano reached them; in spite of the hour, one could feel the heat rising in the room, in the tree-lined streets.

"I don't understand," said Jacob. "Today is Friday. If that lunatic no longer wants to accept the challenge I shall have to do my exhibition, seats at five pesos."

"That lunatic . . ." Orsini started, passing from pity to fury and anger. "No, it's us. We aren't interested in the challenge. We leave at four."

"The man wants to fight? He hasn't backed out?"

"The man wants to fight and he won't be allowed to back out. But we go away."

"Without a fight, before tomorrow?"

"Champion," said Orsini. Jacob's bent head moved in a negative gesture.

"I'm staying. Tomorrow at nine I'll be waiting in the ring. Will I wait alone?"

"Champion," Orsini repeated while approaching the bed; he affectionately touched Jacob's shoulder and lifted the bottle for a small drink. "We leave."

"Not me," said the giant and began to rise, to grow. "I'll be alone in the ring. Give me half the money and go. Tell me why you want to run away and why you want me to run away, too."

Forgetting about the gun without ceasing to grip it, Orsini spoke against the arch formed by the champion's ribs.

"Because there are contracts waiting for us. And that business tomorrow is not a fight; it's only a silly challenge."

Without betraying his uneasiness, Orsini moved away toward the window, toward Jacob's bed. He didn't dare turn on the light; he had no fight in him to win with smiles and gestures.

He preferred the shadow and persuasion by tones of voice. "Maybe it would be best to end it all here and now. I have always been lucky; something has always turned up and it was often better than what I lost. Don't look behind you; just leave him like an elephant without a master."

"But the challenge was ours," Jacob's voice was saying, surprised, almost laughing. "We always issue it. Three minutes. In the newspapers, in the plazas. Money for holding out three minutes. And I always won. Jacob van Oppen always wins."

"Always," Orsini repeated. He suddenly felt weak and weary; he put the gun on the bed and put his hands together between his naked knees. "The champion always wins. But also always, every single time, I first take a look at the man who accepts the challenge. Three minutes without being pinned to the carpet," he recited. "And nobody lasted more than half a minute and I knew it in advance." He thought while saying this: "And, of course, I can't tell him that I sometimes made successful threats to some contenders and that I bribed others to last less than thirty seconds. But maybe I'll have to tell him after all." Aloud he went on: "And now, too, I have done my duty. I went to see the man who picked up the challenge, I weighed him and measured him. With my eyes. That's why I packed the suitcases and that's why I think we should take the four-o'clock bus."

Van Oppen had stretched himself out on the floor, his head leaning against the wall, between the night table and the bathroom light.

"I don't understand it. You mean that he, that small-town storekeeper who never saw a real fight, will beat Jacob van Oppen?"

"Nobody can beat the champion in a fight," said Orsini patiently. "But this is not a fight."

"Ah, it's a challenge!" Jacob exclaimed.

"That's it. A challenge. Five hundred pesos to whoever will remain on his feet for three minutes. I've seen the man." Here Orsini paused and lit another cigarette. He was calm and disinterested: this was like telling a story to a child to make him go to sleep, or like singing "Lili Marlene."

"And that one will hold me three minutes?" van Oppen sneered.

"Yes, he will. He's a beast. Twenty years, hundred and ten kilos—it's only my estimate, but I'm never wrong."

Jacob doubled up his feet till he was sitting on the floor. Orsini heard him breathe.

"Twenty," said the champion. "I, too, was twenty one day and not as strong as now; I knew less."

"Twenty," repeated the prince, turning his yawn into a sigh.

"And that's all? That's all there is to it? And how many men of twenty have I pinned in less than twenty seconds? And why should that hick last three minutes?"

"It's like this," Orsini thought with the cigarette in his mouth, "it's as simple and terrible as to discover all of a sudden that a woman doesn't arouse us, to remain impotent and to know that explanations won't do any good, won't even provide relief; as simple and terrible as to tell the truth to a sick man. Everything is simple when it happens to others, when we remain alien to it and can understand, sympathize, and repeat advice."

The conservatory piano had disappeared into the heat of the inky night; there was the chirping of crickets, and, much farther away, a jazz record was turning.

"He'll hold me for three minutes?" Jacob insisted. "I saw him too. I saw his picture in the paper. A good body to move barrels."

"No," Orsini replied with sincerity and serenity. "No one can resist the world champion for three minutes."

"I don't understand," said Jacob. "Then I don't understand. Is there anything more to it?"

"Yes." Orsini was speaking smoothly and indifferently as if the matter were unimportant. "When we finish this training tour, it'll be all different. It will also be necessary to give up alcohol. But today, tomorrow, Saturday night in Santa Maria—or whatever the name of this hole—Jacob van Oppen cannot clinch and hold a clinch for more than a minute. Van Oppen's chest cannot; his lungs cannot. And that beast won't be thrown in a minute. That's why we have to take the four-o'clock bus. The suitcases are packed and I've paid the hotel bill. It's all settled."

Orsini heard the grunt and the cough to his left and was measuring the silence in the room. He picked up the gun again and warmed it against his knees.

"After all," he thought, "it is strange that I should make so many evasions, take so many precautions. He knows it better than I and for some time now. But maybe this is why I chose the evasions and looked for precautions. And here I am, at my age, as pitiable and ridiculous as if I had told a woman that we were through and was waiting for her reaction, her tears, and her threats."

Jacob had moved back; but the band of light from the bathroom revealed, on his backward-tilted head, the shine of tears. Orsini, still gripping the gun, walked to the phone to order another bottle. He grazed in passing the champion's closely cropped hair and returned to the bed. Raising his legs, he could feel the heavy roundness of his belly against his thighs. A panting noise reached him from the seated man, as if van Oppen had come to the aftermath of a long training session or the end of a very long and difficult fight.

"It's not his heart," Orsini reminded himself, "nor his lungs. It's everything: a six foot six of a man who has begun to grow old."

"No, no," he said aloud. "Only a rest on the road. In a matter of months, it'll all be like before again. Quality, that is what really matters, what can never be lost. Even if one wants to lose it, or tries to. Because there are periods of suicide in every man's life. But they are overcome, forgotten." The dance music had grown louder as the night advanced. Orsini's voice vibrated with satisfaction and lingered in his throat and palate.

There was a knock on the door and the prince moved silently to receive the tray with the bottle, glasses, and ice. He put it down on the table and chose to sit down on a chair to continue the vigil and the lesson of optimism.

The champion had sat down in the shadow, on the floor, leaning against the wall; his breathing could no longer be heard and he existed for Orsini only by virtue of his undoubted and enormous crouching presence.

"Ah yes, quality," the prince resumed his theme. "Who has it? One is born with it or dies without it. It's not for nothing that everybody finds himself a nickname, stupid and comical, a few funny words to be put on the posters. THE BUFFALO OF ARKANSAS, THE GRINDER OF LIEGE, THE MIURA BULL OF GRANADA. But Jacob van Oppen is simply called 'World Champion.' That's all. That's quality."

Orsini's speech faded into silence and weariness.

The prince filled a glass, tasted it with his tongue, and rose to carry it to the champion.

"Orsini," said Jacob. "My friend Prince Orsini."

Van Oppen's big hands lay heavily on his knees, like the teeth of a trap; the knees supported his bent head. Orsini put the glass on the floor after touching the giant's neck and back with it.

He was adjusting his position with a grimace, weariness attacking his midriff, when he suddenly felt fingers encircling his ankle and nailing him to the floor. He heard Jacob's voice slow and gay, lazy and serene:

"And now the prince will drink the whole glass at one go."

Orsini threw himself back to keep his balance. "That's all I needed: that the beast should think I want to drug him or poison him." He stopped slowly, picked up the glass, and drank it rapidly, feeling the grip of Jacob's fingers weakening on his ankle.

"All right, Champion?" he asked. Now he could see the other's eye, a scrap of his lifted smile.

"All right, Prince. Now a full glass for me."

With his legs apart and trying not to stumble, Orsini returned to the table and refilled the glass. He leaned against it to light a cigarette and saw, with the small flame of the lighter, that his fingers were trembling with hate. He came back with the glass, the cigarette in his mouth, a finger on the trigger of the gun concealed in his bathrobe. He crossed the yellow band of light and saw Jacob on his feet, white and enormous, swaying gently.

"Your health, Champion," said Orsini, offering the drink with his left hand.

"Your health," Jacob's voice repeated from above, with a trace of excitement. "I knew they would come. I went to the church to pray that they would come."

"Yes," said Orsini.

There was a pause, the champion sighed, the night

brought them shouts and applause from the distant dance hall, a tug sounded its siren thrice on the river.

"And now," Jacob pronounced the words with some difficulty, "the prince will take another drink at one go. We're both drunk. But I don't drink tonight because it's Friday. The prince had a gun."

For a second, with the glass in the air and contemplating Jacob's navel, the prince invented for himself a life story of perpetual humiliation, savored the taste of disgust, and knew that the giant wasn't even challenging him but was only offering him a target for the gun in his pocket.

"Yes," he said a second later, spat out the cigarette, and took another drink of gin. His stomach rose to his chest as he threw the empty glass on the bed and laboriously moved back to place the gun on the table.

Van Oppen hadn't moved; he was still swaying in the dusk, with a sneering slowness, as if he were performing the classical gymnastic exercises to strengthen his waist muscles.

"We must both be crazy," said Orsini. His memories, the weak heat of the summer's night pressing against the window, his plans for the future were all of no use to him.

" 'Lili Marlene,' please," Jacob advised.

Leaning on the table, Orsini put away the cigarette he was about to light. He sang with a muted voice, with one last hope, as if he had never done anything but hum those imbecile lyrics, that easy tune, as if he had never done anything else to earn a living. He felt older than ever, shrunk and potbellied, a stranger to himself.

There was a silence and then the champion said, "Thanks!" Feeling sleepy and weak, fumbling with the cigarette he had left on the table by the gun, Orsini saw the big whitish body approach him, relieved of its age by the dusk.

"Thanks," van Oppen repeated, almost touching him. "Another time."

Stunned and indifferent, Orsini thought to himself: "It's no longer a cradle song, it no longer makes him get drunk, weep, and sleep." He cleared his voice again and started:

"*Vor der Kaserne, vor dem grossen Tor. . . .*"

Without needing to move his body, the champion lifted an arm from his hip and struck Orsini's jaw with his open hand. An old tradition stopped him from using his fists, except in desperate circumstances. He held up the prince's body with his other arm and stretched him out on the bed.

The heat of the night and of the fiesta had made people open their windows. The jazz for dancing now seemed to originate from the hotel itself, from the center of the darkened room.

VI. THE PRINCE'S STORY

It was a town rising from the river in September, give or take five inches south of the equator. I woke up, with no pain, in the hotel-room morning filled with light and heat. Jacob was massaging my stomach and laughing to speed on its way a stream of insults that culminated in a single one that he repeated until I could no longer pretend to be asleep and drew myself up.

"Old pig," he was saying in his purest German, maybe in Prussian.

The sun was already licking the leg of the table and I thought sadly that nothing could be saved from the wreck. At least—I began to remember—that's what I should think, and my expression and my words should adjust themselves to this sadness. Van Oppen must have foreseen something of this because he made me drink a glass of orange juice and put a lighted cigarette in my mouth.

"Old pig," he said as he filled his lungs with smoke.

It was Saturday morning and we were still in Santa Maria. I moved my head, looked at him, and made a rapid balance sheet of his smile, his gaiety, and his friendship. He had put on his expensive gray suit and his antelope-skin shoes; a Stetson hat was tilted against the nape of his neck. I suddenly thought that he was right, that life was always right in the end, that defeats and victories didn't matter.

"Yes," I said, withdrawing my hand from his, "I am an old pig. The years pass and things get worse and worse. Is there a fight today?"

"Yes," he nodded enthusiastically. "I told you they would come back and they did."

I sucked at my cigarette and stretched myself out on the bed. It was enough to see the smile to realize that Jacob had won, even if he had his spine broken that hot Saturday night, as anyone could foresee. He had to win in three minutes; but I was getting more money. I sat up in the bed and kneaded my jaw.

"The fight is on," I said, "the champion decides. Unfortunately, the manager no longer has anything to say. But neither a bottle nor a blow can abolish facts."

Van Oppen began to laugh and his hat fell on the bed.

"Neither a bottle nor a blow," I insisted. "The fact still remains that, as of now, the champion hasn't enough wind to support a fight, a real effort, for more than a minute. That's a fact. The champion won't be able to throw the Turk. The champion will die a mysterious death at the fifty-ninth second. The autopsy will tell. I believe we agree, at least, on that."

"Yes, we agree on that. No more than one minute," van Oppen assented, sounding young and gay again. The morning was now filling the entire room, and I felt humiliated by my sleepiness, by my objections, by my bathrobe weighed down by the unloaded gun.

"And the fact is," I said slowly, as if trying to take

revenge, "that we haven't got the five hundred pesos. Of course, everybody agrees, the Turk can't win. But we still have to deposit the five hundred and it's already Saturday. All we have left is the bus money and enough for a week in the capital. After that, we're in God's hands."

Jacob picked up his hat and started to laugh again. He was shaking his head like a father sitting on a park bench with his diffident little son.

"Money," he said without asking. "Money for the deposit? Five hundred pesos?"

He passed me another lighted cigarette and put his left foot, the more sensitive one, on the little table. He undid the knot of the gray shoe, took it off, and came over to show me a roll of green bank notes. It was real money. He gave me five ten-dollar bills and could not resist showing off:

"More?"

"No," I said. "It's more than enough."

A lot of money went back to the shoe: between three and five hundred dollars.

And so I changed the money at noon. Since the champion had disappeared—his initialed sweater did not show up that morning for the trot down the Promenade—I went to the Plaza Restaurant and ate like a gentleman, something I hadn't done for a long time. I had a coffee, prepared on my table, the appropriate liqueurs and a cigar, very dry but smokable.

I finished off the luncheon with a tip usually lavished by drunkards or crooks and called the hotel. The champion wasn't there; the rest of the afternoon was cool and gay; Santa Maria was going to have a great evening. I left the newspaper's telephone number with the receptionist so that Jacob could call me about our going to the Apollo together and a little while later sat down at the *El Liberal* morgue with Sports Section and two more faces. I showed them the money.

"So that there should be no doubt. But I'd prefer to hand it out in the ring—whether van Oppen dies of a syncope or has to make a contribution to the Turk's wake."

We played poker—I lost and won—until they informed me that van Oppen was already at the Apollo. It was still more than half an hour before nine; but we put on our jackets and piled into some old cars to drive the few town blocks that separated us from the cinema, giving the occasion an accent of carnival, or the ridiculous.

I went in through the back door and made my way to the room littered with newspapers and photographs and furiously invaded by smells of urine and rancid paste. There I found Jacob. Wearing his sky-blue trunks—the color chosen in honor of Santa Maria—and his world championship belt that glittered like gold, he was doing setting-up exercises. One look at him, at his childish, clean, and expressionless eyes, at the short curve of his smile, was enough to convince me that he didn't want to talk to me, that he wanted no prologues, nothing that would separate him from what he was determined to be and to remember.

I sat down on a bench, without bothering to listen whether or not he answered my greeting, and lit a cigarette. Now, at this moment, in a few minutes, the story would reach its grand finale. The story of the world's wrestling champion. But there would be other stories, too—and an explanation for *El Liberal*, for Santa Maria, for the neighboring towns.

"A passing physical indisposition" looked better to me than "excessive training blamed for Champion's failure." But they wouldn't print the capital C tomorrow, nor the ambiguous headline. Van Oppen was still doing his setting-up exercises, and I lit another cigarette from the first to neutralize the odor of ammonia, not forgetting that clean air is the first condition of a gymnasium.

Jacob was bobbing up and down as if he were alone in the room. He moved his arms horizontally and seemed both thinner and heavier. Through the loathsome smell, to which his sweat added its contribution, I tried to hear him breathe. The noises from the theater also penetrated into the stinking room. Maybe the champion had wind for a minute and a half, but never for two or three. The Turk would remain standing until the bell rang, with his furious black mustache, with the chaste knee-length pants that I expected him to wear (and I wasn't wrong), with his small, hard fiancée howling with triumph and rage near the Apollo stage and its threadbare rug that I insisted calling "the mat." There was no hope left, we would never rescue the five hundred pesos. The noises of the impatient mob that filled the theater grew louder and louder.

"We must go now," I said to the corpse doing its calisthenics. It was exactly nine by my watch; I left the bad smell behind me and walked through darkened corridors to the ticket office. By quarter past nine I had checked and signed the accounts. I returned to the smelly room—the roar indicated that van Oppen was already in the ring—and took off my jacket, after depositing the money in a pocket of my trousers. Then I made my way back through the corridors, reached the theater, and went up on the stage. They showered me with applause and insults, which I acknowledged with nods and smiles, knowing that at least seventy of those present hadn't paid for their ticket. In any case, I would never get my fifty percent from them.

I took off Jacob's robe, crossed the ring to salute the Turk, and had time for only two more clown's tricks.

The bell rang and it became impossible not to breathe and understand the odor of the crowd that filled the Apollo. The bell rang and I left Jacob alone, much more alone and forever than I had left him at so many other daybreaks, on street corners, and in bars, when I began to feel sleepy or bored. The bad thing was that when I left him to occupy my special seat that night I felt neither sleepy nor bored. The first bell was to clear the ring; the second to start the fight. Greased, almost young, without showing his weary weight, Jacob circled, crouching, until he reached the center of the ring and waited with an expectant smile.

Jacob opened his arms and waited for the Turk, who seemed to have grown bigger in the meantime. He waited with a smile until he came close, then made a step back and advanced again for the clinch. Against all rules, he kept his arms up for ten seconds. Then he steadied his legs and turned; he put one hand on the challenger's back and the other, and his forearm as well, against a thigh. I didn't understand this and never understood it for the exact half a minute that the fight lasted. Then I saw that the Turk was flying from the ring, sailing with an effort through the howls of the people of Santa Maria and disappearing into the darkness of the back rows.

He had flown with his big mustache, with his legs flexing absurdly to find support and stability in the dirty air. I saw him sail close to the roof, among the search lights, maneuvering with his arms. The fight hadn't lasted fifty seconds yet and the champion had won—or hadn't, depending on the way you looked at it. I climbed into the ring to help him with the robe. Jacob was smiling like a child; he didn't hear the shouts and the insults of the public, the growing clamor. He was sweating, but not much, and as soon as I heard him breathe I knew that his fatigue came from nerves, not from physical weariness.

Pieces of wood and empty bottles were now thrown into the ring; I had my speech ready and the exaggerated smile for foreigners. But the missiles kept flying and I couldn't be heard above the din.

Then the cops moved in with enthusiasm, as if they had never done anything else from the day they got their jobs. Directed or not, they scattered and organized themselves properly and started knocking heads with their flashing night sticks until all that were left in the Apollo were the champion, the referee, and I in the ring; the cops in the hall; and the poor half-dead boy of twenty, hanging over two chairs. It was then that the little woman, the fiancée appeared from God knows where—I know even less than others—at the side of the Turk. She started to spit on the loser and to kick him, while I congratulated Jacob with all due modesty and the nurses or doctors carrying the stretcher appeared in the doorway.

Translated by Izaak A. Langnas

The Beautiful Soul of Don Damián

JUAN BOSCH

Don Damián, with a temperature of almost 104, passed into a coma. His soul felt extremely uncomfortable, almost as if it were being roasted alive; therefore it began to withdraw, gathering itself into his heart. The soul had an infinite number of tentacles, like an octopus with innumerable feet, some of them in the veins and others, very thin, in the smaller blood vessels. Little by little it pulled out those feet, with the result that Don Damián turned cold and pallid. His hands grew cold first, then his arms and legs, while his face became so deathly white that the change was observed by the people who stood around his bed. The nurse, alarmed, said it was time to send for the doctor. The soul heard her, and thought: "I'll have to hurry, or the doctor will make me stay in here till I burn to a crisp."

It was dawn. A faint trickle of light came in through the window to announce the birth of a new day. The soul, peering out of Don Damián's mouth, which was partly open to let in a little air, noticed the light and told itself that if it hoped to escape it would have to act promptly, because in a few minutes somebody would see it and prevent it from leaving its master's body. The soul of Don Damián was quite ignorant about certain matters: for instance, it had no idea that once free it would be completely invisible.

There was a rustling of skirts around the patient's luxurious bed, and a murmur of voices which the soul had to ignore, occupied as it was in escaping from its prison. The nurse came back into the room with a hypodermic syringe in her hand.

"Dear God, dear God," the old housemaid cried, "don't let it be too late!"

It was too late. At the precise moment that the needle punctured Don Damián's forearm, the soul drew its last tentacles out of his mouth, reflecting as it did so that the injection would be a waste of money. An instant later there were cries and running footsteps, and as somebody—no doubt the housemaid, since it could hardly have been Don Damián's wife or mother-in-law—began to wail at the bedside, the soul leaped into the air, straight up to the Bohemian glass lamp that hung in the middle of the ceiling. There it collected its wits and looked down: Don Damián's corpse was now a spoiled yellow, with features almost as hard and transparent as the Bohemian glass; the bones of his face seemed to have grown, and his skin had taken on a ghastly sheen. His wife, his mother-in-law, and the nurse fluttered around him, while the housemaid sobbed with her gray head buried in the covers. The soul knew exactly what each one of them was thinking and feeling, but it did not want to waste time observing them. The light was growing brighter every moment, and it was afraid it would be noticed up there on its perch. Suddenly the mother-in-law took her daughter by the arm and led her out into the hall, to talk to her in a low voice. The soul heard her say, "Don't behave so shamelessly. You've got to show some grief."

"When people start coming, Mama," the daughter whispered.

"No. Right now. Don't forget the nurse—she'll tell everybody everything that happens."

The new widow ran to the bed as if mad with grief. "Oh Damián, Damián!" she cried. "Damián, my dearest, how can I live without you?"

A different, less worldly soul would have been astounded, but Don Damián's merely admired the way she was playing the part. Don Damián himself had done some skillful acting on occasion, especially when it was necessary to act—as he put it—"in defense of my interests." His wife was now "defending her interests." She was still young and attractive, whereas Don Damián was well past sixty. She had had a lover when he first knew her, and his soul had suffered some very disagreeable moments because of its late master's jealousy. The soul recalled an episode of a few months earlier, when the wife had declared, "You can't stop me from seeing him. You know perfectly well I married you for your money."

To which Don Damián had replied that with his money he had purchased the right not to be made ridiculous. It was a thoroughly unpleasant scene—the mother-in-law had interfered, as usual, and there were threats of a divorce—but it was made even more unpleasant by the fact that the discussion had to be cut short when some important guests arrived. Both husband and wife greeted the company with charming smiles and exquisite manners, which only the soul could appreciate at their true value.

The soul was still up there on the lamp, recalling these events, when the priest arrived almost at a run. Nobody could imagine why he should appear at that hour, because the sun was scarcely up and anyhow he had visited the sick man during the night. He attempted to explain.

"I had a premonition. I was afraid Don Damián would pass away without confessing."

The mother-in-law was suspicious. "But, Father, didn't he confess last night?"

She was referring to the fact that the priest had been alone with Don Damián, behind a closed door, for nearly an hour. Everybody assumed that the sick man had confessed, but that was not what took place. The soul knew it was not, of course; it also knew why the priest had arrived at such a strange time. The theme of that long conference had been rather arid, spiritually: the priest wanted Don Damián to leave a large sum of money toward the new church being built in the city, while Don Damián wanted to leave an even larger sum than that which the priest was seeking—but to a hospital. They could not agree, the priest left, and when he returned to his room he discovered that his watch was missing.

The soul overwhelmed by its new power, now it was free, to know things that had taken place in its absence, and to divine what people were thinking or were about to do. It was aware that the priest had said to himself: "I remember I took out my watch at Don Damián's house, to see what time it was. I must have left it there." Hence it was also aware that his return visit had nothing to do with the Kingdom of Heaven.

"No, he didn't confess," the priest said, looking straight at the mother-in-law. "We didn't get around to a confession last night, so we decided I would come back the first thing in the morning, to hear confession and perhaps"—his voice grew solemn—"to administer the last rites. Unfortunately I've come too late." He glanced toward the gilt tables on either side of the bed in hopes of seeing his watch on one or the other.

The old housemaid, who had served Don Damián for more than forty years, looked up with streaming eyes.

"It doesn't make any difference," she said, "God forgive me for saying so. He had such a beautiful soul he didn't need to confess." She nodded her head. "Don Damián had a very beautiful soul."

Hell, now, that *was* something! The soul had never even dreamed that it was beautiful. Its master had done some rather rare things in his day, of course, and since he had always been a fine example of a well-to-do gentleman, perfectly dressed and exceedingly shrewd in his dealings with the bank, his soul had not had time to think about its beauty or its possible ugliness. It remembered, for instance, how its master had commanded it to feel at ease after he and his lawyer found a way to take possession of a debtor's house, although the debtor had nowhere else to live; or when, with the help of jewels and hard cash (this last for her education, or her sick mother), he persuaded a lovely young girl from the poorer sector to visit him in the sumptuous apartment he maintained. But *was* it beautiful, or was it ugly?

The soul was quite sure that only a few moments had passed since it withdrew from its master's veins; and probably even less time had passed than it imagined, because everything had happened so quickly and in so much confusion. The doctor had said as he left, well before midnight: "The fever is likely to rise toward morning. If it does, watch him carefully, and send for me if anything happens."

Was the soul to let itself be roasted to death? Its vital center, if that is the proper term, had been located close to Don Damián's intestines, which were radiating fire, and if it had stayed in his body it would have perished like a broiled chicken. But actually how much time had passed since it left? Very little, certainly, for it still felt hot, in spite of the faint coolness in the dawn air. The soul decided that the change in climate between the innards of its late master and the Bohemian glass of the lamp had been very slight. But change or no change, what about that statement by the old housemaid? "Beautiful," she said ... and she was a truthful woman who loved her master because she loved him, not because he was rich or generous or important. The soul found rather less sincerity in the remarks that followed.

"Why, of course he had a beautiful soul," the priest said.

"'Beautiful' doesn't begin to describe it," the mother-in-law asserted.

The soul turned to look at her and saw that as she spoke she was signaling to her daughter with her eyes. They contained both a command and a scolding, as if to say: "Start crying again, you idiot. Do you want the priest to say you were happy your husband died?" The daughter understood the signal, and broke out into tearful wailing.

"Nobody ever had such a beautiful soul! Damián, how much I loved you!"

The soul could not stand any more: it wanted to know for certain, without losing another moment, whether or not it was truly beautiful, and it wanted to get away from those hypocrites. It leaped in the direction of the bathroom, where there was a full-length mirror, calculating the distance so as to fall noiselessly on the rug. It did not know it was weightless as well as invisible. It was delighted to find that nobody noticed it, and ran quickly to look at itself in front of the mirror.

But good God, what had happened? In the first place, it had been accustomed, during more than sixty years, to look out through the eyes of Don Damián, and those eyes were over five feet from the ground; also, it was accustomed to seeing his lively face, his clear eyes, his shining gray hair, the arrogance that puffed out his chest and lifted his head, the expensive clothes in which he dressed. What it saw now was nothing at all like that, but a strange figure hardly a foot tall, pale, cloud-gray, with no definite form. Where it should have had two legs and two feet like the body of Don Damián, it was a hideous cluster of tentacles like those of an octopus, but irregular, some shorter than others, some thinner, and all of them seemingly made of dirty smoke, of some impalpable mud that looked transparent but was not; they were limp and drooping and powerless, and stupendously ugly. The soul of Don Damián felt lost. Nevertheless, it got up the courage to look higher. It had no waist. In fact, it had no body, no neck, nothing: where the tentacles joined there was merely a sort of ear sticking out on one side, looking like a bit of rotten apple peel, and a clump of rough hairs on the other side, some twisted, some straight. But that was not the worst, and neither was the strange grayish-yellow light it gave off: the worst was the fact that its mouth was a shapeless cavity like a hole poked in a rotten fruit, a horrible and sickening thing ... and in the depths of this hole an eye shone, its only eye, staring out of the shadows with an expression of terror and treachery! Yet the women and the priest in the next room, around the bed in which Don Damián's corpse lay, had said he had a beautiful soul!

"How can I go out in the street looking like this?" it asked itself, groping in a black tunnel of confusion.

What should it do? The doorbell rang. Then the nurse said: "It's the doctor, ma'am. I'll let him in."

Don Damián's wife promptly began to wail again, invoking her dead husband and lamenting the cruel solitude in which he had left her.

The soul, paralyzed in front of its true image, knew it was lost. It had been used to hiding in its refuge in the tall body of Don Damián; it had been used to everything, including the obnoxious smell of the intestines, the heat of the stomach, the annoyance of chills and fevers. Then it heard the doctor's greeting and the mother-in-law's voice crying: "Oh, Doctor, what a tragedy it is!"

"Come, now, let's get a grip on ourselves."

The soul peeped into the dead man's room. The women were gathered around the bed, and the priest was praying at its foot. The soul measured the distance and jumped, with a facility it had not known it had, landing on the pillow like a thing of air or like a strange animal that could move noiselessly and invisibly. Don Damián's mouth was still partly open. It was cold as ice, but that was not important. The soul tumbled inside and began to thrust its tentacles into place. It was still settling in when it heard the doctor say to the mother-in-law: "Just one moment, please."

The soul could still see the doctor, though not clearly. He approached the body of Don Damián, took his wrist, seemed to grow excited, put his ear to his chest and left it there a moment. Then he opened his bag and took out a stethoscope. With great deliberation he fitted the knobs into his ears and placed the button on the spot where Don Damián's heart was. He grew even more excited, put away the stethoscope, and took out a hypodermic syringe. He told the nurse to fill it, while he himself fastened a small rubber tube around Don Damián's arm above the elbow, working with the air of a magician who is about to perform a sensational trick. Apparently these preparations alarmed the old housemaid.

"But why are you doing all that if the poor thing is dead?"

The doctor stared at her loftily, and what he said was intended not only for her but for everybody.

"Science is science, and my obligation is to do whatever I can to bring Don Damián back to life. You don't find souls as beautiful as his just anywhere, and I can't let him die until we've tried absolutely everything."

This brief speech, spoken so calmly and grandly, upset the wife. It was not difficult to note a cold glitter in her eyes and a certain quaver in her voice.

"But . . . but isn't he dead?"

The soul was almost back in its body again, and only three tentacles still groped for the old veins they had inhabited for so many years. The attention with which it directed these tentacles into their right places did not prevent it from hearing that worried question.

The doctor did not answer. He took Don Damián's forearm and began to chafe it with his hand. The soul felt the warmth of life surrounding it, penetrating it, filling the veins it had abandoned to escape from burning up. At the same moment, the doctor jabbed the needle into a vein in the arm, untied the ligature above the elbow, and began to push the plunger. Little by little, in soft surges, the warmth of life rose to Don Damián's skin.

"A miracle," the priest murmured. Suddenly he turned pale and let his imagination run wild. The contribution to the new church would now be a sure thing. He would point out to Don Damián, during his convalescence, how he had returned from the dead because of the prayers he had said for him. He would tell him. "The Lord heard me, Don Damián, and gave you back to us." How could he deny the contribution after that?

The wife, just as suddenly, felt that her brain had gone blank. She looked nervously at her husband's face and turned toward her mother. They were both stunned, mute, almost terrified.

The doctor, however, was smiling. He was thoroughly satisfied with himself, although he attempted not to show it.

"He's saved, he's saved," the old housemaid cried, "thanks to God and you." She was weeping and clutching the doctor's hands. "He's saved, he's alive again. Don Damián can never pay you for what you've done."

The doctor was thinking that Don Damián had more than enough money to pay him, but that is not what he said. What he said was: "I'd have done the same thing even if he didn't have a penny. It was my duty, my duty to society, to save a soul as beautiful as his."

He was speaking to the housemaid, but again his words were intended for the others, in the hope they would repeat them to the sick man as soon as he was well enough to act on them.

The soul of Don Damián, tired of so many lies, decided to sleep. A moment later, Don Damián sighed weakly and moved his head on the pillow.

"He'll sleep for hours now," the doctor said. "He must have absolute quiet."

And to set a good example, he tiptoed out of the room.

Translated by Lysander Kemp

The Tree

MARÍA-LUISA BOMBAL

The pianist sits down, coughs affectedly and concentrates for a moment. The cluster of lights illuminating the hall slowly diminishes to a soft, warm glow, as a musical phrase begins to rise in the silence, and to develop, clear, restrained and judiciously capricious.

"Mozart, perhaps," thinks Brigida. As usual, she has forgotten to ask for the program. "Mozart, perhaps, or Scarlatti." She knew so little music! And it wasn't because she had no ear for it, or interest. As a child it was she who had demanded piano lessons; no one needed to force them on her, as with her sisters. Her sisters, however, played correctly now and read music at sight, while she ... She had given up her studies the year she began them. The reason for her inconsistency was as simple as it was shameful; she had never succeeded in learning the key of F—never. "I don't understand; my memory only reaches to the key of G." How indignant her father was! "I'd give anyone this job of being a man alone with several daughters to bring up! Poor Carmen! She surely must have suffered because of Brigida. This child is retarded."

Brigida was the youngest of six girls, all different in character. When the father finally reached his sixth daughter, he was so perplexed and tired out by the first five that he preferred to simplify matters by declaring her retarded. "I'm not going to struggle any longer; it's useless. Let her be. If she won't study, all right. If she likes to spend time in the kitchen listening to ghost stories, that's up to her. If she likes dolls at sixteen, let her play with them." And Brigida had kept her dolls and remained completely ignorant.

How pleasant it is to be ignorant! Not to know exactly who Mozart was, to ignore his origin, his influence, the details of his technique! To just let him lead one by the hand, as now.

And, indeed, Mozart is leading her. He leads her across a bridge suspended over a crystalline stream which runs in a bed of rosy sand. She is dressed in white, with a lace parasol—intricate and fine as a spider web—open over her shoulder.

"You look younger every day, Brigida. I met your husband yesterday, your ex-husband, I mean. His hair is all white."

But she doesn't answer, she doesn't stop, she continues to cross the bridge which Mozart has improvised for her to the garden of her youthful years when she was eighteen: tall fountains in which the water sings; her chestnut braids, which when undone reach her ankles, her golden complexion, her dark eyes opened wide and as if questioning; a small mouth with full lips, a sweet smile and the slenderest and most graceful body in the world. What was she thinking about as she sat on the edge of the fountain? Nothing. "She is as stupid as she is pretty," they said. But it never mattered to her that she was stupid, or awkward at dances. One by one, her sisters were asked to marry. No one proposed to her.

Mozart! Now he offers her a staircase of blue marble which she descends, between a double row of lilies of ice. And now he opens for her a gate of thick iron bars with gilded points so that she can throw herself on the neck of Luis, her father's close friend. Ever since she was a very small child, when they all abandoned her, she would run to Luis. He would pick her up and she would put her arms around his neck, laughing with little warbling sounds, and shower him with kisses like a downpour of rain, haphazardly, upon his eyes, forehead and hair, already gray (had he ever been young?).

"You are a garland," Luis would say to her. "You are like a garland of birds."

That is why she married him. Because, with that solemn and taciturn man, she didn't feel guilty of being as she was: silly, playful and lazy. Yes; now that so many years have passed she understands that she did not marry Luis for love; nevertheless, she doesn't quite understand why, why she went away one day, suddenly ...

But at this point Mozart takes her nervously by the hand, and dragging her along at a pace which becomes more urgent by the second, compels her to cross the garden in the opposite direction, to recross the bridge at a run, almost in headlong flight. And after having deprived her of the parasol and the transparent skirt, he closes the door of her past with a chord at once gentle and firm, and leaves her in a concert hall, dressed in black, mechanically applauding while the artificial lights are turned up.

Once more the half-shadow, and once more the foreboding silence.

And now Beethoven's music begins to surge under a spring moon. How far the sea has withdrawn! Brigida walks across the beach toward the sea now recoiled in the distance, shimmering and calm, but then, the sea swells, slowly grows, comes to meet her, envelops her, and with gentle waves, gradually pushes her, pushes her until it makes her rest her cheek upon the body of a man. And then it recedes, leaving her forgotten upon Luis' breast.

"You don't have a heart, you don't have a heart," she used to say to Luis. Her husband's heart beat so deep inside that she could rarely hear it, and then only in an unexpected way. "You are never with me when you are beside me," she protested in the bedroom when he ritually opened the evening papers before going to sleep. "Why did you marry me?"

"Because you have the eyes of a frightened little doe," he answered and kissed her. And she, suddenly happy, proudly received upon her shoulder the weight of his gray head. Oh, his shiny, silver hair!

"Luis, you have never told me exactly what color your hair was when you were a boy, and you have never told me either what your mother said when you began to get gray at fifteen. What did she say? Did she laugh? Did she cry? And were you proud or ashamed? And at school, your friends, what did they say? Tell me, Luis, tell me . . ."

"Tomorrow I'll tell you. I'm sleepy, Brigida. I'm very tired. Turn off the light."

Unconsciously he moved away from her to fall asleep, and she unconsciously pursued her husband's shoulder all night long, sought his breath. She tried to live beneath his breath, like a plant shut up and thirsty which stretches out its branches in search of a more favorable climate.

In the morning, when the maid opened the blinds, Luis was no longer at her side. He had got up cautiously and had left without saying good morning to her for fear of his "garland of birds," who insisted on vehemently holding him back by the shoulders. "Five minutes, just five minutes. Your office won't disappear because you stay five minutes longer with me, Luis."

Her awakenings. Ah, how sad her awakenings! But—it was strange—scarcely did she step into her dressing room than her sadness vanished, as if by magic.

Waves toss and break very far away, murmuring like a sea of leaves. Is it Beethoven? No.

It is the tree close to the window of the dressing

room. It was enough for her to enter to feel a wonderfully pleasant sensation circulating within her. How hot it always was in the bedroom in the mornings! And what a harsh light! Here, on the other hand, in the dressing room, even one's eyes were rested, refreshed. The drab cretonnes, the tree that cast shadows on the walls like rippling, cold water, the mirrors that reflected the foliage and receded into an infinite, green forest. How pleasant that room was! It seemed like a world submerged in an aquarium. How that huge gum tree chattered! All the birds of the neighborhood came to take shelter in it. It was the only tree on that narrow, sloping street which dropped down directly to the river from one corner of the city.

"I'm busy. I can't accompany you. I have a lot to do, I won't make it for lunch. Hello, yes, I'm at the Club. An engagement. Have your dinner and go to bed. . . . No. I don't know. You better not wait for me, Brigida."

"If only I had some girl friends!" she sighed. But everybody was bored with her. If she only would try to be a little less stupid! But how to gain at one stroke so much lost ground? To be intelligent you should begin from childhood, shouldn't you?

Her sisters, however, were taken everywhere by their husbands, but Luis—why shouldn't she confess it to herself?—was ashamed of her, of her ignorance, her timidity and even her eighteen years. Had he not asked her to say that she was twenty-one, as if her extreme youth were a secret defect?

And at night, how tired he always was when he went to bed! He never listened to everything she said. He did smile at her, with a smile which she knew was mechanical. He showered her with caresses from which he was absent. Why do you suppose he had married her? To keep up a habit, perhaps to strengthen the friendly relationship with her father. Perhaps life consisted, for men, of a series of ingrained habits. If one should be broken, probably confusion, failure would result.

And then they would begin to wander through the streets of the city, to sit on the benches of the public squares, each day more poorly dressed and with longer beards. Luis' life, therefore, consisted in filling every minute of the day with some activity. Why hadn't she understood it before! Her father was right when he declared her backward.

"I should like to see it snow some time, Luis."

"This summer I'll take you to Europe, and since it will be winter there, you'll be able to see it snow."

"I know it is winter in Europe when it is summer here. I'm not that ignorant!"

Sometimes, as if to awaken him to the emotion of real love, she would throw herself upon her husband and cover him with kisses, weeping, calling him Luis, Luis, Luis . . .

"What? What's the matter with you? What do you want?"

"Nothing."

"Why do you call me that way then?"

"No reason, just to call you. I like to call you." And he would smile, taking kindly to that new game.

Summer arrived, her first summer since she was married. New duties kept Luis from offering her the promised trip.

"Brigida, the heat is going to be terrible this summer in Buenos Aires. Why don't you go to the farm with your father?"

"Alone?"

"I would go to see you every week on weekends."

She had sat down on the bed, ready to insult him. But she sought in vain for cutting words to shout at him. She didn't know anything, anything at all. Not even how to insult.

"What's the matter with you? What are you thinking about, Brigida?"

For the first time Luis had retraced his steps and bent over her, uneasy, letting the hour of arrival at his office pass by.

"I'm sleepy . . ." Brigida had replied childishly, while she hid her face in the pillows.

For the first time he had called her from the Club at lunchtime. But she had refused to go to the telephone, furiously wielding that weapon she had found without thinking: silence.

That same evening she ate opposite her husband without raising her eyes, all her nerves taut.

"Are you still angry, Brigida?"

But she did not break the silence.

"You certainly know that I love you, my garland. But I can't be with you all the time. I'm a very busy man. One reaches my age a slave to a thousand duties."

". . ."

"Do you want to go out tonight?"

". . ."

"You don't want to? Patience. Tell me, did Roberto call from Montevideo?"

". . ."

"What a pretty dress! Is it new?"

". . ."

"Is it new, Brigida? Answer, answer me . . ."

But she did not break the silence this time either. And immediately the unexpected, the astonishing, the absurd happened. Luis gets up from his chair, throws the napkin violently on the table and leaves the house, slamming doors behind him.

She had got up in her turn, stunned, trembling with indignation at such injustice. "And I, and I," she murmured confused; "I who for almost a year . . . when for the first time I allow myself one reproach . . . Oh, I'm going away, I'm going away this very night! I shall never set foot in this house again. . . ." And she furiously opened the closets of her dressing room, crazily threw the clothes on the floor.

It was then that someone rapped with his knuckles on the window panes.

She had run, she knew not how or with what unaccustomed courage, to the window. She had opened it. It was the tree, the gum tree which a great gust of wind was shaking, which was hitting the glass with its branches, which summoned her from outside as if she should see it writhing like an impetuous black flame beneath the fiery sky of that summer evening.

A heavy shower would soon beat against its cold leaves. How delightful! All night long she could hear the rain pattering, trickling through the leaves of the gum tree as if along the ducts of a thousand imaginary gutters. All night long she would hear the old trunk of the gum tree creak and groan, telling her of the storm, while she snuggled up very close to Luis, voluntarily shivering between the sheets of the big bed.

Handfuls of pearls that rain abundantly upon a silver roof. Chopin. *Etudes* by Fréderic Chopin.

How many weeks did she wake up suddenly, very early, when she scarcely perceived that her husband, now also stubbornly silent, had slipped out of bed?

The dressing room: the window wide open, an odor of river and pasture floating in that kindly room, and the mirrors veiled by a halo of mist.

Chopin and the rain that slips through the leaves of the gum tree with the noise of a hidden waterfall that seems to drench even the roses of the cretonnes, become intermingled in her agitated nostalgia.

What does one do in the summertime when it rains so much? Stay in one's room the whole day feigning convalescence or sadness? Luis had entered timidly one afternoon. He had sat down very stiffly. There was a silence.

"Brigida, then it is true? You no longer love me?"

She had become happy all of a sudden, stupidly.

She might have cried out: "No, no; I love you, Luis; I love you," if he had given her time, if he had not added, almost immediately, with his habitual calm: "In any case, I don't think it is wise for us to separate, Brigida. It is necessary to think it over a great deal."

Her impulses subsided as abruptly as they had arisen. Why become excited uselessly! Luis loved her with tenderness and moderation; if some time he should come to hate her he would hate her justly and prudently. And that was life. She approached the window, rested her forehead against the icy glass. There was the gum tree calmly receiving the rain that struck it, softly and steadily. The room stood still in the shadow, orderly and quiet. Everything seemed to come to a stop, eternal and very noble. That was life. And there was a certain greatness in accepting it as it was, mediocre, as something definitive, irremediable. And from the depths of things there seemed to issue, and to rise, a melody of grave, slow words to which she stood listening: "Always." "Never" . . . And thus the hours, the days and the years go by. Always! Never! Life, life!

On regaining her bearings, she realized that her husband had slipped out of the room. Always! Never! . . .

And the rain, secretly and constantly, continued to murmur in the music of Chopin.

Summer tore the leaves from its burning calendar. Luminous and blinding pages fell like golden swords, pages of an unwholesome humidity like the breath of the swamps; pages of brief and violent storm, and pages of hot wind, of the wind that brings the "carnation of the air" and hangs it in the immense gum tree.

Children used to play hide-and-seek among the enormous twisted roots that raised the paving stones of the sidewalk, and the tree was filled with laughter and whispering. Then she appeared at the window and clapped her hands; the children dispersed, frightened, without noticing the smile of a girl who also wanted to take part in the game.

Alone, she would lean for a long time on her elbows at the window watching the trembling of the foliage—some breeze always blew along that street which ran straight to the river—and it was like sinking one's gaze in shifting water or in the restless fire of a hearth. One could spend one's idle hours this way, devoid of all thought, in a stupor of well-being.

Scarcely did the room begin to fill with the haze of twilight when she lit the first lamp, and the first lamp shone in the mirrors, multiplied like a firefly wishing to hurry the night.

And night after night she dozed next to her husband, suffering at intervals. But when her pain increased to the point of wounding her like a knife thrust, when she was beset by too urgent a desire to awaken Luis in order to hit him or caress him, she slipped away on tiptoe to the dressing room and opened the window. The room instantly filled with discreet sounds and presences, with mysterious footfalls, the fluttering of wings, the subtle crackling of vegetation, the soft chirping of a cricket hidden under the bark of the gum tree submerged in the stars of a hot summer night.

Her fever passed as her bare feet gradually became chilled on the matting. She did not know why it was so easy for her to suffer in that room.

Chopin's melancholy linked one *étude* after another, linked one melancholy after another, imperturbably.

And autumn came. The dry leaves whirled about for a moment before rolling upon the grass of the narrow garden, upon the sidewalk of the sloping street. The leaves gave way and fell . . . The top of the gum tree remained green, but underneath, the tree turned red, darkened like the worn-out lining of a sumptuous evening cape. And the room now seemed to be submerged in a goblet of dull gold.

Lying upon the divan, she patiently waited for suppertime, for the improbable arrival of Luis. She had resumed speaking to him, she had become his wife again without enthusiasm and without anger. She no longer loved him. But she no longer suffered. On the contrary, an unexpected feeling of plenitude, of placidity had taken hold of her. Now no one or nothing could hurt her. It may be that true happiness lies in the conviction that one has irremediably lost happiness. Then we begin to move through life without hope or fear, capable of finally enjoying all the small pleasures, which are the most lasting.

A terrible din, then a flash of light throws her backward, trembling all over.

Is it the intermission? No. It is the gum tree; she knows it.

They had felled it with a single stroke of the ax. She could not hear the work that began very early in the morning. "The roots were raising the paving stones of the sidewalk and then, naturally, the neighbors' committee . . ."

Bewildered, she has lifted her hands to her eyes. When she recovers her sight she stands up and looks around her. What is she looking at? The hall suddenly lighted, the people who are dispersing? No. She has remained imprisoned in the web of her past, she cannot leave the dressing room. Her dressing room invaded by a white, terrifying light. It was as if they had ripped off the roof; a hard light came in everywhere, seeped through her pores, burned her with cold. And she saw everything in the light of that cold light; Luis, his wrinkled face, his hands crossed by coarse, discolored veins, and the cretonnes with gaudy colors. Frightened, she has run to the window. The window now opens directly on a narrow street, so narrow that her room almost strikes the front of an imposing skyscraper. On the ground floor, show windows and more show windows, full of bottles. On the street corner, a row of automobiles lined up in front of a service station painted red. Some boys in shirt sleeves are kicking a ball in the middle of the street.

And all that ugliness had entered her mirrors. Now in her mirrors there were nickel-plated balconies and shabby clotheslines and canary cages.

They had taken away her privacy, her secret; she found herself naked in the middle of the street, naked beside an old husband who turned his back on her in bed, who had given her no children. She does not understand how until then she had not wanted to have children, how she had come to submit to the idea that she was going to live without children all her life. She does not understand how she could endure for a year Luis' laughter, that overcheerful laughter, that false laughter of a man who has become skilled in laughter because it is necessary to laugh on certain occasions.

A lie! Her resignation and her serenity were a lie; she wanted love, yes, love; and trips and madness, and love, love ...

"But, Brigida, why are you going? Why did you stay?" Luis had asked.

Now she would have known how to answer him.

"The tree, Luis, the tree! They have cut down the gum tree."

Translated by Rosalie Torres-Rioseco

Tarciso

DINAH SILVEIRA DE QUEIROZ

The Vilares estate began just beyond the gray stone bridge. A few Babylon weeping willows leaned over the wall, hanging down to the dusty ground as if they sought rest from their suffering. A warm, enervating wind stirred the leaves of the upper branches and shook the windows of the house as if it meant to force them open.

The gardener, kneeling on the ground, was pulling up weeds. He did this with great care in order not to damage the flowers. Now and then he looked up at the sky. The land cried out for water, and there was nothing but that dry, ruinous wind blowing pitilessly on vegetation and on people.

The front door of the house opened and Maninha appeared, delicate, tall, and pale, her hair flying and her white dress fluttering in the wind like a wing.

"If you see an automobile coming across the bridge," she said, "shout and warn them about the ditch."

"All right," replied the gardener, "I'll warn them. Wait there a moment, miss!"

He rose to his feet, holding a bunch of red flowers.

They were so large, so swollen, so lush that they almost seemed artificial.

"These are hardy, miss. There's no wind strong enough to do them in."

Maninha smiled her thanks, took the flowers, and ran back into the house. On entering the living room, she felt the same tense, irritating atmosphere as when she had left there a few moments earlier. Her mother and father were still arguing in that special way of theirs. They continually wounded each other in a war that was at once grim and curiously restrained. No shouting, no weeping, no sudden outbursts of wrath. A cold, methodical battle in which every gesture was studied, every word measured, never wanton or passionate. Maninha passed through the room, with its dark, heavy furniture, like a light breeze all white but for the red spot of flowers in her hand. She went up the iron stairway. Down below, his eyes on his daughter, Carlos Vilares said to his wife:

"I know what those flowers are for, of course. The boy is sick, perhaps very seriously, and all you can think of to do is send your daughter to appease the saints with a gift. Maybe the boy will recover in spite of you."

Carlos said this in an ironic tone, his thin lips drawn back in what was intended as a smile. To his wife, Luisa, the words were a sort of treason. She raised her thin face and stared at him out of the corner of her eye like a bird about to attack its prey with its beak.

"They are flowers for the altar that Tarciso himself made when he was a little boy. Your son was a believer; he had peace of mind. It was you who drove him to doubt, you with your materialism and your stereotyped speeches. It wasn't my faith, it wasn't the flowers which Maninha and I placed at the feet of Our Lady, that confused the boy, that disoriented him. It was you! 'I want my son to be happier than I was, to get more pleasure out of life. Take all the money you want, my son! I never had any when I was your age. Go and have a good time. Break away from your mother's apron strings.' Just remember . . . just remember, it was you who created this crisis for Tarciso—you and your wonderful advice."

Carlos Vilares unbuttoned his jacket and strode back and forth. His steps were calm and measured.

"Yes, I explained certain things to him. Of course. I couldn't let my son be . . . effeminate. How often have I looked at the boy—almost as tall as I am, practically a grown man—and been ashamed of him, of his incredible timidity."

Luisa now turned her thin face toward her husband and fixed him with a flinty stare.

"You sacrificed the boy to your own vanity. The truth is, you suddenly sensed that Tarciso belonged to me. He was mine! None of your eloquence, none of your gross materialism, could possibly convince him. What you did was . . . criminal. Yes! I say it clearly and distinctly and I take responsibility for what I'm saying: You made the boy sick, maybe for the rest of his life!"

"There's no insanity in my family. Can you say as much? That uncle of yours who put on a priest's surplice and went out in the street begging charity for the poor! He threw his money away, he gave it to any bum he could find. The people in my family are normal."

Luisa's face twitched but her voice was firm and hard.

"You? . . . You never acted the way a father should. You showed him indecent books. . . . True, you didn't actually show them to him, you just left them around where you knew he would see them. To Tarciso, to a boy of his innocence, your whole attitude has been a continual shock. That's all that's wrong with the boy."

Carlos passed his hand through his handsome head of gray hair.

"When Dr. Laertes gets here, call me right away."

Luisa never seemed so like an aggressive bird. Her voice rose by a tone: "I called Father Nicolau. My rights are equal to yours. You think Tarciso needs a doctor. I think he needs a priest."

Her husband was about to go up the stairs.

"The poor boy! I'm sorry you had to bring Father Nicolau into this. That way of his—I don't know if it's caution or stupidity—of thinking for half an hour before he says anything. Call anybody you like, call the gardener if you want to—just so long as Dr. Laertes comes. That's the important thing."

Carlos slowly climbed the stairs. Halfway up, he passed Maninha, who was hurrying down to her mother. If he had looked at her, he would have seen that she was agitated. Just as her father entered Tarciso's room, Maninha said: "Mama, I swore I wouldn't but I'm going to tell you anyway. I know the whole thing now. He told me!"

"Did he do something ... awful when he went out? What was it? Tell me, but speak softly on account of your father."

"It's horrible, Mama. I don't think he really did it. I don't know. But he wanted to do it."

Maninha raised her eyes and looked at Tarciso's door. It was closed; there was no danger.

"It all started with some dreams he had. Do you remember when he used to stay up studying, night after night? You were angry with him, and he said he wasn't sleepy. Well, the truth is ... he didn't want to sleep. He was afraid he'd have nightmares. Mama, why should a good person like Tarciso have to suffer so?"

The doorbell rang.

"It must be the doctor," said Luisa. "Tell me the rest later."

She walked rapidly to the front of the house. To her surprise, it was Father Nicolau.

"I came as quickly ... as I could." He paused every couple of seconds to breathe. "Colonel Juliano brought me ... in his automobile. ... What is the trouble?"

He sank heavily into an easy chair before Luisa had a chance to invite him to sit down.

"This wind ... is not good for me. ... The automobile almost ... went into a ditch. ... Right afterward ... your gardener ... warned us about it."

"I'm so sorry. But fortunately it was just a scare, wasn't it? Nobody was hurt."

"True. Now tell me ... what is it? ... Something wrong? ... This young lady. ... ?"

"It's not about me," Maninha broke in. "It's about my brother Tarciso."

Luisa cut her off with an abrupt gesture.

"Tarciso has been acting strangely," she said softly to the priest. "My husband thinks he's sick. Sometimes he runs off without telling us where he's going, and after he comes back he doesn't speak to anyone for hours."

"Ah!" said Father Nicolau. "So Tarciso ... who used to play mass ... when he was little ... runs off mysteriously?"

"We think ... there may be a girl."

"We think he may be having an affair," said Maninha with the gravity of an older sister.

The priest smiled.

"That must be it . . . an excess of adolescent love. ... Maybe petting ... too much petting."

"Mama, can I speak now? Can I tell Father Nicolau?"

"Certainly, Maninha, but softly. Your father might hear you."

"Father Nicolau," Maninha began, "it's a dreadful thing. I don't know how to start."

"My child, imagine ... that you are at the confessional. ... Don't be afraid."

"It's Tarciso's nightmares. At the beginning he always made an effort and woke himself up. ... But after a while he just let himself go on and dream. It was horrible."

Her frightened eyes looked at the priest, then at her mother, then at the priest again.

"He saw men with open sores all over them. Men with no faces. Some with flesh hanging from their bare bones like rags. He saw swollen legs, gangrenous legs. He saw lips eaten away by sores. He saw growths with pus dripping from them. And the worst . . ."

Maninha's eyes were now dim with tears.

". . . the worst of it is that Tarciso liked it all. I wish I could understand. He said to me: 'Maninha, I don't want to keep any secrets from you.' Can I tell you exactly what he said, Father Nicolau, can I tell you no matter how bad it was? He said: 'Not one of those pictures in the books that it's a sin to look at attracted me so much. Instead of feeling sick, I wanted to touch those sores . . . to kiss them . . . to plunge my fingers into the pus.' "

There was a silence. Then Maninha went on, "Tarciso says that at the beginning he didn't feel that way. He saw those horrible men in front of him . . ."

Luisa pressed her lips together. Then she said in a low, distracted voice: "My poor little boy!"

Father Nicolau had turned red. He was breathing very hard and seemed on the verge of apoplexy.

"And then?" he said with difficulty.

The sound of an opening door could be heard.

"Afterward, the dreams began to get confused: those men full of sores were becoming very small, very small, and Tarciso felt big and strong. They put their skeleton arms around him and asked for charity or something. Tarciso didn't know exactly what. 'Don't leave us! Don't leave us!' they shouted. And Tarciso was glad to let them hug and kiss him; he wanted to kiss them too. He had a crazy desire to be like them, to be one of them. My brother couldn't explain just how he felt, just what that terrible attraction was. . . . But suddenly he got scared, he ran away. And the little men with their sores ran after him like a crowd of horrible dwarfs. They kept grabbing at his legs ..."

"So that's what it was!" Carlos, very pale, was standing before Maninha.

"Tell your father," he said. "I've got to know. I have to ... Nothing will happen. I won't do anything. But I have to know. Why should Father Nicolau know more about what goes on in this house than I do? Why do you all hide things from me? Come now, speak!"

"That's all there is to tell, Papa. Except that on the mornings after those terrible dreams, Tarciso ... wanted to go to church."

Carlos shook his head angrily.

"I'm not surprised. Go on."

"When he got to the church stairs, he would just stand there looking at the beggars. They fascinated him. You know, that woman with erysipelas, with the swollen leg; the man with a big sore instead of a nose. ... Tarciso stood there looking at them. Inside him he felt a desire to kiss them, to feel the sore with his fingers, to caress the sick leg. Then he would turn and run, saying, 'Dear God, save me! I'm going mad!' One night he dreamed all night long, dreams that were all confused, with mysterious voices calling him. I don't know . . . and when morning came he went right on dreaming, with his eyes open, going around as if somebody were pushing him."

Carlos looked at Luisa with an expression at once victorious and despondent.

"Didn't I tell you? Do you still say I'm to blame?" And, turning to Father Nicolau: "Luisa thought that certain things I said to my son had shocked him and disoriented him. She thought—can you imagine?—that what she called my materialism was behind all the boy's troubles. Tell her that this thing that's happened to Tarciso is a sickness, a sickness, and that I'm not to blame for it. You can see that!"

Father Nicolau was uneasy.

"At times," he said, "both . . . the father and the mother . . . out of an excess of love . . . can do harm . . . can cause confusion in a child's mind . . . They want to imprint their own souls . . . on the soul of the child. . . . Each tries to stamp his image on the child's heart. . . . They want to destroy his spirit . . . It's a natural egoism, but sometimes . . ."

Luisa lowered her eyes. "Father Nicolau," she said, "let's go to the boy."

"Tarciso is sleeping," said Carlos. "He's exhausted. You shouldn't wake him up."

"Why doesn't the doctor come!" said Maninha. "Tarciso told me that he feels a tremendous strength in him. He says he's going away and he doesn't know where, and he's afraid. . . . I locked his door."

Father Nicolau, visibly perplexed, threw out words at random: "The boy always seemed . . . calm . . . normal. . . ." And turning to Luisa: "My daughter, God is goodness, He is gentleness. . . . Instead of arguing with your husband . . . you should try to meet him halfway. . . . You and your husband should not show Tarciso that you are in conflict. . . . It must certainly have hurt the boy. . . . Poor fellow, he didn't know which one to side with. . . . In his confusion . . . his mind became deranged. . . . That's what happened. . . . Do you agree, Carlos? . . . Don't you agree? . . . And it's important that you . . . not forget at this moment . . . the power of prayer. . . ."

But Carlos darted a glance at Luisa heavy with recrimination. It seemed to say: "Didn't I tell you so?"

Maninha opened the front door. It was getting late. The wind was still blowing. And, she was thinking, Dr. Laertes ought to arrive any moment.

The automobile was moving very slowly. A man leaned out the window of the front seat.

"Keep over on this side," shouted the gardener. "Over this way."

Having crossed the bridge, the car stopped and the man got out.

"I recognized you," he said, "as soon as . . ."

The gardener had turned livid.

"Dr. Laertes!"

"Yes, it's me. Did you think you could run away from the hospital and not get caught?"

The doctor's physical posture expressed authority and competence, like that of a military officer.

"Why did you do it? You deserve to be punished. I ought to send the ambulance here and put you in it, right in front of everybody, and then lock you up. Lock you up in a cell!"

"Doctor . . . I'm not sick. . . ."

He looked imploringly at the doctor and placed his hands behind his back.

"You are sick. You know it as well as I do. Don't hide your hands. Do you think you can fool me?"

The gardener trembled with emotion.

"I'm too old now to get used to living in a hospital. . . . Thirty years digging in the soil, taking care of flowers. Oh, Doctor, what a sad life there for a poor fellow like me who doesn't know how to read and doesn't like listening to the radio all day. Dr. Laertes . . . in the name of God who is in heaven, don't make me go back!"

And the man broke into sobs, like a child. Then he continued: "You don't have to be afraid. I don't really live with the family. I have my own room way in the back of the house. I have my own plates. I cook my own meals. . . ."

"It's useless," said the doctor. "If you don't go with me now, it will be the worse for you. I'll send for the ambulance!"

The sick man wiped his eyes with his shirt sleeves.

"It's not on account of the money they pay me. It's

not even on account of being free to go around wherever I like. . . . It's because I love the little plants that God made. And on account of the boy. He comes out here and we have talks. . . . By my mother's sainted soul, I never saw a child like that! I love him like . . . a son. But, Doctor, believe me, we only talk together, just like I'm talking to you now. I never touch him with my hands."

The doctor looked at his watch and frowned.

"Get ready and let's go. I meant what I said. If you like, make up some sort of excuse for leaving. But hurry!"

And Dr. Laertes walked stiffly toward the house.

When the gardener got to the door of his room, he hesitated. Then he turned and started up the back stairs.

The gardener felt sweat running down his face as if he were carrying an extraordinarily heavy weight. He knocked softly on the door. Then he placed his hand on the knob, but before he had time to turn it the door opened. Perhaps it was the wind. A vague sort of light shone on the wooden bed from the high, half-closed window.

The gardener slowly approached the bed. His forehead was throbbing. "The boy's asleep," he thought. "God protect him, God protect him!"

Tarciso opened his eyes but remained otherwise immobile. He looked about the room and saw the gardener.

"Oh, it's you. Come in . . . sit down. I wasn't sleeping. I only had my eyes shut."

The gardener came closer to the bed.

"I just came . . . to say goodbye."

"You're going away? Why? Don't you like us any more?"

"I'd like to stay here . . . always. I have to go because . . . It's hard for me to tell you. But I wouldn't know how to lie to Tarciso."

"Maybe it's that you're not being paid enough. Would you like me to talk to Papa?"

"No, my son. There's no need to talk with your father. It's that I'm . . . I'm . . . sick. . . ."

"You . . . sick?" Tarciso sat up and said: "You're the picture of health. So strong! I think the truth is you just don't want to live with us any more."

"I want to, but it's dangerous for everybody. The doctor—he's downstairs right now—ordered me to go back to the hospital. I have to stay there. . . . Didn't you ever notice the sores on my hands? I guess not. It's hard to see them through all the dirt."

A ray of orange-tinted light from the declining sun filtered through the dust and fell directly on Tarciso's face. His expression had suddenly changed. His skin was taut, shining, and as smooth as chinaware.

"I thought it was from your work. But . . . Let me see your hands." There was a strangely imperative tone in his voice.

"My boy . . ."

The man approached the brightness of the bed, but when he reached it he stopped and clasped his hands behind his back, for he was ashamed. He trembled. He stammered "No" in a weak, timid voice like that of a child.

"I want to see your hands. Your hands! Come!"

The man seemed hypnotized. He resisted for a few seconds, then extended his hands. They penetrated the brightness, taking on a sort of magic relief. They were mottled and twisted, bruised, purple, and swollen. Tarciso had never really noticed them before. They were there now before his eyes, pieces of flesh marked with proximate death, writhing like two fatally wounded animals.

Then the boy felt a wave of tenderness take possession of him like the sweet fire of love. While the gardener stood as if paralyzed, Tarciso seized the poor, sick hands, slowly placed his lips on them, kissed them.

When Carlos had told Dr. Laertes about his son's illness, the doctor said, with a certain benign gravity: "Fifteen years old. Hmm! It's probably not so serious as you think. It sounds like the sort of emotional crisis that children sometimes go through during puberty. I haven't examined the boy. But, from what you've told me, I think his trouble can be readily diagnosed in the light of modern psychology. His religious fear, inculcated by his mother—forgive me, Father Nicolau—has perverted certain normal sexual tendencies. The open sores, the deformities of which he dreams are nothing but his sexual instinct in disguise. His religious fears make it impossible for him to let this instinct express itself directly."

Luisa and Father Nicolau exchanged glances. Maninha looked at the doctor inquisitively.

Dr. Laertes consulted his watch again.

"Well, let's go and have a look at the young patient."

But a great shout, a man's shout, cut through the air. The gardener opened the door of Tarciso's room, came hurtling down the stairs, and stood before them, laughing and crying like a madman.

"God in heaven! God in heaven!"

Dr. Laertes looked at him sternly and asked: "What is this, man? What's the matter with you? Why are you still here? Do you want me to send for the ambulance to take you away?"

"Let me tell you, Doctor, let me tell you! ... Something happened. ... I want to tell you—but it's hard! I went to say good-by to the boy, up there in his room." Tears were flowing freely down his cheeks. "I only meant to say good-by. I didn't want him to know about my hands. But he found out, he saw them."

Luisa opened her mouth as if to speak but, terror-stricken, remained silent.

"Doctor, what happened ... what happened was that, when Tarciso found out about my hands, his whole face changed. It was so different, he seemed like another person. I was frightened."

They all stood around the gardener in astonishment and fear. They felt that something terrible had happened. The man went on.

"Tarciso took hold of my hands. I wanted to pull them away, but as God is my witness I couldn't move. My arms were like stone! And Tarciso began to kiss my hands. He did it with a kind of firmness but at the same time he was tender and gentle. ... It's hard to describe how he did it. ... And then ... it happened."

The gardener choked a little and could not go on. Then he recovered his voice and blurted: "A miracle! A miracle! Dr. Laertes, look at my hands! That angel of Our Lady, while he was kissing my hands the spots began to disappear. Even the sores ... they're gone! Look!"

And the man extended his hands for the doctor to see. They were pure, smooth, delicate, like those of a newborn child.

While everyone stared, Father Nicolau said softly, as if lamenting: "And I never understood ... I never saw ..."

Maninha rushed up the stairs, shouting, "Tarciso!" She opened the door and, a moment later, started down.

"He's gone," she said. "But I locked the door. I remember doing it."

Maninha, followed by her parents, rushed into the garden. She ran lightly, her white dress fluttering like a sail at sea. She crossed the bridge. Tarciso was ahead, walking rapidly.

"Tarciso, don't go away! Wait, Tarciso—wait for me!"

Despite her desperate effort, she was unable to catch up with him. From far off he waved serenely, saying good-by. Maninha felt dizzy. She thought of the great world of the poor, the sick, the deformed, to which her brother had gone in an ecstasy of love, never to return. The blood-red twilight appeared to concentrate on the figure of the boy, which seemed to grow in majesty as he went farther and farther away.

Translated by William L. Grossman

Warma Kuyay
(Puppy Love)

JOSE MARÍA ARGUEDAS

Moonlit night in Viseca Gorge.

Poor little pigeon, whence have you come,
searching the sand, dear God, along the ground?

"Justina! Ay, Justinita!"

The seagull sings on the glossy lake
filling my mind with pleasant memories.

"Justinay, you look like the wild pigeons of Sausiyok!"

"Leave me alone, Master, go along to your young ladies!"

"And the Kutu? You love the Kutu, you like his toad face!"

"Leave me alone, Master Ernesto! I may be ugly but I can lasso cows, and I make the young bulls tremble with every flick of the whip. That's why Justina loves me."

The cholita laughed, looking at the Kutu; her eyes glittered like two stars.

"Ay, Justinacha!"

"Don't be silly, Master!" said Gregoria, the cook.

Celedonia, Pedrucha, Manuela, Anitacha ... burst out laughing; they shrieked with laughter.

"Master's being silly."

They clasped hands and started dancing in a ring to the music of Julio's lute. Every once in a while they turned to look at me and laugh. I stayed outside the circle, ashamed, beaten for good.

I went off toward the old mill. The whitewash on the wall seemed to move, like the clouds that wander over Chawala's slopes. Eucalyptus trees around the orchard made a long, intense sound, their shadows stretching out to the other side of the river. I reached the foot of the mill and climbed up to the highest wall, and from there I saw the head of Chawala: half black, rearing up, the mountain threatened to fall on the alfalfa fields of the hacienda. It was scary at night. During those hours the Indians would never look at it, and on clear nights always talked with their backs turned to the mountain.

"If you fell on your face, Father Chawala, we'd all be dead!"

Right in the middle of the Witron, Justina sang another song:

May flower, May flower,
first flower of the May,
couldn't you tear youself loose
from that faithless prisoner?

The cholos had stopped in a circle and Justina was singing in the center. Motionless on the cobbles of the big yard, the Indians looked like those stakes you hang hides on.

"That little black dot in the middle is Justina. And I love her, my heart trembles when she laughs, and it cries whenever I see her eyes on the Kutu. So why am I dying for that little black dot?"

The Indians started stomping again, around and around, in time to the music. The lute player kept circling them, cheering them on, whinnying like a lovesick colt. A paca-paca started whistling from a willow tree that nodded on the riverbank; the voice of the damn bird was unnerving. The lute player ran to the fence and threw stones at the willow, all the cholos following him. Soon it flew off and settled in one of the peach trees in the orchard. The cholos were about to give chase when Don Froylán appeared in the door of the Witron.

"Beat it! Get off to sleep!"

The cholos trooped toward the crossbar of the corral. The Kutu remained alone in the yard.

"He's the one she loves!"

Don Froylán's Indians disappeared through the gate of hacienda compound, and Don Froylán followed.

"Master Ernesto!" the Kutu called.

I jumped to the ground and ran toward him.

"Let's go, Master."

We went up to the alley by way of the metal-washing trough that was falling apart in a corner of the Witron. On top of the trough there was an immense iron pipe and several rusty wheels that came from the mines of Don Froylán's father.

Kutu said nothing till we reached the house above.

The hacienda belonged to Don Froylán and my uncle; it had two main houses. Kutu and I were alone in the upper hamlet. My uncle and the other people had gone to dig potatoes and would sleep on that small farm, two leagues from the hacienda.

We went up the steps, without even looking at each other. We entered the corridor and made up our beds there so we would be sleeping in the moonlight. The Kutu lay down without speaking: he was sad and troubled. I sat down beside him.

"Kutu! Has Justina given you the brush-off?"

"Don Froylán has abused her, Master Ernesto!"

"That's a lie, Kutu, a lie!"

"He did it just yesterday, at the canal when she went to bathe with the kids!"

"It's a lie, Kutullay, a lie!"

I hugged him around the neck. I was frightened; I thought my heart would break, it was pounding so. I began to cry, as if I were alone, abandoned in that great black ravine.

"Stop it, Master! Look, I'm only an Indian; I can't stand up to the patrón. Some other time, when you're a lawyer, you will fix Don Froylán."

He picked me up like a yearling and laid me down on my cot.

"Go to sleep, Master! I'm going to talk to Justina now so she'll like you. You'll sleep with her sometime, would you like that, Master? Yes? Justina has some feeling for you, but you're still a boy, and she's afraid because you're the young master."

I knelt on my bed. I looked at Chawala; it seemed dark and terrible in the stillness of the night.

"Kutu, when I grow up, I'm going to kill Don Froylán!"

"Right you are, Master Ernesto, right you are. *Mak'tasu!*"

In the corridor the cholo's thick voice sounded like the snarling of the lion that used to come up to the settlement hunting for hogs. Kutu stood up. He was in great spirits, as if he had just brought down that thief of a puma.

"The patrón arrives tomorrow. We better go to Justina tonight. Sure thing the patrón makes you sleep in his room. Let the moon go in so we can start."

His high spirits made me furious.

"And why don't you kill Don Froylán? Let him have it with your sling, Kutu, from across the river, as if he were a prowling puma."

"His little kids, Master! There are nine of them! But they'll be big by the time you're a lawyer.'"

"You're lying, Kutu, you're lying! You're scared, like a woman!"

"You don't know what you're talking about, Master. You think I haven't seen? You're sorry for little yearlings, but you don't care about men."

"Don Froylán! He's bad! Ranchers are bad; they make Indians like you cry, they carry off other people's cows, or else they starve them to death in their corrals. Kutu, Don Froylán is worse than a wild bull! So kill him, Kutucha, even if by pushing a rock off the Capitana cliff."

"Indian can't, Master! Indian can't!"

He was a coward! He brought down wild stallions, he made colts quiver, he laid open the backs of plow horses with a whip; whenever cows of other cholos wandered into my uncle's pastures, he shot them with his sling from a long way off; but he was a coward. Hopeless Indian!

I looked at him closely: his flat nose, his almost slanting eyes, his thin lips blackened by cocoa. He's the one she loves! And she was so pretty; her rosy face was always well-scrubbed, her black eyes flashed, she wasn't like the other cholas, her eyelashes were long, her mouth called for love and wouldn't let me sleep. At fourteen, I loved her. Her small breasts were like plump lemons; they drove me wild. But she was Kutu's, had been for a long time now, this toad-faced cholo. Thinking of this, my suffering was very much like dying. And now? Don Froylán had raped her.

"It's a lie, Kutu! She must have asked for it, she must have!"

My eyes flooded with tears. My heart was shaking me again, as if it were stronger than my whole body.

"Kutu! The two of us better kill her—you want to?"

The cholo grew frightened. He put his hand to my forehead; it was damp with sweat.

"True! This is how white men love."

"Take me to Justina, Kutu! You're a woman, you're not good enough for her! Leave her alone!"

"Sure, Master, I let you have her, she's all yours. Look, the moon is going behind Wayrala."

The mountains blackened quickly, and little stars sprang out all over the sky. The wind whistled in the darkness, crashing into the peach and eucalyptus trees in the orchard. Farther down, at the bottom of the gorge, the great river sang in its harsh voice.

I despised Kutu. Tiny and cowardly, his yellow eyes made me tremble with rage.

"Indian, you better drop dead, or take off for Nazca! The malaria will finish you off there, they'll bury you like a dog!" I used to tell him.

But the herdsman would just lower his head, humbly, and go off to the Witron, to the alfalfa fields, to the pasture of the yearlings, and take it out on the bodies of Don Froylán's animals. At first I went along with him. At night we would sneak into the corral, hiding as we went. We picked out the slenderest, most delicate yearlings; Kutu would spit on his hands, grip the whip hard, and rip open the backs of the young bulls. One! Two! Three! . . . A hundred lashes. The little ones writhed on the ground, they rolled over on their backs, they cried out; and the Indian kept on, hunched over, vicious. And I? I sat in a corner and enjoyed it. I enjoyed it.

"They're Don Froylán's—who cares? He's my enemy!"

He spoke loudly so as to fool me, to cover up the pain that tightened my lips and filled my heart.

But once I was in bed, alone, a dark driving anguish swept over my soul and I cried for two or three hours. Until one night my heart was ready to burst. Tears weren't enough; I was overcome by despair and remorse. I jumped out of bed and ran to the door, barefoot; I slowly turned the lock and stepped out into the gallery. The moon was already up; its white light washed the ravine; stiff, silent, the trees held their arms up to the sky. I went down the gallery in two leaps, ran across the cobbled alley, jumped the wall of the corral and reached the yearlings. There was Zarinacha, that night's victim, lying on the dry dung, with her muzzle on the ground: she seemed unconscious. I put my arms around her neck. I kissed her a thousand times on the mouth with its odor of fresh milk, and on her great black eyes.

"Forgive me, girl, forgive me!"

I joined my hands, and, on my knees, I humbled myself before her.

"It was that dirty bastard, little sister, it wasn't me. Kutu, that dirty Indian, that dog!"

The salt of my tears kept me feeling bitter for a long time.

Zarinacha looked at me solemnly, with her soft humble eyes.

"I care about you, girl, I do!"

And a perfect tenderness, pure and sweet like the light in that nurturing ravine, lit up my life.

Next morning I found the cholo in the Capitana alfalfa field. The sky was clear and joyous, the fields green, and still cool. The Kutu was already leaving, very early, to look for victims in my uncle's pastures, to relieve his fury.

"Kutu, get out of here," I told him. "No one wants you around here any more. All the Indians laugh at you because you're trash!"

His gloomy eyes looked at me with some fear.

"You're a murderer too, Kutu. A little calf is like a baby. There is no place for you in Viseca, you worthless Indian!"

"Only me, eh? You too. But look at Father Chawala: I'm going to leave ten days from now."

Hurt, more miserable than ever, he galloped off on my uncle's bay.

Two weeks later, Kutu asked for his pay and left. My aunt cried for him, as if she had lost her son.

Kutu had the blood of a woman: he trembled before Don Froylán, he was afraid of almost all the men. They took away his woman and afterwards he went to communities of Sondondo, Chacralla. ... he was a coward!

I stayed with Don Froylán, alone, but near Justina, my heartless Justinacha. And I wasn't unhappy. By that foaming river, listening to the singing of the wild pigeons and the arbor vitae, I lived without hope; but she was under the same sky as I, in that ravine that was my nest. Gazing at her black eyes, listening to her laughter, watching her from a distance, I was almost happy. Because my love for Justina was a *warma kuyay*, I believed I had no right to her yet; I knew that she would have to belong to another, to a grown man who could already handle the long leather thong, who could curse pungently, could fight with whips at the carnivals. And since I loved animals and Indian fiestas and harvests and seedtime with music and *jarawi*, I lived happily in that ravine, verdant and caressed by the sun's heat. Till one day they tore me away from my heaven, to bring me to all this noise and commotion, to people I don't care for and don't understand.

The Kutu at one end and I at another. Maybe he has forgotten. He's in his element; in some quiet little town, even if he's trash, he must be the best herdsman, the best tamer of young mares, and the community respects him. While I live here, bitter and pale, like an animal from the cold plains, taken to the coast, to burning and alien sands.

Translated by Hardie St. Martin

How Porciúncula the Mulatto Got the Corpse Off His Back

JORGE AMADO

The gringo who dropped anchor here years ago was a tight-mouthed and fair-skinned guy. No one had ever seen anybody who liked to drink so much. To say he guzzled the booze isn't to the point, because we all do that, praise the Lord! He'd spend two days and two nights nursing the bottles and not turn a hair. He didn't start blabbing or picking a fight; he didn't begin on the old-time songs, and he didn't spill over with hard-luck stories from way back. Tight-mouthed he was and tight-mouthed he remained; only his blue eyes kept narrowing, a little at a time, one red-hot coal in every glance burning up the blue.

They told lots of stories about him, and some tricked out so neat it was a pleasure listening to them. But all hearsay, because from the gringo's own mouth you couldn't learn a thing—that sewn-up mouth that didn't even open on the big fiestas when your legs feel like lead with the booze accumulating in your feet. Not even Mercedes—with a weakness for the gringo that was no secret to any of us, and inquisitive as only she could be—could squeeze out one clear fact about that woman he killed in his country, or about that guy he kept hounding year in and year out, through one place after another, till he finally stuck a knife in his belly. When she asked about it on those long days as the booze drowned out all reserve, the gringo just kept looking at no one knew what, with those tight little eyes of his, those blue eyes now bloodshot and squinting shut, only to let out a sound like a grunt, not meaning much of anything. That story about the woman with the seventeen knife wounds in her nether parts, I never did get to find out how the thing ended up, it was so bogged down in details; or again, the story about that rich fellow he hounded from one port to another till the gringo stuck a knife into him, the same one he used to kill the woman with seventeen wounds all in her nether parts. I don't know because if he was carrying those corpses around with him he never wanted to get rid of the burden, even when drinking he closed his eyelids and those burning coals rolled onto the floor at everybody's feet. Listen, a corpse is a heavy load, and many's the brave man I've seen who let his load slip into a stranger's hands when booze loosened him up. Let alone two corpses, a man and a woman, with those wounds in the belly . . . The gringo never let his drop, which was why his ribs were bent, from the weight of it, no doubt. He asked for no one's help, but here and there they told about it in detail, and it turned into a pretty good story, with parts for laughing and parts for crying, the way a good story should be.

But what I must tell now has nothing to do with the gringo. Let that one wait for another time, just because it needs time. It's not over one damn little drink—no offense to anyone here now—that you can talk about the gringo and unwind his life's ball of yarn or undo the skein of his mystery. That'll have to wait till another day, God willing. And time or moonshine won't disappear. After all, what are the stills working night and day for?

The gringo only drops in here, as they say, in passing, but he came on that rainy night to remind us the Christmas season was at hand. And of the country he hailed from where Christmas was a real holiday, not like here. Nothing to compare with the feast days of São João, beginning with those of Santo Antônio and going through the days of São Pedro, or those days commemorating the waters of Oxalá, the fiesta of Bonfim, the holy days of obligation of Xangô, and—oh brother!—not to mention the feast of the Conception da Praia, which was some holiday! Since there's no lack of holidays here, why go and borrow one from a stranger?

Now the gringo remembered Christmas just at the time when Porciúncula—that mulatto in the story about the blind beggar dog—changed places and sat down on the kerosene drum, covering his glass with the palm of his hand to keep the voracious flies out of his booze. A fly doesn't drink booze? Your honors will excuse me, but this will sound like nonsense because they don't know the flies in Alonso's place. The flies were really wicked. Crazy for a drop, they'd throw themselves way down into a glass, sample their tiny drop, then out they'd come, weaving and buzzing like May bugs. There was no possible way of convincing Alonso, that headstrong Spaniard, to put an end to such a disgrace. His story was—and he was right—that the flies came with the place he bought, and he wasn't about to get rid of them for being troublesome simply because they wanted a little snort. That wasn't reason enough, since all his customers liked it too and he wasn't going to throw them out, was he?

I don't know if the mulatto Porciúncula changed places to be nearer the kerosene lamp or if he already had the idea of telling the story about Teresa Batista and her bet. That night, as I explained, the lights went out all along that part of the waterfront, and Alonso lit the kerosene lamp grumblingly. He really wanted to kick us out, but he couldn't. It was raining, one of those crazy heavy rains that soaks you wetter than holy water straight through the flesh and to the bone. Alonso was a trained Spaniard who absorbed a lot of his training from being an errand boy in a hotel. That's why he lit the lamp and stood doing his accounts with a pencil stub. People were talking of this and that, swatting flies, skipping from subject to subject, killing time as they could. When Porciúncula changed places and the gringo grunted out his piece about Christmas, something about snow and lit-up trees, Porciúncula wasn't going to let the chance slip by. Driving the flies away and downing a slug of booze, he announced in a soft voice: "It was on Christmas night when Teresa Batista won a bet and started living a new life."

"What bet?"

If Mercedes's question was meant to encourage Porciúncula she needn't have opened her mouth. Porciúncula didn't have to be prodded or coaxed. Alonso put down his pencil, refilled the glasses, with the flies buzzing around convinced they were May bugs, completely drunk! Porciúncula downed his drink, cleared his throat, and began his story. This Porciúncula, he was the best-talking mulatto I ever knew, and that's saying a lot. So literate, so smooth, you'd think, not knowing his background, that he'd worn out a schoolbench though old Ventura hadn't put him into any school but out on the streets and the waterfront. He was such a wizard at telling stories that if this one turns sour in my mouth it's not the fault of the story or of the mulatto Porciúncula.

Porciúncula waited a bit till Mercedes was comfortable on the floor, leaning against the gringo's legs to hear better. Then he explained that Teresa Batista only showed up on the waterfront after her sister was buried, a few weeks later—the time it took for the news to find them where they lived, it was so far away. She came so she could learn directly about what had happened, and she stayed on. She looked like her sister, but it was just a facial resemblance, a surface thing, nothing on the inside, because the spirit of Maria of the Veil no one else had and no one ever will. That was why Teresa all her life remained Teresa Batista, keeping the name she was born with, without anyone finding it necessary to change. On the other hand, who on any day of the week would have thought of calling Maria of the Veil, Maria Batista?

Nosy Mercedes wanted to know who in the world this Maria was and why "of the Veil."

She was Maria Batista, Teresa's sister, Porciúncula explained patiently. And he told how Maria had scarcely arrived in these parts when everyone began to call her Maria of the Veil, and only that. Because of that mania of hers for not missing a wedding, with her eyes glued to the bride's gown. They talked a lot about this Maria of the Veil on the waterfront. She was a beauty, and Porciúncula, with his turn for phrases, said she was like an apparition risen from the sea at night when she wandered around the port. She was so much a part of the waterfront, it was almost as though she'd been born there, when actually she came from the interior, dressed in rags, and still remembering the beating she'd gotten. Because the old man Batista, her father, didn't fool around, and when he heard the story of how Colonel Barbosa's son had taken her virginity, which had been still as green as a persimmon, he grabbed her by the chin and beat the daylights out of her for giving it away. Then he kicked her out of the house. He wanted no fallen woman in his house. The place for a fallen woman is the back alley, the place for a lost woman is the red-light district. That's what the old man said, bringing the club down on his little girl, being so full of rage, and even more of pain, to see his fifteen-year-old daughter, pretty as a picture, no longer a virgin and useless except to be a whore. That's how Maria Batista became Maria of the Veil and ended up by coming to the capital because at home there at the end of the world there'd be no future for her as a prostitute. After she arrived she knocked around from pillar to post till she landed on the Hill of São Miguel, such a child still that Tibéria, madam of the brothel where she'd dragged her bundle, asked her if she thought it was a grade school.

Many of the story's details before and after this Porciúncula got from the mouth of Tibéria, a highly respected citizen and Bahia's best whorehouse madam ever. It's not because she's my friend that I praise her conduct. She doesn't need that. Who doesn't know Tibéria and who doesn't respect her qualities? They're fine folk in there, women as good as their word, hearts of gold, helping half the world. At Tibéria's it's all one big family; it's not each one for himself and the devil take the hindmost—nothing of the sort. Everyone's in accord; it's a close-knit family. Porciúncula was very dear to Tibéria, a familiar of the house, always falling for one girl or another, always ready to fix a leaking pipe, change a burned-out light bulb, patch the gutters on the roof, and with a swift one to the backside he would kick anyone out who dared lose his self-respect and turn into an animal. And it was Tibéria who told him everything, item by item, so he could unravel her story from start to finish without stumbling over any part of it. He was so interested because as soon as he laid eyes on Maria he was madly in love with her, one of those hopeless lovers.

When Maria arrived she was the youngest in the house, not yet sixteen, badly spoiled by Tibéria and the other women, who treated her like a daughter, loading her with elegant dolls. They even gave her a doll to take the place of the Raggedy Ann she used for her engagement and wedding games. Maria of the Veil spent her time on the waterfront; she loved to look out to sea, as people from the interior like to do. She was there at the first hint of nightfall; in moonlight or fog, drizzle or storm, she walked along the sea bank soliciting. Tibéria would scold her, laughing. Why didn't Maria stay inside the brothel, be nice and cozy, dressed in her flowered gown, waiting for the rich men crazy for a fresh young thing like her? She would even arrange for a rich guardian, an old man who'd fall in love and give her a good life in the lap of luxury without her having to go to bed with every Tom, Dick and Harry, at the rate of two or three a night. Right here in the brothel, not to go any further, there was the example of Lúcia, whom Judge Maia came to see once a week, and he gave her everything. Even got porter's jobs for the easygoing Barcelino, Lúcia's sweetheart. Tibéria also was flabbergasted that Maria didn't take to Porciúncula the mulatto, devoured with passion for the girl who slept with everyone but him. She strolled along by his side, hand in hand through Mont Serrat, looking at the sea, or better yet, swaying alongside as a lover would when couples went aboard at night for a moonlight fishing trip. Meanwhile telling the mulatto all about the weddings she'd been to, how beautiful the bride looked, how long her veil was. But when the time came to go to bed and do the right thing, that's when she'd say goodnight and leave Porciúncula drained, stupefied.

This was just how Porciúncula told it that rainy night when the gringo was reminiscing about Christmas. Why I like to hear the mulatto tell stories is, he doesn't twist anything around to make himself look good. He could easily have said he screwed her, many times even. That's what everybody thought, especially those who'd seen them together along the waterfront. He could have bragged, but instead he told it the way it really was, and for a lot of us that was no surprise. Maria slept with this one and that one; she got excited at the right time. It wasn't that she didn't like it. But when it was done, it was done; she didn't like talking about it. Any real emotion in itself, the sort of endless yearning that lovers suffer from not seeing one another, and so forth, well, she never felt that over anyone. Unless she felt it about the mulatto Porciúncula, but then why didn't she go to bed with him? She'd sit next to him on the sand, dipping her feet in the water, jumping with the waves, looking out to the edge of the sea that nobody can ever make out. Who's ever seen the end of the sea? Any of my honorable listeners? Excuse me, but I don't think so.

The one really in love was Porciúncula the mulatto. A night didn't go by when he wasn't watching for Maria on the waterfront, trailing her, wanting to shipwreck himself on her. That's how he told it, hiding nothing; and even then the pain of his love softened his voice. He was more lost than an ownerless dog, sniffing out anything that hinted of Maria of the Veil, while Tibéria went around whispering things in his ear. That's how he began to unravel the net, piecing together the scaffolding of Maria's story up until the event of the funeral.

When Colonel Barbosa's son, a well-heeled student on vacation, screwed Maria, she wasn't quite fifteen but she already had the breasts and body of a woman. A woman to look at but on the inside still a girl playing with her rag doll all day, the kind of doll you can buy for a dollar at the fair. She put together bits of cloth, sewed them into a dress for her rag doll, with a veil and a bridal crown. Any wedding day in church at her end of the world and Maria would be there watching, eyes stuck to the bride's gown. She was thinking only of how good it must be to wear such a gown, all white, with a trailing veil and flowers on her head. She made clothes for the doll, talking to it all the while, and every day contrived a wedding just to see it in a veil and crown. The doll was married to all the animals in the neighborhood, especially the old blind chicken, who made a terrific groom because he didn't run away, but squatted in his blindness, obedient. So when Colonel Barbosa's son told Maria, "Now you're ripe for marriage. Would you like to marry me?" she said yes, if he'd give her a pretty veil. Poor thing, she had no idea that the guy was talking fancy talk and that to get married was highfalutin for getting screwed on the riverbank. That's why Maria, all excited, accepted, and is still waiting to this day for the gown, the veil, and the bridal wreath. Instead she got a beating from old Batista, and, when the story got out, the name of Maria of the Veil. But she didn't lose her obsession. Thrown out of her house, there wasn't a wedding she missed, hiding in the church, because a prostitute isn't allowed to have anything to do with weddings. When that Barbosa fellow, the same one that did her the favor, married the daughter of Colonel Boaventura—a widely discussed wedding!—she was there to see the bride, a beautiful, well-heeled girl, in a dress the likes of which had never been seen, made in Rio, with a train half a mile long and a face veil embroidered all over, something really astonishing. It was after that Maria made her way to this spot and tied up at Tibéria's whorehouse.

A good time for her didn't mean going to the movies, a cabaret, dancing, boozing in a bar, or taking some boat ride. It was just weddings and looking at the bride's gown. She cut pictures out of magazines, brides in veils, store advertisements of bridal outfits. She stuck them all up on the wall at the head of her bed. With new scraps of material she made a new bridal gown for her new doll, a present from Tibéria and the other women. A young girl, still so damn young she could tell Tibéria, "One of these days you'll see me in such a gown." They laughed at her, played tricks on her, jeered at her, but that didn't change her.

Around this time Porciúncula's patience gave out—sick of keeping his animal nature down, of going around with clenched fists, of hearing the talk on the waterfront. Every man has his pride, he saw it was hopeless; he had waited long enough, and he wasn't the type to die of love, the worst death of all. He turned to Carolina, the big husky mulatto who lived just to make love to him. He cured himself of Maria of the Veil with a few drinks and some of Carolina's belly laughs. He didn't want to discuss it any more.

At this point Porciúncula asked for more booze and was served. Alonso would give his eye teeth for a good story, and this one was quickly coming to an end. The end was the flu a few years back that wiped out half of the world. Maria of the Veil fell into a fever; fragile, she lasted only four days. By the time Porciúncula got the news she was already dead. At the moment he was more or less out of circulation because of the hot water he'd gotten into over a guy named Gomes. Gomes, who owned a market stall in Água dos Meninos, had gotten hurt in a card game. Now to cut cards with Porciúncula was to throw your money away. He played because he liked to, and he couldn't take anyone who complained about it afterward.

Porciúncula was letting the storm die down when he got the message from Tibéria, begging him to come right away. Maria was calling for him urgently. She died the very hour he arrived. Tibéria explained the last request she'd made on her deathbed. She wanted to be buried in a bridal gown, with a veil and garland. The bridegroom, she said, must be the mulatto Porciúncula, who was waiting to marry her.

It was a very painful request, but coming from a dead person there was no refusing to honor it. Porciúncula asked how he was going to get a wedding gown, an expensive buy, with the stores closed for the night besides. He thought it was going to be hard but it wasn't. Because all those swarms of women from the brothel and the street, all the old whores tired of life, all suddenly found themselves becoming seamstresses, sewing a dress with a veil and a bridal wreath. They quickly put all their money together and bought flowers, arranged the cloth, got lace, God knows where from, found shoes, silk stockings, even white gloves. One sewed a piece, another put on some ribbon.

Porciúncula said he'd never seen a wedding gown to beat it, so pretty and elegant, and he knew what he was talking about because in the time he'd courted Maria he'd been everywhere looking at weddings and had worn himself out looking at those gowns.

After they dressed Maria, the train of her gown trailed off the bed and bunched up on the floor. Tibéria came with a bouquet and put it in Maria's hands. There never was a bride so serene and sweet, so happy at her wedding.

Standing near the bed, Porciúncula sat down. He was the bridegroom. He took Maria's hand. Clarice, a married woman whose husband had left her with three children to bring up, wept and pulled the wedding ring off her finger—the memory of happier times—and gave it to the mulatto. Porciúncula slowly put it on the dead woman's finger and looked into her face. Maria of the Veil was smiling. Before that moment I don't know, but at the moment she was smiling—that's how Porciúncula described it, and he hadn't been drinking that day, hadn't touched a drop. Tearing his eyes away from that beautiful face, he glanced at Tibéria. And he swore he saw, he truly saw Tibéria changed into a priest, wearing those special garments for consecrating a wedding, with a tonsure and everything, a fat priest who looked a bit saintly. Alonso filled the glasses again and drank up.

It was here the mulatto Porciúncula stopped, and there was no getting another word of the story out of him. He'd unloaded his corpse on us, he'd relieved himself of the burden. Mercedes still wanted to know if the coffin had been white-for-a-virgin or black-for-a-sinner. Porciúncula shrugged his shoulders and swatted flies. About Teresa Batista, the bet she'd won, and the new life she started, nothing was said. And nobody asked. I can't say a thing about it. I'm not someone who tells stories about things he doesn't know. What I can do is tell the gringo's story, because that one I do know, like everyone on the waterfront. But I know it's not the kind of story to tell over one drink like this, if you'll excuse my saying so. It's a full-length story to drink on over a long rainy night, or better yet a fishing trip in the moonlight. Still, if you'd like I could tell it. I don't see any reason why not.

Translated by Edwin and Margot Honig

End of the Game

JULIO CORTÁZAR

Letitia, Holanda and I used to play by the Argentine Central tracks during the hot weather, hoping that Mama and Aunt Ruth would go up to their siesta so that we could get out past the white gate. After washing the dishes, Mama and Aunt Ruth were always tired, especially when Holanda and I were drying, because it was then that there were arguments, spoons on the floor, secret words that only we understood, and in general, an atmosphere in which the smell of grease, José's yowling, and the dimness of the kitchen would end up in an incredible fight and the subsequent commotion. Holanda specialized in rigging this sort of brawl, for example, letting an already clean glass slip into the pan of dirty water, or casually dropping a remark to the effect that the Loza house had two maids to do all the work. I had other systems: I liked to suggest to Aunt Ruth that she was going to get an allergy rash on her hands if she kept scrubbing the pots instead of doing the cups and plates once in a while, which were exactly what Mama liked to wash, and over which they would confront one another soundlessly in a war of advantage to get the easy item. The heroic expedient, in case the bits of advice and the drawn-out family recollections began to bore us, was to upset some boiling water on the cat's back. Now that's a big lie about a scalded cat, it really is, except that you have to take the reference to cold water literally; because José never backed away from hot water, almost insinuating himself under it, poor animal, when we spilled a half-cup of it somewhere around 220° F., or less, a good deal less, probably, because his hair never fell out. The whole point was to get Troy burning, and in the confusion, crowned by a splendid G-flat from Aunt Ruth and Mama's sprint for the whipstick, Holanda and I would take no time at all to get lost in the long porch, toward the empty rooms off the back, where Letitia would be waiting for us, reading *Ponson de Terrail*, or some other equally inexplicable book.

Normally, Mama chased us a good part of the way, but her desire to bust in our skulls evaporated soon enough, and finally (we had barred the door and were begging for mercy in emotion-filled and very theatrical voices), she got tired and went off, repeating the same sentence: "Those ruffians'll end up on the street."

Where we ended up was by the Argentine Central tracks, when the house had settled down and was silent, and we saw the cat stretched out under the lemon tree to take its siesta also, a rest buzzing with fragrances and wasps. We'd open the white gate slowly, and when we shut it again with a slam like a blast of wind, it was a freedom which took us by the hands, seized the whole of our bodies and tumbled us out. Then we ran, trying to get the speed to scramble up the low embankment of the right-of-way, and there spread out upon the world, we silently surveyed our kingdom.

Our kingdom was this: a long curve of the tracks ended its bend just opposite the back section of the house. There was just the gravel incline, the crossties, and the double line of track; some dumb sparse grass among the rubble where mica, quartz and feldspar—

the components of granite—sparkled like real diamonds in the two o'clock afternoon sun. When we stooped down to touch the rails (not wasting time because it would have been dangerous to spend much time there, not so much from the trains as for fear of being seen from the house), the heat off the stone roadbed was a damp heat against our cheeks and ears. We liked to bend our legs and squat down, rise, squat again, move from one kind of hot zone to the other, watching each other's faces to measure the perspiration—a minute or two later we would be sopping with it. And we were always quiet, looking down the track into the distance, or at the river on the other side, that stretch of coffee-and-cream river.

After this first inspection of the kingdom, we'd scramble down the bank and flop in the meager shadow of the willows next the wall enclosing the house were the white gate was. This was the capital city of the kingdom, the wilderness city and the headquarters of our game. Letitia was the first to start the game; she was the luckiest and the most privileged of the three of us. Letitia didn't have to dry dishes or make the beds, she could laze away the day reading or pasting up pictures, and at night they let her stay up later if she asked to, not counting having a room to herself, special hot broth when she wanted it, and all kinds of other advantages. Little by little she had taken more and more advantage of these privileges, and had been presiding over the game since the summer before, I think really she was presiding over the whole kingdom; in any case she was quicker at saying things, and Holanda and I accepted them without protest, happy almost. It's likely that Mama's long lectures on how we ought to behave toward Letitia had had their effect, or simply that we loved her enough and it didn't bother us that she was boss. A pity that she didn't have the looks for the boss; she was the shortest of the three of us and very skinny. Holanda was skinny, and I never weighed over 110, but Letitia was scragglier than we were, and even worse, that kind of skinniness you can see from a distance in the neck and ears. Maybe it was the stiffness of her back that made her look so thin; for instance she could hardly move her head from side to side, she was like a folded-up ironing board, like one of those they had in the Loza house, with a cover of white material. Like an ironing board with the wide part up, leaning closed against the wall. And she led us.

The best satisfaction was to imagine that someday Mama or Aunt Ruth would find out about the game. If they managed to find out about the game there would be an unbelievable mess. The G-flat and fainting fits, incredible protests of devotion and sacrifice ill-rewarded, and a string of words threatening the more celebrated punishments, closing the bid with a dire prediction of our fates, which consisted of the three of us ending up on the street. This final prediction always left us somewhat perplexed, because to end up in the street always seemed fairly normal to us.

First Letitia had us draw lots. We used to use pebbles hidden in the hand, count to twenty-one, any way at all. If we used the count-to-twenty-one system, we would pretend two or three more girls and include them in the counting to prevent cheating. If one of them came out 21, we dropped her from the group and started drawing again, until one of us won. Then Holanda and I lifted the stone and we got out the ornament-box. Suppose Holanda had won. Letitia and I chose the ornaments. The game took two forms: Statues and Attitudes. Attitudes did not require ornaments but an awful lot of expressiveness; for Envy you could show your teeth, make fists and hold them in a position so as to seem cringing. For Charity the ideal was an angelic face, eyes turned up to the sky, while the hands offered something—a rag, a ball, a branch of willow—to a poor invisible orphan. Shame and Fear were easy to do; Spite and Jealousy required a more conscientious study. The Statues were determined, almost all of them, by the choice of ornaments, and here absolute liberty reigned. So that a statue would come out of it, one had to think carefully of every detail in the costume. It was a rule of the game that the one chosen could not take part in the selection; the two remaining argued out the business at hand and then fitted the ornaments on. The winner had to invent her statue taking into account what they'd dressed her in and, in this way the game was much more complicated and exciting because sometimes there were counterplots, and the victim would find herself rigged out in adornments which were completely hopeless; so it was up to her to be quick then in composing a good statue. Usually when the game called for Attitudes, the winner came up pretty well outfitted, but there were times when the Statues were horrible failures.

Well, the story I'm telling, lord knows when it began, but things changed the day the first note fell from the train. Naturally the Attitudes and Statues were not for our own consumption; we'd have gotten bored immediately. The rules were that the winner had to station herself at the foot of the embankment, leaving the shade of the willow trees, and wait for the train from Tigre that passed at 2:08. At that height above Palermo the trains went by pretty fast and we weren't bashful doing the Statue or the Attitude. We hardly saw the people in the train windows, but with time, we got a bit more expert, and we knew that some of the passengers were expecting to see us. One man with white hair and tortoise-shell glasses used to stick his head out of the window and wave at the Statue or the Attitude with a handkerchief. Boys sitting on the steps of the coaches on their way back from school shouted things as the train went by, but some of them remained serious and watching us. In actual fact, the Statue or the Attitude saw nothing at all, because she had to concentrate so hard on holding herself stock-still, but the other two under the willows would analyze in excruciating detail the great success produced, or the audience's indifference. It was a Wednesday when the note dropped as the second coach went by. It fell very near Holanda (she did Malicious Gossip that day) and ricocheted toward me. The small piece of paper was tightly folded up and had been shoved through a metal nut. In a man's handwriting, and pretty bad too, it said: "The Statues very pretty. I ride in the third window of the second coach. Ariel B." For all the trouble of stuffing it through the nut and tossing it, it seemed to us a little dry, but it delighted us. We chose lots to see who would keep it, and I won. The next day nobody wanted to play because we all wanted to see what Ariel B. was like, but we were afraid he would misinterpret our interruption, so finally we chose lots and Letitia won. Holanda and I were very happy because Letitia did Statues very well, poor thing. The paralysis wasn't noticeable when she was still, and she was capable of gestures of enormous nobility. With Attitudes she always chose Generosity, Piety, Sacrifice and Renunciation. With Statues she tried for the style of the Venus in the parlor which Aunt Ruth called the Venus de Nilo. For that reason we chose ornaments especially so that Ariel would be very impressed. We hung a piece of green velvet on her like a tunic, and a crown of willow on her hair. As she was wearing short sleeves, the Greek effect was terrific. Letitia practiced a little in the shade, and we decided that we'd show ourselves also and wave at Ariel, discreetly, but very friendly.

Letitia was magnificent; when the train came she didn't budge a finger. Since she couldn't turn her head, she threw it backward, bringing her arms against her body almost as though she were missing them: except for the green tunic, it was like looking at the Venus de Nilo. In the third window we saw a boy with blond curly hair and light eyes, who smiled brightly when he saw that Holanda and I were waving at him. The train was gone in a second, but it was 4:30 and we were still discussing whether he was wearing a dark suit, a red tie, and if he were really nice or a creep. On Thursday I did an Attitude, Dejection, and we got another note which read: "The three of you I like very much. Ariel." Now he stuck his head and one arm out the window and laughed and waved at us. We figured him to be eighteen (we were sure he was no older than sixteen), and we decided that he was coming back every day from some English school; we couldn't stand the idea of any of the regular peanut factories. You could see that Ariel was super.

As it happened, Holanda had the terrific luck to win three days running. She surpassed herself, doing the Attitudes Reproach and Robbery, and a very difficult Statue of The Ballerina, balancing on one foot from the time the train hit the curve. The next day I won, and the day after that too; when I was doing Horror, a note from Ariel almost caught me on the nose; at first we didn't understand it: "The prettiest is the laziest." Letitia was the last to understand it; we saw that she blushed and went off by herself, and Holanda and I looked at each other, just a little furious. The first judicial opinion it occurred to us to hand down was that Ariel was an idiot, but we couldn't tell Letitia that, poor angel, with the disadvantage she had to put up with. She said nothing, but it seemed to be understood that the paper was hers, and she kept it. We were sort of quiet going back to the house that day, and didn't get together that night. Letitia was very happy at the supper table, her eyes shining, and Mama looked at Aunt Ruth a couple of times as evidence of her own high spirits. In those days they were trying out a new strengthening treatment for Letitia, and considering how she looked, it was miraculous how well she was feeling.

Before we went to sleep, Holanda and I talked about the business. The note from Ariel didn't bother us so much, thrown from a train going its own way, that's how it is, but it seemed to us that Letitia from her privileged position was taking too much advantage of us. She knew we weren't going to say anything to her, and in a household where there's someone with some physical defect and a lot of pride, everyone pretends to ignore it, starting with the one who's sick, or better yet, they pretend they don't know that the other one knows. But you don't have to exaggerate it either, and the way Letitia was acting at the table, or the way she kept the note, was just too much. That night I went back to having nightmares about trains: it was morning and I was walking on enormous railroad beaches covered with rails filled with switches, seeing in the distance the red glows of locomotives approaching, anxiously trying to calculate if the train was going to pass to my left and threatened at the same time by the arrival of an express back of me or—what was even worse—that one of the trains would switch off onto one of the sidings and run directly over me. But I forgot it by morning because Letitia was all full of aches and we had to help her get dressed. It seemed to us that she was a little sorry for the business yesterday and we were very nice to her, telling her that's what happens with walking too much and that maybe it would be better for her to stay in her room reading. She said nothing but came to the table for breakfast, and when Mama asked, she said she was fine and her back hardly hurt at all. She stated it firmly and looked at us.

That afternoon I won, but at that moment, I don't know what came over me. I told Letitia that I'd give her my place, naturally without telling her why. That this guy clearly preferred her and would look at her until his eyes fell out. The game drew to Statues, and we selected simple items so as not to complicate life, and she invented a sort of Chinese Princess, with a shy air, looking at the ground, and the hands placed together as Chinese princesses are wont to do. When the train passed, Holanda was lying on her back under the willows, but I watched and saw that Ariel had eyes only for Letitia. He kept looking at her until the train disappeared around the curve, and Letitia stood there motionless and didn't know that he had just looked at her that way. But when it came to resting under the trees again, we saw that she knew all right, and that she'd have been pleased to keep the costume on all afternoon and all night.

Wednesday we drew between Holanda and me, because Letitia said it was only fair she be left out. Holanda won, darn her luck, but Ariel's letter fell next to me. When I picked it up I had the impulse to give it to Letitia, who didn't say a word, but I thought, then, that neither was it a matter of catering to everybody's wishes, and I opened it slowly. Ariel announced that the next day he was going to get off at the nearby station and that he would come by the embankment to chat for a while. It was all terribly written, but the final phrase was handsomely put: "Warmest regards to the three Statues." The signature looked like a scrawl though we remarked on its personality.

While we were taking the ornaments off Holanda, Letitia looked at me once or twice. I'd read them the message and no one had made any comments, which was very upsetting because finally, at last, Ariel was going to come and one had to think about this new development and come to some decision. If they found out about it at the house, or if by accident one of the Loza girls, those envious little runts, came to spy on us, there was going to be one incredible mess. Furthermore, it was extremely unlike us to remain silent over a thing like this; we hardly looked at one another, putting the ornaments away and going back through the white gate to the house.

Aunt Ruth asked Holanda and me to wash the cat, and she took Letitia off for the evening treatment and finally we could get our feelings off our chests. It seemed super that Ariel was going to come; we'd never had a friend like that; our cousin Tito we didn't count, a dumbell who cut out paper dolls and believed in first communion. We were extremely nervous in our expectation and José, poor angel, got the short end of it. Holanda was the braver of the two and brought up the subject of Letitia. I didn't know what to think; on the one hand it seemed ghastly to me that Ariel should find out, but also it was only fair that things clear themselves up; no one had to out and out put herself on the line for someone else. What I really would have wanted was that Letitia not suffer; she had enough to put up with and now the new treatment and all those things.

That night Mama was amazed to see us so quiet and said what a miracle, and had the cat got our tongues, then looked at Aunt Ruth and both of them thought for sure we'd been raising hell of some kind and were conscience-stricken. Letitia ate very little and said that she hurt and would they let her go to her room to read Rocambole. Though she didn't much want to, Holanda gave her a hand, and I sat down and started some knitting, something I do only when I'm nervous. Twice I thought to go down to Letitia's room. I couldn't figure out what the two of them were doing there alone, but then Holanda came back with a mysterious air of importance and sat next to me not saying a word until Mama and Aunt Ruth cleared the table. "She doesn't want to go tomorrow. She wrote a letter and said that if he asks a lot of questions we should give it to him." Half-opening the pocket of her blouse, she showed me the lilac-tinted envelope. Then they called us in to dry the dishes, and that night we fell asleep almost immediately, exhausted by all the high-pitched emotion and from washing José.

The next day it was my turn to do the marketing and I didn't see Letitia all morning; she stayed in her room. Before they called us to lunch I went in for a moment and found her sitting at the window with a pile of pillows and a new Rocambole novel. You could see she felt terrible, but she started to laugh and told me about a bee that couldn't find its way out and about a funny dream she had had. I said it was a pity she wasn't coming out to the willows, but I found it difficult to put it nicely. "If you want, we can explain to Ariel that you feel upset," I suggested, but she said no and shut up like a clam. I insisted for a little while, really, that she should come, and finally got terribly gushy and told her she shouldn't be afraid, giving as an example that true affection knows no barriers and other fat ideas we'd gotten from *The Treasure of Youth*, but it got harder and harder to say anything to her because she was looking out the window and looked as if she were going to cry. Finally I left, saying that Mama needed me. Lunch lasted for days, and Holanda got a slap from Aunt Ruth for having spattered some tomato sauce from the spaghetti onto the tablecloth. I don't even remember doing the dishes; right away we were out under the willows hugging one another, very happy, and not jealous of one another in the slightest. Holanda explained to me everything we had to say about our studies so that Ariel would be impressed, because high school students despised girls who'd only been through grade school and studied just home ec and knew how to do raised needlework. When the train went past at 2:08, Ariel waved his arms enthusiastically, and we waved a welcome to him with our embossed handkerchiefs. Some twenty minutes later we saw him arrive by the embankment; he was taller than we had thought and dressed all in gray.

I don't even remember what we talked about at first; he was somewhat shy in spite of having come and the notes and everything, and said a lot of considerate things. Almost immediately he praised our Statues and Attitudes and asked our names, and why had the third one not come. Holanda explained that Letitia had not been able to come, and he said that that was a pity and that he thought Letitia was an exquisite name. Then he told us stuff about the Industrial High School, it was not the English school, unhappily, and wanted to know if we would show him the ornaments. Holanda lifted the stone and we let him see the things. He seemed to be very interested in them, and at different times he would take one of the ornaments and say: "Letitia wore this one day," or "This was for the Oriental statue," when what he meant was the Chinese Princess. We sat in the shade under a willow and he was happy but distracted, and you could see that he was only being polite. Holanda looked at me two or three times when the conversation lapsed into silence, and that made both of us feel awful, made us want to get out of it, or wish that Ariel had never come at all. He asked again if Letitia were ill and Holanda looked at me and I thought she was going to tell him, but instead she answered that Letitia had not been able to come. Ariel drew geometric figures in the dust with a stick and occasionally looked at the white gate and we knew what he was thinking, and because of that Holanda was right to pull out the lilac envelope and hand it up to him, and he stood there surprised with the envelope in his hand; then he blushed while we explained that Letitia had sent it to him, and he put the leter in an inside jacket pocket, not wanting to read it in front of us. Almost immediately he said that it had been a great pleasure for him and that he was delighted to have come, but his hand was soft and unpleasant in a way it'd have been better for the interview to end right away, although later we could only think of his gray eyes and the sad way he had of smiling. We also agreed on how he had said goodbye: "Until always," a form we'd never heard at home and which seemed to us so godlike and poetic. We told all this to Letitia, who was waiting for us under the lemon tree in the patio, and I would have liked to have asked her what she had said in the letter, but I don't know what it was, because she'd sealed the envelope before giving it to Holanda, so I didn't say anything about that and only told her what Ariel was like and how many times he'd asked for her. This was not at all an easy thing to do because it was a nice thing and a terrible thing at the same time; we noticed that Letitia was feeling very happy and at the same time she was almost crying, and we found ourselves saying that Aunt Ruth wanted us now and we left her looking at the wasps in the lemon tree.

When we were going to sleep that night, Holanda said to me, "The game's finished from tomorrow on, you'll see." But she was wrong though not by much, and the next day Letitia gave us the regular signal when dessert came around. We went out to wash the dishes somewhat astonished, and a bit sore, because that was sheer sauciness on Letitia's part and not the right thing to do. She was waiting for us at the gate, and we almost died of fright when we got to the willows, for she brought out of her pocket Mama's pearl collar and all her rings, even Aunt Ruth's big one with the ruby. If the Loza girls were spying on us and saw us with the jewels, sure as anything Mama would learn about it right away and kill us, the nasty little creeps. But Letitia wasn't scared and said if anything happened she was the only one responsible. "I would like you to leave it to me today," she added without looking at us. We got the ornaments out right away; all of a sudden we wanted to be very kind to Letitia and give her all the pleasure, although at the bottom of everything we were still feeling a little spiteful. The game came out Statues, and we chose lovely things that would go well with the jewels, lots of peacock feathers to set in the hair, and a fur that from a distance looked like silver fox, and a pink veil that she put on like a turban. We saw that she was thinking, trying the Statue out, but without moving, and when the train appeared on the curve she placed herself at the foot of the incline with all the jewels sparkling in the sun. She lifted her arms as if she were going to do an Attitude instead of a Statue, her hands pointed at the sky with her head thrown back (the only direction she could, poor thing) and bent her body backwards so far it scared us. To us it seemed terrific, the most regal statue she'd ever done; then we saw Ariel looking at her, hung half-way out the window he looked just at her, turning his head and looking at her without seeing us, until the train carried him out of sight all at once. I don't know why, the two of us started running at the same time to catch Letitia, who was standing there, still with her eyes closed and enormous tears all down her face. She pushed us back, not angrily, but we helped her stuff the jewels in her pocket, and she went back to the house alone while we put the ornaments away in their box for the last time. We knew almost what was going to happen, but just the same we went out to the willows the next day, just the two of us, after Aunt Ruth imposed absolute silence so as not to disturb Letitia, who hurt and who wanted to sleep. When the train came by, it was no surprise to see the third window empty, and while we were grinning at one another, somewhere between relief and being furious, we imagined Ariel riding on the other side of the coach, not moving in his seat, looking off toward the river with his gray eyes.

Translated by Paul Blackburn

My Life with the Wave

OCTAVIO PAZ

When I left that sea, a wave moved ahead of the others. She was tall and light. In spite of the shouts of the others who grabbed her by her floating clothes, she clutched my arm and went off with me leaping. I didn't want to say anything to her, because it hurt me to shame her in front of her friends. Besides, the furious stares of the elders paralyzed me. When we got to town, I explained to her that it was impossible, that life in the city was not what she had been able to imagine with the ingenuity of a wave that had never left the sea. She watched me gravely: "No, your decision is made. You can't go back." I tried sweetness, hardness, irony. She cried, screamed, hugged, threatened. I had to apologize.

The next day my troubles began. How could we get on the train without being seen by the conductor, the passengers, the police? Certainly the rules say nothing in respect to the transport of waves on the railroad, but this same reserve was an indication of the severity with which our act would be judged. After much thought I arrived at the station an hour before departure, took my seat and, when no one was looking, emptied the water tank for the passengers; then, carefully, poured in my friend.

The first incident came about when the children of a nearby couple declared their noisy thirst. I stopped them and promised them refreshments and lemonade. They were at the point of accepting when another thirsty passenger approached. I was about to invite her also, but the stare of her companion stopped me. The lady took a paper cup, approached the tank and turned the faucet. Her cup was barely half full when I leaped between the woman and my friend. She looked at me astonished. While I apologized, one of the children turned the faucet again. I closed it violently. The lady brought the cup to her lips:

"Agh, this water is salty."

The boy echoed her. Various passengers rose. The husband called the conductor:

"This man put salt in the water."

The conductor called the Inspector:

"So you put substances in the water?"

The Inspector in turn called the police:

"So you poisoned the water?"

The police in turn called the Captain:

"So you're the poisoner?"

The Captain called three agents. The agents took me to an empty car, amid the stares and whispers of the passengers. At the next station they took me off and pushed and dragged me to the jail. For days no one spoke to me, except during the long interrogations. When I explained my story no one believed me, not even the jailer, who shook his head, saying: "The case is grave, truly grave. You didn't want to poison the children?" One day they brought me before the Magistrate.

"Your case is difficult," he repeated. "I will assign you to the Penal Judge."

A year passed. Finally they judged me. As there were

no victims, my sentence was light. After a short time, my day of liberty arrived.

The Chief of the Prison called me in:

"Well, now you're free. You were lucky. Lucky there were no victims. But don't do it again, because the next time won't be so short . . ."

And he stared at me with the same grave stare with which everyone watched me.

The same afternoon I took the train and after hours of uncomfortable traveling arrived in Mexico City. I took a cab home. At the door of my apartment I heard laughter and singing. I felt a pain in my chest, like the smack of a wave of surprise when surprise smacks us across the chest: my friend was there, singing and laughing as always.

"How did you get back?"

"Simple: in the train. Someone, after making sure that I was only salt water, poured me in the engine. It was a rough trip: soon I was a white plume of vapor, soon I fell in a fine rain on the machine. I thinned out a lot. I lost many drops."

Her presence changed my life. The house of dark corridors and dusty furniture was filled with air, with sun, with sounds and green and blue reflections, a numerous and happy populace of reverberations and echoes. How many waves is one wave, and how it can make a beach or a rock or jetty out of a wall, a chest, a forehead that it crowns with foam! Even the abandoned corners, the abject corners of dust and debris were touched by her light hands. Everything began to laugh and everywhere shined with teeth. The sun entered the old rooms with pleasure and stayed in my house for hours, abandoning the other houses, the district, the city, the country. And some nights, very late, the scandalized stars watched it sneak from my house.

Love was a game, a perpetual creation. All was beach, sand, a bed of sheets that were always fresh. If I embraced her, she swelled with pride, incredibly tall, like the liquid stalk of a poplar; and soon that thinness flowered into a fountain of white feathers, into a plume of smiles that fell over my head and back and covered me with whiteness. Or she stretched out in front of me, infinite as the horizon, until I too became horizon and silence. Full and sinuous, it enveloped me like music or some giant lips. Her presence was a going and coming of caresses, of murmurs, of kisses. Entered in her waters, I was drenched to the socks and in a wink of an eye I found myself up above, at the height of vertigo, mysteriously suspended, to fall like a stone and feel myself gently deposited on the dryness, like a feather. Nothing is comparable to sleeping in those waters, to wake pounded by a thousand happy light lashes, by a thousand assaults that withdrew laughing.

But never did I reach the center of her being. Never did I touch the nakedness of pain and of death. Perhaps it does not exist in waves, that secret site that renders a woman vulnerable and mortal, that electric button where all interlocks, twitches, and straightens out to then swoon. Her sensibility, like that of women, spread in ripples, only they weren't concentric ripples, but rather excentric, spreading each time farther, until they touched other galaxies. To love her was to extend to remote contacts, to vibrate with far-off stars we never suspected. But her center . . . no, she had no center, just an emptiness as in a whirlwind, that sucked me in and smothered me.

Stretched out side by side, we exchanged confidences, whispers, smiles. Curled up, she fell on my chest and there unfolded like a vegetation of murmurs. She sang in my ear, a little snail. She became humble and transparent, clutching my feet like a small animal, calm water. She was so clear I could read all of her thoughts. Certain nights her skin was covered with phosphorescence and to embrace her was to embrace a piece of night tattooed with fire. But she also became black and bitter. At unexpected hours she roared, moaned, twisted. Her groans woke the neighbors. Upon hearing her, the sea wind would scratch at the door of the house or rave in a loud voice on the roof. Cloudy days irritated her; she broke furniture, said bad words, covered me with insults and green and gray foam. She spit, cried, swore, prophesied. Subject to the moon, to the stars, to the influence of the light of other worlds, she changed her moods and appearance in a way that I thought fantastic, but it was as fatal as the tide.

She began to miss solitude. The house was full of snails and conches, of small sailboats that in her fury she had shipwrecked (together with the others, laden with images, that each night left my forehead and sank in her ferocious or pleasant whirlwinds). How many little treasures were lost in that time! But my boats and the silent song of the snails was not enough. I had to install in the house a colony of fish. I confess that it was not without jealousy that I watched them swimming in my friend, caressing her breasts, sleeping between her legs, adorning her hair with light flashes of color.

Among all those fish there were a few particularly repulsive and ferocious ones, little tigers from the aquarium, with large fixed eyes and jagged and blood-thirsty mouths. I don't know by what aberration my friend delighted in playing with them, shamelessly showing them a preference whose significance I preferred to ignore. She passed long hours confined with those horrible creatures. One day I couldn't stand it any more; I threw open the door and launched after them. Agile and ghostly they escaped my hands while she laughed and pounded me until I fell. I thought I was drowning. And when I was at the point of death, and purple, she deposited me on the bank and began to kiss me, saying I don't know what things. I felt very weak, fatigued and humiliated. And at the same time her voluptuousness made me close my eyes, because her voice was sweet and she spoke to me of the delicious death of the drowned. When I recovered, I began to fear and hate her.

I had neglected my affairs. Now I began to visit friends and renew old and dear relations. I met an old girlfriend. Making her swear to keep my secret, I told her of my life with the wave. Nothing moves women so much as the possibility of saving a man. My redeemer employed all of her arts, but what could a woman, master of a limited number of souls and bodies, do in front of my friend who was always changing—and always identical to herself in her incessant metamorphoses.

Winter came. The sky turned gray. Fog fell on the city. Frozen drizzle rained. My friend cried every night. During the day she isolated herself, quiet and sinister, stuttering a single syllable, like an old woman who grumbles in a corner. She became cold; to sleep with her was to shiver all night and to feel freeze, little by little, the blood, the bones, the thoughts. She turned deep, impenetrable, restless. I left frequently and my absences were each time more prolonged. She, in her corner, howled loudly. With teeth like steel and a corrosive tongue she gnawed the walls, crumbled them. She passed the nights in mourning, reproaching me. She had nightmares, deliriums of the sun, of warm beaches. She dreamt of the pole and of changing into a great block of ice, sailing beneath black skies in nights long as months. She insulted me. She cursed and laughed; filled the house with guffaws and phantoms. She called up the monsters of the depths, blind ones, quick ones, blunt. Charged with electricity, she carbonized all she touched; fill of acid, she dissolved whatever she brushed against. Her sweet embraces became knotty cords that strangled me. And her body, greenish and elastic, was an implacable whip that lashed, lashed, lashed. I fled. The horrible fish laughed with ferocious smiles.

There in the mountains, among the tall pines and precipices, I breathed the cold thin air like a thought of liberty. At the end of a month I returned. I had decided. It had been so cold that over the marble of the chimney, next to the extinct fire, I found a statue of ice. I was unmoved by her weary beauty. I put her in a big canvas sack and went out to the streets with the sleeper on my shoulders. In a restaurant in the outskirts I sold her to a waiter friend who immediately began to chop her into little pieces, which he carefully deposited in the buckets where bottles are chilled.

Translated by Eliot Weinberger

Miracles Cannot Be Recovered

ADOLFO BIOY-CASARES

Standing in front of a newsstand in Constitution Station—you still entertained the hope of finding something good to read in those days—I met a young man, Luis Greve, who had been a fellow-student at the Instituto Libre. He asked what I was doing there in the station.

"Taking the train to Las Flores," I said, "but due to an incredible miscalculation I got here an hour and five minutes early."

"Far be it from me to fault you on that one," he said. "I'm going to Colonel Pringle's, and due to an incredible miscalculation *I'm* fifty minutes early. Will you come and have a drink with me?"

We made our way to a bar, ordered, and I remarked, "I've often noticed that in real life things fall in series. Today will probably be full of pointless coincidences."

"Why pointless?"

"Pointless," I quickly explained, not wishing to offend him, "in the sense that they don't prove anything."

"I'm not so sure about that," he said.

"About what?"

"That they don't prove anything. Ever."

Uttered after a pause, the adverb sounded like an explanation—a puzzling explanation, perhaps, that required a question on my part and a further explanation on Greve's. All this, beginning to grow unwieldy, I found discouraging, and, as what I really cared about was convincing him that my qualification was in no way a disparagement of our meeting, I told him the story of the multiplication of Somerset Maughams. Or perhaps I did so simply hoping that a listener might show me how to make literary use of it. Or perhaps because I'm falling into the habit of repeating my own stories.

"It was on a voyage," I began telling him, "aboard one of the Cunard Line ships sailing between New York and Southampton. In the dining room, I shared a table with the only other Argentine aboard—an elderly, somewhat domineering, and thoroughly outgoing woman, with whom I soon struck up a warm friendship.

"I remember the night the passenger list was given out. Each of us, nose in his copy, was lost in the search for his own name. In sudden confusion, as if the omission might turn me into a stowaway, I was unable to find the three magic words. I thought to myself, 'Easy now; let's think this over,' and I had an inspiration. What if, instead of listing my name under *B*, the nincompoops had put it under *C*? Sure enough, there in the C column was a certain *Cesares, Mr. Adolfo B.*, in whom, after one or two doubts, I recognized myself. My friend, who had met with no similar difficulties, had taken her good time and, at last, with a triumphant finger, pointed out to me her correctly printed name. But I was more struck by the name preceding hers. I read aloud, '*Maugham, Mr. William Somerset.*'

"Raising her voice to correct me, my friend read out her name.

" 'No, madam,' I protested, 'I already know your

name. It's just that I was surprised at finding the name of Somerset Maugham, the famous novelist, among the list of passengers.'

"In her look I saw the flash of recognition. Can any of those Argentine ladies of the old school be compared with young girls of today? It's a whole different world, a different intelligence.

" 'Somerset Maugham,' repeated the lady. 'But of course, I read one of his books; it took place in the Pacific. I don't know why, but I've always been fascinated by all the mystery of the East.'

"She asked me if I would recognize Maugham if he were in the dining room.

" 'Yes,' I said. 'I've seen him in photographs. But he isn't here.'

"Looking back on this now, I believe that not finding him was a distinct relief, for the lady said, 'The moment he appears, I'll go straight to him and say that I want him to meet an Argentine writer. What could please him more? I'll tell him that you are a great writer.'

" 'P-please,' I stammered.

" 'That's what's wrong with old Argentines like us,' she said. 'We're too modest.'

" 'It's not modesty. We'll look like a pair of schoolchildren.'

"So as to be spared the dreaded introduction, the next day I avoided my new friend as much as possible. The precaution proved unnecessary, however, since Somerset Maugham, as if he might be in hiding in his stateroom, did not appear anywhere.

"On the eve of our arrival, I accompanied my fellow-Argentine to the ship's commissary and to a shop. Though elderly, she was tireless, and, going both up and down, we ignored the elevators. On a sort of gloomy mezzanine that came to life only when the ship was in port and it became a vestibule, in a leather armchair opposite a photograph of princelings of the

British royal family sat a thoughtful, solitary, oldish man, bundled up like Phineas Fogg for an eighty-day trip around the world, whom I immediately identified as Somerset Maugham. The fearful meeting, perhaps because it had been stayed so many times, now seemed matter-of-fact and even unreal; I actually whispered, or shouted, since my lady friend was a bit deaf: 'It's him.'

"I wished I had not said it. Without an instant's hesitation, her great cape fluttering like a flag, my friend sallied forth. I remember, at the moment, having thought, 'The spirit of our soldiers in the battles of Maipú, Navarro, and La Verde is not entirely lost.' Utterly oblivious of her awkward English, she began tumultuously explaining, 'We wanted to meet you. A great honor. This gentleman is an Argentine writer. We both admire you.'

"The man, absorbed in his thoughts, roused himself with unruffled urbanity. 'May I ask why you admire me?' he said.

"He looked at us with that lofty expression of his—much like a scornful though harmless snake—which photographers have made popular.

"Quickly, because she ignored all scruples, my friend began delivering patriotic protests about the Argentine's not being, though it might seem otherwise, a plumed Indian, and about the fact that foreign novels did, after all, reach Buenos Aires. She closed her outpouring with this question: 'You, Mr. Somerset, don't you believe, as I, that the East has a fascinating mystery?'

"All things have a limit, and I did not want to be misunderstood. Vanity plunged me into the conversation. '*Cakes and Ale* is an unforgettable novel,' I said. 'And I never tire in my admiration of your latest book, your *Writer's Notebook*.'

"The Englishman mumbled something, but I had to ask him (as if my friend's deafness had become contagious) to repeat it. Addressing himself to the lady, he said in a huff, 'You—you are mistaking me for someone else. I haven't written any novel. I am a retired colonel.'

"The only answer she gave was a literal translation of the Spanish phrase 'to fob off a cat for a hare.' We were offended. Coldly, I framed some conventional words of pardon, and we withdrew.

" 'The nerve of that colonel,' my friend commented. 'Why, it's unbelievable. Trying to deceive *me*, of all people—a descendant of the soldiers of the Independence.'

"To annoy her, for she had been to blame for the whole ridiculous thing, I remarked: 'But you're wrong. He wasn't fobbing himself off as someone else—just the opposite.'

"The next morning, in the roadstead off Cherbourg, we watched from the ship's rail as passengers were transferred to a tugboat which would carry them ashore. Pointing to the tug below us, at the side nearest our ship, my lady friend said, 'There he is.'

"Pointing to the opposite side, I contradicted her. 'No, he's over there.'

"He's on both sides," my friend admitted, crestfallen.

In fact, as if due to some unfathomable mirage, we saw in the tug two specimens, so to speak, of Somerset Maugham.

" 'They're the same man,' I said, utterly bewildered.

" 'They're wearing different clothes,' my friend corrected."

As for Greve, he looked off into space like a judge trying to avoid being moved by sympathy. Into the uncomfortable gap I said: "That's all."

He was still a long time in speaking. "You're right," he admitted at last. "An utterly pointless coincidence. Your story doesn't shed a bit of light on mine. Or does it prove that there are moments when anything can happen?"

I was not sure. "Maybe," I ventured to answer.

"Moments," he went on, "that cannot be recovered, since they immediately slip into the past, but that are real—moments that belong to another world, where natural laws can't reach them."

I broke into his digression, asking, "Did you say your story?"

"Something that happened to me. As I was listening to you, I entertained a hope."

"Did I disappoint you? Were you expecting an explanation of a mystery?"

"I don't know what I was expecting. Perhaps there is no other explanation than to suppose it was one of those unique moments we were talking about. What happened to me is very strange. Still, it agrees with what we all feel so deeply—and absurdly—about such things. Do you remember Carmen Silveyra?"

"Poor Carmen, of course I do. So full of life. I used to think she looked . . ." I was going to say I thought she looked like Louise Brooks, a movie actress I had been in love with as a child. In my mind, I recalled the delicate oval of that perfect face—which both women had—white skin, dark eyes and hair, framed by kiss curls.

"Looked how?" he asked with a trace of anxiety.

"I don't know. Irrepressibly young and pretty."

"I'm glad you liked her," he said, quickly adding, "I'm going to commit a desecration. She loved me. I loved her too, but without realizing it. How dumb I was! What I never had any doubt about was that we enjoyed ourselves together. You know how women are. She was always looking for opportunities—inventing them, I should say—to go out with me or to go off on trips, even though in her position it was unwise to be seen with me."

"The inevitable 'position.' All women have a position to maintain—and above all, to risk." I uttered a dry laugh. My witticism—or whatever it was—cheered me again, but it apparently depressed Greve.

"I never knew that," he said. "I may be more naïve than other men. I believed in Carmen's position, and often I dissuaded her from her plans—but sometimes I also let myself be swept along. I have no regrets. How that woman believed in life! Everywhere—in a restaurant, under the stars, boating along the Paraná weekending at some inn—we anticipated (how can I explain?) whole stores of amusement, which of course we always found. On one of our escapades, we went to Mar del Plata.

"I had just sold my car. We took the train, which was risky, since we didn't know whom we might run into. Sitting opposite us was a young woman—we later found out she was a dentist—who was all too ready to engage us in conversation. In a low voice, Carmen steeled me. 'Be firm,' she said. 'Give her an inch and there'll be five solid hours of talk. Such a bore!'

"Carmen was quickly convinced that the only danger on the train was seated opposite us. 'She's no danger,' I said. 'Boring maybe, but that's all. Have we any idea what the other coaches may hold in store for us?'

" 'We won't run into a soul,' she assured me—meaning not a soul we knew.

" 'What hotel are we going to?' I said. I hadn't had time to make room reservations. We had decided on the trip that same day during lunch. Each of us had returned home to pack a bag, and at five o'clock we'd met again at the station. At the last moment, Carmen remembered that she had promised to serve, on Saturday and Sunday, in some benefit drive. We rushed to find a telephone. Carmen got through and made excuses. Later, she told me: 'What luck! I was afraid I'd have to speak to our president, who's the strictest, most respectable thing in Buenos Aires, but her secretary answered, and she's a dear. I told her I was sick in bed. Guess what she said? That the president was sick in bed. So everything's quite marvelous.' To my question about hotels, she answered, 'What about the Provincial?'

" 'Are you mad?' I protested. 'We should find a small hotel, well off the main track.'

"Looking back, I think I was the mad one. It was my miserable mania, always in the name of prudence, to restrain her impulses. I think that if I could be with her now—I say 'think' because nobody, perhaps, can change.

" 'What a bore,' she said. Didn't you mention a certain León, who has a heated hotel and serves good food?'

" 'Everybody goes there.'

" 'In this cold, who'd possibly go there?'

"I didn't answer her, seeing myself as the teacher admonishing the pupil, nor did I overlook the fact that this girl's love was a luxury. Her patience surprises me—it surprised me then.

"All of this conversation I would place in the early part of our journey. What happened in the middle is a blank to me. In the last part, the woman opposite got up her courage to recommend the hotel where she usually stayed—the Quequén—and to inform us that she was a professional (no more than that, as if the one word were sufficient). A while later, however, she specified 'odontologist,' and after that I remember scenes that seem to belong to a dream. For example, when she meddled with (or, more exactly, into) out mouths. Carmen passed her examination with flying colors; I not only flunked but was humiliated. Since none of my imploring looks met with any success, I finally said angrily, 'Please, spare me the details.'

"I thought I was paying for my guilt, which proves that the dentist's entrance into our conversation was probably not exactly as I told it, and that I had done something to pave the way for her. We men have the cowardly defect of being polite to others at the expense of the person we love.

"We stepped off the train into the cold, dark night. At all the cabstands there were long lines of waiting people. We were with the dentist who, with a will of her own, was taking us to her hotel. I had surrendered to her, ready to drag Carmen along. Suddenly I felt my arm being tugged and heard the order, 'Come on!'

"Carmen was pulling me; we ran through the inscrutable darkness into the middle of the traffic along Luro Avenue. I can still hear her stifled laughter. With a raised arm, she hailed a cab. I protested, telling her we ought to have regard for others. A cab driver was about to pass us by, respectful of those in line—especially since it gave him a ready-made excuse for disregarding anyone else—but seeing Carmen, he stopped. He had to. You yourself said it: she was so pretty and so young.

" 'Where are we going?' I said.

" 'To your León's place,' she said, and, when I gave the driver the address, she remarked, 'The Quequén Palace—now I ask you. Can't you just imagine what a Mar del Plata hotel with that name would be like? Quequén! Is that meant to awaken one's desire to leave at once?'

"I've given so many proofs of my idiocy as to depress me. I mean it. Knowing the hotel manager, in my situation, bothered me. Do you know what my situation was? It seems unbelievable. Carmen! Instead of taking pride in her, I felt obliged to explain, to make excuses.

"The hotel welcomed us with the news that the heating system was not working and that, because they were remodeling the kitchens, no meals were being served. So as not to have to brave the cold at that hour looking for another hotel, we stayed. They installed an electric heater in our room. We quickly realized that our options were either to stand away from the contraption and freeze or to get closer to it and burn. We asked for more blankets and climbed into bed with our clothes on. Carmen made a turban of a towel to protect her head from the cold. I assure you her beauty dazzled me.

"A pale sun shone the next day, and we went down to the beach. Lying on canvas in the shelter of a cabana, we warmed up enough to enjoy the morning. We watched the sea, we talked about our travels, and I remember we saw an old couple passing by, their bodies leaning into the wind as if they were plowing the sand. Carmen said that out of season all beach resorts were poetic. That afternoon we had tea in a place at the corner of Santiago del Estero and San Martín, which in later years was torn down. Whenever anyone pushed in or out through the big glass doors, an iceberg seemed to run up the middle of the room. Thinking only of the cold, we stared at those doors with the magic hope, perhaps, of keeping people away.

" 'O my God,' Carmen uttered under her breath.

"A bulky matron had come in, as erect as a haughty sea lion.

" 'She's monstrous, all right,' I said.

" It's her.'

" 'Who?'

" 'The president herself.'

" 'Maybe she won't see you.'

"Before I could finish my sentence, the lady, her eyes glued to our table, stopped short. There was a very long, pregnant moment. I saw a raised forefinger. Perhaps my imagination is overdramatic, but I half expected that finger to point accusingly at Carmen. Then I was astonished. Twice the lady put a finger to her lips. What Carmen asked me, after winking, I could neither confirm nor deny. All I can say is that behind the majestic hulk, a small old man appeared, with a red nose and damp mustache, alien apparently to all that was taking place. In a low voice, Carmen said, 'Am I crazy or did she ask me to keep quiet?' She then added, joyously, 'Like me, she claimed she was ill. Like us, she came to Mar del Plata.'

" 'With the difference,' I pointed out, 'that her little man has caught himself a cold.'

"From that moment on, everything changed. Perhaps the sight, or the caricature, of that mountainous woman in sudden alarm freed me of concern for prudence and of something even worse—my consciousness of uncomfortable circumstances. From that moment on, I gave in to our good luck. I swear that that night the cold lessened. At any rate, I did not get into bed with clothes on; if warmth was lacking, I looked for it in Carmen's body.

"Between us, the old woman's gesture became a private joke. When we were told secrets or were asked not to tell something, we imitated that solemnly absurd finger. Such repeated jokes, as everyone knows, appear foolish. Ours reminded us of the best weekend of our lives.

"The mind is unreliable. Recalling them in order, memories come back that were long forgotten. I remember that we took the one-o'clock train back, but not that Carmen asked me to postpone our return. I now have an image of her lying on the bed, face down, her head sunk into the pillow. I lifted her head to kiss her. Far from gay, she gravely asked that we stay on, looking at me anxiously, as though she were frightened. It was this unexpected anxiety, I believe, that made me uncompromising.

" 'Everyone knows that women go through changes and cycles', I said. 'Haven't they been compared to the moon? If a man recalls this and attributes a woman's fit of weeping to glands or to nerves he appears insensitive. If he forgets and says, when he's about to be jilted, *How you used to cry over me!*, he'll be told he was dreaming.'

" 'You're awful,' Carmen murmured, managing a smile.

" 'If the time for leaving comes, why be tragic about it?'

" 'Then let's stay here for good,' she said.

"My only response was to pack. When my mind is made up—I sometimes boast of this as a virtue—I don't accept changes.

"A few days later, back in Buenos Aires, I found out simultaneously that I missed what we'd had together in Mar del Plata and that Carmen, though as effusive and sweet as ever, no longer clung to me in the same way. She paid me visits, we went walking and we joked, we recalled the old woman's gesture, we took pleasure in everything, but—and this was entirely new between us—I kept feeling inclined to ask her if she loved me less.

"That spring, some friends invited me on a trip to Ushuaia. As Tierra del Fuego had always been of interest to me, I did not want to lose the chance to go. The only obstacle was Carmen. Our traveling together this time presented problems for her; would she let me go alone? To get around difficulties, I went off without a word of goodbye.

"On the afternoon I got back, I found two men at my door. How odd—for me those men have neither faces nor statures nor anything else to distinguish them. They are blotted out of my memory, barely leaving behind a few words and a sort of dizziness. They pestered me with information about a maid who had somehow eluded some investigation or other, when all I wanted was a hot bath and to be alone.

" 'What has this to do with me?" I said.

"They insisted on explanations, and, despite my weariness, I realized that they were talking about an accident. I heard one word—'deceased'—and then two others, spoken with a neutral, unfaltering tone that monotonously brought the sentence to a close—'Carmen Silveyra.' The maid, when she'd been asked to go to the morgue, had locked herself in her room. What maid did they mean? The maid who came mornings to clean the dead woman's apartment. They were asking me to identify the corpse. God forgive me, in the midst of my grief, I felt a certain pride."

"I saw you at the wake," I said.

"I hardly remember a thing about it," Greve answered.

"It must have been a tremendous blow to you," I said, feeling sorry for him. "How lovely Carmen was. To see her suddenly dead was—"

"Was a shock? I was going to say that, but now I think it doesn't express exactly what I felt. Seeing her dead upset me less than the thought that later I'd never see her again. What's incredible about death is that people disappear."

"Some deaths are incredible," I agreed. "One easily falls into superstitions and guilt feelings. It's horrible what happened to you, but you have nothing to blame yourself for."

"I'm not sure," Greve said. "What more can I tell you? My life changed very little. Don't think I didn't miss Carmen; I remembered her by day and I dreamed of her by night. But the past is the past. I got a taste for the country. My journeys to Pringle's became more frequent, my stays there longer. In the dining car of the same train I'm taking today, I met a man who told me wonderful things about traveling abroad, and he encouraged me to set out around the world. As the man owned a touring agency, there were no troubles over tickets. Since Carmen's death, I'm no longer tied to places.

"One evening, as we were flying over the sea, I realized my mistake. The world was full of wonders, but I was looking at them in apathy. Don't think I was overly sad—only indifferent. A tourist goes sightseeing; for that—at the very least—you need hopes of some kind. I began rushing through the last legs of my trip. Instead of staying in a city two or three days, I took the first plane to the next stop on my itinerary. Several times a day, one had to set one's watch forward or back; due to these time changes and to fatigue, I came to feel the unreality of everything—of time and of myself.

"I flew from Bombay to Orly. A short while later, without having left the airport, I boarded another plane back to Buenos Aires. We made a stop in Dakar—it was along about daybreak, I think. I had been dozing; I felt displaced, out of sorts. I know that there, or maybe later, we set our watches back. We were forced off the plane and herded along between wooden barriers, like a long cattle chute, toward a bar attended by Negroes. As we entered this passageway, a voice announced the departure of the Capetown flight, and alongside us, coming down the chute parallel to ours, passengers made their way onto the field. In that countercurrent, I absently noticed a scurry, as if someone were trying to hide among the others. I looked. When she saw she was found out, she decided to greet me. I could have confused one person with another, but nobody with her. She was lovely. I stared at her without understanding. Touching a finger twice to her lips, in parody of our old woman from that far-off weekend in Mar del Plata, she asked me to keep her secret. I faltered. Carmen moved on with her group toward the Capetown plane; I remained there until we resumed our journey."

Translated by Norman Thomas di Giovanni

Encounter with the Traitor

AUGUSTO ROA BASTOS

The news vendor was holding out the change, but he did not reach for it or even remember to reach for it. His attention was suddenly fixed on a man walking past along the sidewalk, swinging a thin walking stick. He started after him. "It's him," he told himself. "It has to be him." A long span of time, crammed with events both large and small, struggled to fit into the flash of a second. In this vivid second, he had recognized the man from behind. For there are certain men with many faces—faces on all sides of them, front and back, faces of an unalterable identity down to the slightest expression—who, for all they may do to pass unnoticed, are unmistakable. This was how, in a single glimpse, he had instantly recognized the man with the stick among the anonymous rush of passersby—even though the man already had his back to him.

But the other man had recognized him at first glance, too, in that instant when his delicate stick wavered in his hands (it was a barely noticeable change of rhythm), not out of fear, nor stupor, nor even surprise, but more in adjustment to a new center of gravity brought on by a sudden shift in time, a rapid change in thoughts. It was like stepping unexpectedly on those slippery tiles that also lurk in the mind. He had seen the first man take the newspaper from the vendor and fold it neatly in three. He had glimpsed the movement of the hand as it tightened around the paper. "It's him," the man with the stick had also told himself. "He's put on weight, but it's him." What convinced him on the way the first man had handed his money to the news vendor. "He still has his pride," he said to himself, not seeing now that the other man had refused his change. The man with the stick did not turn around. He either feigned ignorance or recovered his indifference. It was a custom of his. But his self-possession was not feigned. Were there a trace of simulation in his attitude, one would have said he took pleasure in it. The lacquered cane, with its amber reflection, also regained its rhythmic motion.

The man who followed hurried his pace. The old cause, long stored away but far from over, came alive again in his mind without the loss of a single detail. Now he hung back in his haste to overtake the figure up ahead. The other man walked slowly, barely resting the point of his stick on the pavement or else twisting it in his fingers, not like an aging show-off dandy but out of old habit. "Scarecrow!" muttered the man who was following. "The same as ever!" Then, in control of his mounting anger, he studied the man ahead of him. He was solid and straight, his neck was boyish under his gray hair, and, though his left shoulder drooped slightly and his long legs had lost their youthful spring, there was still—even if faded and out of training—a martial air about him. Or the somewhat cynical mimicry of a martial air. The man with the newspaper noted the other's worn but neat suit and fancied that, with its close-fitting military jacket, it was even cut in the style of those days. Of himself, however, it was obvious that growing obesity had forced him into looser and looser clothing. He passed the back of his hand over his dripping face. Sweat also dampened his rolled newspaper.

"He's right behind me," the man with the stick said to himself. "I wonder if he'll go into all that now. Of course, I haven't given them satisfaction enough. Thirty years we've been dead, but one of them can rise up all at once and pursue me."

The two men were returning to life on a city street, in another country, in a chance encounter which neither of them, perhaps, had ever again expected. But the man with the walking stick suddenly realized that the other man had been in pursuit of him the whole time, and that in the space of a few yards the persecution of all these years was being recapitulated, was coming clear, in all its subtleties. The man was tracking him not from a newsstand, where he had stopped by coincidence, but from much farther back—from that uprising sent to its doom by the report of an informer, from the ensuing court-martial, and from their prison camp out in an arid, desolate land where the coconut palms were like bars and the surrounding waste was a parody of freedom. It was that same savage land of the Chaco which several months later would begin swallowing the flesh and blood of a hundred thousand soldiers. The two men had survived that war for a reason as fortuitous and no more valid than the one that had chosen the victims of the slaughter. And now one of them again found himself pitted against the other, as if nothing had intervened, as if nothing had been enough to atone for the unfounded insult, the hatred, the thirst for vengeance, which only seemed lulled into resentful indifference, while not so much the body but the spirit gradually fattened and aged.

"Stop the fight!" the doctor had shouted at them. "Don't you see this man cannot go on?"

But go on he did, stubbornly, though lacking courage, lacking conviction, with no other will than that of a man who must carry a thing through to the end, or the blind obstinacy of drunkards who invent their own heroism. With his left hand he clutched one side of his bloody face, and the blurred damaged eye looked out from between his fingers into a space that was out of focus—the fadeout of a burning, drenched darkness—under the almost spasmodic sally of the last attack. Sabers glistened in the drizzly dawn that smudged the blackish trees and muffled the clash of weapons until they came to a stop, dripping, the blade of one redder than the other, while neither of the duelers expected or hoped for a reconciliation they knew to be impossible.

"He's still after me," said the tall, gray-haired man to himself. "I can't very well turn and wait for him. What would I say? Can I possibly tell him the truth now—after so many years? He wouldn't believe it. Truth also ages, sometimes faster than men. Besides, truth is not for the weak. And he's fat and sad. All he has is his pride. Even his hatred is no more than a feeling of viciousness now. If only I could be sorry for him, the poor guy! Hatred has to feed on something present to be a faith. My guilt isn't even a memory any longer, because it doesn't exist. It simply does not exist; it never existed—at least not the way other things existed. If I were to turn around, what could I say to him?"

"Traitor! Miserable informer!" one of the accused had shouted, raising his fist at the silent witness. He addressed the man who had presumably bought his freedom with betrayal and who now stood there, testifying with his silence—for at no time did he speak—against his fellow-insurrectionists. The insult came again, more plangent and more furious. The judge gaveled the table, making the papers jump, then leaned back in his chair. His face was livid with anger, as much at the stubborn silence of the one as at the outburst of the other. The rest of the accused stirred *uncomfortably on the benches—one of them in particular, the brother of the man who had been insulted. His head was bowed. He seemed weighed down by an insupportable burden, as if only he were suffering the shame just inflicted on his brother. But every other face was craned toward the insulted man, who seemed not to have heard the words spoken against him. Impassive, he stared out the window at the branches rocking in the wind against the barracks wall.*

"More than one of them has been after me since then," the man with the walking stick thought to himself, unwittingly slowing his pace. "The war wasn't enough. A hundred thousand killed in the Chaos—dead for nothing. And that absurd duel, barely a day after the Victory Parade, between two specters scorched by the Chaco's metallic sun. And again the round of revolutions, conspiracies, and uprisings—each with its new heroes and traitors in an endless chain. Yesterday's executioners, today's victims; today's victims, tomorrow's executioners." He remembered the colonel who had presided over the court-martial. After one of the barracks coups following the war, he too was thrown into prison, where he was beaten every morning with pieces of wire by the barefoot guards who were steeped in hatred. The colonel finally went mad and took to wandering about crooning unintelligibly, covered with thick welts, with new sores, and always with a halo of flies.

The walking stick jerked quickly now, but the pace grew slower with each step, as if the man with the boyish neck might have to snap around at any moment and stand face to face with the person following him.

"More than one of them has been after me since then," the man with the walking stick told himself. "My comrades—my ex-comrades, that is—do not forget me. Some watch me go by and shrug their shoulders, unable to make up their minds about a confrontation.

A lot of time has passed, they figure, and my guilt vegetates under a statute of limitations. In a way, that duel, the very fact of that challenge, partly sealed my rehabilitation. Because who is going to fight with a damned man? Of course, I would never have been able to fight with each of my thirty-seven ex-comrades. But this one has not been placated. He was the most offended, the most excitable. Now he has nothing left but his old pride, the knowledge that his life has amounted to even less than the deaths of the others. He blindly believed, and goes on believing, that I—"

The man had pressed ahead of him, cutting him off, and now stood facing him. He was excitedly waving his newspaper, which was crumpled at one end. The pursued man stopped too. He turned a little, put the walking stick behind him, and leaned on it, both hands at his back.

"Do you know who I am?" he mumbled.

"Naturally."

They glared at each other, the pursuer with eyes that were hard, colored by the old bitterness that made them bulge and that turned the blood vessels bright red; the pursued man with one eye more alive than the other, but tolerant, almost compassionate, though he appeared to be trying not to show the latter sentiment.

"Traitor! Miserable informer!"

The words, worn hollow with time, were now barely an echo of the old courtroom insult, and again they merely struck impassiveness. But then the rolled newspaper cracked like a whip, reaching its destination after a trajectory of thirty years. The eye dropped out and fell to the sidewalk, where it rolled a few inches and came to rest in a crack. The aggressor's hand remained suspended in the air, torn from its initial fury, which the gaping eye socket seemed suddenly to have sucked away. His face, too, was quickly draining itself of anger and bitterness. Its new expression seemed to emanate from within, under an impulse perhaps of mockery and perhaps akin to compassion. It was as if greatness of soul could not be engendered except by a matching wretchedness.

It was hard for the first man to stop staring at the eye he had knocked loose with a flick of his crumpled newspaper. When he turned to his adversary, it was with the helpless surprise of someone who confuses one person with another, whom he nevertheless recognizes.

How, after thirty years, was the second man going to explain that the informer had not been he but his brother, who had died in the Chaco as a hero? He, meanwhile, had gone on living as a dishonored man. With a secret like his, the difference was not so great. How could he ever explain that he liked his role, that he had actually come to enjoy it?

The first man stammered something, an apology perhaps, while he stooped to pick up the dusty eye.

"Don't bother," the man with the stick said. "I have others. That one was already a bit dull."

A few curious onlookers had formed a circle around them. The two pushed through the spectators and went their separate ways.

Translated by Norman Thomas di Giovanni

Macario

JUAN RULFO

I am sitting by the sewer waiting for the frogs to come out. While we were having supper last night they started making a great racket and they didn't stop singing till dawn. Godmother says so too—the cries of the frogs scared her sleep away. And now she would really like to sleep. That's why she ordered me to sit here, by the sewer, with a board in my hand to whack to smithereens every frog that may come hopping out—Frogs are green all over except on the belly. Toads are black. Godmother's eyes are also black. Frogs make good eating. Toads don't. People just don't eat toads. People don't, but I do, and they taste just like frogs. Felipa is the one who says it's bad to eat toads. Felipa has green eyes like a cat's eyes. She feeds me in the kitchen whenever I get to eat. She doesn't want me to hurt frogs. But then Godmother is the one who orders me to do things—I love Felipa more than Godmother. But Godmother is the one who takes money out of her purse so Felipa can buy all the food. Felipa stays alone in the kitchen cooking food for the three of us. Since I've known her, that's all she does. Washing the dishes is up to me. Carrying in wood for the stove is my job too. Then Godmother is the one who dishes out food to us. After she has eaten, she makes two little piles with her hands, one for Felipa, the other for me. But sometimes Felipa doesn't feel like eating and then the two little piles are for me. That's why I love Felipa, because I'm always hungry and I never get filled up—never, not even when I gobble down her food. They say a person does get filled up eating, but I know very well that I don't even though I eat all they give me. And Felipa knows it too—They say in the street that I'm crazy because I never stop being hungry. Godmother has heard them say that. I haven't. Godmother won't let me go out alone on the street. When she takes me out, it's to go to church to hear Mass. There she sets me down next to her and ties my hands with the fringe of her shawl. I don't know why she ties my hands, but she says it's because they say I do crazy things. One day they found me hanging somebody; I was strangling a lady for no reason at all. I don't remember. But then Godmother is the one who says what I do and she never goes about telling lies. When she calls me to eat, it's to give me my part of the food. She's not like other people who invite me to eat with them and then when I get close throw rocks at me until I run away without eating anything. No, Godmother is good to me. That's why I'm content in her house. Besides, Felipa lives here. Felipa is very good to me. That's why I love her—Felipa's milk is as sweet as hibiscus flowers. I've drunk goat's milk and also the milk of a sow that had recently had pigs. But no, it isn't as good as Felipa's milk—Now it's been a long time since she has let me nurse the breasts that she has where we just have ribs, and where there comes out, if you know how to get it, a better milk than the one Godmother gives us for lunch on Sundays—Felipa used to come every night to the room where I sleep and snuggle up to me, leaning over me or a little to one side. Then she would fix her breasts so that I could suck the sweet, hot milk that came out in streams on my tongue—Many times I've eaten hibiscus flowers to try to forget my hunger. And Felipa's milk had the same flavor, except that I liked it better because, at the same time that she let me nurse, Felipa would tickle me all over. Then almost always she would stay there sleeping by me until dawn. And that was very good for me, because I didn't worry about the cold and I wasn't afraid of being damned to hell if I died there alone some night—Sometimes I'm not so afraid of hell. But sometimes I am. And then I like to scare myself about going to hell any day now, because my head is so hard and I like to bang it against the first thing I come across. But Felipa comes and scares away my fears. She tickles me with her hands like she knows how to do and she stops that fear of mine that I have of dying. And for a little while I even forget it—Felipa says, when she feels like being with me, that she will tell the Lord all my sins. She will go to heaven very soon and will talk with Him, asking Him to pardon me for all the great wickedness that fills my body from head to toe. She will tell Him to pardon me so I won't worry about it any more. That's why she goes to confession every day. Not because she's bad, but because I'm full of devils inside, and she has to drive them out of my body by confessing for me. Every single day. Every single afternoon of every single day. She will do that favor for me her whole life. That's what Felipa says. That's why I love her so much—Still, having a head so hard is the great thing. I bang it against the pillars of the corridor hours on end and nothing happens to it. It stands banging and doesn't crack. I bang it against the floor—first slowly, then harder—and that sounds like a drum. Just like the drum that goes with the wood flute when I hear them through the window of the church, tied to Godmother, and hearing outside the boom boom of the drum—And Godmother says that if there are bedbugs and cockroaches and scorpions in my room it's because I'm going to burn in hell if I keep on with this business of banging my head on the floor. But what I like is to hear the drum. She should know that. Even when I'm in church, waiting to go out soon into the street to see why the drum is heard from so far away, deep inside the church and above the damning of the priest—"The road of good things is filled with light. The road of bad things is dark." That's what the priest says—I get up and go out of my room while it's still dark. I sweep the street and I go back in my room before daylight grabs me. On the street things happen. There are lots of people who will hit me on the head with rocks as soon as they see me. Big sharp rocks rain from every side. And then my shirt has to be mended and I have to wait many days for the scabs on my face or knees to heal. And go through having my hands tied again, because if I don't they'll hurry to scratch off the scabs and a stream of blood will come out again. Blood has a good flavor too, although it isn't really like the flavor of Felipa's milk—That's why I always live shut up in my house—so they won't throw rocks at me. As soon as they feed me I lock myself in my room and bar the door so my sins won't find me out, because it's dark. And I don't even light the torch to see where the cockroaches are climbing on me. Now I keep quiet. I go to bed on my sacks, and as soon as I feel a cockroach walking along my neck with its scratchy feet I give it a slap with my hand and squash it. But I don't light the torch. I'm not going to let my sins catch me off guard with my torch lit looking for cockroaches under my blanket—Cockroaches pop like firecrackers when you mash them. I don't know whether crickets pop. I never kill crickets. Felipa says that crickets always make noise so you can't hear the cries of souls suffering in purgatory. The day there are no more crickets the world will be filled with the screams of holy souls and we'll all start running scared out of our wits. Besides, I like very much to prick my ears up and listen to the noise of the crickets. There are lots of them in my room. Maybe there are more crickets than cockroaches among the folds of the sacks where I sleep. There are scorpions too. Every once in a while they fall from the ceiling and I have to hold my breath until they've made their way across me to reach the floor. Because if an arm moves or one of my bones begins to tremble, I feel the burn of the sting right away. That hurts. Once Felipa got stung on the behind by one of them. She started moaning and making soft little cries to the Holy Virgin that her behind wouldn't be ruined. I rubbed spit on her. All night I spent rubbing spit on her and praying with her, and after a while, when I saw that my spit wasn't making her any better, I also helped her by joining in and crying as hard as I could—Anyway, I like it better in my room than out on the street, attracting the attention of those who love to throw rocks at people. Here nobody does anything to me. Godmother doesn't even scold me when she sees me eating up her hibiscus flowers, or her myrtles, or her pomegranates. She knows how awfully hungry I am all the time. She knows that I'm always hungry. She knows that no meal is enough to fill up my insides, even though I go about snitching things to eat here and there all the time. She knows that I gobble up the chick-pea slop I give to the fat pigs and the dry-corn slop I give to the skinny pigs. So she knows how hungry I go around from the time I get up until the time I go to bed. And as long as I find something to eat here in this house I'll stay here. Because I think that the day I quit eating I'm going to die, and then I'll surely go straight to hell. And nobody will get me out of there, not even Felipa, who is so good to me, or the scapular that Godmother gave to me and that I wear hung around my neck—Now I'm by the sewer waiting for the frogs to come out. And not one has come out all this while I've been talking. If they take much longer to come out I may go to sleep and then there won't be any way to kill them and Godmother won't be able to sleep at all if she hears them singing and she'll get very angry. And then she'll ask one of that string of saints she has in her room to send the devils after me, to take me off to eternal damnation, right now, without even passing through purgatory, and then I won't be able to see my papa or mama, because that's where they are—So I just better keep on talking—What I would really like to do is take a few swallows of Felipa's milk, that good milk as sweet as the honey that comes from under the hibiscus flowers—

Translated by George D. Schade

Madness

ARMONÍA SOMERS

When Lorenzo, riddled by El Lampiño's bullets, fell (as you already know, Lorenzo was the louse-ridden bum of Mercado Viejo who had just gotten rabies from El Lañudo, the little dog who protected him and was as much a bum himself), the daguerreotype of that metallic Montevideo afternoon underwent its first change. One: the packing cases, from within which Lorenzo, the fugitive, threatened his executioners with his nails, slobber and teeth, lost their occupant. And two: Lorenzo, who minutes before was standing on his feet waging violent war, immediately after twirling from the force of the bullets fell face up on a mattress of rotten bananas, in its cloud of sweet-sickened flies.

Once more back in the truck, El Lampiño put away his regulation weapon, looked at the driver, who was still rubbing his eyes over what he had just seen, and told him: "It was a case of legitimate defense to avoid further danger. Everyone heard him yell out that he'd bite me if I touched him, and I had no qualms about shooting him as the law allows. And so, it's a matter of mission accomplished, and on to something else."

Mission accomplished . . . The driver started the motor and drove off sweating fear down the dirty street. Joined together by their common job, their two hearts beat dully in a communion of rationales:

". . . Yes, madness, you've got to stamp out the madness in others in order to avenge your own."

"A madness of low wages and an inflated living."

"A madness of little love and many children."

"Of so many ships and not one voyage."

"But yes, what madness that of the Mercado's bum."

"A madness that could blow up all at once."

"That could burst in one big blow-up, rather than petering out in little spurts, like ours has to . . ."

Fortunately, however, not all of these thoughts were expressed. They remained tangled in the net of their thoughts, in the tangential awareness of the scenes they passed, of angry brakings at street corners, of billboard signs announcing the next big soccer game. Only Lorenzo, becoming one with his bananas and flies, was what was real, was what was expressed. And also real was the havoc caused by El Lañudo, as he raced toward the throng like a mad postman, carrying his deathly mail in his teeth. And the scattering of the crowd at the scene. Once the cornering of the man was over, the vendors in the Mercado, and those who stop to watch anything that stirs the air, returned to their lives. Time stalked implacably on, and its slaves had to push the wheel.

Lorenzo lay there waiting to be picked up like some dead dog. The atmosphere around him, of the same blue as El Lañudo's eyes before they became bloodshot, began to clot.

"I'm Alejo, you know? Lorenzo's friend . . ."

The dead man's companion turned his eyes from the body and observed the small, scared blond boy. It was hard to chase him away like another fly. This one was far more solid. He had a real center of gravity. He made the guard uneasy. The man appointed to watch over the dead until the ambulance came felt he had no common ground, no single bridge between himself and this seven-year-old boy with a husky voice and blue eyes who started asking questions and wandered off in his own answers.

"I'm Alejo," he repeated. "Lorenzo's friend. Ma didn't want me to . . ."

"Because of the lice, right?"

"He had sailed on pirate ships . . ."

"Because he used to get drunk on blue firewater boiled with canary seed, right?"

"He could play the harmonica . . ."

"And because that lazy bastard never worked, right?"

"All the dogs in the neighborhood loved him . . ."

Suddenly, and perhaps because of that strange counterpoint between the two tones of voice, one of courage for love, the other of compromise, two such different creeds, it seemed as though the upper lip of the fallen man drew back into a final smile, exposing his incredibly white teeth between two purplish rims. Then, for some reason he could not explain, the man guarding the body kicked it in disgust, trying to alter its new skull-like grimace. Neither could he explain why he hated Lorenzo, who had done nothing more than die because of the unknown El Lañudo. Then, as if emerging from an infinity of parabolas, he heard Alejo's voice:

"And he had beautiful teeth . . ."

Translated by Susana Hertelendy

The Switchman

JUAN JOSÉ ARREOLA

The stranger arrived, quite out of breath, at the deserted station. His large suitcase, which no one offered to carry, had utterly worn him out. He mopped his face with a handkerchief, shading his eyes with his hands, and stared at the rails that tapered toward the horizon. Winded and preoccupied, he checked his watch: it was just train time.

Someone—where could he have come from?—was tapping him gently. Turning, the stranger found himself face to face with a little old man whom he vaguely identified as a station employee. He carried in one hand a red lantern tiny as a toy. He sized up the traveler with a smile, while the latter questioned him anxiously.

"Excuse me—has the train left yet?"

"You haven't been in these parts long . . . ?"

"I've got to get out in a hurry. I'm due in T. first thing in the morning."

"Anyone can see you've missed the whole point of the situation. What you ought to do right off is check in at the Traveler's Hotel." He pointed to an odd, cinder-colored building that would have done as well for a barracks.

"I don't want to rent a room. I want to catch the train out."

"Find yourself a room in a hurry, if there are any still about. If you get a place, rent it by the month. It'll be cheaper that way, and the service is better."

"Are you out of your mind? I'm due in T. first thing in the morning."

"To tell you the truth, it would serve you right if I just let you figure things out for yourself. But I'll give you a piece of advice."

"Now, look here—"

"This part of the world is famous for its railroads, as you know. Up to now, we haven't been able to work out all the details, but we've done wonders with the printing of timetables and the promotion of tickets. The railroad guidebooks crisscross every populated area of the country; tickets are being sold to even the most insignificant and out-of-the-way whistlestops. All we have to do now is to make the trains themselves conform to the indicated schedules—actually get the trains to their stations. That's what people hereabouts are hoping for; meanwhile, we put up with the irregularities of the service, and our patriotism keeps us from any open display of annoyance."

"But is there a train that passes through this city?"

"To say outright that there was would be a plain misstatement. As you can see for yourself, we've got the track, though some of it is a little seedy. In some places, the rails are only sketched in lightly on the topsoil with two strokes of a crayon. As a matter of actual fact, no train is really obliged to stop here, but then there is nothing to prevent one from coming if it wants to. In my lifetime, I have seen many trains pass by and known several travelers who have climbed aboard. If you wait for the right moment, maybe I myself will have the honor of helping you aboard a fine coach where you can travel in comfort."

"But will the train get me to T.?"

"And must it be T. and no place else? You ought to congratulate yourself on just getting aboard. Once on the train, your life will take on some sort of workable direction. What does it matter if you don't get to T. in the end?"

"And must it be T. and no place else? You ought to congratulate yourself on just getting aboard. Once on the train, your life will take on some sort of workable direction. What does it matter it you don't get to T. in the end?"

"For one thing, my ticket is made out to T. It stands to reason, doesn't it, that I ought to be taken to my destination?"

"There are plenty who would agree with you. In the hotel, you will have a chance to talk with people who have taken every conceivable precaution and bought great batches of tickets. As a general rule, the far-sighted ones book passage for every point on the line. Some people have spent whole fortunes on tickets . . ."

"I was under the impression that I needed only one ticket to get me to T. See here—"

"The next fleet of national trains will be built at the expense of a single individual who had just invested a fortune in return-trip tickets for a stretch of rail whose plans, including elaborate tunnels and bridges, haven't even been approved by the corporation engineers."

"But the through train to T.—is it still running?"

"That and a lot more! To tell the truth, there are no end of trains in the country, and passengers are able to use them fairly frequently, considering that there's no regular, out-and-out service to speak of. In other words, no one who boards a train expects to be taken where he really wants to go to."

"How's that?"

"In their eagerness to please the public, the management has been known to take desperate measures in some cases. There are trains running to impassable points. These expeditionary trains take several years to complete their runs sometimes, and the passenger's life undergoes transformations in the interim. Fatalities are not rare in these instances; so the management, anticipating every possible emergency, has added a funerary car and a burial wagon. Conductors pride themselves on depositing the passenger's cadaver—expensively embalmed—on station platforms stamped on the tickets. Occasionally, these emergency trains make runs over roadbeds lacking a rail. A whole side of a coach will rattle dreadfully as the wheels bump over the crossties. First-class passengers—it is another precaution of the management—are accommodated on the side with the rail. Second-class passengers resign themselves to a bumpy passage. There are stretches with no rails at all—there all passengers suffer equally, till the train rattles itself to pieces in the end."

"Good heavens!"

"I'll tell you something. The little village of F. came into existence through one of these accidents. The train tried to tackle unmanageable terrain. Bogged down by sand, the wheels fouled clear up to the axles. Passengers were thrown together for so long a time that many close friendships grew out of the inevitable chitchat. Some of these friendships soon blossomed into idyls, and the result was F., a progressive village full of cheeky little moppets playing with rusty odds and ends of the train."

"Well! I can't say I care for that sort of thing!"

"You must try to toughen your character—perhaps you will turn out to be a hero. You mustn't assume there are no chances for passengers to demonstrate their bravery or their capacity for sacrifice. Once some two hundred passengers, who shall be nameless, penned one of the most glorious pages in our railroading annals. It so happened that, on a trial run, the engineer discovered a grave omission on the part of our road crew—just in the nick of time. A bridge that should have spanned a gorge was missing from the route. Well, sir, instead of reversing direction, the engineer gave his passengers a little speech and got them to contribute the necessary initiative to go on with the run. Under his spirited direction, the train was disassembled piece by piece and carried on the shoulders of the passengers to the opposite side of the gorge, where the further surprise of a rampaging river awaited them. The result of this feat was so gratifying to the management that it gave up the construction of bridges entirely from then on and allowed an attractive discount to all passengers nervy enough to face up to the additional inconvenience."

"But I'm due in T. first thing in the morning!"

"More power to you! I'm glad to see you stick to your guns. You're a man of conviction, right enough. Get yourself a room at the Traveler's Hotel and take the first train that comes along! At least, do the best you can—there will be thousands to stand in your way. No sooner does a train arrive than the travelers, exasperated by the long delay, burst out of the hotel in a panic and noisily take over the station. Often their incredible recklessness and discourtesy lead to accidents. Instead of boarding the train in an orderly way, they jam together in a pack; to put it mildly, each blocks the other's passage while the train goes off leaving them all in wild disorder on the station platform. The travelers, worn out and frothing at the mouth, curse the general lack of enlightenment and spend much time insulting and belaboring one another."

"And the police doesn't intervene?"

"Once, the organization of a station militia at all points was attempted, but the unpredictable train schedule made this a useless and exceedingly costly service. Furthermore, the personnel itself showed signs of venality: they protected only the well-to-do passengers, who gave them everything they owned in return for their services, just to get aboard. A special school was established where prospective passengers received lessons in urbanity and a kind of basic training for spending their lives in a train. They were taught the correct procedure for boarding trains even when the vehicle was in motion or cruising at high speed. Still later, they were fitted with a type of armor plate to prevent other passengers from cracking their ribcages."

"But once on the train, are the passenger's troubles over?"

"Relatively, yes. I would only adivse you to keep your eyes peeled for the stations. For example, you might easily imagine yourself in T., but find it was only an illusion. To keep things in hand aboard the overpopulated trains, the management finds it necessary to resort to certain expedients. There are stations that are set up for appearance's sake only; they have been posted in the middle of a wilderness and carry the name of important cities. But with a little circumspection it is easy to discover the fraud. They are like stage sets in a theater; the people represented are sawdust facsimiles. These dummies show the wear and tear of the weather, but are sometimes remarkably lifelike: their faces show the signs of infinite exhaustion."

"Thank heavens T. is not too far away!"

"But there are no through trains to T. at the moment. However, it might well be that you could make it to T. first thing in the morning, just as you wish. The railway organization, whatever its shortcomings, doesn't rule out the possibility of a trip without stopoffs. Would you believe it, there are people who haven't even been conscious of any problem in getting to their destination? They buy a ticket to T., a train comes along, they climb aboard, and the next day they hear the conductor announce: 'Train pulling into T.' Without any plotting and planning, they get off and find themselves in T., right enough!"

"Isn't there anything I can do to work it out that way?"

"I should certainly think so! But who's to say if it

would really help matters any? Try it, by all means! Get on the train with the fixed purpose of arriving at T. Have nothing to do with the passengers. They will only discourage you with their traveler's tales and look for a chance to publicly denounce you."

"What's that you say?"

"The fact of the matter is that the trains are loaded with spies. These spies—volunteers, for the most part—devote their lives to stirring up the 'constructive spirit' of the management. Sometimes they hardly know what they are saying and talk just for the sake of talking. But the next moment they are ready to impute every possible shade of meaning to a passing phrase, no matter how simple. They know how to ferret out incriminating connotations from the most innocent remarks. One niggling slip of the tongue—and you are likely to be taken into custody; you would then pass the rest of your life in a rolling brig, if you are not actually dumped at a nonexistent station right in the middle of nowhere. Muster all your faith and make your trip; eat as lightly as possible; and don't set foot on the station platform till you see a face you can recognize in T."

"But I don't know a soul in T.!"

"In that case, you must be doubly cautious. There will be many temptations along the way, I can tell you. If you glance out of the train window, you are likely to be trapped by hallucinations. The windows are furnished with ingenious devices that touch off all kinds of delusions in the mind of the passenger. It's easy to be taken in by it all. There is a mechanism of some sort, controlled from the locomotive, that gives the impression, by a combination of noises and movements, that the train is in motion. But the train has actually been at a standstill for weeks on end, while the passengers have been watching alluring landscapes through the windowpanes."

"What's the point of it all?"

"The management has arranged it all with the sensible purpose of reducing the traveler's anxiety and eliminating all sensation of displacement. It is their hope that one day the passengers will leave everything to chance, place themselves in the hands of an omnipotent corporation, and give no thought to where they are going or where they have come from."

"And you—have you traveled the line much?"

"I? I'm only a switchman, sir. To tell the truth, I am a retired switchman, and turn up only once in a while to hark back to the good old days. I never took a trip in my life and never want to. But I hear a lot from the passengers. I know that the trains have given rise to all sorts of communities like the town I mentioned before. Sometimes the train crew will get mysterious orders. They will invite the passengers to disembark, generally under the pretext of admiring the beauties of some particular landmark. They will talk to them about caves, or waterfalls, or famous ruins. 'Fifteen minutes to admire this or that cavern!' the conductor will announce pleasantly. And once the passengers are a comfortable distance away, the train races off full tilt."

"And the passengers?"

"They wander about in confusion from one place to another for a while, but in the end they band together and found colonies. These makeshift halts occur in suitable areas far from civilization and rich in natural resources. Here a choice contingent of young men give themselves up to every conceivable pleasure—chiefly women. How would you like to end up your days in a picturesque hideaway in the company of a pretty young thing?"

The old fellow winked and fixed the traveler with a leer, smiling and benevolent. Just then, a distant whistle was heard. The switchman hopped to attention uneasily and began flashing ridiculous and chaotic signals with his lantern.

"Is this the train?" asked the stranger.

The old-timer began to sprint up the roadbed helter-skelter. When he was a fair way off, he turned about with a cry.

"Good luck to you! You'll make it there by tomorrow. What was the name of that precious station of yours?"

"X.," answered the traveler.

The next moment the man had melted into thin air. But the red point of his lantern kept racing and bobbing between the rails, recklessly, toward the oncoming train.

At the other end of the passageway, the locomotive bore down with all the force of a clangorous advent.

Translated by Ben Belitt

Concerning Señor de la Peña

ELISEO DIEGO

I

Uninhabited for twenty years, the palace rose from a rocky cliff on the outskirts of the village, where winds whirled around it chasing one another in their savage games, and where the sea shatters infinite fists in unending complaint.

Workmen finished storing it a month ago and immediately thereafter twenty truckloads of furniture arrived for its twenty rooms, the way to many of them having fallen into disrepair.

Resting against the portico wall, the gatekeeper, cook, gardener and chambermaid, hired previously by the new owner, watched them come. "They must be a regiment," sighed the cook. And the others nodded sadly.

But at the end of the procession there was only one automobile, and in it nobody but the new Señor de la Peña. "It could be worse," sighed the gardener.

The chambermaid agreed fervently: "It certainly could."

II

"He's a boy, a mere child," said the chambermaid, arranging her hair and trying to see herself sideways in the pantry window.

"Well," said the gardener, leaving his sweaty beret on the kitchen table and wiping his forehead with an enormous red and yellow handkerchief, "a boy with the face of an old man. Who would think . . ." And he proceeded to tell how Señor de la Peña had insisted on hiding pots of roses in among the palm leaves. "Besides," he added with a meaningful look at the chambermaid, "he can barely stand on his two feet."

"Of course," she answered, furious, "what with the backache the poor thing's been given."

III

"He's a simple-minded man of God," declared the gatekeeper, who was also Señor de la Peña's valet. "Buried in his books here, with those clothes that look like a priest's, and always with his 'would you do me the favor of . . .', 'pray be so kind as to . . .', 'so very many thanks . . .' He even begged my pardon when I spilled coffee all over him."

The cook put her hands on her hips: "Priest's clothes! You should have seen him when he came back from riding his horse! All dirty and with his boots covered with . . . A Tartar, that's what I say. And then he asked me for rum, the foul language he used, all for no reason. Eh, not even my dead husband . . . !"

"Come, come," said the gatekeeper absent-mindedly counting some coins, "anyone can have a bad moment."

IV

"An old man," said the gardener, pounding the table with his fist. "I say he's an old man, and it's a disgrace to be talking about him behind his back."

"Listen to him!" shrieked the chambermaid. "An old man! Seeing things! If you're just thinking out loud, all right, but anything else . . ."

"Very well," the gatekeeper broke in, trying to make peace, "a little bald and set in his ways, but not really an old man. Being blond . . ."

"Bald and blond? Black, an Indian!" interrupted the chambermaid, calling on heaven for witness. And they were about to resort to blows when the gatekeeper, who had done his small share of reading and is, in short, an intellectual, detained the belligerent arm of the cook and demanded calm.

"It's very strange," he said. "Apparently we're talking about four different people. And to think about it for a minute, the four of us saw him together only once, when he arrived, so swaddled in furs he could even have been a bear. I wonder if there are three imposters in this house? I propose that we four go and see him right away. He's in his study; I just left him there."

But the cook suggested first sending for her brother-in-law, the village policeman, and, better still, that the five of them peep in at him through the study window.

V

Señor de la Peña was sitting at his desk, but he was not writing. His head leaned against the high back of his chair, motionless in the skylight's leaden glow. "Yes, that's the Señor—he's a boy," said the astonished gardener.

The chambermaid covered her face with her hands: "You were right; he's a horrible old man."

The gatekeeper moved back a step, crossing himself: "He's an absolute devil," he whispered.

The cook, her hands folded over her apron, gazed beautifically at Señor de la Peña. Then the policeman, showing signs of impatience, plucked ill-humoredly at her sleeve. "Whatever are you looking at? There's nothing there at all but an empty chair."

Translated by Elinor Randall

The Dogs

ABELARDO DÍAZ ALFARO

For dogs have compassed me: the assembly of the wicked have enclosed me: they pierced my hands and my feet.
Psalm 22:16

Rucio was now a dilapidated statue. A heap of dulled instincts in which the only thing that seemed to live with any intensity was one eye, a clot of turbid light, an opaque mirror of beings and objects.

His head hanging down, his mane thinning, his spine caved in, his flanks thrusting out a relief of ribs. His fallen croup ending in a limp tail that moved slowly like a useless pendulum of his wrecked body. The mosaic of his mangy hide flowering with sores—oozing stars. When he walked, one foreleg swollen at the frog of the hoof sounded like the clumsy cane of a blind man at night.

The blueflies clung tenaciously to the red sores, but he barely felt them. He moved his tail by reflex, indifferently, and tried to drive them off with a little rippling twitch. But what was the use? They were part of his existence now, of his sluggish travels over the roads. At least they gave him some feeling that he was alive.

Why don't horses die before they reach the roads?

He knew of the suicide of several animals. Josco, the bull, broke his neck on the cliff of Farollón. As a colt he had seen more than one wild-maned high-stepper sacrificed because of a broken leg. That was preferable. *Horses on the road die slowly, day by day, hour by hour.*

He went along the runaway. He had lost that strange instinct that guides animals on moonlit nights. He bent his gaunt head to either side to see the path better, but in the dark mirror of his eye, figures broke and dissolved into ghosts.

But it was the dogs that most made him feel his impotence. Those dogs that never leave the road-horses in peace.

On moonlit nights they dogged him all the more cruelly and venomously. They persecuted him without respite. The barks multiplied—long, dismal barks, harsh piercing ones. They barked in chorus. He was a specter of light, a squalid statue of moonlight. In his staring eye, the dogs were enlarged, became phantasmal. They came stealthily, one by one, dragging themselves along. He listened to the low growls, the panting of black mouths. He could almost feel the red tongues with their silvery drool. Their hard, perverse little eyes on him. The wet muzzles. They rubbed their bristling tails against his dry belly. They sank their fangs violently into his agonized flesh. It was a searing pain, an indescribable pain.

He would kick them as in the old days. He would leave them lying sprawled on the road with frothing, bloodstained mouths. He would make them run away with their tails between their legs. The cowardly dogs . . .

He lost his bearings. The hulk of his body—withered tree in the river wind. The dogs hid behind the dark fringes of brambles, waiting to come back at him with redoubled fury. The barks grew prolonged; they stretched mournfully into the pale night. They faded away gradually, sounding like mad laughter in the distance.

The moonlit night had spent itself. A band of red light gilded the back of Farallón Hill. In the morning Rucio used to feel better. The dogs retired to rest. The light sifting down through the *mamey* trees was warm; it warmed his numb flesh, his side pearled with dew. He listened, absorbed, to the singing of the cocks at dawn, the peaceful whistling of the *guajanas*, the rattling carts of the ox drivers. He felt an urge to go to the top of Farallón. The wind was purer there; it combed the thick rustling grasses, the wild corn. On the summit, a delicate light came down from the nearby sky, softened and caressing. There he would feel free of his misery, of his aimless rambling on the roads, of the cruel barking of the dogs.

He tried to go up. He groped for a foothold for his broken hooves on the rough bulges of the rocks. He advanced painfully. Sweat dampened his discolored ribcage. He stopped to rest a moment. He lowered his head a little. Nearby he could hear the sure, muffled clop of a saddle horse, young and spirited, filling the morning with full-throated neighs, strongly echoing. The rumble of his gut hurt his sleeping ears . . .

His head used to rear back powerfully then, suddenly reined in by a hard hand. He chewed the bridle rebelliously, frothing with the green slaver of his fodder. His mane disheveled by the wind, his back silky, his rump gleaming. His ears sprightly, his rennet rumbling. His eyes, round brown mirrors swallowing the landscape in a headstall of raging suns. A sculpture of muscles and tendons in a willful trot.

A dog's faint barking made him lift his head. The dogs were waking up. A dry bark answered another vibrant one. They scattered in the wind. The dogs were calling one another from sugar mill to sugar mill. Sitting on their haunches, their drowsy heads raked the sky with famished incantations. They were conspiring. Soon they would be on the road. They wiggled through gaps in the *mayus*, they dragged themselves cunningly under barbed-wire fences, they jumped smoothly across the adjacent lands.

The first to reach the road was a tall scrawny black dog. A luminous shadow with flashing white fangs. Others of various breeds, with different coats, followed him. Hunting dogs, house dogs, *sato* dogs, their lowered heads sniffing his elusive spoor, his wavering shadow. Then, catching the scent of his defeated body, they raised their heads. The barks were more rapid now, metallic. They echoed in the rocky places of Farallón. They melted into a single quivering wave. Now it was a pack. He thought he heard the soft padding of restless feet. Before long he would have them right behind his shadow that was shortening with the climb of the sun over the *mamey* trees. He started to tremble. He moved his head from side to side like a pendulum. Terrified, he kept close to the pasture fence posts. He felt a powerful breath on his cheek, a burning snort that sent a shudder through him. In his clouded eye was fixed the tense head of a wild colt, with frightened eyes, frail back and bristling mane. Excited, the colt reared up, lifting his tawny body above the barbed wire, his starred head slashing the radiant blue.

The colt greeted him with an intermittent musical whinny that fell like a whip on the slopes of Farallón. Then he threw himself down on the pasture, his back against the grass, his forelegs pawing the blue in a jubilant excess of spirit.

High spirits such as he had once had. He knew the spaciousness of the pastures and of stampeding along the wire.

The violent barking of a dog exploded in his cocked ears. The bony silhouette of the black dog rose up before him. The hair on its neck bristling, the menacing fangs glittering in the dark jaws. The presence of the black dog drove him wild. Its vicious snarl electrified his nerves, ran over his skull in icy waves. Its eyes with their fixed yellowish light sank into his glassy pupil, blinding him. The dog raised its shadowy head and shattered the morning with an interminable howl. . . . Behind Rucio, other short crisp barks responded. Soon the dance of tails, of mangy backs and dangling tongues, would begin. The dogs were moving in even strides. They hemmed him in, they had him cornered. A whirling mass of shapes in his huge eye. He tried to charge his way out. He sank his mouth grimly against his chest, he dug his hooves like hooks in the earth; but the black dog was leaping recklessly at him, snapping savagely. He backed up, terrified, his ears tensed, his forelegs rigid, showing the white of his eye in fear, petrified on a promontory of bright red earth against a background of solid cloud. One dog buried his fangs into the swollen frog of his hoof. He felt his whole body sway, convulsed with pain. And he pushed ahead furiously amidst the redoubled outcries of the dogs.

He grew winded, and grimly awaited the assault of the pack. . . .

Let them finish him off once and for all. The mangy dogs.

They were backing off, leaving a wake of faint, transparent barks. A silence heavy with sunlight came over the path. Rucio let his head drop, his chin almost on the ground, etched against the depth of the hills flashing with sunlight. Sweat drenched his flanks; it streamed down his legs, down his weak cannon bones, till it soaked the burning earth.

His shadow was now almost an image of his meager body.

He didn't know how long he remained like that, nodding off, the eyelid weighing down the motionless bloodshot eye. He raised his head a little and gradually became aware of his battered flesh, of his bleeding sides, of his stubborn will to reach the summit.

What had become of the dogs? Why were they leaving him alone?

His shadow lengthened on the road. The air was thinner now. It went through his moist nostrils refreshingly; it ruffled his scanty mane. The sun was not punishing his bleeding body much now. He raised his head a bit and in his clouded eye was sketched the summit, on which the shadows were starting to thicken. The Farallón was a sturdy back, saddled with yellow lights.

Rucio tried to take advantage of the dogs' oversight, to get to the top before them, before night tamed the spine of Farallón. He began to move with a measured step, keeping pace with the rhythm of his weightless body. He was leaving a trail of blood on the coarse boulders. He couldn't understand why the dogs had forgotten him. Maybe they were watching him now from the sugar mills, their fierce eyes glowing like coals. The wind rippled the fragrant green of the pastures. An odor of virgin earth filled his emaciated chest.

The colt had scaled the summit of the crag. Head buried in the clouds. Mane trembling in the breeze. The potent neigh spreading out in virile waves over Toa Valley, cracking like a whip over the slopes of Plata, the crags of San Lorenzo.

A deep howl made the silent evening vibrate. They had caught sight of him. A clamor of scattered barks rose up in commotion from the sugar mills.... They weren't coming as before, slow and stealthy. They rushed like swift cloud-racks. Rucio checked himself, baffled. A bitter foaming slaver spilled from his lips. It fell silvery on the road purple with twilight. The barking was more clearly perceptible now. It thickened into a single deep howl, mournful and deathly. The dogs bounded along the road . . . all he had left was a stretch of bare rock. The dogs were fast and his step sluggish. He could barely make out the top of the bluff, crested with bloody lights. The guava trees at the top were dogs of shadow.

The barking was now more intense and ferocious. They howled into the wind. He thought he heard the whistling breath of the black mouths. He stretched his neck in desperation, trying to force his emaciated body to advance. He could hardly hold himself up on his wobbly legs. The wind brought a strange foul stench from the sugar mills, from the road. A stench of mangy backs, ulcerated hides. Bulging with effort, his eye took on the red of the sunset. Again he heard the spongy thud of their restless feet. It drummed in his humiliated ears. He could feel them walking over his back, scratching his withered flesh. They were going to overtake him . . .

He drew up in panic. He tightened his body, drawing in his leg, numb with fear. The chorus of dissonant, tuneless barks exploded behind his croup. Night would soon be falling and the dogs were treading on his heels, on his elongated shadow.

He slanted his head suspiciously from side to side, sensing danger. Nervous, his nostrils flaring. His ears stiffened tensely toward the sky. His eye enormous and rolling wildly.

The dogs closed in aggressively. They growled sourly, baring their pointed teeth, their cavernous jaws. Their tails whirled dizzily.

A stirrup of livid light hung from the bleeding clouds.

The whole pack charged at once. There were more now, from every region, from every direction. They drove their curved claws into his damp flanks, into his flimsy ribcage. The deafening clamor of barks intensified as evening came on. They hammered his ears, they pierced his skull. Rucio turned his head in fury and with his yellowed teeth he tried to tear the dogs loose from his side, but they were fastened to his skeleton, to his faded hide.

He lost his balance and went down on his forelegs, ringed by the jubilant clamor of the quivering pack. He thrashed about on the ground, desperate, defenseless, trying to pull himself above the jumble of mangy backs. He finally managed to dig his knee into the ground and gradually got back to his feet, off balance, determined before the inflamed astonishment of the pack. He was getting winded. His chest pounded unevenly, arhythmically, like a bellows without a fire. A livid froth dripped from his parched flews.

He distended his gasping throat. He stretched his bony head toward the fiery clouds, toward the lustrous sunset.

His wasted body would not respond to the goad, to the spur of his will. The ominous night would surprise him on the road.

With a low snarl, the black dog slipped under his belly and drove his fangs with rage into the inflamed frog of his hoof, into the swollen flesh. A red-hot spur thrust that reached his heart. Every nerve quivered, every sinew. The hulk of his body creaked like a dry tree in the river wind. He plunged ahead, stumbling, hallucinated, driven by a mysterious strength. He stopped, exhausted and stupefied. His head down, his defenseless body tense, his legs paralyzed. Motionless on the wild rocks . . .

His head seemed to be floating now, vertiginous. The wind was thinner. It whistled softly over the rustling pasture grass; it howled on the red cliffs of Farallón. It ruffled his scanty mane. It filled his chest with courage, with scents long forgotten. Rucio sniffed at the deep emptiness. A few more steps and he would roll down to the bottom of the cliff, dashed to pieces on the blue slabs of the river.

The dogs harried him, frenzied, fired up. They pierced his mangled body. Blood streamed down his side. They went for his legs, trying to pry him loose from the summit, but he resisted, stubborn, defiant.

The river's moist vapor gradually took hold of his throat, his chest, his stomach. It coursed down the swollen channels of his veins, giving him new life, like reviving sap. It quieted his fatigue, easing his broken body.

He lifted his head majestically. A clear light, mild and comforting, came down from the close sky, lighting up his darkened eye. It spread gloriously over Toa Valley, it made the slopes seem transparent, it put a nimbus around the clouds. He inhaled all the sweet air of the valley and the river. He felt powerful on the summit, yoked to the clouds, pulled free of the earth, of his misery, of his aimless travels on the roads.

The dogs leaped wildly at his body, at the sunset, but he barely felt them.

His heart began beating violently. A deep, searing bark seemed to break open his chest, shredding his guts. Everything was spinning around now in his one eye—the dogs, the summit, the blood-stained sky. Spine-chilling, obstinate, the eyes with their fixed yellow light flashed in the midst of the commotion.

A cold gust from the base of the hills wrapped around him. It went through his very bones.

A pleasant sensation of peace and well-being slowly invaded his crucified flesh, his tortured bones. He sensed the day's dying, the approach of deep night, of infinite night.

He arched his neck. He lifted his angular head to the clouds in challenge. . . . He set his skeletal figure firmly on the summit. An ashy statue, unflinching before the chiaroscuro of the declining day.

His immense eye gradually filled up with shadows, vague shadows, heavy shadows. A precise and solid shadow.

The dogs weren't barking anymore!...

Translated by Hardie St. Martin

The Smallest Woman in the World

CLARICE LISPECTOR

In the depths of Equatorial Africa the French explorer, Marcel Pretre, hunter and man of the world, came across a tribe of surprisingly small pygmies. Therefore he was even more surprised when he was informed that a still smaller people existed, beyond forests and distances. So he plunged farther on.

In the Eastern Congo, near Lake Kivu, he really did discover the smallest pygmies in the world. And—like a box within a box within a box—obedient, perhaps, to the necessity nature sometimes feels of outdoing herself—among the smallest pygmies in the world there was the smallest of the smallest pygmies in the world.

Among mosquitoes and lukewarm trees, among leaves of the most rich and lazy green, Marcel Pretre found himself facing a woman seventeen and three-quarter inches high, full-grown, black, silent—"Black as a monkey," he informed the press—who lived in a treetop with her little spouse. In the tepid miasma of the jungle, that swells the fruits so early and gives them an almost intolerable sweetness, she was pregnant.

So there she stood, the smallest woman in the world. For an instant, in the buzzing heat, it seemed as if the Frenchman had unexpectedly reached his final destination. Probably only because he was not insane, his soul neither wavered nor broke its bounds. Feeling an immediate necessity for order and for giving names to what exists, he called her Little Flower. And in order to be able to classify her among the recognizable realities, he immediately began to collect facts about her.

Her race will soon be exterminated. Few examples are left of this species, which, if it were not for the sly dangers of Africa, might have multiplied. Besides disease, the deadly effluvium of the water, insufficient food, and ranging beasts, the great threat to the Likoualas are the savage Bahundes, a threat that surrounds them in the silent air, like the dawn of battle. The Bahundes hunt them with nets, like monkeys. And eat them. Like that: they catch them in nets and eat them. The tiny race, retreating, always retreating, has finished hiding away in the heart of Africa, where the lucky explorer discovered it. For strategic defense, they live in the highest trees. The women descend to grind and cook corn and to gather greens; the men, to hunt. When a child is born, it is left free almost immediately. It is true that, what with the beasts, the child frequently cannot enjoy this freedom for very long. But then it is true that it cannot be lamented that for such a short life there had been any long, hard work. And even the language that the child learns is short and simple, merely the essentials. The Likoualas use few names; they name things by gestures and animal noises. As for things of the spirit, they have a drum. While they dance to the sound of the drum, a little male stands guard against the Bahundes, who come from no one knows where.

That was the way, then, that the explorer discovered, standing at his very feet, the smallest existing human thing. His heart beat, because no emerald in the world is so rare. The teachings of the wise men of India are not so rare. The richest man in the world has never set eyes on such strange grace. Right there was a woman that the greed of the most exquisite dream could never have imagined. It was then that the explorer said timidly, and with a delicacy of feeling of which his wife would never have thought him capable: "You are Little Flower."

At that moment, Little Flower scratched herself where no one scratches. The explorer—as if he were receiving the highest prize for chastity to which an idealistic man dares aspire—the explorer, experienced as he was, looked the other way.

A photograph of Little Flower was published in the colored supplement of the Sunday Papers, life-size. She was wrapped in a cloth, her belly already very big. The flat nose, the black face, the splay feet. She looked like a dog.

On that Sunday, in an apartment, a woman seeing the picture of Little Flower in the paper didn't want to look a second time because "It gives me the creeps."

In another apartment, a lady felt such perverse tenderness for the smallest of the African women that—an ounce of prevention being worth a pound of cure—Little Flower could never be left alone to the tenderness of that lady. Who knows to what murkiness of love tenderness can lead? The woman was upset all day, almost as if she were missing something. Besides, it was spring and there was a dangerous leniency in the air.

In another house, a little girl of five, seeing the picture and hearing the comments, was extremely surprised. In a houseful of adults, this little girl had been the smallest human being up until now. And, if this was the source of all caresses, it was also the source of the first fear of the tyranny of love. The existence of Little Flower made the little girl feel—with a deep uneasiness that only years and years later, and for very different reasons, would turn into thought—made her feel, in her first wisdom, that "sorrow is endless."

In another house, in the consecration of spring, a girl about to be married felt an ecstasy of pity: "Mama, look at her little picture, poor little thing! Just look how sad she is!"

"But," said the mother, hard and defeated and proud, "it's the sadness of an animal. It isn't human sadness."

"Oh, Mama!" said the girl, discouraged.

In another house, a clever little boy had a clever idea: "Mummy, if I could put this little woman from Africa in little Paul's bed when he's asleep? When he woke up wouldn't he be frightened? Wouldn't he howl? When he saw her sitting on his bed? And then we'd play with her! She would be our toy!"

His mother was setting her hair in front of the bathroom mirror at the moment, and she remembered what a cook had told her about life in an orphanage. The orphans had no dolls, and, with terrible maternity already throbbing in their hearts, the little girls had hidden the death of one of the children from the nun. They kept the body in a cupboard and when the nun went out they played with the dead child, giving her baths and things to eat, punishing her only to be able to kiss and console her. In the bathroom, the mother remembered this, and let fall her thoughtful hands, full of curlers. She considered the cruel necessity of loving. And she considered the malignity of our desire for happiness. She considered how ferociously we need to play. How many times we will kill for love. Then she looked at her clever child as if she were looking at a dangerous stranger. And she had a horror of her own soul that, more than her body, had engendered that being, adept at life and happiness. She looked at him attentively and with uncomfortable pride, that child who had already lost two front teeth, evolution evolving itself, teeth falling out to give place to those that could bite better. "I'm going to buy him a new suit," she decided, looking at him, absorbed. Obstinately, she adorned her gap-toothed son with fine clothes; obstinately, she wanted him very clean, as if his cleanliness could emphasize a soothing superficiality, obstinately perfecting the polite side of beauty. Obstinately drawing away from, and drawing him away from, something that ought to be "black as a monkey." Then, looking in the bathroom mirror, the mother gave a deliberately refined and social smile, placing a distance of insuperable millenniums between the abstract lines of her features and the crude face of Little Flower. But, with years of practice, she knew that this was going to be a Sunday on which she would have to hide from herself anxiety, dreams, and lost millenniums.

In another house, they gave themselves up to the enthralling task of measuring the seventeen and three-quarter inches of Little Flower against the wall. And, really, it was a delightful surprise: she was even smaller than the sharpest imagination could have pictured. In the heart of each member of the family was born, nostalgic, the desire to have that tiny and indomitable thing for itself, that thing spared having been eaten, that permanent source of charity. The avid family soul wanted to devote itself. To tell the truth, who hasn't wanted to own a human being just for himself? Which, it is true, wouldn't always be convenient; there are times when one doesn't want to have feelings.

"I bet if she lived here it would end in a fight," said the father, sitting in the armchair and definitely turning the page of the newspaper. "In this house everything ends in a fight."

"Oh, you, José—always a pessimist," said the mother.

"But, Mama, have you thought of the size her baby's going to be?" said the oldest little girl, aged thirteen, eagerly.

The father stirred uneasily behind his paper.

"It should be the smallest black baby in the world," the mother answered, melting with pleasure. "Imagine her serving our table, with her big little belly!"

"That's enough!" growled father.

"But you have to admit," said the mother, unexpectedly offended, "that it is something very rare. You're the insensitive one."

And the rare thing itself?

In the meanwhile, in Africa, the rare thing herself, in her heart—and who knows if the heart wasn't black, too, since once nature has erred she can no longer be trusted—the rare thing herself had something even rarer in her heart, like the secret of her own secret: a minimal child. Methodically, the explorer studied that little belly of the smallest mature human being. It was at this moment that the explorer, for the first time since he had known her, instead of feeling curiosity, or exhaltation, or victory, or the scientific spirit, felt sick.

The smallest woman in the world was laughing.

She was laughing, warm, warm—Little Flower was enjoying life. The rare thing herself was experiencing the ineffable sensation of not having been eaten yet. Not having been eaten yet was something that at any other time would have given her the agile impulse to jump from branch to branch. But, in this moment of tranquility, amid the thick leaves of the Eastern Congo, she was not putting this impulse into action—it was entirely concentrated in the smallness of the rare thing itself. So she was laughing. It was a laugh such as only one who does not speak laughs. It was a laugh that the explorer, constrained, couldn't classify. And she kept on enjoying her own soft laugh, she who wasn't being devoured. Not to be devoured is the most perfect feeling. Not to be devoured is the secret goal of a whole life. While she was not being eaten, her bestial laughter was as delicate as joy is delicate. The explorer was baffled.

In the second place, if the rare thing herself was

laughing, it was because, within her smallness, a great darkness had begun to move.

The rare thing herself felt in her breast a warmth that might be called love. She loved that sallow explorer. If she could have talked and had told him that she loved him, he would have been puffed up with vanity. Vanity that would have collapsed when she added that she also loved the explorer's ring very much, and the explorer's boots. And when that collapse had taken place, Little Flower would not have understood why. Because her love for the explorer—one might even say "profound love," since, having no other resources, she was reduced to profundity—her profound love for the explorer would not have been at all diminished by the fact that she also loved his boots. There is an old misunderstanding about the word love, and, if many children are born from this misunderstanding, many others have lost the unique chance of being born, only because of the susceptibility that demands that it be me! me! that is loved, and not my money. But in the humidity of the forest these cruel refinements do not exist, and love is not to be eaten, love is to find a boot pretty, love is to like the strange color of a man who isn't black, is to laugh for love of a shiny ring. Little Flower blinked with love, and laughed warmly, small, gravid, warm.

The explorer tried to smile back, without knowing exactly to what abyss his smile responded, and then he was embarrassed as only a very big man can be embarrassed. He pretended to adjust his explorer's hat better; he colored, prudishly. He turned a lovely color, a greenish-pink, like a lime at sunrise. He was undoubtedly sour.

Perhaps adjusting the symbolic helmet helped the explorer to get control of himself, severely recapture the discipline of his work, and go on with his note-taking. He had learned how to understand some of the tribe's few articulate words, and to interpret their signs. By now, he could ask questions.

Little Flower answered "Yes." That it was very nice to have a tree of her own to live in. Because—she didn't say this but her eyes became so dark that they said it—because it is good to own, good to own, good to own. The explorer winked several times.

Marcel Pretre had some difficult moments with himself. But at least he kept busy taking notes. Those who didn't take notes had to manage as best they could:

"Well," suddenly declared one old lady, folding up the newspaper decisively, "well, as I always say: God knows what He's doing."

Translated by Elizabeth Bishop

Marmosets

CLARICE LISPECTOR

The first time we had a marmoset was just before New Year's. We were without water and without a maid, people were lining up to buy meat, the hot weather had suddenly began—when, dumfounded, I saw the present enter the house, already eating a banana, examining everything with great rapidity, and with a long tail. It looked like a monkey not yet grown; its potentialities were tremendous. It climbed up the drying clothes to the clothesline, where it swore like a sailor, and the banana peelings fell where they would. I was exhausted already. Every time I forgot and absent-mindedly went out on the back terrace, I gave a start: there was that happy man. My younger son knew, before I did, that I would get rid of this gorilla: "If I promise that sometime the monkey will get sick and die, will you let him stay? Or if you knew that sometime he'd fall out the window, somehow, and die down there?" My feelings would glance aside. The filthiness and blithe unconsciousness of the little monkey made me responsible for his fate, since he himself would not take any blame. A friend understood how bitterly I had resigned myself, what dark deeds were being nourished beneath my dreaminess, and rudely saved me: a delighted gang of little boys appeared from the hill and carried off the laughing man. The new year was devitalized but at least monkeyless.

A year later, at a time of happiness, suddenly there in Copacabana I saw the small crowd. I thought of my children, the joys they gave me, free, unconnected with the worries they also gave me, free, and I thought of a chain of joy: "Will the person receiving this pass it along to someone else," one to another, like a spark along a train of powder. Then and there I bought the one who would be called Lisette.

She could almost fit in one hand. She was wearing a skirt, and earrings, necklace, and bracelet of glass beads. The air of an immigrant just disembarking in her native costume. Like an immigrant's, too, her round eyes.

This one was a woman in miniature. She lived with us three days. She had such delicate bones. She was of such a sweetness. More than her eyes, her look was rounded. With every movement, the earrings shook; the skirt was always neat, the red necklace glinted. She slept a lot, but, as to eating, she was discreet and languid. Her rare caress was only a light bite that left no mark.

On the third day we were out on the back terrace admiring Lisette and the way she was ours. "A little too gentle," I thought, missing the gorilla. And suddenly my heart said harshly: "But this isn't sweetness. This is death." The dryness of the message left me calm. I said to the children: "Lisette is dying." Looking at her, I realized the stage of love we had already reached. I rolled her up in a napkin and went with the children to the nearest first-aid station, where the doctor couldn't attend to her because he was performing an emergency operation on a dog. Another taxi—"Lisette thinks she's out for a drive, Mama"—another hospital. There they gave her oxygen.

And with the breath of life, a Lisette we hadn't

known was revealed. The eyes less round, more secretive, more laughing, and in the prognathous and ordinary face a certain ironic haughtiness. A little more oxygen and she wanted to speak so badly she couldn't bear being a monkey; she was, and she would have had much to tell. More oxygen, and then an injection of salt solution; she reacted to the prick with an angry slap, her bracelet glittering. The male nurse smiled; "Lisette! Gently, my dear!"

The diagnosis: she wouldn't live unless there was oxygen at hand, and even then it was unlikely. "Don't buy monkeys in the street," he scolded me; "sometimes they're already sick." No, one must buy dependable monkeys, and know where they came from, to ensure at least five years of love, and know what they had or hadn't done, like getting married. I discussed it with the children a minute. Then I said to the nurse: "You seem to like Lisette very much. So if you let her stay a few days, near the oxygen, you can have her." He was thinking. "Lisette is pretty!" I implored.

"She's beautiful!" he agreed, thoughtfully. Then he sighed and said, "If I cure Lisette, she's yours." We went away with our empty napkin.

The next day they telephoned, and I informed the children that Lisette had died. The younger one asked me, "Do you think she died wearing her earrings?" I said yes. A week later the older one told me, "You look so much like Lisette!"

I replied, "I like you, too."

Translated by Elizabeth Bishop

In The Beginning

HUMBERTO COSTANTINI

This is the story of a great slaughter. When the hunters of horses came out of the east in whooping bands, when the handsome men arrived from over the plains and the mountains, bringing death and annihilation to the last of the earth's ancient men.

This is the story of a great slaughter. Of how that great bloodshed spread its black wing over the whole of Europe, and with its death cry awakened even the least cleft of the rock.

Of how the silent beings who squatted about their fires, the shambling Neanderthal men, woke up one morning and their hearts were filled with wonder before the blossoms of the wild apple. Because spring, at that moment, had taken possession of the land.

A light mist slowly stretching itself rose from the ends of the earth, and vast herds of bearded ponies grazed in peace on the neighboring plain. And the horse had no fear of the stooped head of the cave dwellers.

This is the story of a great slaughter. When the bearded ponies suddenly snuffed the air and smelled fear. And this fear, twitching through their muscles, started them running in terror toward the west.

And the men asked themselves to what such frenzied galloping was owed, such a shaking and tossing of manes. For they had not yet heard the war cry of the hunters from the east.

But the cry materialized. On the crown of a hill, an immense circle of dancers and a great display of colors and feathers. And also of spears and arrows. And again the hearts of the hairy Neanderthal men were filled with wonder, as when they beheld the wild apple trees in flower.

And the singing and the feathers and the rhythmic movements of the dancers drew them with an irresistible force. In wary groups they moved closer and closer, and they felt ashamed of their own thickset hairy bodies. Wanting to approach the beautiful newcomers to make them gifts of mushrooms and fleshy roots.

But the dancers ignored their dark beseeching gaze. The newcomers went on in their play until the sun stood directly overhead in the sky.

This is the story of a great slaughter. When the graceful Cro-Magnons ended their singing and the rhythmic swaying of their bodies painted in three colors and loosed themselves upon the hairy onlookers.

And the spear whistled in the air. And the ax struck out at the squat heads. And death came suddenly, unbidden, decked in feathers, howling, and daubed as for an orgy.

And only those who fled to the mountain saved their lives. For the rest remained behind, their blood soaked up by the earth that the tide of spring had kissed.

And this was the beginning of the great slaughter. One after another came the conquering hordes, all skilled warriors and agile dancers. And all of them hunters of the wild horse and the reindeer. And hunters also all of them, of the stolid inhabitants of cliff and rock.

And the cave dwellers could not grasp how those

beautiful heads harbored so much hate. Those graceful bodies such fierceness.

And that great slaughter lasted many hundreds of years. For the Neanderthal men lived over a great extent of the land. Their eyes, for century upon century, the only eyes to have lifted, questioning the stars.

And that great slaughter lasted many hundreds of years. And the rock dwellers became skillful in the handling of the new weapons. And in place after place the smoke of rebellion often rose up over the land.

But the Cro-Magnon men were bent upon death and annihilation because the presence of the shambling hairy creatures was loathsome to their hearts.

And because the sheltering caves were coveted by them. More even than the flesh of wild horses or the secret sources of red pigment with which they beautified their dead.

And it came to pass that after many centuries none of the race of ancient dwellers were left on the face of the earth. All of them had perished at the hands of the lordly hunters from the east.

The race of hunters multiplied and increased over the whole extent of Europe. And on the rock walls in the caves their beautiful animal drawings looked down in splendor.

* * *

This is the story of the last Neanderthal man. One who lived in the region of the French Dordogne.

This is the story of the last Neanderthal man, and his name was called Grug.

And Grug's age was thirty-six years. Thirty-six were the years of his life when the men from the east became complete masters of the land. And when by blade and by blow they finished off all the old dwellers.

This is the story of the last ancient man on earth. When he abandoned his squatting place and fled to the mountain with the rest of his family group.

And the group was small. Five only were those who

followed his steps. All the others had perished; their blood-tattered corpses strewn over the ground.

And before this, for five years' time, Grug had reigned among his people. His voice was heard on both banks of the river.

Because Grug knew the language of the winds. He knew what dangers lurked in each rustling of the leaves.

And because upon the death of the Old Man, he, the eldest, had led his tribe far from the hunters of the east into the valley of the Garonne where the land was favorable.

And for five years the tribe had remained there. Little more than a few bright points of light disturbing the night.

The water's gladness flowing between the stones. Lichens, snails, and small reptiles in abundance.

Circles of men and women squatting around fires. Their whelps tumbling in play at the river's edge. An appearance of peace.

Until death suddenly caught up with them in the valley of the Garonne.

The untiring hunters sought the river valley. They raised their song in the region of the last Neanderthal men.

They appeared from the end of the valley. Feathers, arrows, and shouts, spreading fear over the land.

Like fire which in its passage destroys all the trees of the forest. Such was their appetite for death.

The tribe wailed under their shafts. The women growled with grief for their brood struck down by the arrows.

The men scattered. Their clumsy bodies scurrying. Fleet arrows tumbled them in the middle of their flight. The arrows caught them at the mouths of their caves.

Death came to and fro through the valley of the

Garonne. It strode the air. It quickened the legs of the rangy hunters of horses.

They killed in the valley and under the rock ledges. They killed alongside the river and in the deep shadow of the caves.

And Grug howled in the midst of his people. By his shouts he attempted to lead the escape. Claiming of the mountain its distant refuge.

But fear turned the men deaf to Grug. Mad scurrying in the valley cut off by death's agile steps.

This is the story of the last ancient man on earth. When he uttered loud cries among his people and he signaled the way to the distant cliffs.

And when five of his family group heeded his call and bound their lives to him. They gathered their fears around the eldest, who was leading them to the mountain.

Two of his women with their whelps. All the others had perished. Their blood-tattered corpses strewn over the ground.

* * *

And first it was a creeping of bodies through thickets. The thorns pained in the flesh.

They questioned the rock. In each movement of their bellies they sought its response.

And then a great silence. A concealment of life among the lower life that droned on the mountainside.

And then they called on the night. They gathered it around them for the protection of their bodies.

And with the night they started out on their march. The moon showed their shadows shambling across a clearing among the thickets.

They crept up the slope. They hushed the fear of the whelps.

They wrested shelter from the mountain. A place to hide their weariness. To conceal their bodies from the hunters.

A spot for their thirst beside the soft patter of water flowing between the stones.

And then again they called on silence. Days and nights squatting in a crevice of the mountain.

Days and nights the voice of the slaughter howling in their ears. Expecting death in each rustling of leaves.

Three days and three nights awaiting some sign in the wheeling of birds. Cowering at the far-off rumble of hooves. Heeding the earth's hidden voice.

Until on the fourth day the war cry of the hunters of the east reached their mountain cranny. (The women clutched the whelps and their flesh shook as with cold.)

And they were able to make out the great display of colors. The circle of dancers, a shifting flower down in the valley.

And then the five increased the silence. They sank their heartbeats in the rock. A nameless waiting beside the trickle of water.

Night after night the wind brought the smell of death. A smell that grated the teeth and made the hair of the flesh stand up.

And endlessly the trickle of water questioned the heavens. Slipping silently over a glimmer of mosses.

But then hunger came to keep them company. Torsos doubled with color prowled about. A sudden startling noise over the stones.

This is the story of Grug and of the five who fled with him to the mountain. And they were the only survivors of the old Neanderthal race.

Of how all at once at the beginning of the sixth day Grug shattered the mountain silence.

And how all at once beside the trickle of water a thin line of red appeared. Over the glimmering mosses, the glimmer of blood.

Because at the beginning of the sixth day, Grug raised his slow hairy frame.

And the women wondered at seeing him stand there. And the whelps did not grasp it because he no longer concealed his hulking frame from the hunters.

The stone ax obeyed Grug's bidding. With blind fury it obeyed the command of his hands.

Five well-aimed blows and little more than a few whimpers. Little more than some eyes questioning Grug's wet black eyes.

Little more than a thin line of red beside the trickle of water. A new glimmer of blood over the glimmering mosses.

* * *

But the hunters responded to the muffled call of the blows. Packs of rangy Cro-Magnons leaping over the stones.

While a hefty male stood over them, higher up the ledge, observing. A magnificent specimen for their hunters' appetite.

But as they reached him their free and easy bearing was blunted. Standing on the rock a terrible stare awaited them. The bloody ax between his hands.

And all of them saw—because this was what they had always heard—that the inferior race was not a race of warriors. All these loathsome hairy beings were tame and cowardly.

And then Grug let out his fighting cry. A howl that seemed to come out of the mountain itself.

And a first corpse fell in blood under his hand. And another's neck went down in the path of Greg's demolishing stone.

Like a bison that turns enraged upon its pursuers, so Grug flailed out in the midst of his earthly enemies.

But the clash did not last long. Two more Cro-Magnons fell under the blows of Grug's ax.

(Five were the blows that awakened the mountain

cranny. Little more than a thin line of red beside the trickle of water.)

But the clash did not last long. For the hunters came in great numbers to vanquish that enraged Neanderthal specimen.

A bone point in his back. But the stone kept obeying his hand.

A bone point in the hip and the groin. But in each one of its blows his hand was still a bearer of death.

An arrow-riddled bison whose last onslaught implants fear and makes the hunters cower in fright.

A bone point piercing his belly. And then the edge of a huge stone bringing him the night.

And the night was a heavy sleep that enclosed him. A memory of faraway bonfires in the valley of the Garonne.

And sweetly the earth called him back.

* * *

This is the story of the last Neanderthal man. When he went out to his meeting with death next to a trickle of water.

This is the story of the last of the earth's ancient men. Of those whom the bearded ponies did not fear. Hundreds of centuries asking the only questions of the stars.

This is the story of Grug. How he died at the hands of the tall hunters from the east. The plumed dancers who embellished the walls of the caves.

And who asked new questions of the stars.

Translated by Norman Thomas di Giovanni

Paseo

JOSÉ DONOSO

I

This happened when I was very young, when my father and Aunt Mathilda, his maiden sister, and my uncles Gustav and Armand were still living. Now they are all dead. Or I should say, I prefer to think they are all dead: it is too late now for the questions they did not ask when the moment was right, because events seemed to freeze all of them into silence. Later they were able to construct a wall of forgetfulness or indifference to shut out everything, so that they would not have to harass themselves with impotent conjecture. But then, it may not have been that way at all. My imagination and my memory may be deceiving me. After all, I was only a child then, with whom they did not have to share the anguish of their inquiries, if they made any, nor the result of their discussions.

What was I to think? At times I used to hear them closeted in the library, speaking softly, slowly, as was their custom. But the massive door screened the meaning of their words, permitting me to hear only the grave and measured counterpoint of their voices. What was it they were saying? I used to hope that, inside there, abandoning the coldness which isolated each of them, they were at last speaking of what was truly important. But I had so little faith in this that, while I hung around the walls of the vestibule near the library door, my mind became filled with the certainty that they had chosen to forget, that they were meeting only to discuss, as always, some case in jurisprudence relating to their specialty in maritime law. Now I think that perhaps they were right in wanting to blot out everything. For why should one live with the terror of having to acknowledge that the streets of a city can swallow up a human being, leaving him without life and without death, suspended as it were, in a dimension more dangerous than any dimension with a name?

One day, months after, I came upon my father watching the street from the balcony of the drawing room on the second floor. The sky was close, dense, and the humid air weighed down the large, limp leaves of the ailanthus trees. I drew near my father, eager for an answer that would contain some explanation.

"What are you doing here, Papa?" I murmured.

When he answered, something closed over the despair on his face, like the blow of a shutter closing on a shameful scene.

"Don't you see? I'm smoking . . ." he replied.

And he lit a cigarette.

It wasn't true. I knew why he was peering up and down the street, his eyes darkened, lifting his hand from time to time to stroke his smooth chestnut whiskers: it was in hope of seeing them reappear, returning under the trees of the sidewalk, the white bitch trotting at heel.

Little by little I began to realize that not only my father but all of them, hiding from one another and without confessing even to themselves what they were doing, haunted the windows of the house. If someone happened to look up from the sidewalk he would surely have seen the shadow of one or another of them posted beside a curtain, or faces aged with grief spying out from behind the window panes.

In those days the street was paved with quebracho wood, and under the ailanthus trees a clangorous streetcar used to pass from time to time. The last time I was there neither the wooden pavements nor the streetcars existed any longer. But our house was still standing, narrow and vertical like a little book pressed between the bulky volumes of new buildings, with shops on the ground level and a crude sign advertising knitted undershirts covering the balconies of the second floor.

When we lived there all the houses were tall and slender like our own. The block was always happy with the games of children playing in the patches of sunshine on the sidewalks, and with the gossip of the servant girls on their way back from shopping. But our house was not happy. I say it that way, "it was not happy" instead of "it was sad," because that is exactly what I mean to say. The word "sad" would be wrong because it has too definite a connotation, a weight and a dimension of its own. What took place in our house was exactly the opposite: an absence, a lack, which because it was unacknowledged was irremediable, something that, if it weighed, weighed by not existing.

My mother died when I was only four years old, so the presence of a woman was deemed necessary for my care. As Aunt Mathilda was the only woman in the family and she lived with my uncles Armand and Gustav, the three of them came to live at our house, which was spacious and empty.

Aunt Mathilda discharged her duties towards me with that propriety which was characteristic of everything she did. I did not doubt that she loved me, but I could never feel it as a palpable experience uniting us. There was something rigid in her affections, as there was in those of the men of the family. With them, love existed confined inside each individual, never breaking its boundaries to express itself and bring them together. For them to show affection was to discharge their duties to each other perfectly, and above all not to inconvenience, never to inconvenience. Perhaps to express love in any other way was unnecessary for them now, since they had so long a history together, had shared so long a past. Perhaps the tenderness they felt in the past had been expressed to the point of satiation and found itself stylized now in the form of certain actions, useful symbols which did not require further elucidation. Respect was the only form of contact left between those four isolated individuals who walked the corridors of the house which, like a book, showed only its narrow spine to the street.

I, naturally, had no history in common with Aunt Mathilda. How could I, if I was no more than a child then who could not understand the gloomy motivations of his elders? I wished that their confined feeling might overflow and express itself in a fit of rage, for example, or with some bit of foolery. But she could not guess this desire of mine because her attention was not focused on me: I was a person peripheral to her life, never central. And I was not central because the entire center of her being was filled up with my father and my uncles. Aunt Mathilda was born the only woman, an ugly woman moreover, in a family of handsome men, and on realizing that for her marriage was unlikely, she dedicated herself to looking out for the comfort of those three men, by keeping house for them, by taking care of their clothes and providing their favorite dishes. She did these things without the least servility, proud of her role because she did not question her brothers' excellence. Furthermore, like all women, she possessed in the highest degree the faith that physical well-being is, if not principal, certainly primary, and that to be neither hungry nor cold nor uncomfortable is the basis for whatever else is good. Not that these defects caused her grief, but rather they made her impatient, and when she saw affliction about her she took immediate steps to remedy what, without doubt, were errors in a world that should be, that had to be, perfect. On another plane, she was intolerant of shirts which were not stupendously well-ironed, of meat that was not of the finest quality, of the humidity that owing to someone's carelessness had crept into the cigar-box.

After dinner, following what must have been an ancient ritual in the family, Aunt Mathilda went upstairs to the bedrooms, and in each of her brothers' rooms she prepared the beds for sleeping, parting the sheets with her bony hands. She spread a shawl at the foot of the bed for that one, who was subject to chills, and placed a feather pillow at the head of this one, for he usually read before going to sleep. Then, leaving the lamps lighted beside those enormous beds, she came downstairs to the billiard room to join the men for coffee and for a few rounds, before, as if bewitched by her, they retired to fill the empty effigies of the pajamas she had arranged so carefully upon the white, half-opened sheets.

But Aunt Mathilda never opened my bed. Each night, when I went up to my room, my heart thumped in the hope of finding my bed opened with the recognizable dexterity of her hands. But I had to adjust myself to the less pure style of the servant girl who was charged with doing it. Aunt Mathilda never granted me that mark of importance because I was not her brother. And not to be "one of my brothers" seemed to her a misfortune of which many people were victims, almost all in fact, including me, who after all was only the son of one of them.

Sometimes Aunt Mathilda asked me to visit her in her room where she sat sewing by the tall window, and she would talk to me. I listened attentively. She spoke to me about her brothers' integrity as lawyers in the intricate field of maritime law, and she extended to me her enthusiasm for their wealth and reputation, which I would carry forward. She described the embargo on a shipment of oranges, told of certain damages caused by miserable tugboats manned by drunkards, of the disastrous effects that arose from the demurrage of a ship sailing under an exotic flag. But when she talked to me of ships her words did not evoke the hoarse sounds of ships' sirens that I heard in the distance on summer nights when, kept awake by the heat, I climbed to the attic, and from an open window watched the far-off floating lights, and those blocks of darkness surrounding the city that lay forever out of reach for me because my life was, and would ever be, ordered perfectly. I realize now that Aunt Mathilda did not hint at this magic because she did not know of it. It had no place in her life, as it had no place in the life of anyone destined to die with dignity in order afterward to be installed in a comfortable heaven, a heaven identical to our house. Mute, I listened to her words, my gaze fastened on the white thread that, as she stretched it against her black blouse, seemed to capture all of the light from the window. I exulted at the world of security that her words projected for me, that magnificent straight road which leads to a death that is not dreaded since it is exactly like this life, without anything fortuitous or unexpected. Because death was not terrible. Death was the final incision, clean and definitive, nothing more. Hell existed, of course, but not for us. It was rather for chastising the other inhabitants of the city and those anonymous seamen who caused the damages that, when the cases were concluded, filled the family coffers.

Aunt Mathilda was so removed from the idea of fear that, since I now know that love and fear go hand in hand, I am tempted to think that in those days she did not love anyone. But I may be mistaken. In her rigid way she may have been attached to her brothers by a kind of love. At night, after supper, they gathered in the billiard room for a few games. I used to go in with them. Standing outside that circle of imprisoned affections, I watched for a sign that would show me the ties between them did exist, and did, in fact, bind. It is strange that my memory does not bring back anything but shades of indeterminate grays in remembering the house, but when I evoke that hour, the strident green of the table, the red and white of the balls and the little cube of blue chalk become inflamed in my memory, illumined by the low lamp whose shade banished everything else into dusk. In one of the family's many rituals, the voice of Aunt Mathilda rescued each of the brothers by turn from the darkness, so that they might make their plays.

"Now, Gustav . . ."

And when he leaned over the green table, cue in hand, Uncle Gustav's face was lit up, brittle as paper, its nobility contradicted by his eyes, which were too small and spaced too close together. Finished playing, he returned to the shadow, where he lit a cigar whose smoke rose lazily until it was dissolved in the gloom of the ceiling. Then his sister said: "All right, Armand . . ."

And the soft, timid face of Uncle Armand, with his large sky-blue eyes concealed by gold-rimmed glasses, bent down underneath the light. His game was generally bad because he was "the baby," as Aunt Mathilda sometimes referred to him. After the comments aroused by his play he took refuge behind his newspaper and Aunt Mathilda said: "Pedro, your turn . . ."

I held my breath when I saw him lean over to play, held it even more tightly when I saw him succumb to his sister's command. I prayed, as he got up, that he would rebel against the order established by his sister's voice. I could not see that this order was in itself a kind of rebellion, constructed by them as a protection against chaos, so that they might not be touched by what can be neither explained nor resolved. My father, then, leaned over the green cloth, his practiced eye gauging the exact distance and positions of the billiards. He made his play, and making it, he exhaled in such a way that his mustache stirred about his half-opened mouth. Then he handed me his cue so I might chalk it with the blue cube. With this minimal role that he assigned to me, he let me touch the circle that united him with the others, without letting me take part in it more than tangentially.

Now it was Aunt Mathilda's turn. She was the best player. When I saw her face, composed as if from the defects of her brothers' faces, coming out of the shadow, I knew that she was going to win. And yet . . . had I not seen her small eyes light up that face so like a brutally clenched fist, when by chance one of them succeeded in beating her? That spark appeared because, although she might have wished it, she would never have permitted herself to let any of them win. That would be to introduce the mysterious element of love into a game that ought not to include it, because affection should remain in its place, without trespassing on the strict reality of a carom shot.

II

I never did like dogs. One may have frightened me when I was very young, I don't know, but they have always displeased me. As there were no dogs at home and I went out very little, few occasions presented themselves to make me uncomfortable. For my aunt and uncles and for my father, dogs, like all the rest of the animal kingdom, did not exist. Cows, of course, supplied the cream for the dessert that was served in a silver dish on Sundays. Then there were the birds that chirped quite agreeably at twilight in the branches of the elm tree, the only inhabitant of the small garden at the rear of the house. But animals for them existed only in the proportion in which they contributed to the pleasure of human beings. Which is to say that dogs, lazy as city dogs are, could not even dent their imagination with a possibility of their existence.

Sometimes, on Sunday, Aunt Mathilda and I used to go to Mass early to take communion. It was rare that I succeeded in concentrating on the sacrament, because the idea that she was watching me without looking generally occupied the first place of my conscious mind. Even when her eyes were directed to the altar, or her head bowed before the Blessed Sacrament, my every movement drew her attention to it. And on leaving the church she told me with sly reproach that it was without doubt a flea trapped in the pews that prevented me from meditating, as she had suggested, that death is the good foreseen end, and from praying that it might not be painful, since that was the purpose of masses, novenas and communions.

This was such a morning. A fine drizzle was threatening to turn into a storm, and the quebracho pavements extended their shiny fans, notched with streetcar rails, from sidewalk to sidewalk. As I was cold and in a hurry to get home I stepped up the pace beside Aunt Mathilda, who was holding her black mushroom of an umbrella above our heads. There were not many people in the street since it was so early. A dark-complexioned gentleman saluted us without lifting his hat, because of the rain. My aunt was in the process of telling me how surprised she was that someone of mixed blood had bowed to her with so little show of attention, when suddenly, near where we were walking, a streetcar applied its brakes with a screech, making her interrupt her monologue. The conductor looked out through his window:

"Stupid dog!" he shouted.

We stopped to watch.

A small white bitch escaped from between the wheels of the streetcar and, limping painfully, with her tail between her legs, took refuge in a doorway as the streetcar moved on again.

"These dogs," protested Aunt Mathilda. "It's beyond me how they are allowed to go around like that."

Continuing on our way, we passed by the bitch huddled in the corner of a doorway. It was small and white, with legs which were too short for its size and an ugly pointed snout that proclaimed an entire genealogy of misalliances: the sum of unevenly matched breeds which for generations had been scouring the city, searching for food in the garbage cans and among the refuse of the port. She was drenched, weak, trembling with cold or fever. When we passed in front of her I noticed that my aunt looked at the bitch, and the bitch's eyes returned her gaze.

We continued on our way home. Several steps further I was on the point of forgetting the dog when my aunt surprised me by abruptly turning around and crying out: "Psst! Go away!"

She had turned in such absolute certainty of finding the bitch following us that I trembled with the mute question which arose from my surprise: How did she know? She couldn't have heard her, since she was following us at an appreciable distance. But she did not doubt it. Perhaps the look that had passed between them of which I saw only the mechanics—the bitch's head raised slightly toward Aunt Mathilda, Aunt Mathilda's slightly inclined toward the bitch—contained some secret commitment? I do not know. In any case, turning to drive away the dog, her peremptory "psst" had the sound of something like a last effort to repel an encroaching destiny. It is possible that I am saying all this in the light of things that happened later, that my imagination is embellishing with significance what was only trivial. However, I can say with certainty that in that moment I felt a strangeness, almost a fear of my aunt's sudden loss of dignity in condescending to turn around and confer rank on a sick and filthy bitch.

We arrived home. We went up the stairs and the bitch stayed down below, looking up at us from the torrential rain that had just been unleashed. We went inside, and the delectable process of breakfast following communion removed the white bitch from my mind. I have never felt our house so protective as that morning, never rejoiced so much in the security derived from those old walls that marked off my world.

In one of my wanderings in and out of the empty sitting rooms, I pulled back the curtain of a window to see if the rain promised to let up. The storm continued. And, sitting at the foot of the stairs still scrutinizing the house, I saw the white bitch. I dropped the curtain so that I might not see her there, soaked through and looking like one spellbound. Then, from the dark outer rim of the room, Aunt Mathilda's low voice surprised me. Bent over to strike a match to the kindling wood already arranged in the fireplace, she asked: "Is it still there?"

"What?"

I knew what.

"The white bitch . . ."

I answered yes, that it was.

III

It must have been the last storm of the winter, because I remember quite clearly that the following days opened up and the nights began to grow warmer.

The white bitch stayed posted on our doorstep scrutinizing our windows. In the mornings, when I left for school, I tried to shoo her away, but barely had I boarded the bus when I would see her reappear around the corner or from behind the mailbox. The servant girls also tried to frighten her away, but their attempts were as fruitless as mine, because the bitch never failed to return.

Once, we were all saying goodnight at the foot of the stairs before going up to bed. Uncle Gustav had just turned off the lights, all except the one on the stairway, so that the large space of the vestibule had become peopled with the shadowy bodies of furniture. Aunt Mathilda, who was entreating Uncle Armand to open the window of his room so a little air could come in, suddenly stopped speaking, leaving her sentence unfinished, and the movements of all of us, who had started to go up, halted.

"What is the matter?" asked Father, stepping down one stair.

"Go on up," murmured Aunt Mathilda, turning around and gazing into the shadow of the vestibule.

But we did not go up.

The silence of the room was filled with the sweet voice of each object: a grain of dirt trickling down between the wallpaper and the wall, the creaking of polished woods, the quivering of some loose crystal. Someone, in addition to ourselves, was where we were. A small white form came out of the darkness near the service door. The bitch crossed the vestibule, limping slowly in the direction of Aunt Mathilda, and without even looking at her, threw herself down at her feet.

It was as though the immobility of the dog enabled us to move again. My father came down two stairs. Uncle Gustav turned on the light. Uncle Armand went upstairs and shut himself in his room.

"What is this?" asked my father.

Aunt Mathilda remained still.

"How could she have come in?" she asked aloud.

Her question seemed to acknowledge the heroism implicit in having either jumped walls in that lamentable condition, or come into the basement through a broken pane of glass, or fooled the servants' vigilance by creeping through a casually opened door.

"Mathilda, call one of the girls to take her away,"

said my father, and went upstairs followed by Uncle Gustav.

We were left alone looking at the bitch. She called a servant, telling the girl to give her something to eat and the next day to call a veterinarian.

"Is she going to stay in the house?" I asked.

"How can she walk in the street like that?" murmured Aunt Mathilda. "She has to get better so we can throw her out. And she'd better get well soon because I don't want animals in the house."

Then she added: "Go upstairs to bed."

She followed the girl who was carrying the dog out.

I sensed that ancient drive of Aunt Mathilda's to have everything go well about her, that energy and dexterity which made her sovereign of immediate things. Is it possible that she was so secure within her limitations that for her the only necessity was to overcome imperfections, errors not of intention or motive, but of condition? If so, the white bitch was going to get well. She would see to it because the animal had entered the radius of her power. The veterinarian would bandage the broken leg under her watchful eye, and protected by rubber gloves and an apron, she herself would take charge of cleaning the bitch's pustules with disinfectant that would make her howl. But Aunt Mathilda would remain deaf to those howls, sure that whatever she was doing was for the best.

And so it was. The bitch stayed in the house. Not that I saw her, but I could feel the presence of any stranger there, even though confined to the lower reaches of the basement. Once or twice I saw Aunt Mathilda with the rubber gloves on her hands, carrying a vial full of red liquid. I found a plate with scraps of food in a passage of the basement where I went to look for the bicycle I had just been given. Weakly, buffered by walls and floors, at times the suspicion of a bark reached my ears.

One afternoon I went down to the kitchen. The

bitch came in, painted like a clown with red disinfectant. The servants threw her out without paying her any mind. But I saw that she was not hobbling any longer, that her tail, limp before, was curled up like a feather, leaving her shameless bottom in plain view.

That afternoon I asked Aunt Mathilda: "When are you going to throw her out?"

"Who?" she asked.

She knew perfectly well.

"The white bitch."

"She's not well yet," she replied.

Later I thought of insisting, of telling her that surely there was nothing now to prevent her from climbing the garbage cans in search of food. I didn't do it because I believe it was the same night that Aunt Mathilda, after losing the first round of billiards, decided that she did not feel like playing another. Her brothers went on playing, and she, ensconced in the leather sofa, made a mistake in calling their names. There was a moment of confusion. Then the thread of order was quickly picked up again by the men, who knew how to ignore an accident if it was not favorable to them. But I had already seen.

It was as if Aunt Mathilda were not there at all. She was breathing at my side as she always did. The deep, silencing carpet yielded under her feet as usual and her tranquilly crossed hands weighed on her skirt. How is it possible to feel with the certainty I felt then the absence of a person whose heart is somewhere else? The following nights were equally troubled by the invisible slur of her absence. She seemed to have lost all interest in the game and left off calling her brothers by their names. They appeared not to notice it. But they must have, because their games became shorter and I noticed an infinitesimal increase in the deference with which they treated her.

One night, as we were going out of the dining room, the bitch appeared in the doorway and joined the family group. The men paused before they went into the library so that their sister might lead the way to the billiard room, followed this time by the white bitch. They made no comment, as if they had not seen her, beginning their game as they did every night.

The bitch sat down at Aunt Mathilda's feet. She was very quiet. Her lively eyes examined the room and followed the players' strategies as if all of that amused her greatly. She was fat now and had a shiny coat. Her whole body, from her quivering snout to her tail ready to waggle, was full of an abundant capacity for fun. How long had she stayed in the house? A month? Perhaps more. But in that month Aunt Mathilda had forced her to get well, caring for her not with displays of affection but with those hands of hers which could not refrain from mending what was broken. The leg was well. She had disinfected, fed and bathed her, and now the white bitch was whole.

In one of his plays Uncle Armand let the cube of blue chalk fall to the floor. Immediately, obeying an instinct that seemed to surge up from her picaresque past, the bitch ran toward the chalk and snatched it with her mouth away from Uncle Armand, who had bent over to pick it up. Then followed something surprising: Aunt Mathilda, as if suddenly unwound, burst into a peal of laughter that agitated her whole body. We remained frozen. On hearing her laugh, the bitch dropped the chalk, ran towards her with tail waggling aloft, and jumped up onto her lap. Aunt Mathilda's laugh relented, but Uncle Armand left the room. Uncle Gustav and my father went on with the game: now it was more important than ever not to see, not to see anything at all, not to comment, not to consider oneself alluded to by these events.

I did not find Aunt Mathilda's laugh amusing, because I may have felt the dark thing that had stirred it up. The bitch grew calm sitting on her lap. The cracking noises of the balls when they hit seemed to conduct Aunt Mathilda's hand first from its place on the edge of the sofa, to her skirt, and then to the curved back of the sleeping animal. On seeing that expressionless hand reposing there, I noticed that the tension which had kept my aunt's features clenched before, relented, and that a certain peace was now softening her face. I could not resist. I drew closer to her on the sofa, as if to a newly kindled fire. I hoped that she would reach out to me with a look or include me with a smile. But she did not.

IV

When I arrived from school in the afternoon, I used to go directly to the back of the house and, mounting my bicycle, take turn after turn around the narrow garden, circling the pair of cast-iron benches and the elm tree. Behind the wall, the chestnut trees were beginning to display their light spring down, but the seasons did not interest me, for I had too many serious things to think about. And since I knew that no one came down into the garden until the suffocation of midsummer made it imperative, it seemed to be the best place for meditating about what was going on inside the house.

One might have said that nothing was going on. But how could I remain calm in the face of the entwining relationship which had sprung up between my aunt and the white bitch? It was as if Aunt Mathilda, after having resigned herself to an odd life of service and duty, had found at last her equal. And as women-friends do, they carried on a life full of niceties and pleasing refinements. They ate bonbons that came in boxes wrapped frivolously with ribbons. My aunt arranged tangerines, pineapples and grapes in tall crystal bowls, while the bitch watched her as if on the point of criticizing her taste or offering a suggestion.

Often when I passed the door of her room, I heard a

peal of laughter like the one which had overturned the order of her former life that night. Or I heard her engage in a dialogue with an interlocutor whose voice I did not hear. It was a new life. The bitch, the guilty one, slept in a hamper near her bed, an elegant, feminine hamper, ridiculous to my way of thinking, and followed her everywhere except into the dining room. Entrance there was forbidden her, but waiting for her friend to come out again, she followed her to the billiard room and sat at her side on the sofa or on her lap, exchanging with her from time to time complicitory glances.

How was it possible? I used to ask myself: why had she waited until now to go beyond herself and establish a dialogue? At times she appeared insecure about the bitch, fearful that, in the same way she had arrived one fine day, she might also go, leaving her with all this new abundance weighing on her hands. Or did she still fear for her health? These ideas, which now seem to clear, floated blurred in my imagination while I listened to the gravel of the path crunching under the wheels of my bicycle. What was not blurred, however, was my vehement desire to become gravely ill, to see if I might also succeed in harvesting some kind of relationship. Because the bitch's illness had been the cause of everything. If it had not been for that, my aunt might have never joined in league with her. But I had a constitution of iron, and furthermore it was clear that Aunt Mathilda's heart did not have room for more than one love at a time.

My father and my uncles did not seem to notice any change. The bitch was very quiet and, abandoning her street ways, seemed to acquire manners more worthy of Aunt Mathilda. But still, she had somehow preserved all the sauciness of a female of the streets. It was clear that the hardships of her life had not been able to cloud either her good humor or her taste for adventure which, I felt, lay dangerously dormant inside her. For the men of the house it proved easier to accept her than to throw her out, since this would have forced them to revise their cannons of security.

One night, when the pitcher of lemonade had already made its appearance on the console table of the library, cooling that corner of the shadow, and the windows had been thrown open to the air, my father halted abruptly at the doorway of the billiard room.

"What is that?" he exclaimed, looking at the floor.

The three men stopped in consternation to look at a small, round pool on the waxed floor.

"Mathilda!" called Uncle Gustav.

She went to look and then reddened with shame. The bitch had taken refuge under the billiard table in the adjoining room. Walking over to the table my father saw her there, and changing direction sharply, he left the room, followed by his brothers.

Aunt Mathilda went upstairs. The bitch followed her. I stayed in the library with a glass of lemonade in my hand, and looked out at the summer sky, listening to some far-off siren from the sea, and to the murmur of the city stretched out under the stars. Soon I heard Aunt Mathilda coming down. She appeared with her hat on and with her keys chinking in her hand.

"Go up and go to bed," she said. "I'm going to take her for a walk on the street so that she can do her business."

Then she added something strange: "It's such a lovely night."

And she went out.

From that night on, instead of going up after dinner to open her brothers' beds, she went to her room, put her hat tightly on her head and came downstairs again, chinking her keys. She went out with the bitch without explaining anything to anyone. And my uncles and my father and I stayed behind in the billiard room, and later we sat on the benches of the garden, with all the murmuring of the elm tree and the clearness of the sky weighing down on us. These nocturnal walks of Aunt Mathilda's were never spoken of by her brothers. They never showed any awareness of the change that had occurred inside our house.

In the beginning Aunt Mathilda was gone at the most for twenty minutes or half an hour, returning to take whatever refreshment there was and to exchange some trivial commentary. Later, her sorties were inexplicably prolonged. We began to realize, or I did at least, that she was no longer a woman taking her dog out for hygienic reasons: outside there, in the streets of the city, something was drawing her. When waiting, my father furtively eyed his pocket watch, and if the delay was very great Uncle Gustav went up to the second floor pretending he had forgotten something there, to spy for her from the balcony. But still they did not speak. Once, when Aunt Mathilda stayed out too long, my father paced back and forth along the path that wound between the hydrangeas. Uncle Gustav threw away a cigar which he could not light to his satisfaction, then another, crushing it with the heel of his shoe. Uncle Armand spilled a cup of coffee. I watched them, hoping that at long last they would explode, that they would finally say something to fill the minutes that were passing by one after another, getting longer and longer and longer without the presence of Aunt Mathilda. It was twelve-thirty when she arrived.

"Why are you all waiting up for me?" she asked, smiling.

She was holding her hat in her hand, and her hair, ordinarily so well-groomed, was mussed. I saw that a streak of mud was soiling her shoes.

"What happened to you?" asked Uncle Armand.

"Nothing," came her reply, and with it she shut off any right of her brothers to meddle in those unknown hours that were now her life. I say they were her life because, during the minutes she stayed with us before going up to her room with the bitch, I perceived an animation in her eyes, an excited restlessness like that in the eyes of the animal: it was as though they had been washed in scenes to which even our imagination lacked access. Those two were accomplices. The night protected them. They belonged to the murmuring sound of the city, to the sirens of the ships which, crossing the dark or illuminated streets, the houses and factories and parks, reached my ears.

Her walks with the bitch continued for some time. Now we said good night immediately after dinner, and each one went up to shut himself in his room, my father, Uncle Gustav, Uncle Armand and I. But no one went to sleep before she came in, late, sometimes terribly late, when the light of dawn was already striking the top of our elm. Only after hearing her close the door of her bedroom did the pacing with which my father measured his room cease, or was the window in one of his brother's rooms finally closed to exclude that fragment of the night which was no longer dangerous.

Once I heard her come up very late, and as I thought I heard her singing softly, I opened my door and peeked out. When she passed my room, with the white bitch nestled in her arms, her face seemed to me surprisingly young and unblemished, even though it was dirty, and I saw a rip in her skirt. I went to bed terrified, knowing this was the end.

I was not mistaken. Because one night, shortly after, Aunt Mathilda took the dog out for a walk after dinner, and did not return.

We stayed awake all night, each one in his room, and she did not come back. No one said anything the next day. They went—I presume—to their office, and I went to school. She wasn't home when we came back and we sat silently at our meal that night. I wonder if they found out something definite that very first day. But I think not, because we all, without seeming to, haunted the windows of the house, peering into the street.

"Your aunt went on a trip," the cook answered me when I finally dared to ask, if only her.

But I knew it was not true.

Life continued in the house just as if Aunt Mathilda were still living there. It is true that they used to gather in the library for hours and hours, and closeted there they may have planned ways of retrieving her out of that night which had swallowed her. Several times a visitor came who was clearly not of our world, a plainclothesman perhaps, or the head of a stevedore's union come to pick up indemnification for some accident. Sometimes their voices rose a little, sometimes there was a deadened quiet, sometimes their voices became hard, sharp, as they fenced with the voice I did not know. But the library door was too thick, too heavy for me to hear what they were saying.

Translated by Lorraine O'Grady Freeman

The Handsomest Drowned Man in the World

A TALE FOR CHILDREN

GABRIEL GARCÍA MÁRQUEZ

The first children who saw the dark and slinky bulge approaching through the sea let themselves think it was an enemy ship. Then they saw it had no flags or masts and they thought it was a whale. But when it washed up on the beach, they removed the clumps of seaweed, the jellyfish tentacles, and the remains of fish and flotsam, and only then did they see that it was a drowned man.

They had been playing with him all afternoon, burying him in the sand and digging him up again, when someone chanced to see them and spread the alarm in the village. The men who carried him to the nearest house noticed that he weighed more than any dead man they had ever known, almost as much as a horse, and they said to each other that maybe he'd been floating too long and the water had got into his bones. When they laid him on the floor they said he'd been taller than all other men because there was barely enough room for him in the house, but they thought that maybe the ability to keep on growing after death was part of the nature of certain drowned men. He had the smell of the sea about him and only his shape gave one to suppose that it was the corpse of a human being, because the skin was covered with a crust of mud and scales.

They did not even have to clean off his face to know that the dead man was a stranger. The village was made up of only twenty-odd wooden houses that had stone courtyards with no flowers and which were spread about on the end of a desertlike cape. There was so little land that mothers always went about with the fear that the wind would carry off their children and the few dead that the years had caused among them had to be thrown off the cliffs. But the sea was calm and bountiful and all the men fit into seven boats. So when they found the drowned man they simply had to look at one another to see that they were all there.

That night they did not go out to work at sea. While the men went to find out if anyone was missing in neighboring villages, the women stayed behind to care for the drowned man. They took the mud off with grass swabs, they removed the underwater stones entangled in his hair, and they scraped the crust off with tools used for scaling fish. As they were doing that they noticed that the vegetation on him came from faraway oceans and deep water and that his clothes were in tatters, as if he had sailed through labyrinths of coral. They noticed too that he bore his death with pride, for he did not have the lonely look of other drowned men who came out of the sea or that haggard, needy look of men who drowned in rivers. But only when they finished cleaning him off did they become aware of the kind of man he was and it left them breathless. Not only was he the tallest, strongest, most virile, and best built man they had ever seen, but even though they were looking at him there was no room for him in their imagination.

They could not find a bed in the village large enough to lay him on nor was there a table solid enough to use for his wake. The tallest men's holiday pants would not fit him, nor the fattest ones' Sunday shirts, nor the shoes of the one with the biggest feet. Fascinated by his huge size and his beauty, the women then decided to make him some pants from a large piece of sail and a shirt from some bridal Brabant linen so that he could continue through his death with dignity. As they sewed, sitting in a circle and gazing at the corpse between stitches, it seemed to them that the wind had never been so steady nor the sea so restless as on that night and they supposed that the change had something to do with the dead man. They thought that if that magnificent man had lived in the village, his house would have had the widest doors, and highest ceiling, and the strongest floor; his bedstead would have been made from a midship frame held together by iron bolts, and his wife would have been the happiest woman. They thought that he would have had so much authority that he could have drawn fish out of the sea simply by calling their names and that he would have put so much work into his land that springs would have burst forth from among the rocks so that he would have been able to plant flowers on the cliffs. They secretly compared him to their own men, thinking that for all their lives theirs were incapable of doing what he could do in one night, and they ended up dismissing them deep in their hearts as the weakest, meanest, and most useless creatures on earth. They were wandering through that maze of fantasy when the oldest woman, who as the oldest had looked upon the drowned man with more compassion than passion, sighed:

"He has the face of someone called Esteban."

It was true. Most of them had only to take another look at him to see that he could not have any other name. The more stubborn among them, who were the youngest, still lived for a few hours with the illusion that when they put his clothes on and he lay among the flowers in patent leather shoes his name might be

Lautaro. But it was a vain illusion. There had not been enough canvas, the poorly cut and worse sewn pants were too tight, and the hidden strength of his heart popped the buttons on his shirt. After midnight the whistling of the wind died down and the sea fell into its Wednesday drowsiness. The silence put an end to any last doubts: he was Esteban. The women who had dressed him, who had combed his hair, had cut his nails and shaved him were unable to hold back a shudder of pity when they had to resign themselves to his being dragged along the ground. It was then that they understood how unhappy he must have been with that huge body since it bothered him even after death. They could see him in life, condemned to going through doors sideways cracking his head on crossbeams, remaining on his feet during visits, not knowing what to do with his soft pink, sealion hands while the lady of the house looked for her most resistant chair and begged him, frightened to death, sit here, Esteban, please, and he, leaning against the wall, smiling, don't bother, ma'am, I'm fine where I am, his heels raw and his back roasted from having done the same thing so many times whenever he paid a visit, don't bother, ma'am, I'm fine where I am to avoid the embarrassment of breaking up the chair, and never knowing perhaps that the one who said don't go, Esteban, at least wait till the coffee's ready, were the ones who later on would whisper the big boob finally left, how nice, the handsome fool has gone. That was what the women were thinking beside the body a little before dawn. Later, when they covered his face with a handkerchief so that the light would not bother him, he looked so forever dead, so defenseless, so much like their men that the first furrows of tears opened in their hearts. It was one of the younger ones who began the weeping. The others, coming to, went from sighs to wails, and the more they sobbed the more they felt like weeping, because the drowned man was becoming all the more Esteban for them, and so they wept so much, for he was the most destitute, most peaceful, and most obliging man on earth, poor Esteban. So when the men returned with the news that the drowned man was not from the neighboring villages either, the women felt an opening of jubilation in the midst of their tears.

"Praise the Lord," they sighed, "he's ours!"

The men thought the fuss was only womanish frivolity. Fatigued because of the difficult nighttime inquiries, all they wanted was to get rid of the bother of the newcomer once and for all before the sun grew strong on that arid, windless day. They improvised a litter with the remains of foremasts and gaffs, tying it together with rigging so that it would bear the weight of the body until they reached the cliffs. They wanted to tie the anchor from a cargo ship to him so that he would sink easily into the deepest waves, where the fish are blind and divers die of nostalgia, and bad currents would not bring him back to shore, as had happened with other bodies. But the more they hurried, the more the women thought of ways to waste time. They walked about like startled hens, pecking with the sea charms on their breasts, some interfering on one side to put a scapular of the good wind on the drowned man, some on the other side to put a wrist compass on him, and after a great deal of *get away from there, woman, stay out of the way, look, you almost made me fall on top of the dead man*, the men began to feel mistrust in their livers and started grumbling about why so many main-altar decorations for a stranger, because no matter how many nails and holy-water jars he had on him, the sharks would chew him all the same, but the women kept on piling on their junk relics, running back and forth, stumbling, while they released in sighs what they did not in tears, so that the men finally exploded with *since when has there ever been such a fuss over a drifting corpse, a drowned nobody, a piece of cold Wednesday meat.*

One of the women, mortified by so much lack of care, then removed the handkerchief from the dead man's face and the men were left breathless too.

He was Esteban. It was not necessary to repeat it for them to recognize him. If they had been told Sir Walter Raleigh, even they might have been impressed with his gringo accent, the macaw on his shoulder, his cannibal-killing blunderbuss, but there could be only one Esteban in the world and there he was, stretched out like a sperm whale, shoeless, wearing the pants of an undersized child, and with those stony nails that had to be cut with a knife. They had only to take the handkerchief off his face to see that he was ashamed, that it was not his fault that he was so big or so heavy or so handsome, and if he had known that this was going to happen, he would have looked for a more discreet place to drown in; seriously, I even would have tied the anchor off a galleon around my neck and staggered off a cliff like someone who doesn't like things in order not to be upsetting people now with this Wednesday dead body, as you people say, in order not to be bothering anyone with this filthy piece of cold meat that doesn't have anything to do with me. There was so much truth in his manner that even the most mistrustful men, the ones who felt the bitterness of endless nights at sea fearing that their women would tire of dreaming about them and begin to dream of drowned men, even they and others who were harder still shuddered in the marrow of their bones at Esteban's sincerity.

That was how they came to hold the most splendid funeral they could conceive of for an abandoned drowned man. Some women who had gone to get flowers in the neighboring villages returned with other women who could not believe what they had been told, and those women went back for more flowers when they saw the dead man, and they brought more and more until there were so many flowers and so many people that it was hard to walk about. At the final moment it pained them to return him to the waters as an orphan and they chose a father and mother from among the best people, and aunts and uncles and cousins, so that through him all the inhabitants of the village became kinsmen. Some sailors who heard the weeping from a distance went off course, and people heard of one who had himself tied to the mainmast, remembering ancient fables about sirens. While they fought for the privilege of carrying him on their shoulders along the steep escarpment by the cliffs, men and women became aware for the first time of the desolation of their streets, the dryness of their courtyards, the narrowness of their dreams as they faced the splendor and beauty of their drowned man. They let him go without an anchor so that he could come back if he wished and whenever he wished, and they all held their breath for the fraction of centuries the body took to fall into the abyss. They did not need to look to one another to realize that they were no longer all present, that they would never be. But they also knew that everything would be different from then on, that their houses would have wider doors, higher ceilings, and stronger floors so that Esteban's memory could go everywhere without bumping into beams and so that no one in the future would dare whisper the big boob finally died, too bad, the handsome fool has finally died, because they were going to paint their house fronts gay colors to make Esteban's memory eternal and they were going to break their backs digging for springs among the stones and planting flowers on the cliffs so that in future years at dawn the passengers on great liners would awaken, suffocated by the smell of gardens on the high seas, and the captain would have to come down from the bridge in his dress uniform, with his astrolabe, his pole star, and his row of war medals and, pointing to the promontory of roses on the horizon, he would say in fourteen languages, look there, where the wind is so peaceful now that it's gone to sleep beneath the beds, over there, where the sun's so bright that the sunflowers don't know which way to turn, yes, over there, that's Esteban's village.

Translated by Gregory Rabassa

A Nest of Sparrows on the Awning

GUILLERMO CABRERA INFANTE

An old couple lives next door and over their terrace hangs a green awning. The awning is rolled up; they never lower it. I've seen them out on the balcony once or twice. They are small, shrunken, and, above all, quiet old people. They only come out to sunbathe, on those two or three days a year when it's cold enough one feels like warming up. If I'm not mistaken, they're Americans, although I've never heard them speak.

One day my wife told me that two sparrows had made a nest on the awning.

"Look"—she said. "One always stays to take care of the nest while the other goes looking for straw."

"That's the female."

"How do you know?"

"Because she's uglier."

"Really?"—she looked at me suspiciously.

In a pocket formed by the crookedly rolled awning, a fat little sparrow watched while her companion tried to enter the opening with his mouth full of dry grass.

"We should tell the people next door"—she suggested. "Otherwise they'll lower the awning and the eggs will fall and break."

My wife looked at me the way one looks at a rare animal: the kindest man in the world.

"They might even have babies," she said with maternal concern, "and they might fall before they can fly." And she added compulsively, as women do: "Why don't you go and talk to them?"

"We'll see."

It was as if I had said "Next century," because her face changed radically and she urged: "You must go right now."

"I can't, honey. I want to finish this book."

The old admiration completely vanished.

"So, finishing a book is more urgent than saving the lives of poor little birds?"

"But, darling, they haven't even finished their nest."

Her tone was more and more demanding. "What do you want, then? To wait until the eggs are in mid-air?"

She had won.

"Okay, I'll go as soon as I finish this page."

But when I got up, she had already changed her mind.

"Look, I think you'd better leave it for tomorrow. It's getting late, and anyway, they've never lowered the awning before."

"Fine, dear. Tomorrow when I come back from work I'll go over and talk to them."

"Okay, but don't keep putting it off."

The following afternoon, when I returned from work, I decided to go and speak to the old couple about the nest. It was a little after five and the day was pleasant. The building I live in is a large apartment house with a central patio, in the middle of which there's a tall and exuberant areca palm. Everything looked pink from the setting sun and a cool, light breeze blew which softened the early-summer afternoon.

After I had rung the bell twice, a freckled, blonde girl came to the door. How old was she? She was dressed in a loose yellow and red-striped gown, tied at the waist with a bright yellow ribbon, and she wore sandals. Her hair fell in a long wave, cutting across her wide and slightly stupid-looking forehead. She wasn't beautiful, but she had the attractive look of an American ingenue. She didn't look like the maid.

"Are the people who live here at home?"

"Sorry. No Spanish."

She didn't speak Spanish and my English was too unsure to explain the whole thing clearly. I realized it would be difficult to communicate.

"The old ones, are they at home?"

"Oh, you mean Grandma and Grandpa," she said in English. "No, they went out. They won't be back till dinner."

She had a voice that didn't seem to come from her. She spoke fast and mumbled the final words, which is why I hardly understood her.

"Well, it's about the sparrows."

She snickered and answered: "That's news to me. I didn't know my grandparents spent their time breeding sparrows."

I didn't think she was capable of making jokes. Realizing I was fidgety, I decided to explain about the nest and the awning so as to get out of this spot. I told her I wanted to make sure they didn't destroy the nest by mistake. Without meaning to, I realized I hadn't even mentioned that I was married and lived next door.

"Won't you come in? I'll tell Grandpa and Grandma when they come back. Meanwhile, you can show me where the nest is."

The apartment was furnished less luxuriously than I had imagined, but it looked comfortable. The kitchen was arranged differently from ours and the living room was larger. When we went out on the terrace the sun reddened the façade of the neighboring buildings. The French blinds on my balcony were closed.

On the awning, the sparrows seemed to be in a

hurry to finish the nest before sunset. One of them returned with a long, curved piece of straw which he couldn't fit into the pocket. He fluttered his wings a bit, tried to hold himself up on the edge of the awning with his little feet and pushed the straw, which bent even more but didn't get into the nest. Something wasn't working, and the sparrow was perplexed. At that moment the female stuck her head out and tried to fly off. Then the male gave up and let the stick fall. He entered the nest and came out again—or was it the female?—flying till he disappeared behind the buildings in the background.

"That's cute," the girl said and laughed. She had a direct, tense laugh, but her body showed no emotion.

It was starting to get cool on the balcony. It had been hot at midday, but now the breeze from the park cooled the terrace. The sun reached only the higher floors of the houses facing us. We went in.

"Would you like to sit down?"

I accepted the invitation too quickly and sat down on a small bench against the windowsill. She was moving toward the living room, but when she saw me, she smiled, turned around, and came to sit on the edge of the bed. It was then I realized my error. I didn't try to correct it.

"What is your name?" I asked the question as if I had said *Tom is a boy.*

"Jill. And yours?"

"Silvestre."

"That's a funny name. I mean, I like it a lot. I don't think I'll ever be able to pronounce it, but I like the way you say it."

"Of course you can."

"No, I can't."

"Try. You only have to say the 'e's like in *better*, both the same."

"I'll never be able to."

"Try, even if only once."

She tried to pronounce my name and said something unrecognizable, which sounded vaguely like "silver tray."

"No, not silver tray. I'm neither a tray nor silver."

"See? I'll never manage to do it right. But I like the way you say it. Say it again."

"Silvestre."

"Say it."

"Silvestre."

"Say it, say it. Say it."

She threw herself back on the bed, laughing. I could see her twisted and white teeth, protected by braces. I didn't like her laugh. I thought she needed braces on her laugh too. When she stopped laughing, she remained lying on her back. Her gown had risen above her knees and I could see her thighs. For a few minutes we didn't say anything.

"Jill, your name is funny too," I said to break the silence. My voice sounded hollow. Another silence.

After a while she said: "There's nothing funny about me. Not even the name. It's silly, out of place, but not funny."

This silence lasted longer than the others. We knew that whoever spoke would probably say something inappropriate. She sat up again. She was serious. She was very serious. She remained calm, but her control had something dynamic underneath: her silence was like a dam holding back a rising river. For a moment I thought that she would speak the next word and that it would be dirty. Would I understand it? I know almost all the dirty words that men say in English, but not the ones women use. However, she just stared at me. Her eyes weren't upset, though. Her twisted mouth was the angry one. But even if her eyes weren't furious, there was something twisted in them too.

She stood up and untied the braided cord that served as a belt. The gown became wider and I realized that it was one of those convertible smocks that changes shape with a belt. Now she was a woman. She was standing, barefoot, her legs firmly planted on the marbled tiles. For once I stopped thinking about her age.

"I like your hair," she said. "I've always liked very black hair. I like black things."

She ran her hand through my hair. Suddenly she bent down and kissed me. Her kiss was rough, and I felt her braces pressing against my lips, then against my teeth and tongue.

I held her firmly by the waist with one arm and tried to caress her breasts, but she pushed my hand away.

"Don't! Oh don't!"

She spoke into my mouth. Her voice wasn't angry, just firm.

Finally she stopped kissing me and simply stood there. Before I could check with my hand if she wore lipstick, I felt a sharp blow on my face, and my head felt hot. By the time I realized she was slapping me, she had already done it several times. My cheeks were burning and a tear fell from my right eye.

"So that's what you're after?" she shouted.

And she left the room in a rage. The last I saw of her was her legs. "She has the legs of a ballplayer," I thought.

I remained there without knowing if I should get up, stay seated, or leave.

Shortly after, I heard sobs and tried to figure out where they came from. Someone was crying in the other room. I went in and found Jill, her arms flat on the table and her head between them. Her shoulders trembled. I felt sorry for her and forgot all about the slapping. Or did I forget because I wanted more kissing? I touched her trembling shoulder.

"Leave me alone," she said, and I don't know why I thought of Greta Garbo.

"Don't cry, please."

From the table came a noise between a suppressed sob and a laugh.

"So you think I was crying?"

She raised her head with an unwholesome guttural laugh.

"You thought I was crying? That's the funniest thing I've heard in a day full of funny things!"

She got up and put her face close to mine so that I'd see she hadn't been crying.

"Me crying? For you?"

And she laughed even louder.

"Fool!"

She moved toward the door and grabbed at the knob, but instead of opening it, leaned her head against the panel. Now she was really crying. Quietly, and yet I was afraid that on the other side of the door the whole neighborhood would hear.

"You fool. Fool, fool!"

I went to her and put my hand on her head. Her hair was strong but soft. She quieted down. After a while she turned the knob and opened the door. I tried to close it, but she insisted with a pull that was both gentle and decided.

"Will we see each other again?"

Then she looked at me for the last time.

"No, I'm going tomorrow. Early in the morning."

She opened the door and I went out. I looked at her and realized that she would cry some more.

"So long."

"Good-by, Silver tray."

Two or three days later I was reading a new book on our balcony. I had tried to forget everything, which I realized was easier than trying to remember. When the door closed, I had stood there for a while. On it was a card that said *Mr. & Mrs. Salinger*. I'd tried to ring, not because I wanted to see her again, but because I wanted to convince myself that it hadn't happened, that I had imagined the whole thing and that nobody would come to open the door, because nobody was there. The house was empty. Nothing had happened. I couldn't remember her face or her voice. Jill didn't exist. My name wasn't Silvestre. The whole thing was a lie.

"Silvestre."

My wife's voice sounded behind me.

"What people!"

"What?"

"Look at those people!"

"What people, dear?"

"Next door. The old folks next door."

I looked up from my book and toward the neighboring terrace. One of them—the old woman—was lowering the awning and the sparrows were fluttering around the green cloth.

"They're lowering the awning."

"So I see."

The little eggs had fallen to the ground. One of them broke against the terrace wall and a viscous yellow stain remained there. The little old lady looked as shocked as the sparrows and ran inside, trembling, calling softly, "Ernest, Ernest!" The two birds chirped and fluttered around the broken eggs. The female sparrow perched beside the spilled yolk and pecked at it. Then she picked a wet little stick out of the white and flew to where the nest had been. Trying to find the former hole, she kept knocking against the green fabric of the awning. More confused than ever, she dropped the straw from her mouth.

My wife was really furious. She went to the edge of the balcony and glared at the next-door terrace. Then she came back to me and loosed her fury in one question: "Didn't you tell them?"

I looked at her and remained mute. How could I explain?

Translated by Suzanne Jill Levine

The Two Elenas

CARLOS FUENTES

To José Luis Cuevas

"I don't know where Elena gets those ideas. She wasn't brought up that way. And neither were you, Victor. But the fact is that marriage has changed her. Yes, there's no doubt about it. I thought my husband would have an attack. Those ideas are indefensible, especially at supper. My daughter knows very well that her father needs to eat in peace. Otherwise his blood-pressure goes up immediately. The doctor told her so. And, after all, this doctor knows what he's talking about. There's a reason why he charges two hundred pesos a visit. I appeal to you to speak to Elena. She doesn't pay any attention to me. Tell her we're willing to put up with everything. We don't care if she neglects her home to learn French. We don't care if she goes to see those newfangled movies at dives full of hippies. We don't care about those clownish red stockings. But that she should tell her father at supper that a woman can live with two men in order to complement herself ... Victor, for your own good you should knock those ideas out of your wife's head."

From the time she saw *Jules et Jim* at a movie club, Elena's had a bee in her bonnet about carrying on the argument at Sunday supper with her parents—the only obligatory family gathering.

When we left the movies we took the MG and went to the Coyote Flaco in Coyoacán for supper. As ever, Elena looked very beautiful in her black sweater and leather skirt and the stockings her mother dislikes. She had also put on a gold chain which supported a jade carving that, according to an anthropologist friend, represents Uno Muerte, prince of the Mixtecas. Elena, who is always so carefree and gay, had an intense expression that night. Her cheeks were flushed and she scarcely greeted the friends who generally gathered at the somewhat Gothic restaurant. I asked her what she wanted to order and she didn't answer. Instead, she took my hand and gazed at me with a fixed stare. I ordered two steak and garlic sandwiches while Elena shook her pale rose hair and stroked her throat.

"Victor, Nibelungo, I realize for the first time that you're right if you're all misogynists. We women were all born to be detested. I'm not going to pretend anymore. I've discovered that misogyny is what love is made of. I know very well that I'm wrong, but the more needs I express the more you're going to hate me and the more you're going to try to satisfy me. Victor, Nibelungo, you have to buy me an old sailor suit like the one Jeanne Moreau wears in the movie."

I told her it was fine with me, provided she kept expecting everything from me only. Elena caressed my hand and smiled.

"I'm well aware that you can't free yourself, darling. But have faith. When you've finished giving me everything I ask for, you yourself will ask to have another man share our lives. You yourself will ask to be Jules and to have Jim live with us and bear the burden. Didn't Christ say so? Let's love one another. Of course."

I thought Elena could be right in the future. I

knew after four years of marriage that with her all the rules of morality learned since childhood tended to evaporate naturally. I always loved that in her—her naturalness. She never negates one rule to set down another, but to open a sort of door like the ones in children's stories in which each page with an illustration contains the announcement of a garden, a cave or a sea, which are reached through the secret opening of the preceding page.

"I don't want to have children for six years," she said one night as she leaned back against my legs while we listened to Cannonball Adderley records in the darkened drawing room of our house. And at Coyoacán, in the same house that we've decorated with polychrome ornaments and colonial masks with hypnotic eyes: "You never go to Mass and no one says anything. I won't go either; let them say what they want." And in the attic that we use as a bedroom and that on bright mornings gets the light from the volcanoes: "I'm going to have coffee with Alejandro today. He's a great sketcher and he'd feel embarrassed if you were there. I need him to explain certain things while we're alone." And as she follows me over the planks connecting the unfinished floors of the group of houses I'm building at the Desierto de los Leones: "I'm going to travel around the country by train for ten days." And while we have a quick coffee at the Tirol in the middle of the afternoon, as she moves her fingers to greet friends who are walking along Calle Hamburgo: "Thanks for taking me to the whorehouse so I could see what it was like, Nibelungo. It was like in the days of Toulouse-Lautrec, as innocent as a story by Maupassant. You see? I've found out now that sin and depravity are not there but somewhere else." And after a private showing of *The Exterminating Angel*: "Victor, what's moral is whatever gives life, and what's immoral is whatever takes away life. Isn't that right?"

And now she repeated it, with a piece of sandwich in her mouth: "Am I not right? If a *ménage à trois* gives us life and joy and makes us better in our personal relations than when there are only two of us, isn't that moral?"

I expressed agreement as I ate and listened to the sputtering of the meat being roasted on the high grill. Several friends saw to it that their slices were done the way they wanted and then came and sat down with us. Elena laughed again and was back to normal. I hit on the bad idea of studying the faces of our friends and imagining each one installed in my house and giving Elena the portion of feeling, stimulation, passion or intelligence that I, having reached my limit, was incapable of bestowing upon her. I watched one friend with his expression of intense interest in her words [sometimes I grow tired of hearing her]. I watched another with his obliging offer to fill the gaps in her reasoning (I would rather her conversation lacked logic or consistency). I watched a third, who was more inclined to frame questions that were precise and, according to him, revealing (and I never use words but gestures or telepathy to draw her out).

But I consoled myself by telling myself that, after all, the little they could give her they would give her after my life with her had reached a certain limit. It would be like a dessert, a cordial, something extra. One friend, the one with the Ringo Starr haircut, asked her in a very precise and revealing manner why she continued being faithful to me, and Elena answered him that infidelity was the rule today, just as Communion every Friday used to be, and she stopped looking at him. The one with the black turtleneck sweater interpreted Elena's reply by adding that my wife meant, no doubt, that now it was fidelity that was getting to be the rebellious attitude. And another, with his perfect Edwardian jacket, only invited Elena with his intensely oblique look to say more: he would be the perfect listener. Elena raised her hand and asked the waiter for an espresso.

We walked arm in arm along the stone-paved street of Coyoacán, underneath the ash trees, experiencing the contrast between the hot day which clung to our clothing and the humid night which, following the afternoon shower, brought out the gleam in our eyes and the color in our cheeks. We like to walk silently, our heads down and holding hands, along the old streets that have been, from the beginning, a meeting point of our mutual inclination toward becoming just like each other.

I think Elena and I have never spoken of this. Nor is there any need to. What I do know is that it gives us pleasure to acquire old things. It's as if we were rescuing them from some painful oblivion or, when we touched them, were giving them new life. When we found them the right place, light and setting in the house, we were in reality protecting them from a similar oblivion in the future. We still have that doorknocker shaped like the throat of a lion, which we found at a hacienda at Los Altos and we fondle it when we open the vestibule door, knowing that each fondling wears it away. In the garden we still have the stone cross that is illuminated by a yellow light and represents four rivers converging from hearts torn out, perhaps, by the same hands that afterward carved the stone. We still have the black horses that came from some carousel that was dismantled some time ago, and the figureheads of brigantines that are probably lying at the bottom of the sea, unless their wooden skeletons are exposed on some shore with solemn cockatoos and turtles in their final throes.

Elena takes off her sweater and lights the fireplace while I look for the Cannonball recordings. I serve two glasses of absinthe and lie back, while waiting for her, on the rug. Elena smokes as she rests her head against my legs and we both listen to the slow sax of Brother

Lateef, whom we got acquainted with at the Gold Bug in New York. Lateef, with his figure of a Congolese sorcerer dressed by Disraeli, with his sleepy big eyes like two African boas, with his little beard of a segregated Svengali and his purple lips pressed against the sax which makes the Negro mute in order to enable him to speak with an eloquence that is very far from the surely hoarse stammering of his daily life. The slow music, with its plaintive affirmation, never succeeds in saying all it wants to. It is, from start to finish, only a search and an approximation full of a strange innocence, lending a pleasure and a direction to our touch, which begins to reproduce the meaning of Lateef's instrument: sheer foreshadowing, sheer prelude, sheer limitation of the foreplay which, because of it, becomes the act itself.

"What the American Negroes are doing is turning the whip around and using it on the whites," says Elena when we take our accustomed places at the enormous Chippendale table in her parents' dining room. "The Negroes' love, music, vitality are compelling the whites to justify themselves. Mind you, the whites now persecute the Negroes physically because they've finally realized that the Negroes persecute them psychologically."

"Well, I'm thankful that there are no Negroes here," says Elena's father as he serves himself the potato soup offered him in a steaming porcelain tureen by the Indian waiter, who during the day waters the gardens of the big house at Las Lomas.

"But what's that got to do with it, Papa? It's as though the Eskimos were to be thankful that they're not Mexicans. Each person is what he is and that's all there is to it. What's interesting is to see what happens when we come in contact with someone who puts a doubt in our minds and we nevertheless know that we need him. And we need him because he negates us."

"Come on, eat. These conversations get more idiotic each Sunday. All I know is that you didn't marry a Negro, right? Higinio, bring in the enchiladas."

Don José observes Elena, me and his wife with an air of triumph. The elder Elena, Elena's mother, in order to save the languishing conversation, tells about her activities of the week gone by. I look at the furniture covered with tulipwood-colored brocade, the Chinese vases, the gauze curtains, and the vicuña skin rugs of this rectilinear house behind whose enormous windows the eucalyptus trees sway in the ravine. Don José smiles while Higinio serves him the enchiladas topped with cream. His green little eyes are filled with an almost patriotic satisfaction, the same I have seen in them when the President waves the flag on the fifteenth of September, although not the same one—it's much more moist—that moves him when he sits down to smoke a cigar in front of his private victrola and listens to boleros.

My gaze fastens on the pale hand of Doña Elena, who plays with a piece of French bread she's rolled into a ball and wearily tells about all the activities that kept her busy since the last time we saw each other. I listen from afar to that cataract of comings and goings, canasta games, visits to soup kitchens for poor boys, novenas, charity balls, searches for new curtains, quarrels with the servants, long telephone conversations with friends, longed-for visits to priests, babies, dressmakers, doctors, watchmakers, pastry cooks, cabinetmakers and picture framers. I keep looking at her pale, long caressing fingers that make little balls with the inside of the bread.

". . . Didn't I tell them never to come and ask me for money because I don't handle anything and I'd gladly send them to your father's office, where the secretary there will take care of them? . . ."

. . . The skinny waist with its languid motions. The bracelet with the embossed copper-and-gold medallions—commemorating the Cristo del Cubilete, Holy Year in Rome and President Kennedy's visit to Mexico City—that strike against one another as Doña Elena plays with the ball of dough . . .

". . . It's enough to give them moral support, don't you think? I tried to get you Thursday so we could go together to the première of *Diana*. I even sent the chauffeur to get in line early. You know what lines are like for premières."

. . . And her arm with its extremely transparent skin, full of veins in the shape of a second skeleton, a glass one, outlined beneath the white smoothness.

". . . I invited your cousin Sandrita and went to pick her up with the car but we whiled away the time with her new baby. He's a delight. She's very put out because you haven't even called to congratulate her. A telephone call wouldn't cost you anything, Elenita . . ."

. . . And her low-cut dress open above her tight jutting breasts like two young animals captured on a young continent. . . .

". . . After all, we belong to the family. You can't deny your blood. I'd like you and Victor to go to the baptism. It's next Saturday. I helped her pick the little ashtrays they're going to give the guests. Just imagine; the time went by so fast while we were chatting that the tickets went unused."

I looked up. Doña Elena was looking at me. She immediately lowered her lids and said we would have our coffee in the living room. Don José excused himself and went into the library, where he has that electric phonograph which plays his favorite records in exchange for a fake twenty-centavo piece inserted in the slot. We sat down to our coffee and the jukebox in the distance made a gurgling sound and began playing *Nosotros* while Doña Elena turned on the television set—but without the sound, as she indicated by placing a finger on her lips. We saw the mute participants of a hidden-treasure program, in which a solemn master of ceremonies guided the five contestants—two nervous, smiling young ladies with their hair done up like beehives, a very stylish housewife and two melancholy, mature dark-complexioned men—toward the check hidden in the cramped study full of vases, paperbook books and little music boxes.

Elena smiled as she sat down beside me in the half-light of that living room with marble floors and plastic calla lilies. I don't know where she got that nickname from or what it has to do with me, but now she began to play word games with it as she caressed my hand.

"Nibelungo. Ni Ve Lungo. Nibble Hongo. Niebla Lunga."

Nibelung? Nor Sees Far? Nibble Mushroom? Long Fog?

The gray, striped, undulating participants looked for their treasure before our eyes, and Elena, squatting, dropped her shoes on the carpet and yawned. Doña Elena, taking advantage of the darkness, looked at me questioningly with those wide-open dark eyes with the deep circles under them. She crossed one leg and arranged her skirt over her knees. From the library we could hear the murmuring of the bolero—*nosotros, que tanto nos quisimos*—and, perhaps, a grunt produced by Don José's digestive stupor.

Doña Elena stopped looking at me so as to fix her eyes on the eucalyptus trees swaying behind the window. I followed her new gaze. Elena yawned and purred as she leaned against my knees. I stroked the nape of her neck. Behind us the ravine which crosses Lomas de Chapultepec like a savage wound seemed to shield a pool of light that was secretly emphasized by the shifting night, which bent the spines of the trees and mussed their pale hair.

"Do you remember Vera Cruz?" the mother said smilingly to the daughter as she looked, however, at me. Elena, asleep against my legs, indicated with a murmur that she did, and I answered: "Yes. We've gone there together many times."

"Do you like it?"

Doña Elena stretched out her hand and let it fall into her lap.

"A lot," I told her. "They say it's the last Mediterranean city. I like the food. I like the people. I like to sit for hours in its arcades eating buttered buns and drinking coffee."

"I come from there," the señora said.

I noticed her dimples for the first time.

"Yes. I know."

"But I've even lost my accent." She laughed, showing her gums. "I got married when I was twenty-two. And when you live in Mexico City you love your Vera Cruz accent. When you made my acquaintance I was already on the mature side."

"Everyone says you and Elena look like sisters."

Her lips were thin but aggressive.

"No. It's that I was just recalling those stormy nights on the Gulf. It's as though the sun doesn't want to be lost—you know?—and mixes with the storm. Everything is bathed in a very pale green light and you suffocate behind the shutters waiting for the downpour to stop. The rain doesn't cool things off in the tropics. It only makes it hotter. I don't know why the servants had to close the shutters every time there was a storm. How nice it would have been to let it break with the windows wide open!"

I lit a cigarette.

"Yes, very heavy odors pour out. The earth gives off its perfume from tobacco, from coffee, from sugar pulp . . ."

"The bedrooms too."

Doña Elena closed her eyes.

"How do you mean?"

"There were no closets then."

She ran her hand over the faint wrinkles near her eyes.

"In each room there was a wardrobe, and the maids were in the habit of placing laurel leaves and wild marjoram in with the clothes. Besides, the sun never dries out some corners very well. It used to smell of mold—how shall I put it?—of moss . . ."

"Yes, I imagine it did. I've never lived in the tropics. Do you miss them much?"

And now she rubbed her wrists against each other and showed the prominent veins on her hands.

"Sometimes. It's hard for me to remember. Imagine, I got married when I was eighteen and they already considered me an old maid."

"And did that strange light that's remained at the bottom of the ravine remind you of all this?"

The woman got up.

"Yes. Those are the spotlights José ordered placed there last week. They look pretty, don't they?"

"I think Elena's fallen asleep."

I tickled Elena's nose and she woke up, and we returned to Coyoacán in the MG.

"Excuse those boring Sundays," Elena said as I took off for the construction site the following morning. Some bond between us and the family and bourgeois life had to remain, even if out of a need for contrast.

"What are you going to do today?" I asked her as I rolled up my blueprints and took hold of my portfolio.

Elena bit a fig, crossed her arms and stuck out her tongue at a cross-eyed figure of Christ that we found one time in Guanajuato.

"I'm going to paint all morning. Then I'm going to eat with Alejandro in order to show him my latest things. At his studio. Yes, he's already finished it. Here at Olivar de los Padres. In the afternoon I'll go to my French class. Maybe I'll have a coffee and then I'll wait for you at the movie club. They're showing a mythological Western: *High Noon*. I agreed to meet with those Negro fellows tomorrow. They belong to the Black Muslims and I'm dying to know what they really think. Do you realize we only know about it from the newspapers? Have you ever spoken with an American Negro, Nibelungo?

"Don't dare disturb me tomorrow afternoon. I'm going to shut myself in and read Nerval from cover to cover. And Juan had better not think he can make an idiot out of me with his *soleil noir de la mélancolie* and his calling himself the widower and the man of sorrow. I caught him at it and I'm going to let him have it tomorrow night. Yes, he's going to 'throw' a masquerade party. We have to go dressed up like Mexican murals. We'd better get that over and done with. Buy me some calla lilies, Victor, darling Nibelungo, and, if you like, dress up as the cruel conquistador Alvarado, who branded the Indian women with red-hot irons before he possessed them. *Oh Sade, where is thy whip?* Ah, and Wednesday Miles Davis is playing at Bellas Artes. He's a bit *passé*, but he stirs up hormones anyhow. Buy tickets. So long, darling."

She kissed the nape of my neck. I couldn't put my arms around her because of the rolls of plans I had in my hands, but I started the car with the aroma of the fig on my neck and the mental image of Elena dressed in my shirt, unbuttoned and tied around her at her navel, and her tight-fitting toreador pants. She was barefoot and getting ready to . . .

Was she going to read a poem or paint a picture? The thought came to me that we would have to take a trip together soon. That brought us closer together than anything else. I came to the *periférico* highway. I don't know why, instead of crossing the Altavista bridge to the Desierto de los Leones, I entered the traffic circle and speeded up.

Yes, I sometimes do that. I want to be alone and run and laugh when someone brings up something unpleasant. And, perhaps, to preserve the mental image of Elena for half an hour after taking leave of her—her golden skin, her green eyes, her endless projects—and to think how very happy I am in her company, how no one could be happier than in the company of a woman who is so lively, so modern, and who ... who ... complements me so.

I go by a glassworks, a baroque church, a roller coaster, a forest of ahuehuete trees. Where have I heard that little word? *Complement.* I circle the Petróleos fountain and turn up the Paseo de la Reforma. All the cars are heading down toward the heart of town, which reverberates in the background behind an impalpable, suffocating pall. I go up to Lomas de Chapultepec, where at this time of day the only ones around are servants and married women, the husbands having gone to work and the children to school. And surely my other Elena, my complement, must be waiting in her warm bed with those very confused dark eyes with circles under them and her flesh as white, as ripe, as yielding and perfumed as clothes in tropical wardrobes.

Translated by Leonard Mades

Weight-Reducing Diet

JORGE EDWARDS

A meteor crossed the night and someone said three wishes could be made.

"What are your wishes, Chubby?"

The fat girl considered. "First," she said, "to fly."

"To fly?"

"Yes," said the girl, "I would like to be able to fly."

"But that's impossible."

"I know," said the girl, "but I would like to. Don't I have the right to ask for anything?"

"All right," they told her. "This means you lose your first wish. What's the second one?"

"The second?" The girl laughed. "I would like to own a pastry shop," she said, "so I could eat pastry all the time . . . with no one bothering me . . ."

The smell of the pastry shop made her mouth water.

"And the third one?"

The girl thought again with her finger on her lips and seemed about to say something, but held it back. She pressed her lips and closed her eyes tightly to drive off the wish—an insane, murderous wish. She thought she had a black soul, a monstrous soul. Later, she recalled that virtue does not lie in lacking evil desires. The devil is continuously active, blowing in our ears the fetid breath of his insinuations. The devil's daring led him to approach Jesus himself. And with the most dangerous and treacherous of temptations, that of power, as the parish priest—who also seemed to feel power's allure—had said, hissing with anger. Virtue, then—and the tone of his voice had, since the conclusion was so logical, descended along a curve of fatigue—consists in rejecting temptation with an iron will, digging your nails into the palms of your hands until they hurt and stamping your foot on a rock.

"What's wrong?"

"Let's go," she said, ill-humored.

When they reached the path, Sebastián hugged her from behind.

"Meanie!" he said.

"Let me go!" she screamed in fury, jabbing his stomach with her elbow.

"Bitch!" howled Sebastián, doubled over.

The light in her mother's room was on. "Tough luck!" thought the girl. She climbed up to her bedroom on the tips of her toes, and the first thing she did was to lift the pillow. All the lumps of sugar had disappeared. "The bedroom is out," she thought.

"Maria Eugenia!" her mother called.

Her pale face glistened with cold cream, and it seemed she had drunk little that night, and was in a bad mood.

"Who gave you permission to go out after dinner?"

The girl lowered her eyes. "They came and picked me up," she said.

"Furthermore," said her mother, "I found the lumps of sugar. If you weigh one gram more than last week your father will punish you. I'm warning you. So don't complain later."

"Let's see . . ." said her father.

"Last week I weighed myself without shoes," protested the girl.

"Well, then, take your shoes off."

She had examined the scale beforehand from all sides, searching for a little screw. Now she stepped barefoot on the scaffold's rubber platform, holding her breath. With her mind she tried to levitate. But the executioner wore his thickest pair of glasses and the inexorable machine showed an overweight of about three hundred grams.

"What's happening is that I'm growing," said the girl. "How could I not increase a little as well?"

"Yes, of course. And what about the lumps of sugar Mommy found under the pillow?"

The girl bit her lower lip. "She turned me in," she said to herself. She put her feet into her shoes without bending. She turned completely red before the cold, sparkling glasses.

"Tomorrow you can't go out at all. Not until you understand!"

"It's not my fault!" cried the girl, biting her lower lip in an effort to stop her tears.

"Not your fault! You spend the whole day eating. Ruminating like a cow!"

The girl burst into tears and ran toward her room hiccupping, sodden, her head lowered. She flung herself on the bed and sobbed for a long time with her face crushed against the bedspread. She would have liked to destroy the flashing glasses, to pierce them with a stiletto so that the eyes would spill like the white of an egg; to suffocate the sharp voice whose inexorable precision drove her up the wall. "One peach only," said that voice. "Stop playing with those crumbs," it said. "Bread is strictly forbidden." And she had an urge to do away with all the bread on the table; to lick the crumbs up on all fours; to empty the platter of peaches and devour five plates of bean soup, deep plates filled to the brim, with fat sausages floating in the center. She imagined that her parents took off and left the pantry open. She settled on the floor among pots of marmalade, jars of peaches in syrup and bricks of quince paste in varied and fascinating shapes. It was a enchanted forest. The ecstasy made her float in the rarefied, sweetish air.... She stabbed the stiletto in and the glasses broke in thousands of pieces. The voice dried out. From pantries of fragrant wood fell torrents of sugar.

But the voice, after the departure to Santiago on Sunday afternoons, left a scientific list of instructions, weaving a metallic net for the rest of the week. No escape was possible. And the girl felt suddenly the desire to throw herself off the highest rock. Anguish left her breathless. To live this way, oppressed by an absurd fatality! Why not the other? But the question remained unanswered. Meanwhile, with its thread of saliva sustained by the gelid glow of the glasses, the voice strung its net of orders, arguments, contradictions, categorical assertions and interdictions. Nothing could stop its hellish fever. No human power.

"It's a real disease," said Perico. "A vice."

"She'll become thin later," said Uncle Gonzalo in a conciliatory attempt. "She has many years ahead of her."

"This little girl," said Perico, "suffers from a respiratory deficiency. And the problem is that the fat oppresses her diaphragm."

"But how can you prevent her from eating sugar!" exclaimed Alicia with a biting edge in her voice.

Uncle Gonzalo stared at her and arched his brows. How can you prevent her! And what does it matter! The diaphragm is one of those typical medical pedantries. Doctors enslaved him for years, until he stopped listening to them. We've got to die of something, haven't we? Those pedants, who believe themselves to be spokesmen for the truth, are the ones who poison the world. And, apropos of nothing, he turned the conversation to the European places he had visited between the two wars. He remembered them, elaborating unfavorable comparisons to the present moment, during his afternoon walk. Uncle Gonzalo spoke for a long time about Budapest, its beautiful women and magnificent restaurants.

"This was sometime in the Twenties, when the Chilean peso still was worth something."

He joined the fleshy tips of his fingers, and his sky-blue, watery eyes submerged in the evocation. The memories had left a painful scar, a scar whose edges opened from time to time like thirsty lips. He kept a few faded pictures with dedications inscribed on them in oblique lines; some wrinkled and yellowed post cards. Pictures and cards which now served to convince him that he hadn't dreamed it all. The process of doubt and verification set into motion the lips of the scar covered with brine and tortured by an insatiable thirst. Lowering his head, Uncle Gonzalo tried to console himself with a sip of his drink.

"It's like the man," he said, "who returns from the future with a flower, after having flown in the time machine. That flower is the irrefutable proof. Do you remember?"

Perico raised his eyes. To save himself further explanation he said yes. "Each day more tiresome and senile," he thought. He was going to tell Alicia to keep him within bounds. But what is gained by saying anything to Alicia! She is completely impervious to reason, to common sense. She nods with her head, very much in agreement, and in a second forgets the whole thing.

"How's that?" asked the girl from her observation post by the swinging door.

"Oh! So you were there!" exclaimed Uncle Gonzalo. "And did not come to greet me!"

The girl approached him and kissed a dry cheek which had a peculiar odor, something between camphor, tobacco, cologne and other undefined substances.

"What's that about the man who flew?" asked the girl.

"He did not fly in space," said Uncle Gonzalo, pleased at being asked, "but rather in time. He'd go in a machine beyond the year two thousand and then he'd return."

Perplexed, the girl stared at him while her father half concealed an interminable yawn. Uncle Gonzalo said that now communism had put an end to all that. That world was gone. Irremediably. And everywhere, due to the insidious influence of communism, which uses thousands of subterfuges, the good things, the real pleasures of the spirit, were beginning to be erased from the map.

"Communism, taxes, the socializing measures, the masses, like locusts, invading and destroying even the remotest corners, the last vestiges of beauty, flattered by unscrupulous demagogues, softened by television, living in a regime of robots, a whole nation brought up with the mentality of a shopkeeper.... The only things they have not succeeded in spoiling are the sea and the mountain range, not for lack of wanting to, but insofar as the work of man is concerned.... Observe the marvels of modern Santiago! Now it's impossible to go anywhere without being forced to rub against the rabble. One should emigrate, but where to? With the progress in communication, the world, instead of enlarging, has become frightfully reduced. If you travel to the remotest hamlet in the Orient you'll find the same Coca-Cola advertisements, the same trash, while the Communists, like ants, ambushed or in broad daylight, gnaw away at the institutions . . ."

The girl was stunned. Uncle Gonzalo crossed his bloodless hands, covered with stains the color of tobacco, and stared over his shoulder with shining eyes as if hostile hordes stood there, on the other side of the door, gathering in the shadows, ready to break into the room and provoke the final unraveling. Noticing that his only remaining listener was the girl, he put an arm around her waist. His right hand delved with difficulty in his trouser pocket and, trembling, he handed her a large bill. The girl made some slight resistance.

"Take it!" ordered Uncle Gonzalo. "Don't be a fool." And he added with a devilish glitter in his eyes: "So you can eat pastry until you burst!"

The eyes of the girl sparkled and remained absorbed, staring into the night. Her uncle stood up, pained. His lungs worked like a worn-out, leaky bellows.

"Your uncle is getting unbearably boring," said Perico.

"Poor old man!" exclaimed Alicia.

The girl felt the bill next to her belly button, pressed by her clothes. The hostile forces truly dominated the universe and the blockage became narrower every day. But she was not as pessimistic as Uncle Gonzalo. She had to defend herself with cunning, silently, without giving one single millimeter of ground, utilizing all the resources allowed by ineffective vigilance overly imbued with its false control and made lax by complacency.

Chewing on an enormous peach, Perico declared that Uncle Gonzalo was becoming completely mushy, totally gaga. The pair of guests, out of consideration for Alicia, smiled kindly.

"And do you know the true story of the pictures?"

"What story?"

Alicia, motioning toward the girl, gestured to Perico to be quiet.

"He used to have strange habits concerning photography. He was a fanatic photographer, fond of taking rather muddy scenes. Do you understand?"

"Perico!" begged Alicia.

"Later I'll explain," said Perico after spitting out the peach pit and wiping his lips with a napkin.

The girl thought of asking permission to eat another peach, but the confusing revelations of her father distracted her.

"Chubby," said her mother, "say good night and go to sleep."

At the first opportunity she would ask Uncle Gonzalo. The art of photography must hide an infallible weapon for dismembering the enemy, for relegating him to the outer shadows. One could make use of the secret, a darkroom protected from intruders and free from the laws that rule time and space. In that darkroom Uncle Gonzalo would bring to light from out of those shadowy depths weird characters: sinister dwarfs, youths with bluish thighs, a being with an enormous belly and the head of a bird, a nun who stuck her tongue out and who would suddenly raise up her skirt and show her behind.... "Who can say?" the girl told herself, surprised at her own wit. She and Uncle Gonzalo were accomplices. They were alone, surrounded by a multitude equipped with glasses, lancets, hair, a thick soft tongue which dripped saliva, red knobby noses. The secret darkrooms could be extended over the whole world, under the very noses of the others, but choosing the right ones presented delicate problems: they should be protected by natural or architectural elements, be outside the common haunts of the knobby-nosed men, and offer facilities for hiding and hoarding, for observing without being observed.... The girl thought the attic fulfilled these conditions. As soon as she entered it, she breathed differently. Her oppression evaporated as if by magic. The crossbeams, the sack of cement, the armchair with a broken leg, the old magazines, all received her with delight. The air crossed the small balcony, and became lost, humming joyfully amidst the beams. In the street, men seemed small and harmless, insects to be pitied. She was the queen of this high land. When she sat in her ancient throne, the spring emitted a triumphant chord. The treasure lay under a loose plank. Now the chests would open to receive with solemnity, in the midst of cheers and the roll of drums, a huge gift, a large bill, which now occupied the place of honor surrounded by the white guard of lumps of sugar under whose command there was a candy cane dressed as a marquis, with tassels, hangings and glittering inlay.

The silence in the rest of the house allowed her to hear better the frantic clamor of the multitude. The fat girl advanced down the center acknowledging the cheers with a slight bow and an aristocratic smile. She was dying of hunger, but would have to await the end of the ceremony before eating the lumps. At the end of her journey she saw from the little window the woman who sold pastry.

"Hey!" she yelled.

The vendor stopped and looked up.

"Do you still have any pastry?"

The vendor searched among the second-floor windows.

"Over here." The girl stuck out a hand.

"I have a few left," the woman said.

The girl rose high and showed her head.

"Could you go over to the back street?"

Confused, the vendor hesitated.

"To the street at the back," the girl insisted.

In the kitchen everything was in order, shining and empty. Celestina surely snored. Olga had left. And besides, Olga was not dangerous. And the siesta habit would keep Celestina for many hours out of commission, open-mouthed and covered with sweat. The girl ran noiselessly toward the wooden fence. She became restless seeing that the street was deserted, but soon the vendor tiredly climbed the slope.

The bill was enough to buy twenty pastries. After counting them all, only one remained inside the basket.

"Can't you throw it in?" asked the girl.

"All right," said the woman with a gesture of resignation.

"That's it," said the girl, staring behind her, suddenly assaulted by the fear that Celestina with a perfidious smile would be spying on her. "Don't tell anyone that you sold me these pastries, okay?"

Glum, the vendor shrugged her shoulders. "I don't have to go around telling things," she said. "Who would I tell it to?"

"My Uncle Gonzalo," said the girl, "gave me the money to buy the pastries, but . . ."

Expressionless, the vendor watched her attentively. She waited for a second, and since the girl did not complete the sentence, she took her leave. The servants' quarters were plunged in a quiet, sticky drowsiness, gently underlined by the hum of insects around the gladiolas at the edge of the yard. There, in the open, repressing a howl of Apache vengeance, the girl gave an enormous bite into the cake and then brandished it above her head. She was answered by the roar of a bloodthirsty mob. Singing hymns of war, the girl climbed up to the dark interior of her armored fortress, her nest of eagles.

Between the trees, the sea dazzled, tranquil as a cup of milk. The distant cries of swimmers became confused with the murmur of the waves. Her burden lightened, the vendor soon reached the road's curve and disappeared. The street was again deserted, heated by rays which made the light vibrate and gave to the sounds a spongy, sweet consistency. She licked her lips and decided to eat another one. They were extremely light; they melted in her mouth. She ate another, and the white crumbs, dissolving on her tongue, gave her a sense of ecstasy—something airy, angelic: pure delight. The wishes made on the falling star, to which she had candidly confessed, provoking the mockery of her obtuse, ignorant companions, had come true with added interest. For example, her graneries had become crammed with magical goods, among whose virtues was that of providing weightlessness. The woman who had brought them to her advanced to the end of the street without touching the ground; as soon as she went around the bend of the road, she became smoke. She was, doubtless, a messenger from the secret alcoves of Uncle Gonzalo. Once there again, she would loosen her braids and emit siren-like cries, swinging her hips. During her mission she had faked a sullen, suspicious attitude while fulfilling the instructions which had been given to her. That way she could circulate fearlessly, protected by the hidden powers controlled by her masters. If Uncle Gonzalo, who had planned it all to the smallest detail, gave the girl a bill, it was so that the transaction would have all the appearance of normality. But the bill did not exist; it became smoke together with the vendor at the curve of the road. No one else saw the vendor. And the cakes needed only to enter into the cavity of her mouth to become foam, breeze, and the body that swallowed them was transformed into a balloon lighter than air: the breeze itself could lift it away.

At that moment there was a fanfare and the floodgates of the attic opened. All at once, light, and a mischievous, whimsical breeze entered, bringing the distant shouts of bathers and the quacks of a flock of wild ducks flying in a straight line. The clear, immense sky appeared. The girl barely had time to fish out two cakes for her journey; the breeze allowed for no delay or objection. The beating of her panic-stricken heart only quieted once she found herself above the hills, far from the danger of being torn apart by branches or the sharp edges of crags. Floating slowly, she thought that from his darkroom her Uncle Gonzalo controlled the operation and rubbed his hands with an ironic smile of satisfaction. She discovered that by blowing upward she descended, and that it was enough to move her hands as if they were wings to gain altitude. It was beautiful to contemplate the sinuous white line of the breakers which separated the coast line's reef from the peaceful, open blue. From time to time, over one or another elevation, a quiet jet of water sprang. It sprang and fell slowly and then broke out again at a more distant spot, while the successive ridges of the sea swelled till they reached the interior of the bay. When she observed them again, the flock of ducks appeared farther down, flying about halfway between herself and the water.

Blowing strongly, she neared the beach and watched the bathers at a closer distance. They, unaware of the unusual presence, continued their innocent games. The girl got bored with watching these fooleries and continued her flight toward the south. It was better to contemplate the seaweed covering the rocks by the shore; caressed and swept by the surge, they remained always in place, turgid, slippery, undulating and firm. She could imagine the suction of the foamy ebb, and the restless bubbling of the crabs, baffled in their holes by the sudden violence of the tide. They clasped the wall insanely with their tense musculature and, in the depths, the sea urchins mobilized their antennae and continuously devoured and digested, transforming all kinds of living organisms into elemental clay and yellow tongues.

She made out Perico and Alicia on a nearby beach and maintained a prudent distance. But a rare and lucid faculty allowed her to capture their conversation even to its slightest subtleties. Perico spoke of certain possible applications of science in the year two thousand. His glasses sent out sparks. Alicia, lying on her back, with her face protected by a hat, was thinking that cellulitis had definitely installed itself in her muscles; that her will could no longer combat it. She had already eliminated sugar, bread, cookies and cakes, but twilight would come and she could not resist the temptation of cocktails. At dusk, things were seen in a different light. What did cellulitis matter! Life was short and abstinence excessively sad. Afterward, nothing happened. Three or four times, totally drunk, she had climbed to a secondfloor bedroom with the husband of a friend or a passing bachelor. Perico, who boasted of his tolerance, who sustained modern, scientific ideas about these subjects, hit her one time with his thick open hand with all his strength. It's one thing to act with freedom; it's another to behave like a goddam whore! He pulled her out of the bedroom by one arm, not even alluding to the presence of the other fellow, who had spent better moments in his life. Without caring about appearances, he pushed her downstairs with a determination she had never imagined him capable of, and, in the garden, with one blow, he threw her to the ground, where, as she fell, she crushed one of the new, thorny bushes. "Shut up!" he ordered and pointed at the girl's window. But the girl, with no need for hysterical crying, had understood everything. She slept lightly. She knew by heart that voice, a little vulgar, lascivious, which two or three times in the last year had gone up the stairs followed by other steps, in search of the rear bedroom. The indistinct filthy murmur frightened her. She hid her head under the sheet, while her heart throbbed as if it were about to jump out of her mouth, and the idea that the door might suddenly open, that it might open and that the voice might enter and inundate the dark room filled her with terror. The night of the fight, she thought panic would no longer let go of her. She was covered with cold sweat. But the sobs which slowly tapered off in the garden, the gentleness of this crying, let her sink into a heavy sleep, bathing all her muscles in tranquilizing honey, and placed oil on her lips.

This happened two or three times to Alicia, but usually nothing came of it. Anyway, this was the same as nothing. Except for the dryness in her mouth, the undefined uneasiness, a pain which she could not locate with precision, the signs of hangover, and next morning cellulitis, which had made frightening progress. She ordered Celestina to prepare a bit of fish and a little lettuce for lunch, and there was to be no sugar on the breakfast table. Useless precautions, because as soon as darkness descended on the sea, after nine in the evening, things took on a different look. What did cellulitis matter!

Perico was saying that in the year two thousand an amputated arm or leg could be made to grow again under specific treatments. There would be ways of changing the human body in order to adapt it to new conditions of life, to supersonic speed, to regular trips to the moon and to explorations of other planets. A friend watched him, awed, thinking that doctors are fascinating, that she had been a fool to marry a poor bureaucrat, and Alicia, on the other hand, had gotten into bad shape; her legs were full of little lumps, really ugly, her only advantage being that she was such a shameless bitch—which is, one must admit, in current times an enormous advantage. Alicia had always been that way, even in school; she would introduce a friend to her, in all naïveté, and the following week he'd be taken. Afterward they would pass her by scarcely bothering to greet her. Over here a girl's got to be really alert! If you just look away for one second . . . Perico, swollen with satisfaction, continued his dissertation, sprinkling it with incomprehensible, fascinating words . . .

The girl, losing altitude, saw men whose veined eyes shone in the night like fireflies of incandescent blue. They possessed pointed ears; vibrating, transparent wings; legs like toothpicks, covered with long hair; and broad gristly feet. All of a sudden there was no one on the shore. Breathing was very hard. The sky took on an ashen, gloomy aspect, announcing cataclysms and afflictions. She noticed that the sea was boiling and that from the lower slopes of the hills came forth a great cloud of dust, as if the earth were quaking. On the beach and over the rocks there were fat fishes, with great perpendicular fins and light gray bellies turned upward. The difficulty in breathing became more desperate by the minute.

"How did you behave?" asked her father. "Did you eat anything between meals?"

"Nothing," said the girl. She stretched her arms, thrusting out her breasts, which were beginning to show, and then scratched her back. Slyly, she passed her tongue over her lips.

The cook had appeared on the living room's threshold. "Tell me, Celestina, did the girl eat anything between meals?"

"Nothing, it seems," said Celestina and shrugged her shoulders.

Her father joined his hands and, with a sigh, let himself fall into an armchair. Alicia told Celestina to bring ice, lemon and sugar. Uncle Gonzalo rubbed his eyes and signed in turn, in a prolonged and deep manner. At that moment, his facial tics were more rapid, more agitated than usual. They were accentuated by the nervous drumming of his fingers and the rocking of his right foot, which was crossed over the left.

"The afternoon was quite pleasant," said Uncle Gonzalo, who seemed to be thinking of something else.

"Pleasant," said Perico, covering a yawn.

"Shall I make drinks for everyone?" asked Alicia, cocktail shaker in hand.

"Yes," said Perico. "Why not? There's never enough for you . . ."

"I'm thinking of inaugurating a system of only one single cocktail an afternoon," said Alicia.

"Hum!"

Perico, with a mocking air, made himself comfortable.

The eyes of Uncle Gonzalo, lost beyond the windows leading to the garden, in the cluster of dark bushes, met the eyes of the girl and gave her a fast wink. The girl answered with a smile of complicity. With a shaking hand, Uncle Gonzalo grasped his cocktail glass. He drank the first sip with a grimace of distaste.

"Very pleasant!" he said before the grimace had disappeared completely. "A marvelous afternoon!" And the girl knew he was saying it to divert the attention of the others. She understood that he was thinking of something totally different. His fatigue filled with dissatisfaction, the rocking leg, the eyes wandering toward the bushes in the shade, everything was part of a subtle feint. Her uncle was an eminent artist of deceit. The girl realized it now perfectly. Light had come into her spirit—an overwhelming evidence. Just the merest wink and the circle of conclusions she had drawn that afternoon in the intimacy of her refuge closed itself. Uncle Gonzalo looked at her again and that gesture was the final confirmation, the missing detail for the day to attain its roundest culmination. The girl felt her own clairvoyance and observed the others, those who did not share the secret, with an attitude that had passed disdain and reached a compassionate, even friendly sympathy.

Translated by Susana Hertelendy and Lita Paniagua

Sunday, Sunday

MARIO VARGAS LLOSA

He held his breath an instant, dug his nails into the palms of his hands, and said quickly: "I'm in love with you." He saw her redden suddenly, as if someone had slapped her cheeks, which had a smooth and pale sheen to them. Terrified, he felt confusion rising and petrifying his tongue. He wanted to run off, be done with it; in the still winter morning, he felt the surge of that inner weakness which always overcame him at decisive moments. A few moments before, among the vivid, smiling throng in the Parque Central in Miraflores, Miguel was still saying to himself: "Now. When we get to Avenida Pardo. I'll take a chance. Ah, Rubén, if you knew how I hate you!" And even earlier, in church, looking for Flora, he spotted her at the foot of a column and, elbowing his way brusquely through the jostling women, he managed to get close to her and greet her in a low voice, repeating tersely to himself, as he had done that morning, stretched on his bed watching the first light: "Nothing else for it. I must do it today, this morning. Rubén, you'll pay for this." And the previous night he had wept for the first time in many years, realizing that the wretched trap lay in wait for him. The crowd had gone on into the park and the Avenida Pardo was left empty. They walked on along the avenue, under the rubber trees with their high, dense foliage. "I have to hurry," Miguel thought, "or else I'll be in trouble." He glanced sideways, round about him. There was nobody; he could try it. Slowly he moved his left hand until it touched hers. The sudden contact told her what was happening. He longed for a miracle to happen, to put an end to that humiliation. "Tell her, tell her," he thought. She stopped, withdrawing her hand, and he felt himself abandoned and foolish. All the glowing phrases prepared passionately the night before had blown away like soap bubbles.

"Flora," he stammered, "I've waited a long time for this moment. Since I've known you, I think only of you. I'm in love for the first time, truly. I've never known a girl like you."

Once again a total blankness in his mind, emptiness. The pressure was extreme. His skin was limp and rubbery and his nails dug into the bone. Even so, he went on speaking painfully, with long pauses, overcoming his stammer, trying to describe his rash, consuming passion, till he found with relief that they had reached the first oval on the Avenida Pardo, and he fell silent. Flora lived between the second and third tree after the oval. They stopped and looked at one other. Flora by now was quite agitated, which lent a bright sheen to her eyes. In despair, Miguel told himself that she had never looked so beautiful. A blue ribbon bound her hair, and he could see where her neck rose, and her ears, two small and perfect question marks.

"Please, Miguel." Her voice was smooth, musical, steady. "I can't answer you now. Besides, my mother doesn't want me to go out with boys until I finish school."

"All mothers say that, Flora," Miguel insisted. "How will she know? We'll meet when you say so, even if it's only Sundays."

"I'll give you an answer, only I have to think first," Flora said, lowering her eyes. And after a moment, she added, "Forgive me, but I have to go. It's late."

Miguel experienced a deep weariness, a feeling which spread through his whole body, relaxing it.

"You're not angry with me, Flora?" he asked, feebly.

"Don't be an idiot," she answered brightly. "I'm not angry."

"I'll wait as long as you want," said Miguel. "But we'll go on seeing each other, won't we? We can go to the movies this afternoon, can't we?"

"I can't this afternoon," she said softly. "Martha's invited me to her house."

A warm flush swept violently through him and he felt himself lacerated, stunned, at the reply he had expected, which now seemed to him torture. So it was true what Melanés had whispered fiercely in his ear on Saturday afternoon. Martha would leave them alone; it was the usual trick. Later, Rubén would tell the gang how he and his brother had planned the set-up, the place and the time. In payment, Martha had claimed the privilege of spying from behind the curtain. His hands were suddenly wet with anger.

"Don't, Flora. We'll go to the matinee as usual. I won't speak about this. I promise."

"No, I really can't," said Flora. "I've got to go to Martha's. She came to my house yesterday to invite me. But afterwards I'll go with her to the Parque Salazar."

Not even in those final words did he feel any hope. A moment later, he was brooding on the spot where the slight blue figure had disappeared, under the majestic arch of the rubber trees of the avenue. It was possible to take on a simple adversary, but not Rubén. He remembered the names of the girls invited by Martha, one Sunday afternoon. He could do nothing now; he was beaten. Once more there arose that fantasy which always saved him in moments of frustration: against a distant background of clouds swollen with black smoke, at the head of a company of cadets from the Naval Academy, he approached a saluting base set up in the park; distinguished people in formal dress, top hats in hand, and ladies with glittering jewels, all applauded him. Thick on the sidewalks, a crowd in which the faces of his friends and enemies stood out, watched him in awe, murmuring his name. Dressed in blue, a broad cape flowing from his shoulders, Miguel marched at the head, gazing off to the horizon. He raised his sword; his head described a half circle in the air. There, in the center of the stand, was Flora, smiling. In one corner, ragged and ashamed, he noticed Rubén. He confined himself to a brief, contemptuous glance. He went on marching; he disappeared amid cheers.

Like steam wiped off a mirror, the image disappeared. He was in the doorway of his house, hating the whole world, hating himself. He entered and went straight up to his room. He threw himself face down on the bed. In the half-dark under his eyelids appeared the girl's face. "I love you, Flora," he said out loud—and then came the face of Rubén, with his insolent jaw and his mocking smile. The faces were side by side, coming closer. Rubén's eyes turned to mock him while his mouth approached Flora.

He jumped up from his bed. The wardrobe mirror gave him back a face both ravaged and livid. I won't allow it, he decided. He can't do that, I won't let him pull that on me.

The Avenida Pardo was still empty. Increasing his pace, he walked on till it crossed Avenida Grau; there he hesitated. He felt the cold—he had left his jacket in his room and his shirt alone was not enough to protect him from the wind which came from the sea and which combed the dense foliage of the rubber trees in a steady swish. The dreaded image of Flora and Rubén together gave him courage and he went on walking.

From the door of the bar beside the Montecarlo cinema, he saw them at their usual table, occupying the corner formed by the far and left-hand walls. Francisco, Melanés, Tobías, the Scholar, they noticed him and, after a second's surprise, they turned toward Rubén, their faces wicked and excited. He recovered himself at once—in front of men he certainly knew how to behave.

"Hello," he said, approaching. "What's new?"

"Sit." The Scholar drew up a chair. "What miracle brings you here?"

"It's a century since you've been this way," said Francisco.

"I was keen to see you," Miguel said warmly. "I knew you'd be here. What are you so surprised about? Or am I no longer a Buzzard?" He took a seat between Melanés and Tobías. Rubén was opposite him.

"Cuncho!" called the Scholar. "Bring another glass. Not too dirty a one." When he brought the glass and the Scholar filled it with beer, Miguel toasted "To the Buzzards!" and drank it down.

"You'd have the glass as well!" said Francisco. "What a thirst!"

"I bet you went to one o'clock Mass," said Melanés, winking one eye in satisfaction, as he always did when he was up to something. "Right?"

"Yes, I went," said Miguel, unperturbed. "But only to see a chick, nothing more."

He looked at Rubén with a challenge in his eyes, but Rubén paid no attention. He was drumming on the table with his fingers and, the point of his tongue between his teeth, he whistled softly "La Niña Popoff."

"Great," Melanés applauded. "Great, Don Juan. Tell us, which chick?"

"That's a secret."

"Among the Buzzards, there are no secrets," Tobías

reminded him. "Have you forgotten? Come on, who was it?"

"What's it to you?" said Miguel.

"A lot," said Tobías. "I have to know who you go with to know who you are."

"There you are!" said Melanés to Miguel. "One to zero."

"I'll bet I can guess who it is," said Francisco. "Can't you?"

"I know," said Tobías.

"Me too," said Melanés. He turned to Rubén, his eyes and voice all innocence. "And you, brother, can you guess? Who is it?"

"No," said Rubén coldly. "And I couldn't care less."

"My stomach's on fire," said the Scholar. "Is nobody going to order a beer?"

Melanés drew a pathetic finger across his throat. "I have not money, darling," he said in English.

"I'll buy a bottle," Tobías announced with a grand gesture. "Who'll follow me? We have to quench this moron's fire."

"Cuncho, bring a half dozen Cristals," said Miguel. Cries of enthusiasm, exclamations.

"You're a real Buzzard," Francisco affirmed.

"Crazy, crazy," added Melanés. "Yes, sir, a Top Buzzard."

Cuncho brought the beers. They drank. They listened to Melanés tell dirty stories, crude, exaggerated, and lushed-up, and a bitter argument on football broke out between Tobías and Francisco. The Scholar told a story. He was coming from Lima to Miraflores on a bus. The other passengers got off at the Avenida Arequipa. At the top of Javier Prado, Tomasso got on, the one they call the White Whale, that giant albino who's still in the first grade, lives in Quebrada, get it?—pretending to be interested in the bus, he began to ask the driver questions, leaning over the seat from behind, at the same time slicing the cloth of the seat back systematically with a knife.

"He did it because I was there," the Scholar said. "He wanted to show off."

"He's a mental degenerate," said Francisco. "You do things like that when you're ten. At his age it isn't funny."

"The funny thing is what happened next," laughed the Scholar. " 'Listen, driver, don't you know that that monster is destroying your bus?' "

"What's that?" said the driver, braking suddenly. Ears flaming, eyes wide with fright, Tomasso the Whale forced his way out the door.

"With his knife," the Scholar said. "Imagine the state he left the seat in."

The Whale finally managed to get out of the bus. He set off at a run down the Avenida Arequipa. The driver ran after him shouting: "Grab that creep!"

"He got him?" Melanés asked.

"I don't know. I got out. And I took the ignition key as a souvenir. Here it is."

He took a little silver key from his pocket and placed it on the table. The bottles were empty. Rubén looked at his watch and stood up.

"I'm off," he said. "See you."

"Don't go," said Miguel. "Today I'm rich. I invite you all to eat."

A shower of hands clapped him on the back; the Buzzards thanked him noisily, cheered him.

"I can't," said Rubén. "I have things to do."

"All right then, go, my boy," Tobías said. "Say hello to Martha for me."

"We'll be thinking about you, brother," said Melanés.

"No," Miguel shot out. "I'm inviting everybody or nobody. If Rubén goes, it's off."

"You hear him Buzzard Rubén?" said Francisco. "You've got to stay."

"You've got to stay," said Melanés, "no question."

"I'm going," said Rubén.

"The thing is that you're drunk," said Miguel. "You're going because your're afraid of screwing up in front of us, that's all."

"How many times have I taken you home nearly passed out?" said Rubén. "How many times have I helped you up the railing so your father wouldn't catch you? I can hold ten times more than you."

"You could," said Miguel. "Now it'd be difficult. Want to try?"

"With pleasure," said Rubén. "We'll meet tonight, here?"

"No. Right now." Miguel turned to the others, arms open. "Buzzards, I'm making a challenge."

Fortunately, the old formula still worked. In the midst of the noisy excitement he had provoked, he saw Rubén sit down, pale.

"Cuncho!" shouted Tobías. "The menu. And two baths of beer. A Buzzard has just made a challenge."

They order steaks *a la chorrillana* and a dozen beers. Tobías put three bottles in front of each of the competitors. The others had the rest. They ate, scarcely speaking. Miguel drank after each mouthful and tried to show some zest, but the fear of not being able to hold the beer grew in proportion to the acid taste in his throat. They finished the six bottles just after Cuncho had taken the plates away.

"You order," said Miguel to Rubén.

"Three more each."

After the first glass of the new round, Miguel felt a buzzing in his ears. His head was spinning slowly; everything was moving.

"I need to piss," he said. "I'm going to the john." The Buzzards laughed.

"Give up?" asked Rubén.

"I'm going to piss," shouted Miguel. "Have them bring more if you want."

In the lavatory, he vomited. Then he washed his face thoroughly, trying to remove every revealing sign. His watch said half past four. In spite of the overwhelming sick feeling, he felt happy. Now Rubén could do nothing. He went back to the others.

"*Salud!*" said Rubén, raising his glass.

He's furious, Miguel thought. But I've stopped him now.

"There's corpse smell," said Melanés. "Someone here's dying on us."

"I'm like new," affirmed Miguel, trying to overcome both his disgust and his sickness.

"*Salud!*" repeated Rubén.

When they had finished the last beer, his stomach felt leaden; the voices of the others reached him as a confused mixture of sounds. A hand appeared suddenly under his eyes, white and large-fingered, took him by the chin and forced him to raise his head. Rubén's face had grown. He was comical, all tousled and angry.

"Give up, kid?"

Miguel pulled himself together suddenly and pushed Rubén, but before the gesture could be followed up, the Scholar intervened.

"Buzzards never fight," he said, making them sit down. "They're both drunk. It's all over. Vote."

Melanés, Francisco and Tobías agreed, grumblingly, to declare a draw.

"I already had it won," said Rubén. "This one's incapable. Look at him."

Indeed, Miguel's eyes were glassy, his mouth hung open, and a thread of saliva ran from his tongue.

"Shut up," said the Scholar. "You are no champion, as we say, at beer-swilling."

"You're not beer-drinking champion," added Melanés. "You're only the swimming champion, the scourge of the swimming pools."

"Better keep quiet," said Rubén. "Can't you see you're eaten up with envy?"

"Long live the Esther Williams of Miraflores," said Melanés.

"Over the hill already and you hardly know how to swim," said Rubén. "Don't you want me to give you lessons?"

"Now we know it all, champ," said the Scholar. "You've won a swimming championship. And all the chicks are dying over you. The little champ."

"Champion of nothing," said Miguel with difficulty. "He's a phony."

"You're about to pass out," said Rubén. "Will I take you home, girl?"

"I'm not drunk," Miguel insisted. "And you're a phony."

"You're pissed off because I'm going to see Flora," said Rubén. "You're dying of jealousy. Do you think I don't catch on to things?"

"Phony," said Miguel. "You won because your father is Federation President. Everybody knows that he pulled a fast one, just so you would win."

"And you most of all," said Rubén, "you can't even surf."

"You swim no better than anyone else," said Miguel. "Anybody could leave you silly."

"Anybody," said Melanés. "Even Miguel, who is a creep."

"Permit me to smile," said Rubén.

"We permit you," said Tobías. "That's all we need."

"You're getting at me because it's winter," said Rubén. "If it weren't, I'd challenge you all to go to the beach to see if you'd be so cocky in the water."

"You won the championship because of your father," said Miguel. "You're a phony. When you want to take me on swimming, just let me know, that's all. On the beach, in Terrazas, where you like."

"On the beach," said Rubén. "Right now."

"You're a phony," said Miguel.

"If you win," said Rubén, "I promise I won't see Flora. And if I win, you can go sing somewhere else."

"Who do you think you are?" stammered Miguel. "Bastard, just who do you think you are?"

"Buzzards," said Rubén, spreading his arms, "I'm offering a challenge."

"Miguel's not in shape now," said the Scholar. "Why don't you just toss for Flora?"

"You keep out of it," said Miguel. "I accept. Let's go to the beach."

"They're crazy," said Francisco. "I'm not going to the beach in this cold. Make a different bet."

"He's accepted," said Rubén. "Let's go."

"When a Buzzard makes a challenge, everyone holds his tongue," said Melanés. "Let's go to the beach. And if they're scared to go in, we'll throw them in ourselves."

"They're both drunk," the Scholar insisted. "The challenge doesn't stand."

"Shut up, Scholar," roared Miguel. "I'm a big boy. I don't need you to look after me."

"All right," said the Scholar, shrugging his shoulders. "Suit yourself, then."

They went out. Outside, a quiet grayness hung in wait for them. Miguel took deep breaths; he felt better. Francisco, Melanés and Rubén walked ahead, Miguel and the Scholar behind. There were a few idlers on the Avenida Grau, mostly maids dressed up, out on their free day. Gray-looking men, with long lank hair, followed them and watched them greedily. They laughed, showing gold teeth. The Buzzards paid no attention. They walked with long strides, excitement slowly growing in them.

"Feeling better?" said the Scholar.

"Yes," replied Miguel. "The fresh air's done me good."

At the corner of Avenida Pardo, they turned. They walked, deployed like a squadron, in the same line, under the rubber trees of the walk, over the flagstones bulged from time to time by huge tree roots which occasionally broke through the surface like great hooks. Going down Diagonal, they passed two girls. Rubén bowed to them, very formally.

"Hello, Rubén," they sang out together.

Tobías imitated them, fluting his voice.

"Hello, Prince Rubén."

The Avenida Diagonal gave out on a short bend which forked; in one direction wound the Malecón, paved and shining; in the other, there was an incline which followed the downward slope and reached the sea. It is called the "bathers' descent" and its surface is smooth and shines from the polish of car tires and the feet of bathers from many summers.

"Let's give off some heat, champs," shouted Melanés, breaking into a run. The others followed him.

They ran against the wind and the thin fog which came up from the beach, caught up in a whirlwind of feeling. Through ears, mouth and nostrils, the air came in, into their lungs, and a feeling of relief and clear-headedness spread through their bodies as the slope steepened and suddenly their feet obeyed only a mysterious force which seemed to come from deep in the earth. Arms whirling like propellers, a salty tang on their tongues, the Buzzards ran down in full cry to the circular platform over the bathing huts. The sea disappeared some fifty meters from the shore, in a thick cloud which seemed ready to charge against the cliffs, the high dark bulk of which spread all along the bay.

"Let's go back," said Francisco. "I'm frozen."

At the edge of the platform there was a banister stained here and there with moss. An opening in it indicated the head of the almost vertical ladder which led down to the beach. The Buzzards looked down from there at a short strip of clear water, its surface unbroken, frothing where the fog seemed to join with the foam from the waves.

"I'll leave if this one gives up," said Rubén.

"Who's talking about giving up?" retorted Miguel. "Who do you think you are?"

Rubén went down the ladder three rungs at a time, unbuttoning his shirt as he did so.

"Rubén!" shouted the Scholar. "Are you crazy? Come back!"

But Miguel and the others also went down, and the Scholar followed them.

From the terrace of the long, wide building backed against the cliff, which contains the changing rooms, down to the curving edge of the sea, there is a stretch of smooth stones where, in summer, people took the sun. The small beach hummed with life then, from early morning until twilight. Now the water was well up the slope, there were no brightly colored umbrellas, no elastic girls with bronzed bodies, no melodramatic screams of children and women when a wave succeeded in splashing them before receding backward over the groaning stones and pebbles, there was not a strip of beach to be seen under the flooding current which went up as far as the dark narrow space under the columns which held up the building; and in the surge of the tide, it was difficult to make out the wooden ladders and the cement supports, hung with stalactites and seaweed.

"You can't see the surf," said Rubén. "How will we do it?"

They were in the left-hand gallery, the women's section; their faces were serious.

"Wait until tomorrow," said the Scholar. "At noon it will be clear. Then you can judge it."

"Now that we've come all the way, let it be now," said Melanés. "They can judge it themselves."

"All right by me," said Rubén. "You?"

"Fine," said Miguel.

When they had undressed, Tobías joked about the veins which spread across Miguel's smooth stomach. They went down. The wood of the steps, steadily worn for months by the water, was slippery and very smooth. Holding the iron rail so as not to fall, Miguel felt a shiver run from the soles of his feet to his brain. He figured that, in some ways, the mist and the cold were in his favor, that success would depend not so much on skill as on endurance, and Rubén's skin was already purple, risen all over in gooseflesh. One rung lower, Rubén's neat body bent forward. Tensed, he waited for the ebb and the arrival of the next wave, which came evenly, lightly, leading with a flying crest of foam. When the top of the wave was two meters from the ladder, Rubén leaped. His arms stretched like arrows, his hair streaming with the dive, his body cut the air cleanly, and fell without bending, his head not dropping, his knees straight, he entered the foam, hardly going down at all, and immediately, making use of the tide, he glided forward; his arms appeared and disappeared in a frenzy of bubbles, and his feet were leaving behind a steady, flying wake. Miguel in turn climbed down one rung and waited for the next wave. He knew that the bottom there was shallow, that he would have to dive like a board, hard and rigid, without moving, or he would scrape the stones. He closed his eyes and dived; he did not touch bottom but his body was lacerated from forehead to knees, and he stung all over as he swam with all his strength to bring back to his limbs the warmth which the water had suddenly drained away. In that stretch of sea beside the Miraflores beach, the waves and undertow meet, there are whirlpools and conflicting currents, and last summer was so far away that Miguel had forgotten how to ride the water without using force. He did not remember that you had to go limp, let go, let yourself be carried with the ebb, submitting, swimming only when a wave gets up and you are on the crest, on that shelf of water where the foam is, which runs on top of the water. He forgot that it is better to suffer with patience and a certain resistance that first contact with the sea ebbing from the beach, which tumbles the limbs and makes water stream from eyes and mouth, not to resist, to be a cork, to gulp air, nothing more, every time a wave comes in without force, or through the bottom of the wave if the breaking crest is close—to cling to a rock and wait out patiently the deafening thunder of its passing, to push out sharply and keep forging ahead, furtively, with the arms, until the next obstacle, and then to go limp, not struggling against the undertow but moving slowly and deliberately in a widening spiral and suddenly escaping, at the right moment, in a single burst. Farther out, the surface is unexpectedly calm, the movement of surf small; the water is clear and level, and at some points you can make out dark, underwater rocks.

After fighting his way through the rough water, Miguel stopped, exhausted, and gulped air. He saw Rubén not far away, looking at him. His hair fell in curls on his forehead; his teeth were bared.

"Let's go."

"Okay."

After swimming a few moments, Miguel felt the cold, which had momentarily gone, surge back, and he stepped up his kick, for it was in the legs, above all in the calves, where the water had most effect, numbing them first and then stiffening them. He was swimming with his face in the water, and every time his right arm came out of the water, he turned his head to get rid of his held breath and to breathe again, immediately dipping his forehead and chin, lightly, so as not to check his forward motion, and to make instead a prow which parted the water, the easier to slip through. At each stroke he would see Rubén with one eye, swimming smoothly on the surface, not exerting himself, scarcely raising a wash, with the ease and delicacy of a gliding gull. Miguel tried to forget Rubén and the sea and the surf (which must still have been some distance away, for the water was clear, calm, and crossed only by small, spontaneous waves). He wanted to keep in mind only Flora's face, the down on her arms which on sunny days gleamed like a small forest of gold thread, but he could not prevent the girl's face from being succeeded by another image, shrouded, dominant, thunderous, which tumbled over Flora and hid her, the image of a mountain of tormented water, not exactly the surf (they had once reached the surf, two summers ago, with its thundering waves and greenish-black foam, for out there, more or less, the rocks ended and gave way to mud, which the waves brought to the surface and stirred up with clumps of seaweed, staining the water), instead a sea on its own wracked by internal storms, in which rose up enormous waves which could have lifted up a whole ship and upset it quickly and easily, scattering passengers, lifeboats, masts, sails, buoys, sailors, bull's-eyes and flags.

He stopped swimming, his body sinking until it was vertical. He raised his head and saw Rubén drawing away. He thought of calling to him on some pretext, of shouting for example, "why don't we rest a moment?" but he refrained. All the cold in his body seemed to be concentrated in his calves; he felt the muscles growing numb, the skin tightening, his heartbeat accelerating. He moved his legs weakly. He was in the center of a circle of dark water, enclosed by the fog. He tried to make out the beach, or at least the shadow of the cliffs, but the fog which appeared to dissolve as he penetrated it was deceptive, and not in the least transparent. He saw only a short stretch of sea surface, blackish, green, and the shrouding clouds, flush with the water. At that point he felt fear. The memory of the beer he had drunk came back and he thought "That could have weakened me, I suppose." Suddenly it seemed that his arms and legs had disappeared. He decided to go back, but after a few strokes in the direction of the beach, he turned and swam as easily as he could. "I won't make the beach alone," he thought: "Better to be close to Rubén. If I poop out I'll tell him he's won but we'll get back." Now he was swimming carelessly, his head up, swallowing water, stiff-armed, his eyes fixed on the imperturbable shape ahead of him.

The activity and the energy relaxed his legs, and his body recovered some warmth. The distance between him and Rubén had lessened and that calmed him. Shortly after, he caught him up; flinging out an arm, he touched one of Rubén's feet. Immediately the other stopped. Rubén's eyes were very red, his mouth open.

"I think we've gone off course," said Miguel. "We seem to be swimming sideways on to the beach."

His teeth were chattering, but his voice was firm. Rubén looked all around him. Miguel watched him, tense.

"You can't see the beach any more," said Rubén.

"Not for some time," said Miguel. "There's a lot of fog."

"We haven't gone off," said Rubén. "Look. There's the surf."

Actually, some waves were reaching them with a fringe of foam which dissolved and suddenly formed again. They looked at them in silence.

"Then we're close to the surf," Miguel said, finally.

"Sure. We've been swimming fast."

"I've never seen so much fog."

"Are you very tired?" asked Rubén.

"Me? You're crazy. Let's go."

He immediately regretted that reply, but it was now too late. Rubén had already said, "Okay, let's go."

He had counted twenty strokes before he decided that he could not go on. He was hardly moving forward; his right leg was semi-paralyzed by cold, his arms felt limp and heavy. Panting, he called out, "Rubén!" The other one kept on swimming. "Rubén, Rubén!" He turned and began to swim toward the beach, or to splash, rather, in desperation; and suddenly he was praying to God to save him, he would be good in the future, he would obey his parents, he would not miss Sunday mass, and then he remembered having confessed to the Buzzards, "I go to church only to see a chick," and he was struck by the certainty that God was going to punish him by drowning him in those troubled waters which he was desperately battling, waters beneath which a terrible death was awaiting him and, beyond that, possibly Hell itself. Into his distress there suddenly swam up a phrase used occasionally by Father Alberto in his religion class, that divine mercy knows no limits, and while he flailed at the water with his arms—his legs were hanging down like lead weights—moving his lips, he prayed to God to be good to him, he was so young, and he swore that he would become a priest if saved, but a second later he corrected that quickly and promised that instead of becoming a priest he would offer up sacrifices and other things and dispense charity, and then he realized that hesitation and bargaining at so desperate a time could prove fatal, and suddenly he heard, quite close, wild shouts coming from Rubén, and, turning his head, he saw him, some ten meters away, his face half submerged, waving an arm, pleading:

"Miguel, friend Miguel, come, I'm drowning. Don't go!"

He remained rigid a moment, puzzled, and then it was as if Rubén's desperation stifled his own, for he felt his courage and strength return, and the tightness in his legs relax.

"I have a stomach cramp," Rubén hissed out. "I can't go on, Miguel. Save me, whatever you do, don't leave me, pal."

He floated toward Rubén and was about to go to

him when he remembered that drowning men always manage to hang on like leeches to their rescuers, drowning them with them, and he kept his distance, but the cries frightened him and he realized that if Rubén drowned, he would not reach the beach either, and he went back. Two meters from Rubén, a white shriveled mass which sank and then rose, he shouted: "Don't move, Rubén. I'm going to pull you by the head, but don't try to hang on to me. If you hang on we'll both drown. Rubén, you're going to keep still, pal. I'm going to pull you by the head but don't touch me." He kept a safe distance, stretching out a hand until he grasped Rubén's hair. He began to swim with his free arm, doing all he could to help himself along with his legs. Progress was slow and painful. He concentrated all his efforts and scarcely heard Rubén's steady groaning, or the sudden terrible cries of "I'm going to die; save me, Miguel!" or the retching that convulsed him. He was exhausted when he stopped. He supported Rubén with one hand, making a circular sweep on the surface with the other. He breathed deeply through his mouth. Rubén's face was twisted in pain, his lips drawn back in a strange grimace.

"Friend Rubén," gasped Miguel, "there's not far to go. Have a shot at it. Answer me, Rubén. Shout. Don't stay like that."

He slapped him sharply, and Rubén opened his eyes; he moved his head weakly.

"Shout, pal," Miguel repeated. "Try to move yourself. I'm going to massage your stomach. It's not far now. Don't give up."

His hand went underwater and found the tightness of Rubén's stomach muscles, spreading over his belly. He rubbed them several times, slowly at first, and then strongly, and Rubén shouted: "I don't want to die, Miguel; save me!"

He began to swim again, this time pulling Rubén by his chin. Each time a wave caught up with them,

Rubén choked, and Miguel shouted at him to spit out. And he kept swimming, not resting a moment, closing his eyes at times, in good spirits because a kind of confidence had sprung up in his heart, a warm, proud, stimulating feeling which protected him against cold and fatigue. A stone scraped one of his feet, and he shouted aloud, and hurried. A moment later he was able to stand up, and he reached out his arms to support Rubén. Holding him against himself, feeling his head leaning on one of his shoulders, he rested a long time. Then he helped Rubén to move and loosen his shoulders, and supporting him on his forearms, he made him move his knees. He massaged his stomach until the tightness began to yield. Rubén had stopped shouting and was doing all he could to get moving again, massaging himself with his own hands.

"Better?"

"Yes, pal. I'm fine. Let's go."

An inexpressible joy filled them as they made their way over the stones, leaning forward against the undertow, oblivious of the sea urchins. Soon they caught sight of the groins of the cliffs, the bathing house, and finally, close to the water's edge by now, the Buzzards, standing in the women's gallery, looking out.

"Listen," Rubén said.

"Yes."

"Don't say anything to them. Please don't tell them I was crying for help. We've always been good friends, Miguel. Don't do that to me."

"Think I'm a creep?" said Miguel. "I won't say a thing, don't worry."

They came out shivering. They sat down on the foot of the ladder, with the Buzzards buzzing around them.

"We were ready to send our condolences to your families," said Tobías.

"You've been in over an hour," said the Scholar. "Tell us, how did it come out?"

Speaking steadily, drying his body with his shirt, Rubén explained: "Nothing at all. We got to the surf and then we came back. That's how the Buzzards do things. Miguel beat me. By nothing more than a hand's reach. If it had been in a pool, of course, I'd have made him look silly."

A rain of congratulatory handclaps fell on the shoulders of Miguel, who had dressed without drying himself.

"Why, you're becoming a man," Melanés said to him.

Miguel did not reply. Smiling, he thought that that very evening he would go to the Parque Salazar. All Miraflores would know, thanks to Melanés' ready mouth, of the heroic trials he had come through and Flora would be waiting for him with shining eyes. Before him was opening a golden future.

Translated by Alastair Reid

Notes on the Contributors

MACHADO DE ASSIS (1839–1908). As Dudley Fitts said of the great Brazilian writer: "Machado de Assis was a literary force transcending nationality and language, comparable certainly to Flaubert, Hardy, or James." The son of a mulatto house painter and a Portuguese, he early developed a desire to became a man of letters. His collected works number thirty-one volumes, among the best known of which are *Epitaph for a Small Winner*, *Quincas Borba*, and *Dom Casmurro*. William L. Grossman, his translator, calls him "perhaps the most completely disenchanted writer in occidental literature." But, curiously, allied to this is a wonderful liveliness, irony, and wit.

RUBÉN DARÍO (1867–1916), a Nicaraguan by birth, was both poet and prose writer. His first major work, *Azul*, introduced French Symbolism to the New World, and also the aesthetic approach which went with it. The book had a great effect on the future of Latin American writing both as inspiration and something to be opposed and grown out of. He later served, as so many writers have done, in the diplomatic corps as Minister to Paris. Modernism, to him, was essentially a move toward the free-wheeling imagination and toward style. His real name was Felix Rubén García Sarmiento, but he chose to adopt the cognomen Darío, from a distant ancestor.

LEOPOLDO LUGONES (1874–1938), from Argentina, knew Darío well. He also could be termed a Modernist, with, too, a non-realistic approach, which led him to seek new forms of expression. An erudite man, he translated *The Iliad* and other classics, while his psychological and imaginative interests connect him with such North American writers as Edgar Allan Poe. He also took a shrewd look at the advance of science, as Ysur suggests. Borges speaks of Lugones as "a great writer . . . . whom I very much admire. . . ." He committed suicide in 1938.

HORACIO QUIROGA (1878–1937), a Uruguayan, on the other hand, in general dealt, as William E. Colford says, "with the two dominant themes in Spanish American literature—Man against Nature, or Man against Man, with a hostile natural environment in the background. . . ." He goes on to say, in speaking of *Cuentos de la Selva* (Jungle Tales), from which *the Alligator War* is taken: this collection and another, "have animals and reptiles as the protagonists. They are unique in the Spanish language, and fully worthy of being compared to Kipling's tales of the jungle. . . ." Depression and ill health brought on his suicide in 1937.

ROMULO GALLEGOS (1884–1969) is best known for his novel *Doña Barbara*, which appeared in English in 1931. He had a varied career as novelist, short-story writer, essayist and playwright, as well as professor of literature and philosophy. In 1948 he had the distinction of being the first democratically elected President in Venezuelan history; shortly afterward, he was ousted by a military regime, and during the subsequent disctatorship lived in Mexico. He had a deep interest in the different cultural strains in Venezuela and in its folklore. Among his many works are *Cantaclaro*, *Canaima* and *Pobre Negro*. Though very different, he had—in common with Upton Sinclair and Sinclair Lewis—the courage to face and write about the social problems that he recognized.

RICARDO GÜIRALDES (1886–1927), wrote the noted translator and editor Harriet de Onís—"in *Don Segundo Sombra* . . . distilled the essence of the pampa, and the gaucho, the two cornerstones of Argentine mythology. . . ." Güiraldes traveled extensively in Europe, lived for some time in France and knew English well. It is interesting that he was a friend of Valery Larbaud, the distinguished French poet who wrote *Poems of a Wealthy Non-Professional* (1908), which purported to be the work of one A. O. Barnabooth, a young South American. This appeared in 1955 as *Poems of a Multimillionaire*, expertly translated by William Jay Smith. Leopoldo Lugones had this to say of the Argentinian's novel: "Güiraldes possesses in the highest degree that gift whereby the writer reveals himself in his entirety with the natural synthesis of a bird in its song. To say of him that he painted the life of the country well because he knew it well, is to confuse the gift of painting with its instruments. He painted the country well, not because he knew it, but because he was an artist."

GABRIELA MISTRAL (1889–1957), who won the Nobel Prize in Literature in 1945, was the first Latin American writer to do so. Though principally a poet, she also wrote prose, and was a teacher, educator and journalist of note. In the course of her career she taught at Barnard College, was Consul of Chile in Madrid, and represented her country at the League of Nations and the UN. Her works include *Sonetos de la muerte*, 1915, *Desolación*, 1922—which many believe includes her finest work—and *Lagar*, 1954. Her *Selected Poems*, in a translation by Langston Hughes, appeared in 1957, and a more recent volume, *Selected Poems of Gabriela Mistral*, translated by Doris Dana, was brought out by the Johns Hopkins University Press in 1972. She was a lyric poet among whose themes were love and its loss, and her sense of justice. Her real name was Lucila Godoy de Alcayaga.

ALFONSO REYES (1889–1959), Mexican poet, essayist and critic, was, as is a tradition in Latin America, a diplomat as well. Beyond this, he was well known as a classical scholar, and his translation of *The Iliad* is considered to be the best in Spanish. Luis Harss and Barbara Dohmann, in their valuable critical work *Into the Mainstream*, say of him: "There was that ingrained sense, so often described by another intelligent observer, Alfonso Reyes, that the American continent as a whole, and Mexico in particular, had not only been discovered but invented. It had started as a European utopia . . ." as the case of Emperor Maximilian and his Carlotta so sadly showed. In his preface to *El arco y la lira*, Octavia Paz says that Reyes' *La experiencia literaria* and *El deslinde* "illuminated" him.

CÉSAR VALLEJO (1892–1938), the noted Peruvian poet, spoken of as "a lone eminence in his lifetime," is, as James Wright has observed, one in whom "we may see a great poet who lives neither in formalism nor in violence, but in imagination. . . ." The jacket copy for *Twenty Poems of César Vallejo*, chosen and translated by John Knoepfle, James Wright and Robert Bly, The Sixties Press, states: "He had a tremendous feeling for, and love of, his family—his father, his mother, and his brothers—which he expresses with simple images of great resonance. There is a tenderness as in Chaucer. . . ." A more recent volume, *Neruda and Vallejo: Selected Poems*, edited by Robert Bly, A Seventies Press book, brings together a remarkable contrast. He has also been translated by Clayton Eshleman.

ANÍBAL MONTEIRO MACHADO (1895–1964), a Brazilian, received a law degree, but soon turned to his basic interest, writing. As William L. Grossman says in his *Modern Brazilian Short Stories*, ". . . in 1919, [he] was appointed public prosecutor in a town in Minas. By temperament he was ill-suited to this position . . . as he put it, 'I always felt like taking the accused home for a cup of coffee. . . .' " I quote Mr. Grossman further: "He began a novel in 1926, worked on it intermittently for six years, then left it in a drawer for twenty-eight years, after which he completed it. . . . He also wrote essays, prefaces, prose poems, and two plays. . . ."

JORGE LUIS BORGES (1899–), the great Argentine writer, has said about himself: "My father was very intelligent and, like all intelligent men, very kind. Once, he told me that I should take a good look at soldiers, uniforms, barracks, flags, churches, priests, and butcher shops, since all these things were about to disappear. . . ." And then: "It was he who revealed the power of poetry to me—the fact that words are not only a means of communication but also magic symbols and music. . . ." In 1961, Borges shared the International Publishers' Prize with Samuel Beckett, and has since received many honors, among them honorary degrees from Oxford and from Columbia. Some ten volumes of his work, translated by Norman Thomas di Giovanni in collaboration with the author, are being published by Dutton, the latest of which is *A Universal History of Infamy.* ". . . . I am never bored, because I am always existing," Borges told the critic Frank MacShane recently at a lecture given at Columbia University. Mr. MacShane comments: "This feeling for existence, pulling experience and meaning together . . . accounts for the richness Borges represents. . . ."

MIGUEL ÁNGEL ASTURIAS (1899–), won the Nobel Prize for Literature in 1967. At present he is Ambassador from Guatemala to France and lives in Paris. But, as Mr. Harss and Miss Dohmann maintain, he keeps going back to touch base at home: "That's why I have to keep going back to Guatemala. Because when I'm away I stop hearing its voice. Not so much the voice of the people as that of the landscape. I start losing my feel for it, and then I can't handle it so well anymore." There is great range in his work, from the delicate, fanciful *Leyendas de Guatemala*, with their strong Mayan influence and overtones of such Indian classics as the *Popol Vuh*, to a later novel, *El Señor Presidente*, which was a bitter attack on the dictator Estrada Cabrera. A remarkable novel, perhaps blending both attitudes, *Hombres de Maiz* (Men of Corn), followed. Influenced to a degree by surrealism in his earlier work, he then turned to his "Banana Republic" trilogy, the first volume of which was *Strong Wind*. It might be said that his ten novels are all marked by his concern for the poor and downtrodden; his overall view has some affinity with Kafka's.

ROBERTO ARLT (1900–1942), son of German immigrants to Argentina, was a friend of Ricardo Güiraldes, though a very different sort of man and writer. Arlt lived on the fringes of poverty and brought to his work a deeply realistic and also almost surrealist picture of life in the poor sections of Buenos Aires. He worked as a journalist, and despite an early death he wrote several novels and many short stories and plays. Among his later books are *Los siete Locos* (The Seven Madmen) and *Los Lanzallamas* (The Flamethrowers). Though his work has been given increasing attention abroad, he is undeservedly neglected in English.

ALEJO CARPENTIER (1904–), was born in Cuba of a French architect father and a Russian mother who studied medicine in Switzerland, and this varied background very likely has something to do with the great range of his interests: a man of many talents and many travels. Aside from his writing, he has also been involved with architecture, journalism, musicology and politics. In 1956, his remarkable novel *The Lost Steps*, depicting the passage of urban sophisticates back into the primeval upper reaches of the Orinoco, was published in this country. This was followed by *The Kingdom of This World*, 1957, and *Explosion in the Cathedral*, 1963. Recently, *War of Time*, short stories, have appeared in English. Darius Milhaud has set some of his work to music. At present he is Cultural Attaché at the Cuban Embassy in Paris.

PABLO NERUDA (1904–), the Chilean poet, received the Nobel Prize for Literature in 1971. His expanse of work covers a veritable personal and political universe. An early book was called *Twenty Poems of Love and One Ode of Desperation*. He was then understandably a more romantic, even surrealist, poet than he is today. In his early twenties he was appointed to the consular service of Chile, and spent time in India and other countries of the Far East. It was then that he worked on the three volumes of *Residencia en la Tierra*. Later on, back in Chile, he met Lorca, and in 1934 was posted to Spain. The Civil War, in which he became deeply involved, followed. There is a parallel here with Whitman, with whom Neruda has great affinity, and our Civil War. Among other works are: *España en el Corazón*, 1937, and *Odas Elementales*, 1954. As one critic has said of him, the recent poems have a greater simplicity, "and an emphasis on poetry that is 'useful and usable, like metal and cereal.'" His real name is Neftalí Ricardo Reyes y Basualto; his pseudonym, Neruda, was taken from a Czech poet and essayist, Jan Neruda, 1834–1891, whose poetry has been compared to that of Heine. *Ballads and Romances* and *Plain Themes* both appeared in 1883, titles that suggest J. N.'s place as precursor.

LINO NOVÁS-CALVO (1905–   ), born in Spain, went to Cuba as a child. After completing his studies, he lived in Spain, working as journalist, translator, writer; later, in Cuba, he taught at the Havana Normal School. In 1960 he left Cuba for the United States and is now a professor at the University of Syracuse. His works include *La Luna Nona y Otros Cuentos*, *Cayo Canas*, and *No Sé Quien Soy*. He has also brought the literature of North America to the attention of the South through such translations as that of Faulkner's *Sanctuary*. In contemporary Cuban writing, he has been a leader in the trend toward "magic-realism."

ARTURO USLAR PIETRI (1906–   ), is a writer, lawyer, and Doctor of Political and Social Science at the University of Venezuela. From 1929 to 1934, he lived in Paris, and came to know many of the writers active at that time. From 1946–1951, he taught at Columbia University. He is a member of both the Academy of the Language and the Academy of History. Among his works are two books of short stories, *Red* and *Treinta hombres y sus sombras*, and a novel, *Las lanzas coloradas*. He too is an exponent of "magic-realism." As Professor Anderson-Imbert says of his story *La lluvia*: "Reality is so subjectively treated that frequently the reader seems to be following the scenes of a dream. . . ."

JOÃO GUIMARÃES ROSA (1908–1967), like so many Latin American writers, had a variety of careers and talents. Born—with Swabian ancestry far in the background—in Minas Gerais, Brazil, a province in touch with both city and hinterland, he practiced medicine as an army doctor and also in the *sertão*, that vast highland covering nearly a third of Brazil. This untamed area indeed provided a rugged frame for his writing; many of his stories—and at times the rhythms of his prose—reflect a hard and simple life on horseback. His prose, though—there is an unpublished book of verse—is anything but simple. The book, *Sagarana*, short stories, appeared in English in 1966, and a novel, *The Devil to Pay in the Backlands*, was also published here by Knopf, as was *The Third Bank of the River*, a further collection. As William L. Grossman says: "He is noted for the unconventionality of his prose and for the mystical, telluric quality, at once brutal and tender, of his stories."

JUAN CARLOS ONETTI (1909–   ), of Uruguay, has been likened to Faulkner, in that he has concentrated, in his case, on an urban, special environment, and on the predicament and haunted loneliness of those who live in cities. To a degree, he stems from the tradition of Roberto Arlt, with perhaps a dash of Jean-Paul Sartre added. He is, in any case, one of the major figures of his generation. Among his works are *El Inferno tan temido* and *El Astillero*, 1960. In 1961 he received the National Prize for Literature of Uruguay. In an interview in 1961 he is quoted as saying: "All I want to express is the adventure of man."

JUAN BOSCH (1909–), of the Dominican Republic, has also achieved that marriage of literary and political concerns that is so often evident among Latin American writers. Though he is widely traveled, his work in general concerns itself with the problems of the Dominican people. He was President of his country after the overthrow of the Trujillo dictatorship; seven months later he was himself overthrown. After a period of exile in Puerto Rico and Europe, he has returned to his own country. Among his works are *Camino Real, Indios, La Muchacha de la Guaira,* and *Cuentos Escritos en el Exilio*. Basically a writer of short stories, he has brought to his books a sense of style and a knowledge of human beings, their soil, and their fate.

MARÍA-LUISA BOMBAL (1910–), the Chilean writer, has a degree from the Sorbonne. Her two novels are *La última niebla* and *La amortajada*. Writing in a Proustian and poetic vein, she is aware of the subconscious and of the reality of dream. As Professor Anderson-Imbert says of "The Tree," the profound psychological analysis of a woman is no less impressive than the contrapuntal technique followed in the story: point and counterpoint of a domestic drama and a concert. . . ." After living for a while in the United States, she now resides in Buenos Aires.

DINAH SILVEIRA DE QUEIROZ (1911–), the Brazilian writer, was the first woman to receive the Machado de Assis prize, awarded by the Brazilian Academy of Letters. She has lived abroad and traveled widely, with her husband, a diplomat; they now make their home in Brasilia. As well as novels, she has also written a book for children and plays. A book of stories, *As Noites do Morro do Encanto*, appeared in 1957, and more recently a new volume, *Comba Malina*, showed a new side to her talent.

JOSÉ MARÍA ARGUEDAS (1911–1969), the Peruvian writer and sociologist, was half Indian and spoke the Quechuan language fluently. From this divided background came his deep understanding of Indian, mestizo and white psychology. Also a poet in the Quechuan language, he brings to his short stories many poetic interludes and impressions, many hair-raising images. "Warma Kuyay" itself turns out to be a bucolic, though harsh, poem; it gives us a country landscape: true, forbidding, sensitive, cruel. His use of Indian words, idiom, psychology separated his writings off from all others. Among his books are *Warma Kuyay*, 1935; *Runa Yupay*, 1939; *Los Ríos Profundos*, 1958; and *Todas las Sangres*, 1964. He committed suicide in 1969.

JORGE AMADO (1912–), from the Atlantic coastal province of Bahia, in Brazil, published his first novel at the age of nineteen. Since then, his career has included being a lawyer and journalist, as well as novelist. He might be called a regionalist, concerned as he is with the lives of the people of Bahia and also being a propagandist for social justice, as the two are often intertwined. *Gabriela, Clove and Cinnamon*, Knopf, 1962, was his first novel in what might be called a comic vein, and this was followed recently by *Dona Flor and Her Two Husbands*, 1969. His work has great vitality and spontaneity, humor and a relation to folkways; in many instances the influence on him of the ocean makes it appear almost as a personality of magnetic force. He is a member of the Brazilian Academy and has been Visiting Professor at Pennsylvania State University.

JULIO CORTÁZAR (1914–), an Argentinian born in Brussels, has lived in Paris since 1952. A highly intellectual, highly imaginative writer, he has worked in many styles. His first book, *Los Reyes*, based on the myth of Theseus, Ariadne and the Minotaur, suggests, perhaps, one aspect of his mind: Theseus is presented as a sturdy square, the Minotaur as the hero. Others of his novels are *The Winners*, 1965, and *Hopscotch*, 1966, which had an enormous effect. He is also author of three volumes of short stories, some of which are indeed more nightmare than story. One of these books, *End of the Game*, included the story "Blow-up," out of which the considerably more blown-up, but splendid, film by Antonioni came. Cortázar works currently as a translator for UNESCO.

OCTAVIO PAZ (1914–), the distinguished poet, attended the National University of Mexico, and fought on the Republican side in the Civil War in Spain. Diplomat, essayist, editor, with a strong metaphysical bent, he is best known for his poetry. A long poem, *Sun Stone*, is one of the ten volumes that have appeared. There is also a remarkable study of Mexican character and culture: *The Labyrinth of Solitude*, originally published in 1950. As the English-language jacket states, "Far more than an interpretation of his own country alone, this book is also a penetrating commentary on the plight of Latin America today as a whole, an enlightening view of the North American—'who wanders in an abstract world of machines, fellow citizens, and moral precepts'—and a universally applicable evaluation of the situation of modern man." *Postdata*, 1970, written after the student massacre and other events of 1968, provides a certain revision of his earlier views.

ADOLFO BIOY-CASARES (1914–), of Argentina, is a novelist and short-story writer. Two of his novels (*Diario de la guerra del cerdo* and *Sueño de los héroes*) and two story collections (*Historias fantásticas* and *Historias de amor*) will be published shortly in English translation. His *The Invention of Morel*, which won the First Municipal Prize in Buenos Aires in 1941, appeared here in 1965. He has also collaborated with Borges on film scripts and, under the joint pseudonym of H. Bustos Domecq, in three lively volumes of satire on various literary fashions and factions. In praise of Bioy's work, which shows the influence of Wells and Priestly, Borges has written that "In Spanish, works of reasoned imagination are infrequent and even very rare."

AUGUSTO ROA BASTOS (1917–), of Paraguay, served as a boy in the Chaco War between Bolivia and his own country. For the past twenty-five years he has lived in Buenos Aires, where he formerly worked as a journalist, teacher, and writer of film scripts. He has published several story collections, the earlier *El trueno entre las hojas* (1953) and the latest *Moriencia* (1970). His important novel *Son of Man* (1960), about the Chaco War, brings a complex treatment of time to the naturalistic strain so persistent in South American fiction. A recent Guggenheim Fellow, Roa Bastos is at work on a novel about the nineteenth-century Paraguayan dictator Francia. As in the case of José María Arguedas, he has developed a mestizo language, a mixture of Guaraní and Spanish.

JUAN RULFO (1918–), the Mexican novelist and short-story writer, studied at the Universities of Guadalajara and Mexico City. In his first novel, *Pedro Páramo*, and his book of stories, *The Burning Plain*, 1967, he presents a vision of the harsh actualities of peasant life with strokes as sure as those in a painting by Orozco. As Mr. Harss and Miss Dohmann say of him in *Into the Mainstream*, "He is a stoic who does not inveigh against treachery and injustice, but suffers them in silence as part of the epidemic of life. His theme is simply human sorrow in dispossession."

ARMONIA SOMERS (1918–), the Uruguayan writer, is well known as a teacher and for her books on pedagogy. *La Mujer Desnuda*, her first novel, appeared in 1950. Her real name is Armonía Etchepare de Henestrosa.

JUAN JOSÉ ARREOLA (1918–), "Mexico's master of hermetic fiction" as *TriQuarterly* has it, brought out his first volume, *Varia Invención*, in 1949. This was followed by two other books which joined together, appeared in English translation as *Confabulario and Other Inventions* done by George D. Schade. In 1954, Arreola established a publishing house, *Los Presentes* (Writers Today) to bring out the work of younger artists. He himself is a sophisticated man who works in a variety of forms and might be said to have affinity with Kafka and Borges. In 1963 he turned to the novel, with *La feria* (The Fair).

ELISEO DIEGO (1920–), Cuban poet and short-story writer, teaches at the University of Havana. He has traveled widely in Europe and the United States and has a broad knowledge of English literature. In addition to poetry, he has published works of prose, including the volume of short stories, *Divertimientos*, 1946. His work is light, ironic, and often employs the apparatus of fable, as in the tale here included.

ABELARDO DÍAZ ALFARO (1920–), the Puerto Rican writer, graduated from the Polytechnic Institute at San Germán with a degree in sociology and psychology. He worked for some years in rural sections of his country. At present, he writes programs about life on the island for station WIPR. A series of sketches of rural life, *Terrazo*, which appeared in 1947, was his first literary success. He is a writer who has observed the daily lives of the peasant, the *jíbaro*, with great sympathy, and his realistic stories widen out to a larger significance.

CLARICE LISPECTOR (1922–), a Brazilian, brought out a collection of short stories, *Lacos de Familia*, in 1960. In this was included the remarkable "The Crime of the Mathematics Professor," which has appeared in various anthologies, notably *Modern Brazilian Short Stories*, edited and translated by William L. Grossman, University of California Press, 1967. Other works are *Algun Contos*, 1952; *The Apple in the Dark*, a novel, Knopf; and one more recent: *Passion According to G. H.* She is a writer perceptively concerned with human and spiritual values; sensitivity and style are among her attributes.

HUMBERTO CONSTANTINI (1924–), of Argentina, has published several volumes of short stories, in addition to a book of monologues and a book of poetry, *Cuestiones con la vida* (1966). His most recent collection of stories, *Hablenme de Funes* (1970), won a Second Municipal Prize in Buenos Aires. *In the Beginning*, when it came out in *Mundus Artium* in 1970, was the first of his works to appear in English translation.

JOSÉ DONOSO (1928–), the Chilean novelist, has been a

teacher, editor and journalist. He attended the University of Chile and spent two years at Princeton on a Doherty Foundation Fellowship, receiving a degree from that institution in 1951. His first collection of short stories won Chile's Municipal Prize in 1956, and in 1962 he received the William Faulkner Foundation Prize for Chile, for his novel *Coronation*. Donoso's work reflects urban life, and its complications, madness, opulence and decay. He is cognizant both of the complexity of social formulas and of the irrationality of the human beings, or human structures, inhabiting them. His most recent novel, *The Obscene Bird of Night*, is soon to appear in English. The title is taken from a cautionary letter Henry James, Sr., wrote to his sons.

GABRIEL GARCÍA MÁRQUEZ (1928–), though born in Aracataca, Colombia, has spent much time in Mexico and Europe. After attending the University of Bogotá, he worked for a time as a journalist and editor, which occupation took him abroad. Among his books appearing in this country are *No One Writes to the Colonel*, 1968, and an extraordinary novel, *One Hundred Years of Solitude*, 1970. There is a strong influence of Faulkner in his work—the family chronicle descending from generation to generation, the passionate and irrational histories. But again the similarity is limited to certain aspects. These themes recur: ". . . and once again she shuddered with the evidence that time was not passing, as she had just admitted, but that it was turning in a circle." And: "Only then did Ursula realize that he was in a world of shadows more impenetrable than hers, as unreachable and solitary as that of his great-grandfather." His nature as a writer, his compassion, irony and intelligence are matched by his style, vital and seemingly capable of doing anything at all he wants done.

GUILLERMO CABRERA INFANTE (1929–), the Cuban writer, now lives in London, though he has recently spent some time in this country on a Guggenheim Fellowship. He has been at times a movie critic, editor and diplomat. Fer a while Cultural Attaché to the Cuban Embassy in Brussels, he resigned his post in 1965 and has since lived abroad. *Así en la paz como en la guerra*, 1968, a collection of short stories, has been widely translated. *Tres Tristes Tigres*, a novel, won the Premio Biblioteca Breve award in 1964. It recently appeared in this country as *Three Trapped Tigers*. The novel, as the publishers (Harper & Row) jacket describes it, is a "celebration of night." There are shadowy influences to be discerned: Faulkner, Shakespeare, Hemingway, but especially Joyce. It is full of parodies, allusions, puns, which are handled with great skill. Perhaps there is also a touch of Isherwood's *Goodbye to Berlin*. It is an evocation of a different time—Havana under another sky.

CARLOS FUENTES (1929–), the Mexican novelist, is the son of a diplomat and spent his early years in a number of cities of North and South America. By the age of four, he had learned English. For a time in the diplomatic service, he then studied law, but had already moved toward a career of letters. His first book, *Los diaz enmascarados*, was published in 1954. Soon after, he started a literary magazine, *Revista Mexicana de Literatura*, which held that "a culture can be profitably national only when it is generously universal." The days when writers concentrated on the nature of the "Mexican soul" were, for him, over. His interest in politics has remained passionate. Speaking of Pancho Villa, he says: "The Mexican Revolution was . . . an act of national self-recognition." Villa exemplified "the strong intuitive need to break away from the closed compartments of Mexican life, to contaminate Mexico with its own songs, colors, slang, passions. . . . " Among other works of his translated into English are *Where the Air Is Clear*, Farrar, Straus & Co., 1960, and *The Death of Artémio Cruz*, 1964.

JORGE EDWARDS (1931–), of Chile, was born in Santiago. He studied philosophy and law at the University of Chile. Before entering the diplomatic service, he was involved in a variety of professions, as lawyer, farmer and journalist. He lived in Europe from 1962–1967. He has three volumes of short stories to his credit. *Gente de la ciudad* received the Literary Prize of Santiago in 1961.

MARIO VARGAS LLOSA (1936–), from Peru, studied at various universities there and received his doctorate from the University of Madrid. For several years thereafter he lived in Paris. His first two novels have been translated into English as *Time of the Hero*, 1962, and *The Green House*, 1969. "I wouldn't write as I do," he said in a recent interview in *Caribbean Review*, "if I hadn't read Flaubert or Faulkner, whose influence in Latin America has been gigantic. . . . In the contemporary novel, after Joyce, Proust and Kafka—that grand trilogy—Faulkner has carried the narrative furthest in terms of construction of an imaginary world. Faulkner's world was an underdeveloped world. Yoknapatawpha County could be in Colombia, Peru, Mexico, Bolivia. . . . It is a world we Latin Americans recognize." His most recent book concerns itself with the Colombian novelist: *Gabriel García Márquez: Historia de un deicidio*, 1972.

Notes on the Translators

WILLIAM L. GROSSMAN fiirst brought the work of Machado de Assis before the North American public. He has also translated and introduced *Modern Brazilian Short Stories*, published by the University of California Press. He is a professor in the School of Commerce at New York University.

BEN BELITT's most recent book of poems, *Nowhere but Light*, was published by the University of Chicago Press in 1970. His translation of a play by Neruda, *Splendor and Death of Joaquim Murieta*, Farrar, Straus & Giroux, appeared in the fall of 1972, and translations of the same poet's *New Poems: 1968–1970*, Grove Press, will come out thereafter. An essay on Borges and Kafka will be in *TriQuarterly*.

WILLIAM E. COLFORD edited and translated the stories for *Tales from Spanish America*.

PATRICIA EMIGH was a Fulbright scholar in Madrid, 1968–1969, and is finishing her M.F.A. degree this year at Columbia's School of the Arts. She is also at work on a volume of short stories.

WILLIAM JAY SMITH is widely known as a poet, translator, writer of children's verse, anthologist and critic. He was recently Consultant in Poetry at the Library of Congress. His most recent book is *New & Selected Poems*, Delacorte Press.

HARDIE ST. MARTIN was born in a British colony of a U.S. father and Latin American mother. He now lives in Barcelona.

He has translated *Twenty Poems* of Blas de Otero for the Sixties Press, and among other things, the novel *Gazapo* by Gustavo Sainz, and *The Obscene Bird of Night*, a major work of José Donoso, for Knopf.

ROBERT MEZEY studied at Kenyon and the University of Iowa, and is the author of several books of poems, the most recent being the selected *The Door Standing Open*, Houghton Mifflin. He now lives near Barcelona.

NORMAN THOMAS di GIOVANNI graduated from Antioch College and in 1965 edited a selection of the poems of Jorge Guillén. In 1968, invited by Jorge Luis Borges, he went to live in Buenos Aires. In collaboration with the author, he is translating ten of Borges' books, the first volume of which, *The Book of Imaginary Beings*, appeared in 1969, published by Dutton. He is also working on a novel and is currently living in England.

FRANK MacSHANE, educated at Harvard, Yale and Oxford, is head of the literature division of the School of the Arts at Columbia. His books include *Many Golden Ages*, an anthology; *The American in Europe*; and a book on Nepal. *The Life and Work of Ford Madox Ford*, a literary biography of the novelist and editor, appeared in England in 1965.

FRANCES PARTRIDGE translated *El Señor Presidente* by Asturias for Atheneum and Gollancz in 1969, and Rita Guibert's forthcoming *Seven Voices* for Knopf.

PAUL BOWLES is well known as a poet and short-story writer and in the thirties spent some fifteen years as composer, music critic and collector of folk music. Putnam's has recently brought out his autobiography, *Without Stopping*, and a collection of his poems, *The Thicket of Spring*. He lives in Morocco.

LYSANDER KEMP, poet and translator, is now senior editor of the University of Texas Press. Among his translations are *The Labyrinth of Solitude: Life and Thought in Mexico*, by Octavio Paz; Juan Rulfo's novel, *Pedro Páramo*, and the *Selected Poems of Rubén Darío*.

ROSALIE TORRES-RIOSECO is the wife of Arturo Torres-Rioseco, literary critic and authority on Latin American literature, and chairman of the Spanish Department at the University of California at Berkeley.

EDWIN and MARGARET HONIG live near Providence, Rhode Island, as he is in the English Department at Brown. Edwin

Honig's translation of the Portuguese poet Fernando Pessoa's *Selected Poems* was published recently by Swallow Press. A play, *Calisto & Melibea*, was brought out by Hellcoal Press, Brown University.

PAUL BLACKBURN, poet and scholar, brought out an anthology of twelfth-century troubadour poetry, *Proensa*, in 1953. Among his translations from the Spanish are *The Poem of the Cid;* also *End of the Game and Other Stories*, and *Cronopios and Famas* by Cortázar, and a book of poems by Picasso. His own *Early Collected y Mas: Poems 1951–1961* is about to appear.

ELIOT WEINBERGER, as well as translating *Paz, Eagle or Sun?*, will have several translations in a forthcoming anthology: *New Poetry from Mexico*. Mr. Weinberger lives in New York City.

GEORGE D. SCHADE is Professor of Spanish at the University of Texas. His translations include many selections of prose and poetry in the special issue of *The Texas Quarterly*, 1959, devoted to Mexican letters. Also, *Confabulario and Other Inventions* (1964), by Juan José Arreola, and *The Burning Plain* (1967) by Juan Rulfo.

SUSANA HERTELENDY, from Brazil, lives in New York. Among other things, she translated Josué de Castro's novel *Of Men and Crabs*, brought out recently by Knopf. She is now at work on an anthropological study of the Xingu Indians of Brazil for Farrar, Straus & Giroux.

LITA PANIAGUA has a B.A. degree in English literature and is currently chairman of the English Department at Harlem Prep School. She edits the newsletter for the World Association of Women Journalists and Writers and has worked as reporter and editor in Mexico.

ELINOR RANDALL, who has translated three novellas and a play by Ramón Sender, has also put many Latin American poets into English. Her work has appeared frequently in such magazines as *El Corno Emplumado*, the *New Mexico Quarterly*, *Mundus Artium*, *TriQuarterly*, etc. She is currently working on a volume of the selected writings of José Martí, the great Cuban poet and patriot of the last century.

ELIZABETH BISHOP, who received the Pulitzer Prize for Poetry in 1955 and the National Book Award for *The Complete Poems* in 1969, has lived for some years in Brazil. Her translation of *The Diary of Helena Morley* appeared in 1957, and she, along with Emanuel Brasil, edited *An Anthology of Twentieth-Century Brazilian Poetry*, published by Wesleyan University Press.

LORRAINE O'GRADY FREEMAN has translated work by the Chilean novelist José Donoso, among other Latin American writers.

SUZANNE JILL LEVINE has translated Manuel Puig's *Betrayed by Rita Hayworth* and most recently was co-translator of G. Cabrera Infante's *Three Trapped Tigers*, published by Harper & Row. She has just finished work on three short novels by José Donoso, Carlos Fuentes and Severo Sarduy.

LEONARD MADES has a Ph.D. from Columbia in comparative literature of the Renaissance. He has taught Spanish literature at Rutgers and Columbia and is now Professor of Romance Languages at Hunter College. Among other contributions, he is author of *The Armor and the Brocade: A Study of "Don Quixote" and "The Courtier."*

GREGORY RABASSA is Professor of Romance Languages at Queens College and was a Fullbright-Hays Fellow in Brazil in 1965–66. He is known for his notable translations of complex novels, among them García Márquez' *One Hundred Years of Solitude* and Cortázar's *Hopscotch*, which won for him the National Book Award's translator's prize in 1967.

ALASTAIR REID, poet and man of letters, was born in Scotland and has lived for some time in Spain. He has translated principally the poetry of Borges and Judas Roquín, and much of his work appears in the recent Delacorte Press edition of Neruda's *Selected Poems*. A book of Neruda's, *Extravagaria*, which he did, has just come out in England. He is now working on a *New and Selected Poems* of his own.